PRAISE FOR
THE UNMAPPING

"An extremely pacy, suspenseful cli-fi novel that—in its central conceit—finds an apt, hard-hitting metaphor for the uncanny and disorienting reality of our times, and follows through on it with courage."

—Caoilinn Hughes, author of *The Alternatives*

"Bold, inventive, and genre-defying, *The Unmapping* is a thrilling exploration of human nature, survival, and the unknown forces that shape our world. At once surreal and eerily prescient, the book deftly conjures the disorientation of a city upended and rearranged by a mysterious phenomenon, and the fragility of the systems that underpin our lives. I was in Robbins's thrall from page one."

—Nada Alic, author of *Bad Thoughts*

"What a powerful way to get at the essential fact of our time—that the world we've always known is now shifting around us, and we must come together to confront that reality."

—Bill McKibben, author of *The End of Nature*

"*The Unmapping* is a madcap adventure—a big concept novel with a lot of heart—and most importantly, it's great fun."

—Bud Smith, author

"*The Unmapping* is a timely and original novel that reads like a satisfying twenty-first century rendering of *The Twilight Zone*. Fans of China Miéville will delight in this quickly paced narrative that is unafraid to tackle the most pressing issues of our time. Robbins has a dazzling imagination matched by sparkling prose and a nose for plot. A great read."

—Nickolas Butler, internationally bestselling author of *Shotgun Lovesongs* and *A Forty Year Kiss*

"*The Unmapping* is a deeply imaginative novel about the Anthropocene: the impermanence of our cities, the ubiquitousness of emergency, and the hope that can still be found in the grassroots. How will the world look when all our homes leave us—and how will we rebuild when we wake up and find them gone? A jolting debut from a veteran climate activist with much to offer the world of fiction."

—Johannes Lichtman, National Book Foundation 5 Under 35 honoree and author of *Such Good Work* and *Calling Ukraine*

"A tour de force, *The Unmapping* is an allegory for this moment of disorientation, when climate change, predatory capitalism, and hubristic technology have left us unsure of our place and path. Yet Robbins weaves a thread of warm humanity through the book, hinting at how we may find our way again."

—Marcia Bjornerud, author of *Turning to Stone* and *Timefulness*

"*The Unmapping* is a wildly imaginative and thought-provoking novel that feels urgently, almost painfully, relevant. Yet it radiates a constant warmth, a testament to Robbins's unique voice. This novel will make you think, but it will also make you dream."

—David Yoo, author of *The Choke Artist*

"What a fun, mind-bending read! In the vein of Peng Shepherd, *The Unmapping* gives the reader an utterly original concept, a multilayered speculative puzzle, and a plot that unfolds at breakneck speed. In a world where we're all feeling a bit lost, I'm glad I found *The Unmapping*."

—Mark Cecil, author of *Bunyan and Henry; Or, the Beautiful Destiny*

"Robbins has crafted a resolute thrill ride, with a tender heart, that depicts an unravelling world frighteningly like our own."

—Max Hipp, author of *What Doesn't Kill You Opens Your Heart*

"*The Unmapping* is an ambitious and masterful exploration into the apogee and folly of human endeavor, and our inexorable talent for delusion. Robbins's themes and storytelling speak to my adult fears and anxieties the way Stephen King did in my youth. In *The Unmapping*, nothing is safe. Not the characters, not their perceptions and beliefs, not even the ground beneath their feet."

—Alan ten-Hoeve, author of *Notes from a Wood-Paneled Basement*, editor at Farewell Transmission Lit

THE
UNMAPPING

THE
UNMAPPING

A NOVEL

DENISE S. ROBBINS

Published by Mareas Books, an imprint of
Bindery Books, Inc., San Francisco
www.binderybooks.com

Acquired by Marines Alvarez
Edited and designed by Girl Friday Productions
www.girlfridayproductions.com

Cover design by Charlotte Strick
Cover illustration by Ibrahim Rayintakath

ISBN (hardcover): 978-1-964721-07-1
ISBN (paperback): 978-1-964721-06-4
ISBN (ebook): 978-1-964721-08-8

Library of Congress Cataloguing-in-Publication data has been applied for.

Printed in the United States of America

First edition
10 9 8 7 6 5 4 3 2 1

PART ONE

1

Early morning in Manhattan: hushed in a blanket of quiet. But even that quiet is not a true quiet. Cars pass by in steady rhythm. Wind breathes through the sidewalk trees. A single siren sounds, disappears, and arrives again: the heartbeat of the city. And one lonely person walks to work before the world wakes up.

The time is 4:10 and the person is Esme Green and the exact location is unknown, though she doesn't know it yet. It's dark as dark, and the streetlights and headlights around her illuminate nothing more than empty sidewalks, calm roads, and the air, misting with a coming storm. Building facades appear briefly in the lights, and everything about them is incorrect. A bodega where a row house should be. A karaoke bar that belongs in Chinatown. A recycling facility that was never there before, churning through mountains of dirty bottles and unrecyclable receipts. But Esme doesn't notice. She opens her umbrella. There are more important things to think about.

There's a pebble in her shoe.

No, not that.

That terrible fight with her fiancé.

No, not that either.

A hurricane is coming to New York City.

Hurricane Janus had blown through Saint Lucia, torn through Jamaica, and strengthened in the Caymans, before it then veered northeast, hovering alongside the Atlantic Coast in a precise path that refused to touch land or spiral away, supercharging on bathtub-temperature waters in the Carolinas, whipping up the seagulls at Virginia Beach into a frenzy, then swerving to the right at Atlantic City toward the open ocean, where it met the cold front now bringing it back northwest toward the shore. The winds are chaotic and make Hurricane Janus difficult to predict: The forecasters give a range of projections that don't agree about whether it will be a "weak miss" or "catastrophic." But all of them agree the storm is a freak. A freak storm in a freak season, with so many storms named that they've gone through the alphabet twice, and now it's November 6, which means it's too late in the year for a cyclone of this magnitude.

Esme doesn't worry about the "how" or "why" of Hurricane Janus. Her job is "what next." She's on the early shift at Watch Command in the New York Emergency Management Department, where she will provide the data her bosses need in order to recommend if and when New York should order evacuations. Others in her department have been organizing emergency shelters in schools, libraries, and hotel basements. Still others are in charge of a cadre of helicopters in preparation for a post-storm rescue. Everything they have has been put into this. This means Esme needs to be at full attention, which requires a clear mind, which comes only after her morning walk, when she presses the reset button in her head and concentrates on one thing and one thing only: the walk itself. Streets and sidewalks. Feet on pavement. This glimmering city and its incredible life.

Esme can walk to work without looking, her feet know the way so well. Turn right on Tenth when you get outside and then it's straight up, through midtown to uptown, as Tenth becomes Amsterdam, until you're there, in front of the Emergency Management Department building. It's a towering conglomeration of steel and glass with walls set back, like a fifty-layer wedding cake, to allow every floor a piece of sunlight. She views this building like churchgoers view their sanctuary. Here lie answers. Solutions. Strategies. Rapid responses. Death happens, yes, but here it makes sense. Here they can do something to stem the black tide of horror that lives beneath the glistened surface of the city that never sleeps. Fires and floods, storms and crashes, blackouts, pandemics, and terrorist attacks. It's a numbers game and they do what they can. The reality of this, the pure rationality, energizes Esme. So normally, by the time she arrives after her thirty-minute walk, she's ready. To confront and defeat death. To save one life, then another. And to live. To live in this moment and love it.

Yet today, she's distracted. That pebble is still lodged underneath her heel. It's not so bad, especially when she shifts her weight to her toes, but every so often, just as soon as she has forgotten, it gives a sharp sting. No matter how she flails or kicks her foot to move the pebble to the side, it stays put. And the wind is picking up, blowing her curly brown hair all over her face. And her umbrella comes upturned. So although Esme would very much like to live inside her head, to narrow in on this moment, and that one, then that one—interruptions keep butting back in. And every time they do, it breaks her concentration and brings her mind to her foot, after which more thoughts tumble in, all of which lead to her fiancé, Marcus.

No.

Not yet.

Esme puts her umbrella away and ties her hair up, letting the chilly mist collect on her face and neck. This mist is an early warning from Hurricane Janus, which, if it hits land, will do so by midnight, but they'll know by noon and begin the evacuations. Precautionary evacuations have already been ordered, but no one listens to those. It's when shit hits the fan, when the first windows pop, that people realize: This is serious. So today is important. Today, at her computer, Esme will be surrounded by a dozen different feeds, and she'll be able to take it all in, losing herself in information and transmissions. She will relieve the exhausted night shifter from desk sixteen and he will be grateful for the extra few minutes she provides. Then she will work. Oh, she will work. She will learn which electricity lines go down the moment it happens. She will have a running forecast at the bottom of the screen, and through it she will feel the weather worsen. In the pixels she will feel the winds come, the dark clouds swirl, the rain spit sideways. If the hurricane intensifies, she will play a small part in saving many lives this day, and then she will go home, exhausted, victorious, and Marcus will be so proud that he'll tell his mother, and his mother will be so proud that she'll finally decide on a wedding venue, which Esme is pretty certain Marcus's mother keeps avoiding as an excuse to put off the wedding because she thinks Marcus deserves better—but does he? Does he?

Stop.

Thoughts of last night circle in her head like loose coins in a dryer. She tries to turn off the memory but too late: There it is, the fight with Marcus is repeating itself in its full glory. Their fights take on a certain rhythm. First, something upsets Esme. Then she goes quiet. Then he gets angry that she's quiet, because it means she's upset without telling him why. Then she tells him why, and she cries, and he's too angry to care. Then she goes to sleep and he goes out and the next day they're fine. But yesterday, for the first time, she exploded with anger. Their fights are usually about one of two things, and last night, it was both. Number one: the wedding thing. Number two: the late-night thing. Yes, she has to wake up at ungodly hours in the morning and therefore goes to bed at ungodly hours in the early evening, but he often leaves in the evening, right after dinner, and doesn't come back until she's asleep, so she goes to sleep alone, every single night. And there's something about the fact that she always goes to sleep alone that makes her feel empty. Of course she understands that this is the nature of journalism these days, at least according to Marcus: late-night, beer-fueled interviews with sources that require a little social lubrication. And yes, she understands he's on the verge of a breakthrough about something she doesn't quite understand, but she's tired of going to bed alone, so would it kill him to stay home once in a while? Yet she loves him dearly, so they ended the fight, as always, in a silent and gripping hug, clutching each other for dear life. She wants him to succeed. And she wants to marry him. She wants to marry him immediately, today. After four years of being engaged, why aren't they married? Because his mom is paying for it, that's why, and she hasn't decided on a venue, and as Marcus said, *Don't you want this day to be perfect?*

Stop.

The wind. The mist. The streets. The sidewalk. There's graffiti on the ground, but each slab of sidewalk has a different picture, incomplete: half a snake, half an eyeball, half a body part she won't name. Three halves don't make a whole. Something isn't right. How could she have not noticed this graffiti before?

Pain stabs through her foot. Fucking pebble. Esme takes off her shoe.

◆ ◆ ◆

In the coffee shop down the street, a young man prepares for a five o'clock opening. No need to know his name; there are too many names already. In any given day, there are hundreds. Thousands. They never stick. The stories, though, they're like glue. Coffee man—can we call him a man? He's just on the outside of eighteen, but "boy" feels inaccurate, too young for all he's been through. He's on his way to becoming a real man, somehow. College isn't in the realm of possibility. He'll make enough cash to move out of this hellhole, then find a cabin in the wilderness where he can chop wood. Or something. He's not strong enough to lift one of those massive chain saws yet but could be, with practice. Or he'll keep making coffee, sure, just somewhere else. Somewhere far away. He likes the smell of the fresh-ground beans, the power of the grinder as it pulverizes—he feels it now, vibrating like a jackhammer—the sound of the drip machine's final gasp. Ah. Coffee. It's alive and makes him feel like he's creating something. Like he's the manic scientist heading a crazy experiment. Maybe lightning will strike and the coffee beans will all stand up and march out the door. They will rise up and swarm the people that, for centuries now, have stolen them from their forests. They will shove themselves down the people's throats until they choke. Everyone except for the coffee man, who has shepherded the beans into existence, and who, today, has fully embraced his status as the man in the coffee shop.

It's officially his home. As of last night, he's moved in for real. He brought a thin sleeping bag, a toothbrush and toothpaste, a block of hard laundry soap, and a handful of clothes, all of which he'd stuffed into an empty coffee-bean bag. It is time and he is ready, now, to leave his former home forever. Sleeping here also provides the extra convenience of not having to commute, which, at that hour, all the way from the far edge of Queens to the Financial District, is asking for trouble. It's an hour-and-a-half subway ride, yet the long commute was by design; he wanted to work somewhere with money, somewhere far from his family. The job itself he hates and loves, depending on the hour. Hates the rich men in fitted suits who can never look him in the eye, the rich women in heels who stare at him a little too hard, with pursed, condescending lips. Loves the tips. Good lord, the tips. He can take a little pity if it comes with President Jackson. *Twenties or pennies,* he wrote on the jar, and no one has pennies anymore.

Except maybe his brother. His brother, aged twenty, who got hooked on some new cheap pill and now spends his life either high and warm or low and mean or sleeping on the couch, stinking up the two-bedroom apartment they share with their parents in Queens, who are both too busy working round-the-clock janitorial jobs to notice. Maybe there'd be some pennies in his brother's pockets that he'd found on the street when he was searching for his next big hit. Maybe he'd scavenge penny after penny until he could build himself a penny tower that he'd then knock down. The worst thing is the smell. How can his parents, janitors, not notice the smell? Probably their own noses have been blasted by cleaners. Everything in the apartment smells from the brother who can't bother to shower or wash or control his rages. There are pizza boxes piling up by the door. Moths feasting on the couch. Coffee grounds spawning new life-forms in the sink. Everything in decay.

Not here in his coffee shop. Here, the clothes shimmer in the light.

Yes, he thinks, this is going to be a good day, despite the ache in his neck from sleeping in a corner of the storage closet and the pain in his head from sitting up and smacking into a cabinet. He's grateful for the chilly air and linoleum floors, and for the coffee, now gurgling into metal carafes, ready for the first customers, who'll arrive at five on the dot. He fires up the foaming machine and whips the cream and shuffles the most appealing-looking pastries to the front of the pastry box, and then, ready twenty minutes ahead of schedule, steps over to the windows so he can rearrange the plastic flowers. Later he'll thank the Lord he moved as far away from the kitchen as possible, because behind him, the methane-powered pastry oven has been severed from the city's underground gas pipeline, which, for the past several minutes, has been releasing everything it can down beneath the floorboards, so several liters of methane are pooling beneath the floor and flowing into the area beneath the hallway by the bathroom, waiting for something, anything, to set it off, a spark of static, a flick of flame . . . but it wouldn't be a flicker, it wouldn't be a spark, it would simply be the fact that too much gas is in too small a space, and the heat of pressure builds and builds, as the coffee man rearranges the plastic peonies, admiring how real they look, that translucent shade of blue, thinking about how someone once told him that, in nature, there is no true blue, there's only the deepest purple, and how if one thing looks like another thing, isn't it the same? And he is still thinking about the plastic flowers when the coffee shop explodes.

●   ◆   ●

She thought she smelled gas. As Esme emptied her shoe, only to find that it wasn't a pebble at all, but a rolled-up sale sticker, it was a half thought, half registered. Gas. Now she knows. Reality asserts itself. Leaking gas. The world rocks with impossible noise and it's everywhere and everything and now there is a shop with a blown-out window and a cloud of flame behind it and a hurricane of smoke. Her cell phone is open and 911 is on the other end of the line.

"Nine one one, what's your emergency?"

"Gas explosion. Upper midtown, Tenth Avenue. Must be a severed line. Turn off the gas on this block. NOW."

"Ma'am, where are you? And are you sure?" Esme recognizes this voice as Willy, who falls asleep on the job at least once a week, and the rest of the time has one foot in a drug-addled dream.

"Yes, I'm fucking sure. There is a ball of fire in front of my face behind a blown-out shop front and—a man! Oh, god. Someone's hurt." Esme sees a man on the ground, blasted away from the explosion site, and as she runs closer, over the roar of flame, she hears him moan. "Turn off the gas and send us an ambulance and please connect me straight to Lana Tully." *Or anyone more competent than you,* she wants to add. She runs up to the man on the ground. It looks like he landed on his shoulder. Probably the best place to land. A man can handle a broken shoulder.

"Ma'am, what is your location?" It's still Willy.

"Tenth Avenue, like I said, somewhere between, god, I don't know, Fiftieth and Fifty-Fifth. Are you okay?" She says this last bit to the man on the ground. "You're just a kid." He looks like he's still in high school. When he rolls over, she sees he is bleeding out from a shoulder wound, a blood-covered piece of metal beneath him. Instructions from first-aid training flood through her brain. Don't touch the body. Do stop the bleeding. Which one is correct? She took the class two years ago. That's a lot of blood. It's flowing out madly. He must have severed an artery. If so, he has just minutes to live. Unless she can stop the bleeding. Esme sticks her phone between her ear and neck and pulls the belt off her pants to use as a tourniquet.

"Please calm down," says Willy. "I need you to be more precise with your location."

"Willy, it's Esme. A man is hemorrhaging a life-threatening amount of blood in front of my face. Does the exact location matter? Do I have permission to tie up your arm? Say yes." The man barely nods. She ties the belt around his arm as quickly as she can. When the blood stops, she wants to fall over and cry. Instead she runs toward the nearest intersection. The location does matter. Of course it does. She's only wearing one shoe. The other was dropped on the sidewalk. Every neuron in her body is laser focused on running as fast as she can while avoiding all the debris and glass on the ground, and time has slowed to a standstill and yet suddenly she is there, looking up at the street signs.

It's all wrong.

Esme knows her route to work better than she knows herself. Take a right from her apartment building, go up Tenth Avenue straight for two miles until you hit Sixtieth. But one street sign says she's on Parsons and Twenty-Second. And the one across the street says Pearl Street.

Those streets are supposed to be in two different boroughs.

Now, with a full-body click of recognition, Esme knows.

She remembers Marcus's face when he told her. Those deep, brown dimples that usually deepen when he smiles, that distract her from his words and make her want to poke them and laugh—they'd disappeared. He was worried. He worried something terrible was happening, and that it would come for New York; it wasn't a question of if, but when. But everything he told her seemed so irrational, so impossible, that she couldn't help but laugh, until he laughed, too, and his dimples reappeared. And then he stopped talking about it. He didn't say a thing.

"Your location, ma'am?"

Esme checks the map on her phone, finds her blue GPS dot.

"Hudson Street and Charles Street," she tells him. "Northwest corner."

"You're in Greenwich Village? You said midtown."

"Now I'm saying I'm on Hudson and Charles. And where are *you*?"

2

Arjun Varma knows something is wrong right away. He doesn't know if it's the normal "something's wrong" or a bigger "something's wrong," but he knows. This is a city where many things are wrong all the time. There are people dying and getting lost and messing around and calling 911 for fun. There's the hurricane coming, people going crazy with apprehension. There are the couple who live above him and fight with what must be violence, the people who pass out on the street, the people who call the police on those people, but none of that is his place. He doesn't make the calls; he doesn't even decide which calls need his response—he just goes where the Emergency Management field team manager tells him to go.

This morning, in bed with his sheets to his chin and a compressible pillow in his arms, he wakes with anxiety all the way down. He's not sure if his crinkly feelings are intended to keep him inside or set him out, but when faced with the two choices, he much prefers to go out; he can't stand his father right now, and the feeling is reciprocated, and it's not Arjun's place to complain. Literally. It's his father's place. So Arjun walks from the bedroom to the living room with the massive floor-to-ceiling windows that provide a good view of Central Park, the best view in the city, according to his father. It might not be the best-best but it's close, Arjun thinks, as he puts his feet in velvet slippers and pulls on a velvet robe, both of which are a little luxurious for his taste, but the floor is freezing and his father keeps the air-conditioning on cold, even in winter, and it's nice to feel luxurious, like it's a dream, just temporary, which it is; he'll move out eventually—he's twenty-three, for goodness' sake—but New York rents, you know, he's waiting for a good deal to open up. He's been waiting two years.

Now he walks to the window and sees not Central Park but a river. A river, frothing in the wind of a coming storm, and he knows.

The Unmapping is here. It's five thirty in the morning and he takes his phone off Do Not Disturb, and the frantic texts and hurried emails all rush in, confirming this new reality.

He worried this would happen. Ever since he heard about the small town in the thumb of Wisconsin called Gleamwood City. In this little town pretending to be a city, all the houses decided one day that they didn't want to stay put. Every day at four in the morning, they'd rearrange. You went to bed one place, woke up somewhere else. That's it. How? No one knows. No one really saw it, anyway, even the ones that stayed up till four to watch. You blinked and then it happened. Or at least it felt like you blinked. You'd peel your eyes open and stare and wait and still, a blink. That's what people said. There were videos, sure, but anyone could splice a video, and the fact that their narrators were so insistent that this was real, really really real, gave the notion that it was almost certainly made up, especially when they'd ask "Why would I make this up?" and the answer would be right there: *To get idiots like me to watch, for the clicks, for the views, for the sponsorships, for the sunset night-lights you're trying to sell.*

Unmapping? Un-possible. Completely impossible. No one else worried. And yet. Now it's here.

The big boss provides GPS coordinates of the Emergency Management Department building and requests everyone join as soon as they can. Pin where you are so you can return home, the email states, as do the texts and voicemails. This directive is of utmost importance. Pin your location. Ensure your own safety, then come in ASAP. If you need guidance, contact your superior. Arjun is not scheduled to start until one in the afternoon today, because he'll be working all night, and he was planning to come an hour early so he could eat lunch with Esme, but it's five thirty in the morning and they want him to come ASAP. ASAP is the most American word in the history of American words. You feel the all-caps in your head. Come in ASAP, the mass text states. But there's only one text message on his phone he cares about.

ESME: Need you. When will you be in?

"Need you." Did she mean "we need you" or "I need you"? Yes, they are lunch friends, and yes, she understands that he is one of the only lonely people in the entire Emergency Management Department that takes the job seriously. At least at their level. Everyone in the suits looks very serious all the time. Everyone in the seats and on the streets makes it all seem like some party or joke. He knows they need to cope. When you see death and more death day after day, you need something. But can't they cope in a better, more productive way? Like Arjun, who works on triple speed when nervous. Everything makes him nervous and his nerves flit around through his hands, through his fingers. It turns people away, he knows, but the more he knows this, the more his fingers flit. And now they dance around his phone as he considers what to say to Esme.

He rereads her text. It came at five a.m. Earlier than the other messages.

ARJUN: Soon. How did you get there so quickly?

Stupid. What a stupid question. You think she has time to answer such a stupid text from stupid Arjun? But, as the dot-dot-dots show, she's typing a response. And how did she find the building, truly? She's amazing. That's how.

ESME: Long story. Will tell you later.

She responds! Right away! She's supposed to be paying attention to her screens, but she responds to his text instead. This is not because she's distracted. There's no way. He's watched her and seen how she loses herself in concentration at her computer, taking in five video feeds at once, typing with an intensity of focus that could be broken only by a jackhammer. His job requires a different sort of concentration, a one-thing-at-a-time sort of concentration. He's on the field team, which means during emergencies, he'll be in on the action. Whatever that may be. The first rule of emergencies is you never know what will happen until it happens. That's what makes it an emergency. Otherwise it's just a bad day.

Now it's five thirty in the morning and something huge has happened, something bigger than a hurricane. The Unmapping. What does it mean and what will happen and how will Arjun get to work? He's already spent several minutes leaning against the window, lost in thought. Now he jumps up and gets himself together: one morning clonazepam. One favorite fedora. No social media—no time, he needs to get going.

He looks at Esme's GPS coordinates. She's in Manhattan, where he's supposed to be, and he's in Brooklyn, looking at the East River. How will he cross the river? He will go outside and figure it out. He'll run or taxi or steal someone's bike. Instead, when he goes outside, he sees a subway station down the street and hears the screeching song of the trains' stops and starts, so he heads into the station, a decision made subconsciously but backed up after the fact with rationality: Trains are faster than taxis.

The F train pulls up to the platform right as he approaches, a magical moment that makes him nervous but also excited—and what's the difference? Nerves are nerves—because he can't say for certain where it will take him, but the train ahead has screeched away and another one is coming, so either they're all going to die or everything is fine, and since he's a member of the Emergency Management field team, it seems important for him to discover what happens either way, so he gets on. The train takes him deep into a tunnel that, according to the map on his phone, heads straight for the river.

Then his service cuts out.

Whenever this happens, Arjun worries. He knows he shouldn't worry, but his nerves don't get the memo. He likes feeling connected. Hates the idea that something could happen and no one would know. He takes off his fedora, smooths the rim, and puts it back on. Whenever he's here, or anywhere with no service, a flood of disasters pours through his brain. Like floods! A flood could pour into this train, drowning each one of them. They are under a river, after all. He's sharing this train with three others: a mother, a toddler, and a college-aged kid. If the train stopped and the floods came, who would Arjun save first? Obviously the toddler. But what is a toddler without her mother? And aren't college kids the future?

But the floods don't come, the air is dry as ever, and everything seems fine as they shuttle through the tunnel beneath the river. Until the train jerks to a halt. They have no service. No answers. They are trapped.

• ◆ •

With so many people in this jungle of a city, you can never be alone in your pain. While you cry, a truckful of tears falls to the ground. When you have a stroke, someone else strokes harder. Is that supposed to make you feel better? It does not. Arjun and his three trainmates are not alone in being trapped beneath the ground.

Elsewhere in the city, there is a boy.

He will have a name, but not yet. Now he is the boy who runs. Over the past year, his legs have grown like extendable curtain rods. Every day he runs, his strides become longer and his legs carry him farther. He leaps through the air and soars so high he wonders when that one final stride will let him fly.

The boy who runs isn't sure if he's twelve or thirteen. He's never celebrated a birthday, because his mom hardly remembers the month he was born and she lost the birth certificate long ago. His mother, now sober, had another son with another man first, and this son, the boy's older half brother, is his favorite person in the world. The brother is funny and loud and stupidly nice. He gives every peddler he sees at least a whole dollar. He holds doors and bows low. He gives the kid who runs gifts of candy and nice sneakers. He's taught him everything he knows.

The brother also wants him to join his new gang.

He calls it a "startup gang." "We're breaking barriers," the brother says, "making gang activity more accessible. No violence, no retaliation." He believes they'll be able to coexist alongside extant gangs without stepping on anybody's toes. "We have a completely different market on both ends," he says, "both in supply and demand." It started when he made a friend with inventory access in a pharmaceutical company. This friend managed the machines, and he had another friend who oversaw outgoing supply. The brother was so friendly it made you want to do anything for him. He eventually persuaded his friend to join a scheme that would make good money while doing good for the world. The kid gathered that the brother's friend had somehow programmed the factory's machines to lower the amount of opioids dumped in each pill while tricking the guys who do quality control, leaving a whole lot of surplus to send to the brother. The friend was glad to rip off the pharmaceutical company. Plus, their plan would help addicts get weaned off opioids by reducing the dosage in each pill over time. It was a perfect business model, the brother said, that would allow their supply to grow. And profits would be shared with people in need, increasing buy-in and stability, all while the neighborhood slowly eased its drug addiction. The kid thought the brother was ripping a lot of people off and that someone would probably catch wind one day. And how would it work with the other gangs around? But the brother had an answer for everything, even if the answers didn't make sense; the brother was smart and said big, important words like "epidemic" and "redistribution." The brother had gone to college and one year of medical school until he was kicked out due to something about missing painkillers, which the brother said he was framed for, but he didn't have the money for a lawyer or anything like that. Besides, he told the kid, he could do more work healing people in the real world. The brother thought he was changing the world. He called his gang the "Underground Neighborhood Collective for Unity and Trust," or UNCUT for short.

The brother wanted the kid to join UNCUT so he could run from one side of the Bronx to the other carrying loads. He saw how fast he was. "You're talented," said the brother. "You should put that talent to good use." And the kid saw the appeal. He liked running. And he liked the gifts of candy and especially the shoes. So he said he would help. UNCUT seemed a lot better than the other gangs around, with angry faces and silent stares. He kept running and started learning. He was ready for a role.

Until the brother showed up at the house covered in blood.

"I'm fine," he said to the kid, "but I need your help." With the assistance of internet tutorials, the brother showed the kid how to sterilize a needle and sew up his skin, which had been torn open underneath the armpit by a passing bullet. "Barely nicked me," said the brother. When the brother was all sewn up, he washed off the blood and put on a new shirt and never mentioned it again.

But the kid remembered. He remembered the blood. The blood all over his hands. It stained his favorite Nikes and the stain is still there no matter how hard he scrubs.

The kid still wanted to run. He wanted to run away.

It was the night before the Unmapping, though he didn't know it yet. Everything was normal except the beating in his chest that told him: tonight. Tonight it was time to leave. He packed a backpack of comic books, candy, and five bottled waters, then waited until everyone was asleep. It took a long time, because his brother comes home late and then always checks on the kid to make sure he's okay, waking him up in the middle of the night with presents and promises. This night, the brother showed up at three. His present: a brand-new flip phone. "You keep swiping mine," said the brother. "So I guess you need one." No retaliation. Only ever a hand extended. The kid felt guilty. He liked to use his brother's fancy phone to look at maps and watch videos of the world's best runners. This phone was a sore replacement. It was a dumb phone; it barely even had a screen. He hated it and felt even more guilty for hating it. But that wasn't all. The brother also gave him a portable charger. The kid didn't say anything in response. "For when you're on the go. You've always been my family, but now, you're one of the team. We're thicker than blood. Uncut love."

The kid loved his brother, this was true. But this didn't stop him from wanting to leave. At 3:35, when his brother was deep in snores, the kid grabbed his backpack full of snacks and water. He packed the phone and charger, too, because of course that would be useful. Then he ran.

How good it was to run. No one else around, no cars even, not on these streets at that late-and-early hour. It was starting to mist, which felt good on his face. He was running as hard as he ever had and could feel his skin heating up. It never slowed him down, this heat; it only ever powered him forward. Even in the dark, he knew these streets well. After months and months of running, he'd made a perfect mental map. And he knew his destination. He'd found a new home. An old, abandoned home actually, at the tip of Hunts Point, with the Bronx River nearby. It was locked but he knew how to jimmy open the back door, and inside were rooms upon rooms to sit in and comic books to read and food to feast on like a king, thanks to the Chinese restaurant next door that threw away bags full of delicious noodles every night. He ran past a huge half-made high-rise with crisscrossing beams that looked like the ribs of a giant skeleton. There was the cowboy bar his brother snuck him into once. There was the hair salon and the other hair salon. There was the sound of gunshots. Wait, that wasn't normal. Nor was that man running through the streets, away from the gunshots, nor the cop running after him, down to the right, where the kid was supposed to go.

So he turned left and kept running. Fear in his chest. The

gunshots pulsing in his ears. Was it the cop or the man or both? Didn't matter. His brother's blood dripped through his mind. The kid didn't notice the cop car with its lights off until it was too late.

The police car turned on its lights and followed.

He was a Black kid running at night. He knew what happened to Black kids running at night when gunshots were in the air. So late. Three forty-five in the morning. Or was it four already? This was a mistake. He should have run off during the day. But it was too late for that: here he was, with a bag full of candy, a bag that could be mistaken for something. Cops could say anything. Everything could be a great mistake and the kid could end up bleeding all over and that could be the end. Blood on his newest Nikes. No one to clean them. In his grave, would they let him keep the shoes? The cop car was following him. He was running and the cop car was following with its lights on and the more he ran, the more he needed to run, because what else could he do? He ran down an alley and down another alley but there were people there, too, and he didn't know if he knew them, but he knew things about people in alleys at night, so he turned back into another alley, to find, shit, a dead end. He thought he had his mental map but it was gone, flown away as he flew down the alley, and now he was on another street, too dark to see. Which street was it? The cop car had turned down this street, too, capturing the kid in the glare of streetlights. He was off, into an alley. The car pulled over and the cop got out and yelled: "HANDS UP. STOP RUNNING."

The kid would never stop running. He ran faster than any fat cop. Once the cop was out of his car, the kid had the upper hand. Down one alley with an opening on the other side, then another, in the middle of the street now, unworried, turning back briefly in the middle of an intersection to confirm, yes, he was gaining distance, the cop was falling further behind, surely regretting the decision to get out of his car, but wait, no, there was another cop car coming the other way—but he knew this street, the way it widened and narrowed, and once he knew, he knew, he was unstoppable, so he lost the car easily in an alley, then ran, and was almost there, his new home, old home really, with a good basement hideaway, impossible to see, yes, they wouldn't be searching through everything, no, they would lose him and give up, yes, and he would be victorious. He saw it all clearly—

And he was wrong. Something got mixed up in his running, in his fear, so that what he thought he knew, he didn't. But here was something. An empty lot. It wasn't his favorite abandoned house, but it looked like it had a few good places to hide. He clambered over the fence. The emptiness extended into the earth. He crawled down the side of what used to be a basement. There were pipes and planks that were ideal for climbing. Down he went, until he reached the bottom, with two concrete walls pierced by pipes, and he found a space beside them, between the walls, on the ground beneath the pipes, touching the dank soil. He was safe. He didn't know how safe he was.

When the clock struck four, darkness overtook him. It felt like a giant eyelid closing. Above him, a moment prior, there was the dim night sky, the halos of orange streetlights. Now he couldn't see anything. Pressed between concrete walls, with knees on soil and backpack in hands, he waited for this darkness to pass.

The cops wouldn't find him. That was no longer the problem. The problem was how he'd find his way out.

◆　◆　◆

The subway is shut down. There is no cell service and the subway is shut down. Arjun is sitting on his fingers to keep them still and telling himself: Wait. Wait. Wait. How many times has he been sent to deal with panic attacks for people who can't handle a simple subway stop? Not many, but enough. It's always nothing. Usually nothing. An inspection, a miscommunication, a minor malfunction. But sometimes it's something. A train runs off the tracks, a spark becomes a fire. Once in a while there is something, and why not today? Of course today. It's a miracle the subway was running in the first place. Stupid. Stupid. How could he get on a train? He could have taken a cab. He could have walked; he could have run. He could have ordered a helicopter. Anything but be underground at a time like this.

A time like what? What is happening? Arjun has wondered when it would happen, whatever "it" was, and what the bosses would do when it did. During the big department meeting three months ago, after Department Commissioner Kelley gave her general updates and opened the floor for questions, someone in the crowd asked about the threat of the so-called Unmapping, noting the strange videos coming out of Wisconsin. But the bosses told everyone not to worry, because first of all, nothing was happening, at most a mass hallucination, and second of all, even if there was something happening, it was a freak thing in a freak town that would never happen to New York City, the citiest of cities, the impermeable, impenetrable, not with them at the helm, no, and third of all, it didn't look that bad. But fourth of all, it definitely wasn't real. "Has anyone seen it with their own eyes?" asked Commander Bill Cummings. "Raise your hand. If you've seen the Unmapping, raise your hand." And Esme raised her hand. Esme! They asked her to explain, inviting her to the microphone stand in the audience. "My fiancé saw it," she said quietly. "And who is this fiancé?" asked Commander Cummings. "Is he trustworthy? Does he have proof?" Commissioner Kelley immediately jumped down his throat: "That is a completely inappropriate question to ask. Esme says her fiancé saw it. That's all we need to know." She pulled Commander Cummings and the other bosses aside so they could whisper to one another, then returned to the crowd to announce that they would assign an incident commander to this case, and that the incident commander would in fact be Bill Cummings, who declared: "We will refrain from making a plan until it becomes clearer that this is an actual possible threat." And because the incident commander has the final say, is where the buck stops, Commissioner Kelley and the other deputy commissioners thanked the man who raised the issue and said it was time to move on. They had bigger concerns at the time, as Arjun already knew, like a late-breaking heat wave and a tornado watch and sea levels rising and opioids and car crashes and cybersecurity and the publication of their forthcoming picture book featuring a superhero named Preparation Heroine. Working title.

And now here he is, stuck beneath the East River in a broken-down subway car. "No, no, no," Arjun whispers. This is the worst-case scenario. But no. The worst-case scenario would be a flood. Or a fire. Would it be worse to die by drowning or by burning? Maybe it would be a kindness to snuff out the little girl on the train before she suffers. "No, no, no." Nothing's happened, though, Arjun reminds himself. He pulls his fedora low over his head and, underneath the brim, peers at the others. The mother and her toddler. The college kid, it seems now, isn't related to them, but is making funny eyes at the little girl, making her laugh, while the mother looks more tired than afraid. If they've shut down the subways, they'll need to evacuate. He can do that!

He knows his way around. He has a mental map. He can lead them through the tunnels, kick away the evil rats. Warn the girl, *Stay away from that rail, it'll kill you!* He'll pick her up and she'll hug him when they're free, and the mother will ask how she can repay him for saving them, and he'll say, *No need, ma'am, it's my job. Just make the world a little kinder today.* If he were wearing his Emergency Management polo, yes, he would most certainly do this, or something like it. He would stand up right now and tell everybody: *Be calm! Stay with me and you'll be okay. I know this city. I breathe this city.*

But the thing is, he's not wearing his Emergency Management polo, so if he tries to stand up and take charge of the situation, he won't look like anyone important, just one crazy man on a crazy train telling people to evacuate, all due to a routine stop for maintenance. No. So he'll stay seated for now. But if this keeps up, then he'll definitely take charge and Do Something. He'll walk through the cars to get to the conductor. He'll figure out the problem and solve it. Save them. Arjun rests in the satisfaction of this image. Arjun that could be. Arjun that still might be, if something worse happens. For now, he can wait. He readjusts his hat and sits on his fingers.

The subway jolts back to life. It moves slowly, then picks up speed. They arrive at the station at East Broadway and a voice announces: "Subway closed indefinitely." But they made it to the other side of the river. To Manhattan. Arjun leaves the train, keeping track of the other three passengers to make sure they're okay, and they seem fine, so he heads off unnoticed. They don't know he could have saved them. Maybe later that day, maybe next week, he'll see them again, and he'll save them then. But now Arjun nods goodbye to these poor souls, these sad and scared people who don't even know they just shared a ride with a hero.

3

The Unmapping. It's impossible and it's here and there's no time for Esme to wonder about the "how" or the "why," only "what next." The answer to this question is nearly as impossible. The simple fact is that there are too many problems for one human to respond to. Thirty gas explosions in thirty different neighborhoods. Five water mains bursting, one of which flooded a row of basement apartments. One empty row house collapsing when pulled away from its support wall. Hundreds of people now lost after leaving their houses thinking nothing was wrong. An earthquake in Queens throwing a subway train off its tracks. "A goddamn earthquake?" Esme hears someone nearby yell out. Oh, and it's now raining. Hard.

The mood is disbelief, with a side of humor to hide the horror. For once Esme doesn't mind her colleagues' nonchalance. First of all, she has no time to mind. Second of all, it makes sense. They need to look away. She yearns to look in, she wants to look deeper, but there is no time for probing questions. Not while there are floods and fires and missing people to find.

It feels right, being here, in this grand room with its high ceilings surrounded by screens with news reports and video feeds and, everywhere you look, life. Being here has always felt right. Problem, answer. Problem, answer. Too many problems? Take them one at a time. If only you could fit an hour in a minute. If only Esme could pull time apart and walk inside it. On a busy day, she achieves timelessness. A single moment passes and then it's hours later and she's ready to collapse, like after a good hard run in the rain.

An hour ago, she followed her intuition to check her GPS pin, and her intuition was correct. She still exists in the eyes of the sky. There's a satellite up there and it sees her. Thank you. Then, standing by the bleeding man and the ball of flame, Esme explained carefully on the phone with the dispatcher, Willy, how GPS works, and walked him through the process of discovering his own GPS coordinates. Lucky, lucky: He and the Emergency Management Department were just two blocks away. He could then request the gas line be turned off and dispatch an ambulance from downstairs with EMTs that could stabilize the kid until they found the nearest hospital. The flames before her lowered until they disappeared into roiling smoke. And then, and only then, Esme was finally transferred on the phone to Night Commissioner Lana Tully to tell her everything she knew. While on the phone with Tully, she stood over the coffee man, shielding him with her body from passing cars, waiting for the ambulance. She reached Tully only for Tully to tell her to call Incident Commander Bill Cummings instead.

"Cummings is in charge of all things Unmapping," she reminded Esme.

"But I'm on the phone with you now," Esme said. "He's probably asleep."

"Call him. Wake him."

"If he doesn't pick up?"

"Call his wife."

"If his wife doesn't pick up?"

"Call the deputy incident commander."

"Has a deputy been assigned yet? I thought Cummings kicked the can on everything."

"If Cummings doesn't pick up after five tries, then you can call me back. If what you're saying is true, Esme, the last thing we need right now is a breakdown of the process. You of all people know how important it is. We need to be acting with one brain so we don't collapse."

"At least you need to turn off the gas."

"We just turned off the gas."

"I mean across the whole city."

Tully, after a beat, agreed. And Esme, as she flagged down the EMT for the coffee shop man, rang Commander Cummings five times until he finally woke. And then, while running the two blocks it took to get to the Emergency Management Department building, Esme told Cummings what to do.

Bring everyone in. Send out the GPS coordinates. Follow your pins. Take taxis. Guide them closer to the office pin. Whatever it takes. Send out a mass emergency text to everyone else in the city, urging them to stay home. Find the hospitals. Find the shelters.

Cummings, groggily, said yes to all she recommended, except for the emergency mass text. "Are we sure?" he said. "Don't want to cause, you know, panic."

Esme thought about arguing but held her tongue. She'd made her case and it wasn't her place to talk back. She could only make recommendations and ask questions. By then she'd arrived at the building and gone up the elevator to Watch Command, where no one seemed to realize anything was off, despite the fact that the fire trucks they'd sent to another gas explosion had gotten lost, as had the ambulances. It was a strange morning, but that was every morning in this building, where all the city's emergency services converged in a whirlwind of activity. All the strange calls they'd gotten seemed disparate and unconnected. Commissioner Tully was in the back of the room, grimly watching pour-over coffee drip into a new cup. When Cummings's directive came through on all the screens in the office, someone groaned. *Unmapping protocol forthcoming,* the text said in large red letters. *Stand down and stand by for instructions.* Esme took the small spare station in the back and waited for someone to tell her what to do. Her normal supervisor was missing and Tully would only say: "Wait for Cummings." Esme's usual computer at desk sixteen was still occupied by the night shifter. "Another goddamn earthquake?" came a voice from behind her. Now a blackout on Forty-Fourth Street. She texted Marcus. Stay home. Be safe. Call me when you can.

But Cummings was late. He sent an update that his taxi got lost, again and again. Eventually Esme texted him to ask if he might assign Tully as deputy incident commander—or at least interim incident commander—to take over until his arrival. He listened. Now Esme can work. Tully assigns each person on Watch Command to monitor a distinct geographic subdivision and provide recommendations for the incident report logs extant in the queue. No one may act on those recommendations until a clearer structure is established, but they will gather the data and prepare for action. Esme is assigned to the south tip of Brooklyn. Could you still call it Brooklyn? In her range of GPS coordinates she notes three different fires and ten blocks of power outages. They need firefighters and utility workers. She finds Engine 161 where a synagogue should be, but her searches for utility offices run dry. Through security camera footage she sees the Empire State Building on the beach at Coney Island. She checks her phone. No call back from Marcus. She reviews 911 transcripts. The first couple of 911 dispatchers assumed they were being pranked. They either hung up or said "We're looking into this" and let them off gently. Now that they've gotten the memo, they're telling everyone to stand down. No matter the emergency, stand down. Confusion. "Where are you? What are your coordinates?" Now there are calls coming in from panicked people on the subway. Why are they stuck on the subway? Esme poses this question to Commander Cummings, who's finally arrived, who explains they shut it down in response to the reported earthquake as a precautionary measure.

"But there are thousands of people now stuck between stations," says Esme.

His face pales; he says he assumed the subway trains would keep going to the next station first before shutting down. "That's protocol. Who are you?"

"It seems protocol was forgotten," says Esme, "because four thousand subway cars are currently trapped between stations, and unless we want to commit all our field forces to evacuating them, we need them to move." Cummings agrees. The subway trains reach their next stations. And then they shut down. He's finally agreed to send out a mass text. Now, yes, there are calls of panic. Real heart attacks. And how can they reach them? If the caller doesn't know their coordinates: brute force. Ambulances will be sent out all throughout the city, picking up whoever needs one. And the lost? Here come the calls of the people who are lost. And those who have lost their loved ones. And nothing from Marcus. Each report of a missing person makes Esme's heart flinch. Every action has a consequence, and the consequences are piling up. A blackout on one street causes an overload on another. The lack of power turns off electric sump pumps, which leads to flooded basements, which leads to damaged electric panels, and on it continues. Every gas line is off, but what about the few buildings that need it for heat in this storm? They'll have to hand out emergency blankets. How? Somehow. There has to be a way. Marcus. Can't Marcus call back? He hasn't called back. But he's certainly not awake yet. Commander Cummings paces back and forth, frowning so hard his whole chin curves down. He's constantly on the phone through a Bluetooth earpiece. Esme catches him saying something about the mayor's office on one pass through. Something about power plants next. Something about fire. And then, seemingly to no one: "What's *happening*?"

◆   ◆   ◆

It's been happening for three months in Gleamwood City, Wisconsin. You've never heard of Gleamwood City and it hasn't heard of you and everyone is happier that way. Gleamwood City: the town that built itself on aluminum Christmas trees. When everyone decided it was time to create something more permanent than a smelly green tree, Gleamwood City was there. And later, when everyone decided aluminum was too expensive, that plastic would be better instead, Gleamwood City was there, too, adding a PVC wing to its manufacturing complex. When everyone decided that no, it was time to go back to the woods, the real thing, the true trees, then Gleamwood City was ready for that, too, creating TruTrees, the perfect fake Christmas trees that smell just like reality. Aluminum, plastic, any kind of tree, Gleamwood City has it all. Right on the edge of Door County, there's an aluminum forest surrounded by the real thing—living trees—and more beauty than one set of eyes can take in.

A cliffside view of Green Bay. Five bald eagles' nests to see on any given day. Caves and coves and one picturesque lighthouse. The TruTree manufacturing complex has an observatory up high where not only can you see the view, you can launch into it in a paraglider. As long as you avoid the smokestacks, you can see the manufacturing complex in all its glory. The grocery store, cafeteria, bowling alley, bank, gym, pub, and medical center are all right there. Three libraries and twenty club rooms. And the people. Inside the plant, two thousand people work round the clock. Outside the plant, dotted alongside a street that runs a pleasing spiral from the center to the limits, are all the prefabricated homes. Each house is fifty feet down from the next, so when the trees are full, you feel all alone. Which is just what they want. During the day: community. Every other moment: privacy. Within city limits, no one cares about the Far East, Middle East, or anything east of Lake Michigan. Take a step outside, and no one thinks about Gleamwood City.

There is a man in Gleamwood City who runs the *Gleamwood City Weekly*. Reporter, editor, photographer, the whole shebang. His business card says *Newsman*, and for the past two decades, he's been happy to live incognito, unknown, alone. Ever since his scandal at the *Post*, the story that led to his ousting. The topic, the time? Doesn't matter. Drained out the brainhole. All that matters is that his editors had a story in mind and they wanted him to find the facts until that story was true. And so there were anonymous sources; there were always anonymous sources, and one finally said what was needed . . . and of course it was a lie. And of course the newsman got caught.

But here in Gleamwood City, no one knows about his sordid past, and if they did, they wouldn't care. Gleamwood City is the ideal place to start over. It's a version of life that says: *You're perfect as you are and anything you want is here.* You can hunt and fish, sail, camp, ride horses, practice yoga, make jam, and lucid dream. Each home is outfitted with a fireplace, television, and high-end Jacuzzi. And of course three aluminum Christmas trees. It's the American dream all wrapped up in one neat Christmas-wrapped package. Anyone can be happy here. Everyone is happy here.

The newsman needs none of the fancy things. All he needs is a pen and paper and the drive to find Truth, whatever that may be. Here, Truth is less about big society things, more about the little world they live in. Weather, new curtain designs, the upgrade to the bowling alley. The missing cat. The other missing cat. When the newsman told his dad about the job, his dad barked back, "So you're writing church announcements for your little cult?" But no, there's no church in Gleamwood City. No religion whatsoever, if you don't count Christmas. No drugs or hard liquor either, sure, but the light beer is refreshing. Maybe a lot of them wear the same bright red work outfit at all hours of the day, but the coveralls are comfortable and versatile and everyone finds it liberating to offload that decision. They believe in their little city and in each other. Sure, there's the morning song and the evening hug, and yes, the newsman has to post a weekly affirmation from the factory manager in his newspaper, and maybe a little hagiography of Gleamwood City here and there, but it's never anything untrue. Cult? What's a cult, anyway? Most everyone's a slave to something. Social media, CNN, the perfect green lawn. All that matters is, when the newsman writes about the little place he lives in, he finds his own piece of truth, and he's happy. And his dad? Now dead. Dead and not in any great beyond. The newsman? Here. He is very alive and here. His three aluminum trees are silver, green, and purple.

But when Gleamwood City became "unmapped"—that's

what the newsman calls it—he listened to the pit in his stomach that told him: Stop. Step out of this beautiful little bubble and do something. It wasn't all that bad, really, this so-named Unmapping. Gleamwood City was still easy to navigate. Everything you needed was at the complex, and as for your house, well, every single house was on that one spiraling road. You simply had to drive around a little farther until you found your destination. Maybe the numbers seemed out of order, and maybe a certain tree you liked in the forest across the street wasn't there anymore. Tough cookies.

But still. This—the Unmapping—was a story that mattered. The pit in his stomach told him so. *Truth.* So he tried writing about it for the *Gleamwood City Weekly.* But no one really wanted to be interviewed about that. He asked Management questions, and they gave him canned answers. And what would be the point of telling everyone what they can already see for themselves? What could he say, other than, *Boy, isn't this weird?* No. This story went beyond Gleamwood City borders.

The world needed to know.

He sent photos to producers at every national news station. Photos, for instance, of his house in different locations. The responses were skeptical at best and mocking at worst, because who could tell the difference between one Midwestern yard and the next? One reporter responded about how beautiful it must be for everything to look the same even when it's different. So the newsman invested in a videophone, but they didn't believe his videos either. Then he invested in a real video camera, which was ridiculously expensive and a huge waste besides, its quality barely better than his phone. But that pit in his stomach told him to keep trying, so he learned how to mail merge and sent email invitations to every website and blog he could find, inviting them to see it themselves. The pit said: *Tell the truth!* but the old hungry reporter brain said: *Make it snappy!* So he told the pit *Shut up, I'm trying* and turned up the shock and awe—*Pandemonium in a Sleepy Town*; *World Ending in Door County?*; *Aluminum Trees Driving Us Mad?*—whatever it took to get someone to listen.

A blogger named Marcus took the bait. This Marcus wrote for a news website called Bluzz, which appeared to gravitate toward conspiracy theories but had a huge following, with thousands of comments on every post. Marcus, in an email, said he was making a trip to Chicago anyway, so he'd stop by after and see what there was to see.

When Marcus said this, the newsman felt a different kind of sinking pit in his stomach. Like, shit. Someone's really listening. This is really happening. There was no explicit rule against what he was doing, but the newsman felt he was breaking some internal code. What happens in Gleamwood City stays in Gleamwood City? Nope. Not anymore. So he told this guy Marcus to create a fake name and say he was the newsman's distant cousin. Marcus was immediately like, "Michael. I'm Michael." Okay, sure, Michael. The newsman went to pick him up from the airport in Green Bay, and when he saw him, the newsman knew: This reporter was hungry. It reminded him of his younger self. At least, if his younger self was a little more attractive and a lot more Black. They got through check-in at the entrance of Gleamwood City without issue, and when the newsman pulled into his driveway, he sighed in relief and swallowed his saliva. His tongue gets dry when away from town for too long; the return is a Pavlovian joy.

The newsman served Marcus light beers on a too-warm night on his front porch. Eventually, the newsman was comfortable enough to ask: "So, 'Michael.' What's Bluzz?"

"It has dual meanings," said Marcus. "It's the buzz, you know, what people are talking about. But Black. You know, for Black people. So there's that. But also, we publish stories that don't get the light of day. The undercurrent of life. What people *should be* talking about, if only they could see it. The hum. The sound beneath the sound."

"Conspiracy theories?"

"They're only theories if they're untrue." Marcus winked. Did he really just wink? The newsman wished he could pull off a wink. Marcus told the newsman they were trying to launch an outlet in Chicago. "You should apply," he said, gesturing to the newsman's video setup. "We could use a videographer."

The newsman pointed to his very white face. Marcus shrugged.

Either way, the newsman wasn't trying to leave Gleamwood City, Unmapping and all. He told Marcus he was happy here, writing and thinking and drinking light beers and shooting squirrels on weekends. "I want to die here," he said. "In about twenty years."

"Maybe we'll find the fountain of youth by then," said Marcus. "Aim for fifty."

At three in the morning, the newsman made a pot of coffee. Marcus followed him inside to admire his decorations. "All these aluminum trees," said Marcus. "I thought you said the big thing now was making manufactured trees that look real. TruTrees. Right?"

"I like the nostalgia of aluminum." The newsman shrugged. "The dream of this town. Besides, aluminum's not flammable, while the TruTrees are . . . well, never mind about that."

The two of them returned outside with coffee and sat together on his porch swing. That evening, the newsman's house looked out over the brink of a cliff. The day prior, there was a forest, and the night before that, a different piece of forest. Tonight, the newsman was on the edge of town, overlooking Lake Michigan. A few steps farther and he'd fall off the map.

Marcus set up his camera and tripod for a live viewing. The newsman shifted in his seat. Time melted away most of his beer buzz, but now his strong cup of coffee replaced it with something more. The waters ahead seemed to have stilled in anticipation. He could swear he heard something hold its breath in the sky.

Then it happened.

The newsman always tries to peel his eyes open, but he always blinks right at four. Or it feels as if he blinks even when he's sure he hasn't. There is no flash of light, no sudden darkness, no shifting or sighing or smashing of streets torn up and thrown back down. Just a simple moment, a nanosecond, in which the world is one way beforehand and quite another after that.

On this night, before them, the lake view disappeared, replaced by a forest filled with buzzing, chirping insects.

Marcus cheered, then cheered again, all full of joy. He said words that had no place to go. "I can't believe . . . it's really . . . wow . . . and all this . . . but . . . no . . . it's happened. It's really really motherfucking real." Such emotion was not what the newsman expected. But this joy infected the newsman nonetheless. So he stood up, lifted his arms to the sky, and joined in on the whooping. Who saw this? Did anyone see this? Could the sky see back? He still wonders if this is what it would be like to go to church: praying for something incredible, and when that something incredible happens, you can feel it somewhere deep inside your stomach, inside your heart, and you believe.

◆ ◆ ◆

Esme believes in the system. She believes that when she passes on data, it will get to the right place and lead to the right action. She believes that doing what she's told to the best of her ability will create the best outcome. That everybody has their role and that if each person in each role is doing their job with care and dignity, then they can solve anything. One person cannot stop a disaster but two hundred people can work as a group that becomes more than the sum of its parts.

But when she discovers the outage on Coney Island is spreading unchecked—from one block to ten to thirty, spanning three square miles—and that her incident ticket has no follow-ups in the log, she sends a message directly to Commander Cummings, asking who's looking into this—and gets no response. Not good. Not correct. Not how the system is supposed to work. In a storm, people need power, and workers need to follow protocol by responding to incident tickets. Esme switches over to the satellite images to see if she can figure out what went wrong, but the video is useless, nothing but clouds. Why has nobody followed up on this? Where is Cummings? She's about to send him another message when he appears at her desk, which is closest to the entrance.

He leans down and asks her quietly, smelling like mouthwash, "Which one here is Esme Green?"

"That's me."

"Of course." He stands up straight and smooths his purple shirt cuffs. His tie is tied so tightly his skin wobbles around the rim of his collar. Something about the loose neck makes him seem very old and tired, even as she guesses he's in his late thirties or early forties. "I got your outage ticket. Sorry for the delay. Turns out we didn't assign you a division manager yet. Your outage ticket was passed up to me. Do you . . . ah . . . What would you recommend?"

Esme suggests he make sure the field team is investigating the outage, because it's still spreading unchecked. That he get the utility team out there, find the line workers, and maybe create a task force devoted to this. "And while we're at it, a task force for water utilities, too, and definitely for gas. Keep all the gas off until every valve can be checked. Which should not be today's priority. Prioritize life safety. And the shelters. Who's in charge of helping the shelters switch directives? We'll need a system for people who get lost. A two-way missing person registry: one for the lost, one for the looking." He takes her recommendations solemnly, then leaves without committing to anything. She refreshes her ticket log—at least the Coney Island outage status has switched from "reported" to "pending."

The smell of pizza awakens her stomach. Could it already be lunchtime? But no, it's for the night shifters, most of whom stayed on an extra shift, and who are running on their own clocks. It's only ten a.m.

It's already ten a.m.

Esme texted Marcus hours ago and he hasn't texted back. But he must be awake by now. No, he's still asleep. He forgot to set his alarm and without an alarm that man can sleep. Esme closes her eyes and tries to picture Marcus snoring softly underneath their flannel sheets, with the alarm clock dead on its side, feeling this vision as strongly as if she were summoning it into being.

She remembers when he first told her about the funny town claiming to become "unmapped." Marcus was no stranger to conspiracy theories or wild stories, and this didn't seem like anything different, so she didn't take it seriously, and he didn't seem to either. "It's a free trip," he said. "A new place. If I don't find anything weird, at least it'll be a good character piece. This Man Believes His Town 'Unmaps.' Why Does He Believe and Could It Really

Happen?" He admired conspiracy theorists, he told her, because they were often smarter than he was. "They just choose to use their intellect for something that is probably, almost definitely, wrong." Like flat-earthers. Esme couldn't explain how gravity worked. She didn't know how to measure the curvature of the earth, or why the path of the stars told one story and not another. Flat-earthers could do all that and more. "It's good to question things," he said. "We've stopped questioning things. And what happens when you don't question anything? You become a slave."

If the conversation ever got this far, Esme knew to cut it. There were many layers of meaning there. Slavery and racism, yes, topics Marcus cared about, of course, with a deep pain that Esme could never satisfactorily feel no matter how hard she tried. But also, church. He was talking about church, and the only way he ever talked about church lately was by talking around it. It was a sticking point between Marcus and Esme, and between Marcus and his parents, and between Marcus and himself. His parents were strict Catholics in a Protestant town, and when Marcus was growing up, they drove an hour each way to church every Sunday. And he hated it. He hated every minute of it.

He used to be more open about it, this disagreement with the Catholic Church, in a way that wouldn't make him spiral into rage. When they were in college in DC, he told her how he felt. "They tell you you're made of sin," he said the night they'd made love for the first time, when they were freshmen, after he'd kicked out his roommate and leaned a chair against the door. "They say you should feel guilty all the time, just for being alive." His dorm room smelled of cheese puffs but his blanket and sheets were freshly washed with pine-scented laundry soap. As he spoke, he brushed the curls out of Esme's face, and even in the dark, she admired his beauty.

She'd always admired it, and everything about him. She knew his face well enough to outline it in the dark. Esme and Marcus grew up in the same town in southwest Virginia but rarely spoke during grade school or high school, he being popular and she being shy. At college, though, they got together and stayed together and Esme didn't question her luck. So she was there when he poured out his heart, as if he needed her, a connection to his childhood, to complain about his childhood. It's like he realized only while talking to Esme that it was physically possible for him to complain about church without getting struck down by lightning, or, more realistically, without the complaints somehow getting back to his parents or priest. Here, he could talk and live freely. He could have sex with Esme, for instance. He could have sex with a man if he wanted to! Not that he wanted to. It was all Esme, all the time. And it was new, this questioning, and he loved it; he said it felt like he could breathe for the first time in a decade. "Back home," he said, some later evening in some other dorm, "if you question anything, you're sinning. If my mom ever heard me wonder whether or not Jesus really rose after three days dead? I think she'd die of a heart attack. Then she'd come back from the dead three days later and kill me."

"And then she'd make you come back alive three days after that so she could kill you again," Esme joked.

He didn't laugh. "It's exactly the sort of thing I'd get excommunicated for. Like, seriously, what if I asked, what if Jesus never died on the cross? It's a little suspicious that he supposedly died after six hours, when it took days for most to die by crucifixion. What if he lost consciousness, then revived in his tomb? He'd still have been real and everything he said would have been said. Why do we have to believe in some impossible miracle in order to believe in him? He had some cool things to say, but everything we say about him is wrong. Think about Christmas. I can't say when he was born but I guarantee it was not in December. There is literally no evidence to suggest that. Yet we spend all day on December twenty-fifth in church, talking about this birth, telling this story, when we could be asking bigger questions. Maybe I'd actually be a believer if they let me ask questions. Like, there's some good research out there about how Noah's flood fits in with geologic history, for example. But no. In church there's no research. No such thing as geologic data. There's just: This happened. Don't ask questions. Believe. Why? Because you have to.

"It's not just church, though. Everywhere you go, people tell you to 'believe the science.' Why? Because the people in power say so. Trust the science once meant trust the doctors who are secretly trying to end your existence. Ask Black women in North Carolina in the 1960s. I'm sure they were told to 'trust the science' before they were put under the knife and medically sterilized."

"So now you don't believe in science?"

"I believe in science. I believe in the scientific process of asking questions."

"But what about climate change?" When people said they "believed the science," she knew they were often talking about climate change. And Esme had agreed with the sentiment, because global warming's truth seemed so clearly past debate. Even her father had started complaining about the punishing summer heat and the alarmingly mild winters and strange spring storms and choking wildfire smoke. So Esme had signed up for a class on the science of global warming, excited to apply her statistical studies to something useful.

"What about climate change?" he asked.

"Do you believe in climate change?"

"I'm not saying I don't. I'm just saying I don't understand the models myself. How many people really do?"

"I want to learn."

"You're one in a million. But even you will probably only learn one side of things. It has to fit in a curriculum that makes a point. Do you think you'll study any models that suggest it's not happening?"

Esme didn't know, but still his question displeased her on a gut level she couldn't explain.

"Think about what else scientists tell us," Marcus said gently, noticing her displeasure. "They tell us there's dark matter behind everything, pushing the universe apart. They tell us that cells can never really touch or else they'll explode. That when we feel like we're touching, it's not real. Well, it certainly feels real to me when I put my hand on the stove until the skin burns off. It feels real when we kiss."

And he kissed her.

"You're one in a million," he said again. "I know what I'm saying makes you uncomfortable. I'm not trying to make you feel that way."

"It's okay," she said. "It's okay to be uncomfortable."

"When I talk like this," he said, "most people run away."

"I'll never run away."

A flood is reported in the South Ferry subway station. Esme passes on the report. Shut it down and protect all associated electric works.

She wonders how Marcus would feel about all this. Whether he would feel as terrified as everyone else, or vindicated. There had been many conversations over the years as Esme watched Marcus question anything and everything. She stood by him through all of it, though, and came to admire this side of him, even as he argued with his professors and got put on academic probation. And he stood by her, sticking up for her against his mother, who didn't want him dating any non-Catholic, let alone an atheist. Marcus made Esme a more interesting person. She shined in his light. And then he brought them here, to New York, so he could begin work at his dream job at Bluzz. He was happy, he told Esme, because every day brought him closer to the truth.

But when Marcus returned from Gleamwood City, the site of the so-called Unmapping, his attitude changed. He didn't want to ask questions. He didn't want to talk. He came home late from a delayed flight and woke Esme up when he got into bed, even though he was being careful with the covers, clearly trying not to wake her. She turned around to face him and asked how it was. He kissed her hard for a very long time, pushing her head gently into the pillow. She grabbed his waist and stroked his shoulders. It was hot in their apartment, the building's broken air-conditioning sputtering warm air uselessly around the room, and his skin was sticky with sweet-smelling sweat. She pulled him closer. She could feel the hardness underneath his boxers. Her hand reached down to grab the waistband.

But he pushed her away.

"I'm exhausted," he said.

"Okay."

He kissed her on the cheek and turned over.

Esme leaned up on her elbow. "So you saw it?"

Marcus was quiet.

"Did you see the Unmapping?"

She could hear him breathing. At all hours of the day, even while asleep, he breathed hard. Eventually he said, in a near whisper, "Yes. It's nothing."

"What do you mean 'it's nothing'?" She brought her voice low to match his. "You saw it."

"I said probably nothing."

"No you didn't. You said it's nothing."

"Well, I'm saying it now. It's probably nothing."

"But you saw it. With your eyes?"

"Yes. I saw it with my eyes."

"And what was it like?"

It took him so long to respond she thought he'd fallen asleep. But eventually he whispered: "It made me feel . . . untethered."

That was three months ago. But their fights, every single argument Esme and Marcus ever had, they all felt present. All because of last night. Last night they had the worst fight they'd had in years. Every little hidden thing that drove a wedge between them had been brought to the surface and laid bare.

Hours later, he still hasn't responded to Esme's texts or phone calls. If he's awake, it might be that he's still upset with her. She hopes that's the case. It's a grim wish, to hope that he's too angry with her to call. But she'd prefer that to anything else. So many people are already missing. Some may have already died.

Blackout, flood, row house collapse. The screen before her barely registers in her mind anymore. She pulls out a notepad and writes: *Marcus*. She's sent him five texts as the morning has gone on, but he hasn't responded. She tries calling him now. The phone doesn't ring. Straight to voicemail. She texts him again: Tell me you're okay. Marcus. Please just tell me you're okay. His phone is dead. And what about him? If he's home, he must have found some way to charge it. If he's anywhere else, he could find a pay phone. Do pay phones still exist? Or he could hassle a stranger to borrow their phone. Marcus is very good at persuasion. Wouldn't he do anything he could to get in touch with her? Wouldn't he want her to know he's okay?

Email!

She hasn't emailed him yet. Maybe he's awake and working but his phone is on Do Not Disturb mode and he is very busy with all there is to write about and he assumes Esme is also busy, too busy to check in on him, and he's planning to message her later, having no clue that she's worried. So she sends him an email, trying her best not to panic. There are many reasons why a man doesn't answer his phone. It's not worth considering until you know. He'll email her back and everything will be fine.

There is no other alternative.

4

Arjun's first task of the day: Meet with the evacuation field team. Second task: Who knows. There is a process to these things, and taking instructions is just as important as implementing them. He knows that whatever happens will be exciting. Most days, being on the field team means being errand boy for the department's PR activities. They host fairs at local schools, hand out food at various parks, and carry out trainings in corporate offices, and Arjun's the one running around and picking things up and putting them down and doing whatever else anyone tells him to do. During emergencies, though, it means real action. His team leader, Liz, told him and the others to meet "ASAP" in the lunchroom, but no one else is here yet, so he takes the opportunity to lean against the glass and watch Esme in Watch Command.

Who watches the Watch Command? Arjun. It's not creepy. It's admiration. And it's not just Arjun watching Esme. It's everyone watching everything, others pressing their own faces to their own glass windows to see what there is to see. The room is magnificent. Five stories high. They knocked out the insides of a former office building so they could have this giant atrium in the Emergency Management Department. It's like getting fresh air although it's all conditioned here. Up top there are skylights, but no one needs to see the real sky when they can see the fake one through their monitors, which are everywhere, with screens not only at the individual worker stations but also peering down from every angle, displaying news stations and 911 transcripts and police scanner maps and more, and a two-story screen at the front of the room. Whenever anything big happens, it's always on those screens. There's something about the mechanics of how everything fits together, all that energy fluttering from computer to computer, that feels almost beautiful. Yes, beautiful. He knows he shouldn't feel any positive feelings right now, not with what's happening out there, still so much unknown—how many explosions, however many injured or dead—but he can't help it; he's excited, and the feeling seems to pervade the room, people running left and right just to give their energy somewhere to go. That's what Arjun needs. His nerves need an outlet, and usually that's his fingers, and sometimes it's his feet, drumming on the ground, and most often it's driving, driving fast—he likes speed, he likes his job on the streets; he's meant to be out there, saving lives, not in here, watching them get saved.

But still, today, it feels like the energy is here and he wants it. He wants to be the keyboard underneath Esme's delicate fingers. No. He wants to be her friend, that's it. Who cares that he's in love? Not Arjun. What's love? Who knows. She's three years older than him, but she's the only one in Watch Command that's given him her number; nothing like that, she has a fiancé, but on his first day, two years ago, they ate lunch together in the break room, and when he told her it was his first day, she said he could join her for lunch in the future or text her if he needed anything, and she rubbed her engagement ring to make sure he saw it, but he was grateful nonetheless. Now he has a friend in this huge building of steel and glass that he can eat lunch with and that

he can text when he comes up with a joke about the head commander and she can respond "lol," and for one glorious hour on
each day that his job brings him to the office, he eats lunch with
Esme after she clocks out of the morning shift, and they make
each other laugh and tell each other about their lives, and for that
hour, his fingers settle.

Now his fingers drum on the glass as he watches the Watch
Command and the poor night shifters falling over each other in
the back and the people running and Esme. Esme, at a different
desk than usual, but there she is, long, curly hair all the way
down her back, her round cheeks and delicate nose and eyes
that are gray like a clouded sun. She looks like she'd be at home
in a French garden, or at least a movie about a French garden,
starring an Esme wearing a long peasant skirt, although she
only ever wears simple work-appropriate clothes: loose pants
tied with a belt around the waist and simple V-neck shirts or
collared button-downs. In the French movie, though, her round
cheeks would be red from too much wind, and her small, serious mouth would contemplate death. Tragic and quiet. He likes
the seriousness of her face and likes it even better when he can
make her laugh. Now it's all serious as she takes in five screens
at once, typing, clicking. The tempo of his fingers is all over
the place, like one of those improvisational jazz songs people
pretend to understand. He wonders if maybe he'd like one of
those songs if he listened to it right now, if he just needs to be in
the correct mood to appreciate it, fully discombobulated, like
the mood he's in right now. He checks his social media. Earlier,
he posted Crazy Day with a picture of an explosion that was
emailed around the department, and now it has two likes, which
is two more than usual, and which translates to two flutters of
the heart.

Arjun watches as Commander Bill Cummings walks through Watch Command, looking flustered. He's aware that this Commander Cummings is newly in charge of the department's Unmapping response, but Arjun will never speak to him, nor to any of the deputy incident commanders, nor to the interim incident commanders, nor to the branch managers or division heads or anyone who works above him except his task force team leader, who will presumably remain Elizabeth Flynn. Liz was assigned to lead the evacuation field team branch of the hurricane response. Now they have something else to respond to. And then there's his partner, Miles, who, when they're on emergency duty, does the hard stuff while Arjun takes the wheel. Miles does the stuff Arjun hopes to do himself one day. Diving into flooded streets. Saving cats from trees. Miles hasn't arrived yet either and isn't picking up his phone, so there's nothing for Arjun to do but wait.

He texts Esme. I made it.

And he watches as her entire body jolts. Her phone is on her desk and it lights up and she nearly falls out of her chair as she picks up the phone, which she stares at for a moment. Then she puts it down and continues typing at her computer.

She saw his text. Then she ignored it. She's busy, they're all busy, but still. It hurts. Earlier she texted Need you. Now what? She changed her mind? *Don't need you*? *Don't like you*? *Go away, I'm busy*? She is busy, and he should be, too, but he's not; he's waiting, and he wants . . . He doesn't know what he wants. He sits down against the wall and pulls his hat over his face. He wants to melt. He doesn't melt. His phone buzzes in his pocket.

ESME: Yay! Glad ur ok. Catch up later

And that's all he needs to melt for good, to feel his fingers settle, like the best clonazepam. Which he forgot to take that morning. Duh. In the chaos of the morning, of course he forgot. Now he pulls a bottle out of his backpack and puts one pill in his hand. But wait. Did he forget earlier? Maybe not. It's become an automatic thing: Wake up, take the pill. Yes. He counts the number of pills left in the container and confirms that yes, he did take one. He puts the bottle away and wonders what he should text Esme now to keep the conversation going, but no, she probably is too busy to respond, and he'll be anxious all over again; better to leave it here, with her implication that she wants to catch up. But when? Later. Figure it out then.

"Arjun." His boss Liz has arrived and is standing behind Arjun in the lunchroom. The others on the field team are there, too—they must have arrived in a clump—wearing their navy-blue polos with the big white letters. Arjun forgot to wear his work shirt this morning. Another piece of the day lost to chaos. They said come right away and so he came and how could he have known to put on the uniform? The others knew. There they all are, standing polo to polo in the lunchroom, where they always have meetings because somehow, in this massive complex, there are no dedicated offices for the field teams.

"Time to get going," says Liz.

"Where? Why? To do what?" asks Arjun.

Liz explains. Arjun and the field team will soon fan out in their navy-blue vans, which match the navy-blue polos and are all safely parked in the building's basement parking lot—Liz confirmed it. They are assigned to be present at the place of the emergency, which, today, is every block in New York City. Then, in their assigned neighborhoods, they will bring lost citizens to the designated shelters, addresses forthcoming—dozens of shelters have already been put in place in preparation for the hurricane, but someone needs to find them. That's why the field team, as they span the city, will also help to find and note the shelter locations as they search for distressed citizens, prepared to bring them to safety.

That's stage one.

"What's stage two?"

"Not your problem."

"Where's Miles?"

"Family emergency. You'll be on your own."

On his own! Now Arjun can play music as loud as he wants. Drive as fast as he wants. And be the one to drag burning bodies out of a mountain of flame. Well. Not quite. According to Liz, ambulances and fire trucks are on the case for things like that. Arjun and the others, in addition to driving people to shelters, will be handing out GPS devices. They will each be given hundreds of these devices, tiny black boxes that can be programmed to be found easily through a GPS tracking app. She tells them all this very quickly, as her phone is buzzing and she has other places to be, but where? Not Arjun's concern. And what do these GPS devices have to do with evacuations? He'll figure it out. And what if the evacuees don't have the right app? Or no smartphone on which to download apps? She pretends she doesn't hear these questions; she's brought the team to a pile of boxes in the back, and here she reads from a clipboard and assigns them vans and neighborhoods. Arjun's assigned to Coney Island. "Drive carefully," she says. "Very carefully." Arjun's heart sinks a little. "Approach every intersection with caution. Stoplights and stop signs don't apply today. We'll send a map with shelter coordinates as soon as we get them. In the meantime, load up with bottled water, granola bars, towels, and Mylar blankets. And those GPS devices. It's beginning to rain. Your subjects will be scared, nervous, anxious, volatile. Above all, focus on their physical safety.

People need help. And you're there to help them. You each may very well save several lives today."

Arjun puffs his chest out.

Liz checks her phone. "Oh, and now they want me to tell you that stage two is data collection. Find anything strange? Call it in."

"Strange like what?" asks Arjun.

But Liz is already running off, and she calls out behind her, "You'll know when you see it!"

Arjun and the others pile up supplies on carts to bring down to their vans, which are, indeed, parked safely in the basement lot. How many seats should be saved for supplies, and how many for the people he is going to save this day? He isn't sure. He tries to fit all the boxes he can into the back and one seat. That leaves eleven seats, which, if each person he saves holds a baby on their lap, would mean twenty-two souls in his hands. That's a good number, two twos. He turns the key in the ignition, flips on the radio. Most of the stations are fuzzy, but he finds one that works, currently on a commercial about how Arjun may be entitled to compensation. He listens to the lawyer, Jack or John, talk about his "golden heart" as he pulls out behind the other vans, moving slow beyond slow before him; he wants to fly down the street and leap his van over a bridge. His nerves are wild, even post-clonazepam, but he keeps his jitters to his fingers, drumming the steering wheel, the radio now switched to jazz that he can blast, and so he concentrates on the tempo of the song instead as the van inches forward. The song is interrupted by an emergency report. It's nothing he doesn't know. The thing is, there's still a hurricane coming, and it's been downgraded from a Category 3 to a Category 2, but according to the radio, the projections are still all over the place, showing it smashing into Manhattan or consuming every grape of Martha's Vineyard or spiraling away back into the sea. Back to the jazz. He finally leaves the parking lot, into the rain.

It's coming down now. And worse, it's dark. Angry black clouds promise something even darker. So dark you need street-lights, headlights, house lights. The van before him turns left at the next intersection, and he turns right. It may not be a hurri-cane yet but the wind feels apocalyptic; he's dodging bags of gar-bage that are scattered in the streets from a trash day that never arrived. A bagel bag lands on his front windshield; he smears it off with his wipers. Rain spurts onto his windows in rounds that sound almost like gunshots. How could anyone be outside in this? But that's his goal: Find those in need, those who are stuck outside, who need shelter. He crosses town, passing disaster after disaster—a burned building, a fire truck collision, a small swarm of ambulances—but he's not needed. Other emergency vehi-cles have all gotten there first. "Good," Arjun mutters. But also. What about Arjun? He sees another Emergency Management Department van pulled over, and a mother and two babies get in-side. Good for them. When will he get to save babies? Reminder: It's better if you don't. It's better not to be needed. To see people already getting the help they need. But maybe just one little res-cue today? Why not one? This will be a historic day that everyone will remember, and Arjun is ready for his story.

He makes his way down Brooklyn to the beachfront at Coney Island, as assigned, which is where it's supposed to be. He is quickly learning what has stayed the same: parks, trees, the shoreline, the pavement on the streets. And what has changed: everything else. His own headlights brighten the sheets of rain three feet in front of his van, which will have to be enough. He reaches a neighborhood that is in a total blackout. The stoplights are off. There are unlit signs in unlit windows. There are old shops and new shops and rubble where shops used to be. And there is the ocean. The ocean is right there. Yes, the unlit buildings are on the left, and on the right it's dark, so he almost didn't see it, but it's there. The waves. The nothingness. And where are the people? There must be people. He drives down the boardwalk. There is one house with light. A tan two-story house with pink shutters, a big wraparound porch, and a mansard roof with dormer windows. And in these windows on the roof, there is light. Oh, how there is light. It's so bright it makes him want to eat it. It makes him think: This is a miracle. A miracle.

◆　◆　◆

The wife on the couch in the house on the beach sits alone with her hands in her lap. Every light is lit, every screen and stereo turned on and turned up: three laptops and three phones and one wireless radio; she has them all running in a digital cacophony. The radio has on commentary about things that she'd rather ignore but can't: missing people, power outages, curfew updates, injured people, water outages, and storm updates—it's a Category 1 and it's headed toward Long Island. The phones are each playing different white noise playlists: "Two hours of static," "Three hours of rain," and "Romantic crickets." One laptop is playing her favorite video of three eaglets in their nest, waiting for their father to return. One laptop plays a video of Salmon River Falls, calm and serene. One is just a photo of her husband—blonde and beautiful and joyful as he sits on the stern of a canoe—who in real life is still somewhere out there, walking in the rain, trying to make his way home. She'd found his SOS spotlight and pointed it out the window. A little lighthouse on a blackout street.

The radio switches from updates to music. Apparently the news has run out of news. It's a relief. She keeps thinking they'll list the names of dead bodies and that her husband will be one of them, so whenever the news alerts interrupt the stream, her muscles freeze up until they end. Now that's done. For the time being. Yet she is still paralyzed. A Frank Sinatra song plays softly, underneath the hum of static, rain, crickets, eagles, and waterfalls, underneath the memories of her husband, who walked away hours ago after he told her: *Be safe. Be prepared. I'll be back.* She clutches her empty stomach.

Empty of food, empty of life. But the wife is not hungry; she's not anything. She's waiting, is what she is. Waiting to get pregnant. Waiting to leave this place for good. For the past seven years, she's wanted nothing more than to leave the city. Ever since she met her husband, who told her about his dream to move somewhere with real eagles and real crickets and a real waterfall. Before that, she wanted nothing. She floated through life unable to say why she made one decision or another. Getting through the week, the day, the moment. She has few memories of that time. Her life before him. Dropping out of high school, waitressing at some restaurant or strip club or another, making money, spending money, hating money. He woke her up. He saw her, wanted her, told her his dream. And she wanted the same thing, she realized. To move to a house in the woods, have four kids, leave everything behind. It may have simply been the fact that he wanted something and that she wanted to want something, but the more time she spent with him, camping in the woods, the more this want became a reality. They got married right away, she at twenty-one and he at twenty-eight. "I don't want a ring," she told him. "Build me that house in the woods instead." And he built it. It took seven years but he actually did it.

Their house in the woods is small, no denying it, but it exists. The two-room cabin sits near Salmon River Falls, a day's hike to Lake Ontario. First room: the bedroom. Next room: the everything room, with a showerhead and a latrine and an electric stove and a sink hooked up to a filtration system built to weather the elements. Outside, dozens of raised beds ready to grow the hardiest vegetables. Underground, the steel-walled cache with floss, knives, PVC pipes, duct tape, and two thousand jars of pickled foods, which they'd canned themselves over the years. Once they move there, he says, they'll be able to hunt all the deer they can eat, grow everything else they need, and teach their future children to forage in the woods, but it's always good to have extra.

Her former friends call him a prepper and she has to agree, he's prepared, but she hates the way they say that word. They say the word "prepper" and mean the word "idiot." They mean unhinged. They mean crazy. But her husband's not crazy. He's almost painfully sane. A stockbroker in the Financial District, he eats eggs for breakfast, ham sandwiches for lunch, and salad for dinner. And then there's the other side of him, the one that watches a constant stream of instructional videos on how to keep chickens and bees, how to forage for medicine, how to make soap, beer, moonshine, and cheese, and this part of him seems very sane, too. Then there's the third side of him, the secret side, that comes out when they're up tenting by their cabin, when he's putting things together while she's heating up burgers over the fire, when he lets himself go wild, the side that howls at the moon and shoots his gun at the stars and takes her in his arms and kisses her madly. Something about that person seems the most sane of all, even when he's pretending he has a Southern accent, because it's the most *him* he'll ever be. Living in the city, it feels like you're inside even when you're outside; no matter where you go, you're surrounded by walls. In the woods, she feels open. Wide open. And yet it's been seven years of marriage and although he built that house in the woods, they're still in the city. But she's patient. It's not ready, he keeps saying. The septic tank has problems. Or the water filtration system is too fragile. Or maybe he's just waiting. He's waiting for society to break down. He says he sees how fake it all is, how fragile, the financial system where he works, yes, and everything else, too, these systems holding everything together. "I press a button and a company goes bankrupt," he says. "I press two and make someone a millionaire. I press three and an industry collapses." She hopes it's hyperbole but can never be sure with him. At some point, he tells her, there's going to be a global shock so shocking they'll never bounce back and no amount of magic buttons will be able to fix it.

So what if he says the world will end? He's funny and smart and not only did he build her a house in upstate New York, he bought her one on Staten Island, with a yard and a porch and a walnut tree to boot. But now that's gone. The tree, the yard. At least their home still has its wraparound porch and all the fixings he's set up to keep this place safe, with its own solar panels and battery-operated power station and a year's supply of water and canned food, because you have to have a backup plan to your backup plan, so if civilization collapses while they're in the city, they'll be fine for a long time here, too. Still, this whole day has been a strange one. First, they woke up to no power. Then they realized: no yard. Instead of a yard, they have an ocean. Coney Island. Their house is on Coney Island, looking at the roiling waves, when it should be snug in their Staten Island enclave, looking out on their walnut tree. At least she still has the video of the eagles and the lake and the crickets.

The blackout is no issue. Her husband almost seemed happy to see the entire block go dark. When he turned on their backup power, and everything worked as it should, he picked up his wife and kissed her so hard with his scratchy stubble that she thought her lips might fall off. He was that young boy in the woods again, and there was nothing she could do to tell him no. Nor would she want to. His giddiness infected her.

Until he told her he had to leave.

Their car. Where was their car? The hole in the plan was the car. Presumably, it was in their detached garage on Staten Island. Her husband put on his raincoat. "I'm going to bring it back. Then we're leaving today." But how would he get there? Walk in a hurricane. It was a five-hour walk from Coney Island to their address on Staten Island, where, he assured her, their car would be waiting for him. Five hours? In a hurricane? Oh, and he had to cross the Verrazzano-Narrows Bridge, where there were no sidewalks. Not even a bike lane. In the dark, in the rain, on the side of a highway, he'd be walking, somewhere, and she'd be home, waiting for him.

"Be careful," he told her, and though she wanted to say the same, she could tell that nothing she said would stop him. It was that look. That look that he often reserved for her. A look of pure devotion. Now he's gone and anything might happen. They keep saying names on the radio.

She's getting to her favorite part of the eagle video. The nest is in the middle of an open spring prairie, with grasses glazed gold in the sunlight. The view switches to a close-up of the father, flying through the sky, returning to the nest with a meal. Then to the eaglets, whose tiny beaks are facing up and open in anticipation. She turns up the sound. They're ready for their father. No matter what happens out there, she can watch this video and the father will always return home. She's watched it fifty times already.

For all her husband has done to prepare, he's forgotten one thing. He's forgotten the fear.

Someone knocks at the door.

• • •

Arjun knocks on the door of the house on the beach with the lights. It opens almost immediately, then slams shut. In between, he catches a brief glimpse of pale fingers, nails unpainted and smooth. The lock turns.

"I'm here to help," he calls through the door with a megaphone.

"Go away," a female voice responds.

"Can I ask you a question?"

"You're not my husband."

"Who is he? Where is he? I can help find him."

He knocks again and again. No one answers. How do they have electricity? A miracle. He needs to know the answer. The lights turn off. Then on again. He knocks and no one answers. "Ma'am, I'm with the Emergency Management Department. I'm here to help!" But he feels helpless. Who is he, himself, this strange man at the door? If he were a lonely lady and there was a mysterious, solitary man knocking on his door in the middle of a storm on the most chaotic day in history, he probably wouldn't open it either. He berates himself for forgetting his work shirt. He hates the department's van. It's so dark! Not official looking like those candy cane ambulances. No sirens or anything. Just a dark and creepy van, and a man shouting through the door: "I'm here to help!" He can hear his own desperate voice.

A wild wind steals the fedora from his head. "Hey!" He runs after it but it's impossible to see, the rain now coming down in sheets. He nearly runs into a man who's standing in the street. There are dozens of people. Looking up at the sky. Why are they looking at the sky? He looks where they are looking. He sees clouds; he sees rain. He doesn't see his hat. The winds keep coming and the hat is nowhere to be seen. His favorite fedora. His only fedora. It was a buttery bronze that made his skin glow. He looks up. A cloud moves. He sees now what they are seeing.

The Empire State Building.

He didn't recognize the bottom half. Now he can just barely see the top. Especially unlit, especially in the rain. But it's there. The bottom floor is made of shops, a pharmacy and salad restaurant with black walls and silver chrome lettering. Then there are limestone offices with vertical windows framed in red. And then the entrance. If you don't know what you're looking at, it's not exciting. Two silver revolving doors flank one golden doorway. Above this, three oblong olive-green rectangles are striated with aluminum stripes, like a triad of religious tablets. And then you see, in golden letters above the rectangles, the shining words: *Empire State*. And the windows go up, framed in aluminum. And they keep going up. And farther, and farther, until you can't see anything else. It's the Empire State Building and today it's on Coney Island, looking out at the ocean, and there are dozens of people on the street, looking up.

Arjun shouts into his megaphone. "Take shelter!" he says. "You are all exposed to the elements!" Some glance at him, but the rest ignore him. "This is an emergency situation! I am here to take you to a shelter!" The few that looked at him now look away. They don't want to leave. He pushes closer to the entrance of the Empire State Building and tries again. "Return to your homes!

If you are lost, I can help! I'm with the Emergency Management Department and I'm here to help!" The rain gets into his mouth. He spits it out. It gets into his eyes and stings. He squints through it at everyone around him, who all barely seem to notice him, despite all his yelling. Some wave their hands around their ears as if shaking off a mosquito. There must be at least fifty people here, perhaps a hundred, and he wants to catch their eyes, but doesn't. No one has eyes for Arjun. They want to stare at this miraculous building that can see the ocean and they want to take it in. He takes a hint, puts down his megaphone, and looks up. The sight of it pierces him. It sticks straight from the sky down into his chest. Like a ship breaking ice in a storm, it splits him into pieces.

Miracles upon miracles. And who is Arjun? Nobody. In the face of all this, he is nobody.

5

"Good work today, everyone," Commander Cummings says, standing at the front of the atrium, where everyone in Watch Command can see him. It's 12:50 in the afternoon and the morning shift is about to wrap up. After hours in his new role, Cummings seems more comfortable in his skin—even if he still has to glance at the name cards he asked everyone to tape to their computers. He had to learn fifty new names today and a hundred new responsibilities. There was no preparing for this.

Which is partially his fault, Esme remembers, as Cummings was the one whose plan was to not make a plan. He never seems to think beyond the present moment. But this is a useful trait during an emergency. If you threw a ball at him, he'd catch it. His attitude is that of a football coach at Super Bowl halftime when they're down by twenty points. He claps a single clap when he walks into a room. She half expects him to ask everyone to put their fists together and say, "Go team."

Instead he tells them all about the task forces they've been setting up and urges anyone who is willing to please stay on after their shift and help out, instructing them to pick their assignments in the main meeting room on the fifteenth floor. Esme barely listens as she watches the second hand move around the clock. It's 12:51. Nine minutes until Esme leaves. Twenty-nine minutes until she returns home to find Marcus, if she jogs when she gets outside. Twenty-four if she runs as fast as she can. When she gets home, she'll hug him so hard it'll hurt his stomach. She'll grip him for one full minute, maybe two, until she is assured that he is real. Then she'll slap him dramatically, like in those noir movies, asking why he didn't text her back, and he'll explain that his phone was dead and he wasn't checking his email and he just thought staying home was the smartest thing to do. He's still not picking up his phone and he hasn't responded to her email. She tries not to panic.

There must be a reason.

The reason is hidden behind a curtain, or maybe balled up and put in the back of the junk drawer, but it's somewhere and Esme will search every drawer of her mind until she finds it. When she learns the reason, she will laugh until she cries. Or just cry. Last night, she considered what life might be like without him. In her darkest moment, she wondered, for the first time, if he never truly wanted to get married. When he proposed, he told her he didn't want to get married right away, but if they lived together, they had to be engaged if they didn't want to give his Catholic mother a conniption. They couldn't afford to live here on their own and didn't want to roll the roommate dice. He won the lottery for affordable housing in a studio apartment in Chelsea, so they took a train up to view it together on a rainy afternoon the weekend before college graduation. The building was hideous but the apartment was acceptable and when the apartment tour was over, he got down on one knee and presented a plain ring, made of a metal that looked like tarnished silver. There was no diamond; he doesn't like diamonds, and she doesn't either, which she'd mentioned to him before, but still, she didn't say she didn't like any other kind of gem or stone, and this ring had nothing. It was just a plain band. In time she came to love it. He told her it was made of iron, the same metal found in meteorites, and that wearing it could both increase her body's iron levels and enhance her vision at night, "so you can see the stars, even in the city." She didn't quite believe that, but she liked that he liked it, as well as the fact that it looked like a wedding band. Already they'd jumped to wedding bands without even getting married. But still, she wants to get married, and so does he; he loves her. Present tense. He may have proposed four years ago and he might not stand up enough to his mother, but he loves her. His mother insists on her Catholic church, but Esme's not Catholic and it wouldn't be allowed, so Marcus wants to get married literally anywhere else. Their compromise is that his mother gets to pick the venue, as long as it's not a church. And supposedly she travels to secular venues every weekend—"godless," she calls them—and finds further fault with each one of them: The lighting is off or the acoustics are terrible or there's not enough space for the band.

Esme sometimes wonders if she should convert to Catholicism to make things easier, but Marcus is fiercely opposed. "Don't let us force you." Is it forced if she makes the decision herself? She doesn't believe in it, no, but has considered doing it for Marcus. She decided to attend a baptism once. She'd seen the church flyer taped to a transformer box, but the tape was coming loose, and as she walked toward it, it freed itself and flew to the ground. She picked up the flyer and saved it in her pocket, planning to keep it only until she found a recycling bin. The next Sunday morning, she found it again when she was turning out her pockets for laundry. Pathway Pilgrim Church, it was called, a name that she liked, though she couldn't say why. The flyer had a drawing of the church, a small brick thing with three colorful stained glass windows, each with an eight-pointed star.

When she was looking at this flyer after pulling it out of the laundry, she realized the baptism was later that day. So, on a whim, she told Marcus she was in the mood for a solo walk, and she'd finish the laundry later. He didn't complain. The church was in Brooklyn in the middle of a row of brick houses, and itself was made of brick, too, so was almost unrecognizable as a church until you saw the stained glass windows and the small wooden cross on the tip of the gabled roof. It was sunny and hot out but the air inside was dusty and cool. Red and green light floated through the glass. The pews were light tan wood with pink fabric cushions. She was ten minutes late to the baptism on purpose so she wouldn't have to speak to anyone; the proceedings were underway when she arrived. She sat in the back and listened. As the baptized baby in a too-big fluffy lace outfit mewled its complaints, the elderly pastor with a gingery silver beard spoke. He said a lot of things Esme doesn't really remember but the overall effect frightened her. He said something about how we all die with Jesus and will soon be brought back to life. Something about the angels we submit to. And an extensive monologue on Satan and evil. This tiny baby was about to embark on life in a world of sin, the reverend said, and would always be in a struggle against Satan, as evil is everywhere. Esme left before it ended.

Could she ever say those words, ones she doesn't believe in, just to appease Marcus's mother? She isn't sure. She believes words have power. She believes that "I love you" means something, that "I want to marry you" means something even more, and that one day, at the altar, "I will love you forever" will mean the most. Vows. She fantasizes often about the vows she would write. She even started little scratchlings here and there. But none of them seem good enough. Maybe that's why it's taken so long. What if nothing seems good enough because nothing, truly, can capture the impossibility and glory of love? When she returned to the apartment, after the baptism, and Marcus asked about her day, she fessed up. She couldn't hide anything from him. And why would she want to? When she showed him the flyer and his face darkened, she realized maybe she had been hiding it subconsciously. She knew how he felt about organized religion. He hated that he was baptized as an infant, too young to even think about making his own choice. He didn't believe in it, he told Esme, and if she did, it might make things difficult. "I've told you how I feel about Catholicism," he said. But Pathway Pilgrim wasn't a Catholic church; it was something called Congregational, although she didn't really know what that was or whether it made a difference. "But I don't believe in it," she told him. "The baptism freaked me out. I can't do it. I can't convert." And he said, with a sigh of relief, "Good."

And finally it's one o'clock. Commander Cummings dismisses the crew. Esme packs up her things. The winds are strong enough to make her umbrella useless, so she stows it in her bag. Her rain jacket will have to be sufficient. She zips up and looks around. All around her, many of her colleagues have been replaced by the afternoon shift. Faces she vaguely recognizes are replaced by those she doesn't. Except that of Commander Cummings. Who has come over to her desk and now looks at her, expectantly.

"Commander Cummings."

"Esme Green." He says her name as if for the first time.

"How can I help you?"

"I'm glad you asked. I was wondering if you'd like to stay on to meet with the electric grid task force. Tully talked you up, big-time. She said you have the data chops and the intuition we need to move quickly."

Esme peers at the clock on her computer.

"I think we all agree these are extraordinary times and that we need the best of us putting our heads together. Our response today will shape everything. We want your head. We need your head."

"Well—"

"We have lunches. They're not the best, we haven't had time to find a deli, but we have some extra brown bags. Sandwiches and cookies. They're in meeting room 3B, along with the rest of the task force. You can head straight there, no need to pass through the fifteenth floor. They're expecting you now."

"Now?"

"Yes."

On the one hand, it's nice to be told what to do. On the other, it's been hours, and she's losing the ability to concentrate. It's not just her mind that's falling away: it's her legs, it's her chest, it's every cell in her body that longs for Marcus to respond. Her shoulders need his hands and her ears will soon stop working if they do not hear his calm voice say, *Don't worry, I'm okay.* Every part of her wants to know where he is. It feels unnatural, her being here, in this uncomfortable chair, surrounded by screens, everything screaming irreality.

"Can I make a quick phone call first?"

"Of course."

In the hallway, she calls Marcus five times, but each time is sent directly to voicemail. She thinks about calling his boss, Rick, but what would Rick know? Or his mother, but she doesn't have her number. No—Marcus will call her when he can. He'll want to make sure she knows he's okay. Step one in a disaster:

Alert your family. Then she realizes she's been so busy and so worried that she hasn't yet contacted her father to assure him of her own safety. So she calls a number she hasn't dialed in years, to Coal Hollow, Virginia.

•   •   •

In Coal Hollow, the phone rings but no one answers. Esme's father is an hour away in Roanoke, cleaning windows at the city council building. He never got a cell phone, so is unreachable most of the day, like when he is off at work, and when he is in the forest in his backyard, and even when he is sitting on his front porch, too far from the phone in his bedroom to hear it, particularly when the cicadas buzz up their motors. He still doesn't know anything is wrong in New York City. He hasn't heard Esme's voice in months; she understands why he hates the phone, how badly it makes him stutter. He needs to see a person in person to talk to them, and even then it's difficult. Instead of phone calls, they write each other emails. He writes her updates about changes to the town, which is less of a town these days and more of an amalgamation of country homes in a five-mile radius around a stream called Coal Hollow Creek. Pronounced *crick*. Coal Hollow also has the basic necessities, holdovers from the days it was a coal-mining community: a gas station, a supermarket, and a doctor's office. Three different bars and two good roads. But Esme's father hates doctors and isn't much of a bar man or into anything that involves talking to strangers. He's a janitor who appreciates a job that doesn't expect anything from you. The floors don't ask questions or wait impatiently for answers. They don't get frustrated when he stumbles over his p's and g's. Esme is an easy name to say, but Green is not, and even after being a Green his whole life, he still can't say it. Why? He'll never know why, and if you ask, it'll make everything worse. But he can type it. He can type anything. So he emails Esme when the town puts in a new stop sign at the end of Main Street, and when the stop sign disappears, stolen by either rebellious teenagers or pissed-off adults who always blew through it anyway. Esme writes back about the strangest 911 transcripts she reads: chickens running through the Upper West Side, noise complaints about fire trucks, someone convinced he's being chased by a dinosaur, pickle juice thrown on a dog—many rants, many objects inserted into alarming orifices. He likes the chaos of the city that comes through in these little tidbits. That's enough chaos for him. He writes about how the pine tree ridge behind their house looks in the evening light. She writes about Marcus and their one-day wedding, which Esme's father doubts will ever take place, but he'll never tell her that.

Now he's wiping down a window at the city council building and overhears a councilmember yell on the phone, something about New York, something about an emergency. He wonders about Esme then. He wishes he could call her, or that perhaps she'll call him when she gets home from work, when he has a phone to answer. He realizes at the same time that he won't make the call and he won't pick up if she tries him either.

Later, there will be a voicemail from Esme, and he will hear just enough to know she is okay. Then he will write her an email asking for an update and telling her he expects a prompt response. After he finishes, he'll go on a walk in the forest behind his house, to the glade of clovers in the middle of the trees that he cleared long ago, and lie on his back, looking at the dark sky, the sputtering clouds, feeling the clovers on his bare arms, and feeling, beneath the clovers, his love lying six feet underground. Esme's mother. The only one who could stop the stutter. There was no funeral: After all he went through with the coroners, he was sick of formalities, even sicker of authorities. He bought a cheap wooden box on the internet, and when it arrived, he had to nail it together anyway, making him wonder why he even bothered to order something he could have made himself. He found a patch of land in the forest behind his house that was far enough away no one would notice or care. He got his wife's garden shovels from the shed and did all the digging by hand, then called three of her friends to help lower her box. Some things, you don't have to explain. Like how to lower a coffin. After he wrapped the box in nylon straps and each person took hold, they brought it down swiftly and in synchrony. Every moment was agony as his wife was taken farther away from him, creating a new distance he would never be able to close. So he was grateful for the speed of the whole thing. Then one of them said a prayer as little Esme, just six years old, cried and cried, drowning out the words, which he appreciated, because he was not in the mood to hear about God but also not in the mood to tell his wife's friend to stop. That was it. Now every evening, lying on the clover field where she's buried, he remembers her and thinks about what he could have done differently, always coming to nothing, feeling a deep ache that's almost like relief; then he will go back inside and pick up the landline to consider giving Esme a call, to tell her how much has changed, like the new woman in his life, something he's afraid to tell Esme, but would be happy to show her, so maybe he'll ask her to visit. Even thinking about it, the ache is too much; Esme's voice is his wife's voice, more so every day, and it still sticks him in the heart like a knife, but so does his yearning for his daughter. He misses the days they spent with each other in near silence, cooking for one another, reading together on the front porch, hearing her hum as she washed the dishes, watching her ride her bicycle, or just knowing that she'd be in her bedroom, with the door closed, lying on the floor reading books or doing homework. She was always content to be alone. He knows she will be okay up there in the big city, the city that would never welcome someone like him, because no matter where she goes, she has her own self, her own world, and yet he misses her, so he will write another email.

•   •   •

"You've reached the Green Machine. Please leave a message."

Her father recorded this sentence fifty different times before the words would leave his lips without a stutter. Esme hasn't called him in years and now she doesn't know what to say, but she imagines he will want to hear her voice, and so, in a quiet corner of the hallway, she calls, saying something quickly about how she's fine, things are fine, it's handled, she's okay.

She hangs up and walks down the hallway toward the elevators, replaying the voicemail she just left in her head. The number of times she said that she's fine and she's okay might set off alarm bells with anyone other than her father, but she knows this will satisfy him. Anything so that he doesn't also have to pick up the phone or leave the southwest corner of Virginia. God forbid.

Not that he believes in God, or anything else, especially since Esme's mother died. No one could say why she died. No bleeding in the brain. No infection, no stroke, no aneurysm. Never any drugs, no risky behavior. The coroners interrogated his father. They asked about the family history of a thousand different diseases. They asked him if she liked to cliff dive. Really? You have a dead woman on the table in front of you with a body entirely intact, very clearly not dead from any physical accident, and you're asking about cliff diving? It was her heart, they guessed at first, it had to be her heart. But there was no cardiac event they could identify: no sign of heart attack, disease, or arrhythmia. They carried out blood tests and ultrasounds, tested her tissue samples a hundred ways, opened up her unbeating heart and her unbreathing lungs, removed the contents of her lifeless stomach. Ultimately, they could provide no reason. And if there was no reason for her death, what was the reason for anything?

For a long time, nothing made sense. But Esme continued going to elementary school, even if she was now a pariah, for no one her age wanted to talk to someone so touched by death. But her teachers took care of her. She discovered she was good at math, and not only was she good at it, she loved it. Her teachers asked her to solve problems and she solved them. Everything made sense. Everything had an answer. There were a million wrong answers but only one right one. This attitude brought her here, to the Emergency Management Department, where there were a million problems in any given day, and although she might not solve them all, most of them had an answer, and she could focus on that, and feel better.

A nearby television shows a water main bursting on Ocean Avenue.

Esme checks her texts. Then she turns her phone off and on again to check the voicemail.

Still nothing from Marcus.

She puts her phone away, hands shaking.

The thing is, Marcus runs.

He is unable to think before he runs, while he runs, and for two heart-pounding minutes after. He is a whirlwind. In the mornings, between the time he gets out of bed and is out the door in running shoes, anything that falls in his path is subject to destruction. A cup of water or mug of coffee? Crashed. Last night's takeout boxes? Smashed. He has no mind for anything except getting out the door, waking up in the streets with the sidewalk rushing away underneath his feet and his heart pumping and lungs pumping and arms pumping, too, and he returns an hour or two later with the biggest smile, huffing, spent, collapsing on the couch, stinking of sweat and joy. Only then can he think. Esme can very easily imagine Marcus getting up, bleary-eyed, grabbing his shoes and phone for music, and running out the door before the rest of him is even conscious. Then he'd realize, several blocks or even miles later, that something is very wrong. Then it'd be too late. And what then? His phone dies. Or falls into a puddle and breaks. And he'd be out there, in the rain and the cold, in his small running shorts and blue windbreaker, with nowhere to go and no way to call home. But safe. He would find a shelter and be safe.

This, she's now decided, is the most likely explanation. She pictures his smile. His joyful collapse.

But also, anything can happen.

Esme needs to know. She needs the facts in her hands. She needs to see his face and kiss his dimples and tell him to never leave again. What's the point of this job if it comes with no Marcus? She's here, in this city, because of him.

She's in the elevator now. Hand hovering over the buttons. Cummings wants her to go up to the third floor. But someone else gets in the elevator with her and presses Lobby before she can say no.

There are fifteen hours left before the city turns over again. But only four hours before it gets dark. And if he gets lost in the dark? If you don't find a missing person within the first day, your chances of ever finding them plummet.

This is a statistical fact.

Esme likes facts.

The elevator doors open in the lobby.

Esme walks through them.

The electric grid task force can handle one less person. Especially someone like Esme, who's now completely lost the ability to concentrate on anything other than Marcus. She half expects someone to stop her or ask her where she's going. No one does. She is disobeying orders for the first time in her life. She's surprised to discover this makes her feel nothing. This is an emergency. New rules apply.

Outside, the rain immediately gets in her eyes and makes them sting; she blinks and the world looks like it's floating in a swimming pool; she blinks again and her vision clears. She holds her hands above her eyes as she runs. But her lungs betray her, so she half walks and half runs, running when she can, wheezing and walking when she must; there are stop signs in the middle of the sidewalks, and the stoplights don't match one another, but Esme doesn't care—she needs to make sure Marcus is okay. His phone still goes straight to voicemail. She runs past the blown-out coffee shop, a host of ambulances, streets clogged with confused cars that don't know where to turn, stoplights pointed the wrong way, and so many people, standing in the rain, until there, on her right, is her apartment building. She pounds up the stairs—how can she know where an elevator will go?—but exhausts herself by the tenth floor, taking the elevator the rest of the way. Its path is true, bringing her to the forty-third floor, and the hallway in her building remains gratefully the same, leading to her apartment. She reaches it with sopping hair and freezing hands and pulls her keys from her pocket.

But the front door is unlocked. And Marcus is gone.

6

Arjun's hat is gone. It's no big deal. But also, it is. And not just because he's sentimental. It was a gift from his mother, who still lives in Delhi, who refused to move with Arjun and his father to America. A week before the big move, she took Arjun to a hat shop to get it custom-made. She couldn't understand why anyone would ever buy nice clothes off the shelf. To her, if you wanted something nice, you got it made and that was that. You pushed your way through crowded market alleyways, taking hairpin turns around incense shops and walking through clouds of chicken meat and grease and dog and sweat and cloves and cardamom and fenugreek, until you found the best shop, the one that smelled like camel leather. And then they spent thirty minutes measuring you all over, even for a hat, because not only do they need the size of your head, they need your height and girth so they can make sure the hat's crown and brim are perfectly proportionate. It was a happy day when she brought Arjun to the hat shop. She knew he liked detective shows. That was how he prepared for the move to America, by watching television shows in English, repeating lines he'd heard over dinner. "Every man has his price, and every dame has a secret." "When the going gets tough, the tough get investigating." He was fifteen.

"You're only getting this one hat, beta," his mother told him when they went to pick it up the next day, as he touched the buttery leather for the first time and glimpsed himself in a dusty hand mirror. "So don't let your head get too big in America."

"I won't," he said, admiring himself in the mirror, the way his eyes looked dark and mysterious underneath the hat's brim. He stuck out his jaw to make it look more square and manly. "From here on out, I promise to only get dumber. My head will shrink to the size of a pin."

"Not that either," she said, pinching his cheeks. "Stay exactly as you are."

"That's impossible."

"You're my Arjun. You can do the impossible."

Now he's sitting in his van, touching his hatless head, pulling his fingers through the thick black mass of hair that got matted underneath the brim. He was angry when he realized his mother wouldn't be joining him and his father in leaving India. She told him only a day before they left that she had changed her mind. Her father was ill, she said, and her mother was dead, so someone needed to take care of Arjun's grandfather. "He has a million friends!" Arjun complained, but his mother said that wasn't enough, he needed blood. "So bring him with!" said Arjun, even though he didn't really like his grandfather, who coughed all the time and smelled like sour cigarettes. But his grandfather refused to leave, because he'd spent his whole life in this city, from the slums to, now, the top floor in a nice condo building. He said he'd made it to the pinnacle of life and didn't want to get any closer to the sun or else his eyes would burn out. He said the only thing he had left to do in his life was to keep praying to God, smoke a cigarette, and eat kaju katli, that silvered cashew candy. And the local tobacco was shit but the world's best cashew candies were right down the street, as was the temple. Every day in this home was paradise according to Arjun's grandfather, because he could wake at the crack of dawn, stumble over to the temple, pray for an hour, and return with cigarettes and candy. He couldn't exactly bring a whole temple to America, could he? So his grandfather stayed and his mother stayed, too, and Arjun hasn't been back since. It's been eight years. He misses the hat because he misses his mother, yes—she calls frequently, but he misses her cooking, her scent, her bad jokes that sometimes get jumbled in the static—but also everything the hat had made him feel. That he would be a movie star without the movie. The hero of his own life. A man with a hat, walking the streets of New York City.

The radio is turned up as loud as it can go, but even so, it's hard to hear over the rain pelting his windshield like pellets from a BB gun, and then his music gets interrupted by news briefs and public service announcements. "A child is reportedly trapped beneath a building in Hunts Point in the Bronx"—BAM BAM BAM BAM—"If you have electricity, please conserve to protect the grid"—BAM BAM BAM—"Thirty-car pileup on the street formerly known as Flatbush"—BAM BAM—"If you must drive, drive safely, but if you can, stay home"—BAM BAM BAM— "Storm downgraded from a Category 1 hurricane to a tropical storm"—BAM.

"Sure feels like a hurricane," he mutters and cannot hear himself. Eventually he gives up on untangling his hair and scratches his head mightily until the matted knots become a nest. If he had gel, he could slick it back like the cops in *Miami Vice*. That was the other touchstone of his cultural education. It consisted of two things: hard-boiled mysteries and *Miami Vice*. These two things contradict each other. One says that detectives wear hats and big jackets. The other says they wear hair gel and sunglasses and white leisure suits, never a hat. He figured he'd live in New York first, wearing hats and jackets, then move to Miami, wearing a slick button-down. And then when he moved to New York, he discovered that there is no consistency to anything. People wear leisure suits, sunglasses, gelled hair, cowhide, feathers and leather and platform boots. They wear sweatpants and suits and ball gowns and sometimes nothing at all. When he walks around in his fedora, no one gives him a passing glance. He blends in. He considers that a success.

Arjun's phone rings. He checks the ID. It's his team leader, Liz.

He picks it up right away. "Liz," he shouts, but he cannot hear a thing with the rain banging down, even after turning off the radio. "One moment, please," he shouts, and puts his car into drive. "One moment," he says again as he sees an empty-looking parking garage and pulls in. "Okay! Go!"

"Arjun."

"Did you get the memo, Liz? I called it in earlier. The Empire State Building is on Coney Island."

"That's nice," says Liz.

"Did you know the Empire State Building has its own zip code? More than a thousand businesses work there. It's like its own little city. Anyways, I think that's what's caused the blackouts over here. I imagine the grid was not prepared to handle a load as big as what comes from the Empire State Building. But there's one house, completely unaffected. It was fully lit up. Its address was listed in black iron letters on the door: 1103 Lamberts Lane. What can you tell me about that address?"

"We'll look into it."

"It looked like they had solar panels. There must be something else about it, though. Perhaps they run on their own battery system. Is this the kind of thing that goes through zoning? Perhaps we can learn from it—"

"We'll look into it, Arjun. It's time for you to go home."

"But I haven't really done anything yet."

"You've made your best effort, right?"

"I guess."

"You guess?"

"Yes."

"Do you have in-building parking? An attached garage? And how are you on gas?"

"Yes, in the basement. I'm okay."

"Keep a tracker in your van, just in case your parking lot ends up somewhere else. Gas stations are closed, so when you're running low, find a nearby shelter. We've sent out the coordinates. They'll have gas for you."

"Gas stations are closed?"

"Yes. The pumps are nowhere near their storage containers. They've been sealed off."

"Okay."

He hangs up the phone. The day has been a complete failure. Which, in a way, Arjun reminds himself, is a good thing. A day not saving anybody means a day where no one needed to be saved. But that's not true. The music keeps getting interrupted with names of those who are lost or missing. But why hasn't Arjun seen any of them? Those are a lot of names. But this is a big city. But surely he must have passed by at least one of them. But how many buts can you fit in one head? Eleven butts could fit in the seats of the van besides Arjun, but it's empty, except for the boxes of supplies he's been munching through as the day goes by. Again he blames the van. In the dark, you can barely see the words *Emergency Management*. If only he were in a fire truck. Or even a NYC Parks Enforcement Patrol vehicle. Or a tow truck or anything with a little light you can put on top of the car and look official. Or go the other way and join the Secret Service, with a car so dark you can't see a thing, but you know it's important, whatever it is. Not this ratty van with the seats that feel like cat scratchers.

Time to go home. Fine. He checks the map on his phone. It turns out he's not too far from the pin where his home should be. This morning he woke up in Brooklyn, and now he's back in Brooklyn. The streets are the same streets with the same number of lanes and the same potholes, although the sidewalks and their signs and stoplights have all been rearranged. It's a ten-minute drive to get home, and there's a shelter on the way. Ten minutes. That's only two songs' worth of time, or one if it's an improvisational jazz number. But it will probably take longer to get through the lawless intersections that have no guidance. And his fingers aren't ready for sleep. They are wilding out on his steering wheel, drumming to a song he can't name, the one always playing in his head on repeat.

Arjun opens his social media feed. His "Crazy Day" explosion photo has now received ten likes and two reposts. He likes each repost, then scrolls through the feed. Most people are posting things similar to Arjun's post, with photos of the closed-off tunnels and explosions and the occasional flood. Some people are talking about what they are doing to get through the storm without electricity or gas. Romantic candles and portable phone chargers are being sold on the online marketplace, with vague approximations of where they are or promises for delivery. Others are talking about the boy who's apparently trapped beneath a building in Hunts Point in the Bronx. Where exactly, they're not sure. Arjun tries to remember if he's ever been to Hunts Point.

He vaguely remembers its proximity to Rikers Island, where the Bronx River meets the East. This missing boy. What is his name? He tries to find it. Then he gets a notification. His heart pops. His post has gotten one more repost, which he likes. And then his alarm goes off. It's time for his evening clonazepam, and he hasn't thought about his anxiety all day. Too busy thinking about other things. He pops his pill dry, backs out of the parking garage, and turns on the radio.

Classical music plays from the speaker. He's not a classical music man, but today, maybe, he should be. It swells beautifully just as the rain begins to subside. So that's why they said it was just tropical. The storm really is beginning to fade. Then the music cuts out. There's a voice. The voice he's heard all day, the mayor repeating a warning. They've blasted her voice out of speakers on every corner. And now she's in his car. This voice. He doesn't even know her name. Mayor Mayor.

"Go home and stay home." The mayor's voice is calm and collected. "If someone goes missing, don't go out looking. Call the authorities and submit a ticket. Don't be a hero. We'll get through this. We're strong. We're together. We're New York."

Don't be a hero. It feels like she is chastising Arjun specifically. It feels like a challenge.

Arjun drives toward Hunts Point to search for a missing boy.

. . .

A woman nearby, walking in the rain, has many regrets. For starters, she straightened her bleached blonde hair with an iron, but this was a mistake: Even underneath her yellow hooded coat and red umbrella, the rain steals in and within minutes she can feel it all frizz. And the sweat on her neck. Her raincoat is uncomfortably hot, her skin swollen with heat. The nylon grabs her skin through her thin black dress, her favorite dress, the one that smooths the lumps while accentuating the curves. If she were feeling sensible, she would have worn something with more coverage. But this is not a sensible night.

She's on her way to a date. Yes, tonight. She hasn't met him in person yet but she feels like he knows her better than anyone. And she knows him, too, at least as much as she can gather from their conversations and her internet searches. It's not stalking if someone puts it all out there. His life story is splashed on the "About" page at Bluzz, which he founded. After much research she's concluded that he's definitely not a serial killer. If so he'd have to have taken on five different identities by now. Instead her date has one very strong identity. New York, New York, New York. For as long as he can remember, the website says, he's been hitting the pavement, gathering stories from strangers. From people living on the street to working on Wall Street, he could get anyone to talk. *All you gotta do is ask questions,* he wrote. *Everyone's dying to tell their story.* He hired journalists from all over the world, from southwest Virginia to the Philippines—so he said in an interview that she'd watched five times already, studying the movements of his lips. She loves his look and his voice and his words and so watching his mouth is the perfect amalgamation. "You should be a nature documentary narrator," she told him once in a video chat, just wanting to watch him talk. "Tell me about the hardship of being a penguin." He proceeded to tell her about the penguins in the Bronx Zoo that were quite possibly being fed radioactive kibbles. Then he told her about the rats' hideaways in the subway tunnels, how their congregations are an open secret, but the city refuses to exterminate them, be-cause this group includes some of New York's most famous rats:

Pizza Rat, Bubble Tea Rat, all the rats that have brought the city fame and its residents joy, and though everyone complains, they won't be gone anytime soon. "Tell me about pigeons now," she said. "Why the purple feathers?" But he responded, "They're diurnal. I'm nocturnal. I don't know a thing about pigeons." His nocturnal nature made things difficult when she tried to schedule an in-person meetup. His work hours were her free hours. He slept until five in the afternoon, then worked all night. But sometimes he took breaks from work to call her.

"Did you know," he told her one night, "that the governor of New York technically died and was resuscitated?"

She didn't know.

"Did you know that honking a car horn is literally illegal in New York?"

She didn't know that either.

"Did you know that people who have their first date in a hurricane are more likely to have children together?"

"Really?"

"Not sure, actually. Want to find out?"

That was earlier today, when their video call extended from a fifteen-minute chat to a five-hour conversation. She took breaks only to refresh her makeup and fix her hair and make sure the video camera was positioned the right way, pointed at her good side from above to highlight the eyes and hide the double chin. She felt good, with her bleached hair straightened to a shine, and a liquid eyeliner pen that didn't smear once. She thought if she were on a reality television show, she'd be considered "the pretty one." Contoured cheeks, bronzed forehead, and a perfectly dewy nose. Fake eyelashes that looked real. She'd spent days figuring out the best places to take photographs for her dating profile. It was all worth it when he said: "You're beautiful." And:

"Your selfies are like works of art." And: "I can't believe we're still talking, it's been five hours." She couldn't believe it either. She didn't have a drop to drink and yet she felt liquid and warm and open. She refrained from her normal nervous habits of asking him if he was having a good time and did he like her hair and did he think she was too fat and it's not some kind of fetish, right? Instead she talked about her childhood, her secrets, her dreams, things she had kept unspoken. They also talked a little about the Unmapping. It was his news outlet, after all, that had broken the story. His lead reporter had traveled all the way to Gleamwood City to prove its veracity.

"It reminds me of tree blindness," she pondered. "The Unmapping."

"Tree blindness?"

"You know how most people can't tell one tree from another? And even when you learn about things like maple and oak, it's still difficult, especially in winter when there are no leaves. Any given tree is obviously extremely different from any other tree, like with its bark pattern and branches and height and everything. And yet we see one tree and to most people, it's just a tree. Maybe trees feel the same way about humans. About houses. One house is just like another house. What's the difference?"

"That's incredibly profound," he said. "Can I steal that?"

"Go ahead," she said, pleased. He gave shape to her inchoate thoughts, made her want to quit her boring copyediting job. He made her want to ask questions, to discover the world. To discover, by extension, herself. That's why she's here, after growing up with her parents in New Rochelle and having lived with them throughout and even after community college, because they loved her so much and doted on her so much it was hard for her to leave, even as they never let her go to the city, warning of its dangers. Her mom cried for two hours when she dyed her curly brown hair silvery blonde, and her dad cried for three when she told them she was moving out, when she explained that, after twenty-three years of life, she needed to find herself, which was hard to do with them breathing down her neck.

"What does that mean, find yourself?" her father sobbed. "You're right here."

She didn't quite know what it meant, only that she had to do it. And that she had to do it in the city, on her own. And she loved it here. Every step she took, there was something beautiful to see. She found beauty in the neon lights reflected in dirty puddles. She loved how she looked in the dark and dirty bar mirrors. She loved watching her clothes spin in the washer at the laundromat. She loved cooking her own food with turmeric and cayenne and bright green kale, trying to get every color of the rainbow on each platter. She even appreciated the time someone stole her clothes from the dryer, because she told herself to learn from this lesson, and the robbery necessitated a wardrobe refresh. Is that what finding yourself means? Being fully responsible for yourself.

Whatever it was, today she got close. Five hours of talking and they were getting closer to the truth. Or closer to each other. Or . . . something. "I'm enamored by you," he said suddenly, at the five-hour mark. His comment was so abruptly romantic it still makes her blush, even now, in the chill of the rain as she walks in the night.

"I want to see you in person," she said. "Can you come over?"

"There's a stay-at-home order," he said. "But I have a feeling that's not meant for people like you. It's meant for people like me."

"Like you?"

"People with a certain amount of melanin, shall we say."

So they agreed that she'd walk to his apartment. She insisted.

After weeks of chatting virtually, she needed to see the real thing. Yesterday, she lived in Queens while he lived in Manhattan, but today, they're both in north Brooklyn, which feels like fate. He offered to stay online with her the whole time she walked to make sure she was okay.

"You don't need to do that," she said.

"You sure?"

"I'd rather listen to music."

That was the truth. Music would calm her. Now that she was finally going to meet him in person, she needed the smooth sedative of bubblegum pop. It could transport her through time as she moved through space, and when she arrived, she'd feel like no time had passed at all. Before they hung up, he reminded her to set up a pin at her house so she could get home later that night. "Duh," she said, though she hadn't thought of it.

She packed a small bag with makeup, her wallet, and her pepper spray. Her mother's warnings were always in her ear and it didn't hurt to be prepared, even on a night like tonight, pouring rain, when no one would be out. She was ready to be there. To close her eyes and listen to the music and wake up in his arms.

Too late, she realizes her mistake.

The wind is making the rain go sideways into the headphones, which sputter out from an electrical failure. She puts away her phone. It's cold. Yesterday it was warm and now it's cold. She tightens the scarf around her neck. And yet she's sweating between her legs and on her chest. She's cold and hot and her legs are exposed to the rain. It's a one-mile walk, nothing unreasonable. But now, thirty minutes into it, she wants to die. This rain is one thing. The wind is another. Why didn't anyone warn her about the wind? But she must already be nearly there, so at this point it's easier to finish it.

The streets are empty. A single taxi approaches but drives by too quickly for her to flag it down. No one else is walking on the streets on this rainy, windy night. No one is as stupid as her.

Except for them.

Three people are on the sidewalk just ahead of her, standing in a circle, laughing. They push each other around, taking up the whole walkway. There are no streetlamps here, so she doesn't see them until she practically bumps into them. They have rain jackets pulled low over their faces and no umbrellas, but she can tell by their voices that they are young. Teenagers, maybe even younger.

"Excuse me," she says.

The boys don't move off the sidewalk.

She checks the street for cars—it's empty—and moves to step around them, into a gutter filled with water, which seeps into a hole in her rain boot.

The boys move with her, into the street, blocking her way.

"Hi," she says. "Can I help you?"

"This is the part where you give us your stuff," says one of them, holding up a kitchen knife. She can hardly see the blade in the dark, except for its glint of light.

His face is so young.

"Is this a joke?"

But there's no laughter anymore.

The other two boys have knives in their hands, too.

The rain is pouring down.

Later, she'll wonder if there was something she could have said. She could have talked them down, asked if they really wanted to do this, if this was the road they wanted to go down; they're still young, they can turn things around; she could have offered to pay them to let her keep her stuff, anything they wanted, or maybe she could have hidden her phone. How? Somehow. They should be home right now. So should she. Why didn't they follow the stay-at-home order? Why didn't she? Everything feels upside down. They're out to experience whatever this is. So is she. But why the knives? One big knife and two small paring knives. She has pepper spray in her purse. But there are three of them. And they're ready. They're so young.

In the moment, she barely registers what's happening. Kids. Knives. Purse. Headphones. Rain dripping down her jacket from her neck to her spine.

"Hurry up," says another boy.

She holds out her bag. They tell her, impatiently, to just give them the phone and wallet, not the whole bag. She obliges. The kids laugh and run off.

If her body stopped working in those few seconds, now it revs up to top gear. Heart pounding. Breath coming in gulps. Nausea. She doesn't know what to do. Go find her date's apartment? She's close at this point, a few blocks away. But how many blocks? One? Five? And what's the address? What's the apartment number? She's already forgotten. And what about the way back? Has she been walking thirty minutes? Twenty-five? Thirty-five? She needs to find him, but then what? No, who cares about the date; let him wait—she needs to go back home, while her feet hold some memory of the route. In this rain?

She turns back and starts running, straight until the road curves, which she doesn't remember from before; she must've gone too far. She turns back and runs in and out of side streets to look for something familiar. A taxi drives by—she waves to pull him over, but the driver doesn't notice. Another taxi appears from around the corner and she runs into the street in front of it to wave it down. It rolls to a stop. She dashes to the driver's-side window, which is barely cracked; she can't see inside, only her own reflection scattered by drips. "Please," she says. "I'm lost. Can you help me find my apartment?" She catches her breath; her lungs scream from the running, and what if they come back? And what if someone else finds her instead? She has nothing left to give. She's never felt so alone. She wanted to find herself tonight. But what if someone else finds her first?

"You don't know where you're going?" says a man with a strong Brooklyn accent from inside the cab.

"It's somewhere around here." She resists the urge to reach inside the window. It smells like cologne, which makes her hungry.

"Sure," he says. "Five dollars a minute."

"I don't have any money," she says.

The car pulls away, drenching her with water.

Another car drives down the road. A dark blue van with bright headlights that flash in her eyes, blinding her. She covers her face. Even without her beckoning, the van pulls over. Who is inside? What do they want? She has nothing left to give.

"I'm with the Emergency Management Department," says a voice from the van. "I'm here to help."

◆　◆　◆

He set out to rescue a boy in Hunts Point, and instead he rescues a beautiful blonde woman. What's her name? Already forgot, would be stupid to ask again. His one rescue and he forgot. She was mugged on the way to a date, she says, and could she borrow his phone to call him? He hands it to her. Then she says she doesn't know her date's phone number. "His name is Rick. Rick . . . Rick. Can you look up his number in some sort of city system?" She hands the phone back to him.

"Last name Rick? I cannot call Rick Rick."

"Wait, I can look up his last name, if I can just borrow your phone again—"

"Apologies, ma'am, we need to get you to the shelter." Arjun searches the map Liz sent him with a list of shelter GPS coordinates. The closest one is in the lobby of a nearby Holiday Inn. He puts his phone on the dashboard and sets up the navigation system. His gas is at a quarter tank. More than enough to get him there. He could even drive fast. It's a straight shot down I-278. He will drive and drive and save the day.

He's just about to pull onto the highway when the phone rings, disrupting the navigation.

Esme.

Arjun pulls over and accepts the call. Esme's voice is frantic. "Can you pick me up?"

7

Esme spends approximately ten minutes in her apartment before going on the search for Marcus. Those ten minutes are a complete waste. In that time, the apartment is turned inside out and Esme is no closer to finding Marcus. She's ripped the blankets off the bed, upturned the closet, and opened every cabinet in the kitchen. No Marcus. She's torn apart his office, searching for notes amid the piles of printed papers. But no, he's not nestled in the spoons or hidden under the bathroom sink. He's not sleeping in the oven. He's gone.

There's only one explanation. He went on a run. He got out of bed, ignored the texts and phone calls, put on his shoes, and went out the door. The man can run far. He can run a half marathon without thinking much about it. Esme doesn't know his running route. Why doesn't she know his running route? In DC, when they were in college, he occasionally convinced her to jog with him, and he would even take it slow to match her pace as they ran through his favorite neighborhoods. Capitol Hill was a given, its rich row houses filled with politics and history. Kalorama was even better, home to embassies and ambassadors. Esme liked looking at the rustic bricks and flower gardens. Marcus liked imagining conspiratorial plots happening beneath their feet. He was convinced that the president of Iran secretly lived in Lincoln's cottage, and that there was a nonzero possibility of aliens in the naval observatory, controlling the world's clocks as best fit their own machinations.

But these days she works while he sleeps and he runs while she works and she doesn't run anymore. Marcus runs in the rain, snow, sleet, or heat; it doesn't matter, he's out in the elements. Ready to come back with that big smile, stinking of sweat and joy.

She can still smell the deodorant on his pillow.

Esme steps through the glass door to the balcony, which is big enough for two people to stand close together, but not much else, where she has a view of a small chunk of the city. Normally, in Chelsea, she has a view of the High Line. Now she sees only Marcus, everywhere. They're on the forty-third floor of a highrise and the few people on the ground look like toy pieces in a board game. Each one could be Marcus. But they aren't. She wants to scream his name but that would only make her feel small. She looks for a bright blue windbreaker. Marcus's windbreaker. In this rain he'd be wearing it, no question. The city sways. Her building moves slightly in the strong storm winds, which have been downgraded from hurricane to tropical but are still strong enough to make her heart leap.

Time to search.

It's pouring sideways rain, which will make Esme's umbrella mostly useless. But she has planned her route carefully. She will walk around every single block surrounding their apartment building, turning four times until she's back where she started, then one block farther out, taking this wider circuit around the original, up and down connecting streets, calling out Marcus's name all the while, and so on until the night grows late or her feet fall off from walking. And hope, and hope, that if she doesn't find him, it's because he found the building, this ugly building, easy enough to recognize by its rusted copper doorway and moldy concrete and tiny dots of balconies that make it look like a beehive. It's an ugly building with an ugly name: Gleamwood Gardens, which Esme complained about when they first moved in. There is no tree or plant called gleamwood, so how can you have a garden for a plant that doesn't exist? Not just one garden, but multiple gardens? There isn't even a courtyard or any plants on their roof. It's affordable, however, thanks to the housing lottery, and their apartment is well decorated, with floating shelves to hold candles and photo frames, a beautiful wooden bookshelf Esme found on the street, and peel-and-stick wallpaper with lemon trees. Esme is proud of their apartment and usually likes to keep it clean. She is suddenly embarrassed by the mess she made. What will he think when he gets home to this? She leaves him a note on the kitchen table: *If you get home, call me ASAP*, and adds her phone number, in case his phone has died, but what if he can't find the note amid the mess? What if he thinks something happened to *her* and he goes out to find her and the cycle continues until both of them are lost? They'd spiral outward into a fractal of lostness until they ended up dead on the bottom of the Hudson River.

Not worth worrying about that. She commits to walking until she can't any longer. At least until four in the morning, when the city unmaps again. No. Until ten o'clock, the new curfew. Or until someone forces her to go home due to the stay-at-home order. But she knows they won't enforce that. It's more of a suggestion. So she will walk until her legs fall off and then she will find her way back to her GPS marker. It will take a long time; it's crude and inefficient, but it's the only thing she can do. She tries to decide whether he'd first go east or west; it must be one or the other, to run to a river, to see the sun, to escape the city's permanent shadows. And then, at the river, north or south? Two choices would be one thing, but four is impossible. He never told her, and now, she knows nothing. She should have asked. She should have watched him leave. She should know everything about him, or at least things like this. What goes on in his head when they're not together?

The rain is picking up, in thick sheets now. It soaks through her thin felt gloves and reaches down the neck of her jacket. She rounds the first block, then the second, and is relieved to confirm that the Hudson River is where it's supposed to be, along with the Hudson River Park.

She can barely hear her calls of "Marcus" over the rain as she pushes into the streets, through every empty alleyway, passing by glassy skyscrapers, noting each vacant street cart and parking lot and construction site, as if mentally recording these buildings will provide her with some clue: Marcus likes hot dog stands but hates gyros, likes fruit juice but hates ice cream. He loves Chinatown but hates Little Italy. They went to this sushi restaurant once, on their anniversary, even though he admitted later that he hated the idea of sushi. She walks up to the former 30s, down to the former 10s, up to the former 40s. After she reaches the southern tip of the island, she goes only north, which feels like accomplishing something, like climbing a mountain. The parks, like the rivers, have stayed where they are, but their statues and monuments have been shuffled around and the public bathrooms have now been replaced by bodegas. She tells herself more stories about where Marcus might be, why he's fine: His phone's dead and he hasn't memorized any numbers to make a call with a borrowed phone. He's found shelter in a coffee shop. He's in a deli, chatting up the cashier. He's popped into a church for a bagel, because even though he doesn't like church, churches always show up with bagels in times like these, bagels from the beyond. He's found a shelter, yes, that's it; he's still lost but keeping calm and focusing on finding somewhere safe. Marcus always keeps her calm; he's good at it. She's not. No, she is not good at keeping calm, which she realizes as the ground pulses in the rain, as black despair throbs in her chest. It feels pointless but there's nothing she can do but move on, keep walking, keep searching, keep calling out his name. The mayor's voice comes now from speakers that Esme can't see. "Don't be a hero. Go home and stay calm." Esme knows the speakers are scattered throughout the city for emergency announcements just like this, but where? They're hiding. They're unimportant. Every ten steps, a new sliver of life where Marcus might be found. And yet there's nothing. Not even a shoelace. If only she could find a scrap of his jacket. Some sign that he ever existed.

"Don't be a hero." The mayor's voice is calm and that only makes Esme feel worse. The streets are crowded with rain, and sometimes an ambulance, sometimes an Emergency Management vehicle. An ambulance rushes down a low-lying street that will soon become a river, and the wheels spray Esme, a great solid wave that overtakes her whole body; her phone is in her rain jacket pocket but her face is exposed, her gloves are sopping wet; she'd shake them off and keep going but an emergency van drives by on the same street and sprays her once more, soaking every single centimeter of exposed skin.

"Go home and stay calm." The water on the street feels warm at first but quickly turns cold. The November heat wave has chilled in the storm. A shudder takes her. The buildings surrounding her look as if they lean over her, like they will fall at any moment, on Esme; despair tightens behind her eyes; she takes deep breaths to keep calm—rain jacket fabric, fingers on fingers, water on face—and rests upon these sensations.

"Don't be a hero." That announcement from the mayor keeps cropping up on every block. Esme keeps looking for the source of the voice but doesn't see it. She wants to smash it. Who is the mayor to tell her to stay home? Who is she to intrude on this, the worst day of Esme's life? Who is she?

◆   ◆   ◆

The mayor of New York City has a three-week headache. She's thrown everything she can at it: ibuprofen, acetaminophen, aspirin, caffeine, acupuncture, rishi healing, yoga, tarot, massages and crystal therapy, and enough water to fill a koi pond; all of it has been consumed and aimed at her head, but the pain has only gotten bigger and fuller. The doctors have carried out all sorts of tests and concluded that she's fine, just needs to sleep more and cut out the caffeine, but the caffeine is the only thing that gives her any relief: When she goes without it, she can't think, she can't work, so what is she supposed to do, let the city die?

The night before the Unmapping, the headache was the worst it'd ever been, waking her up in the middle of the night and keeping her awake until four a.m., when she finally found some relief with sleep. The dream came quickly: gambling with the mayor of Atlantic City, playing on a new Christmas-tree-themed slot machine. They shared a seat; she sat on his lap. He put his hairy white hand on her smooth brown one and they pulled the lever together. Three golden trees. Cha-ching. And ring.

The hotline by her bed rang, a blaring tone on what looked like an old-fashioned rotary, even though the phone was completely digital. It was loud. And not just the sound of the phone.

Everything *felt* loud. A red light burned onto the back of her eye-lids. Her bed's stiff quilt sandpapered her skin. The air conditioner spit out cold. This was no ordinary wake-up call. This call came straight from the Emergency Management Department.

She sat up straight, her dream disappearing in a blink.

"Don't make me think," she said. "Just tell me what to do."

The head commissioner didn't tell the mayor what to do. Instead, Commissioner Kelley told the mayor everything she knew, which was not very much, other than the fact that the Unmapping was here. "I thought that was a joke," said the mayor. Then she was passed through to the Emergency Management Department press office, where a young, peppy woman said they'd send a script for a press announcement, and they should schedule a virtual press conference ASAP so the mayor could explain why they were issuing an emergency stay-at-home order.

"Stay-at-home order?"

"Yes. Which means you better not leave Gracie Mansion. We don't want to look like hypocrites, do we?"

Who was this woman, giving the mayor orders? She didn't even know her name.

"You have our number if you need anything. Have a great day!" The woman on the other end of the line clicked out.

Have a great day? The mayor supposed it was a gut reflex to end a phone call this way. Still. It felt like spite. That young woman, that girl, didn't know what it was like to carry the responsibility of a city's safety. And to feel it all crashing down.

That phone call feels like weeks ago, though it's only been—the mayor checks her watch—fourteen hours. Since then, after a record five minutes to do her hair and makeup and put on her go-to power suit, she has spent every possible moment receiving or relaying information. Everyone has come out of the woodwork to talk to her today. Despite the stay-at-home order, dozens of people keep showing up at Gracie Mansion. They work for her, but still. They come without warning. To her home. Drinking her coffee. Every time she goes to the kitchen, the coffee maker is in the process of rebrewing. But she has no time to wait for the new pot. If she stays still for more than ten seconds, someone new will find her and pull her away. The sanitation commissioner needs to know what to do about the landfill retaining walls disappearing. The health commissioner demands more fuel for the hospital backup generators. The Gracie Mansion building manager requires her advice on what to do with all the aluminum Christmas trees. Who cares about the aluminum Christmas trees? "Well, there are about four hundred of them stacked in the driveway, getting in the way." The director of Yankee Stadium wants five acres of tarp to cover up the grass. Two thousand people are reported missing. Three thousand. And a much larger number of people have shown up lost, knocking on whatever door looked friendly enough to accept them. The libraries-turned-shelters are dealing with drug sales in their basements. Fifty children are missing. Sixty. Seventy. Gunshots are reported in Times Square. The mayor's press secretary says the mayor needs to record a video public service announcement that they can blast through speakers set up around the city and play on a loop on every digital billboard.

"Can't you just pull from the press conference footage?" she asks.

Her press secretary says no. "It's different." So for five quiet minutes, the mayor goes into a soundproof room to read from a script, with no one asking questions, and no one telling her anything terrible, and she doesn't even remember what was in the script—something about staying home, staying safe, we'll figure things out, blah blah blah—but when she finishes, her social media manager tells her, "That was sick."

"Thank you?"

Her scheduling assistant hands her a phone. She holds it to her ear; it's ringing. A man picks up with a broken voice. "He-eh-llo?" The mayor looks at her scheduling assistant in a nonverbal plea for assistance. He's holding a notebook that says: *His name is Brian. Survived a gas explosion in refrigerator, which catapulted out of his house and landed three yards over. Currently in hospital. Tell him the city cares.*

The miracle is that her headache disappears, at least for a moment. But as soon as she remembers, it comes back, stronger than ever. This happens multiple times. It disappears, and when she notices, it's back. People speak to her and she lives half on the surface of their conversation, half in the pain in her head. *It's all in your head,* she tells herself often, a grim joke that makes her want to laugh, or else scream. Just because it's all in her head doesn't mean it's not real. There is a very real pain. After saying a few kind words to this Brian character, who can only moan in response, she walks into her bedroom to find the directors of transportation and finance deep in conversation, and when they see her, they pull her in. They disagree over whether or not they will be able to bring buses back online, because with the subways out until further notice, people need a way to get around, and the buses will be useless with their stops all shuffled, won't they? But the environment head says no, they will be essential, and we can't give up on our efficient public transportation options, right? At least for the people who don't flee the city. It'll just take a week or so to figure out.

"A week?" asks the mayor. She's been planning to take a private preholiday break with the Atlantic City mayor and his son at her house on the shore. "When do you expect this to be over?"

They give her a look, like *You poor thing.*

"And what do you mean by—never mind."

She wants to ask what they meant about people fleeing the city, then decides it's too much for her to handle right now. She walks straight out of the bedroom and into the master bathroom for two minutes of quiet. Maybe she should offer to do another PSA. Or anything to get back to the silence of the soundproof room. She rolls down her pantyhose, sits on the toilet, and tries to urinate—nothing comes out, she's severely dehydrated—when her cell phone rings. She sends the call to voicemail, but it rings again, and one more time, and then she hears someone bang on the bathroom door.

"Occupied," the mayor calls out. "Obviously."

"It's the White House on the phone," says her scheduling assistant.

The mayor pulls up her tights and fixes her skirt and opens the bathroom door. Her assistant holds out a landline phone with a long cable leading from the hallway. The mayor grabs the phone. "Connecting you now to the president of the United States," says a voice. She goes back into the bathroom and closes the door. The phone clicks and there is silence. But not the silence she wants. It is a silence that expects. It's waiting for her.

The mayor takes a deep breath. "Mr. President." She tries to speak quietly to keep the bathroom echo out of her voice. "It's an honor."

"Ms. Mayor," he says. "What the hell is going on?"

She almost responds, *Are you fucking kidding me with this question?* But she holds her tongue and says instead, "They're calling it the Unmapping."

"The Unmapping."

"Yes."

"I'm asking you what's going on and you're telling me it's the Unmapping."

"Yes."

"I hate to break it to you, Mayor, but sometimes I actually watch the news."

She sighs. "It's fucking crazy, whatever's happening. What do you want me to say? Ask me a question and I'll tell you what I can."

His voice gets quiet. "Is it real?"

"Is it real?" The pain in her head comes back with a vengeance, pulsing all the way to her shoulders. She swallows it down. "Mr. President, I don't know how to answer that. Whatever is happening out there is very real, whether or not anyone believes it. We have had very real car pileups and very real gas explosions and very real blackouts and a very real minor earthquake. Wait—that one was a false flag. But there are very real hospitals full of very real premature babies hooked up to life support at risk of shutting down from power outages."

"Right, then," says the president. "I meant no offense, my friend. Tell me. What's causing this thing?"

"Our people are working on it."

"I'd like to hear what you think. Man to man. It's not terrorism, right? Some next-level 9/11 or anything like that?"

"Why don't you tell me? Man to woman."

"My sources say it's not terrorism."

"Mine, too," she says, pressing on her temples. "Let's see. Most people who've had time to actually think about this believe it has something to do with global warming. The energy we put into our atmosphere creates entropy. Entropy, by definition, is the degree of randomness. Theoretically it's possible for you to jump through a brick wall—all of the cells in your body could bypass all of the molecules in the brick—it's just a matter of probability. The theory is that global warming makes the unlikely more likely."

"Entropy. What am I, a scientist? Nobody knows what entropy is."

"I know. Let me try again. Heat is basically air with energy, with each individual particle moving more quickly. But what's actually moving is the particles, not the empty space. The movement of these particles causes entropy, which basically means unusable heat. As in, we can't do anything productive with it. Like, we can turn normal heat into energy at power plants when we aim that heat toward a generator. But we can't turn entropy into energy. It's irreversible. It's like making a smoothie. You mix in your bananas with your apples, but then you can't undo it. You can't turn a smoothie back into a banana. A banana has structure. In a smoothie, the structure breaks down and is irreversible."

"So global warming is making us into a giant smoothie."

"Not yet, but maybe someone's turned on the blender. I know it all sounds crazy and I'm sure I'm not saying it right, but it's happening, so we need to entertain crazy ideas, and this one sounds like the least crazy, to be honest."

"What are the other ideas?"

"It's something like brain chemistry. If you consider the planet an organism, you're at the mercy of its whims. Animals in stressful situations will act strategically to avoid threats—mostly we're talking about predators, but also, say, floods and storms— until their strategies no longer work. At a certain tipping point, their brain floods with a stress hormone, and their behavior switches from strategic to random. It's almost the same as the entropy argument. There's too much energy, too much stress, and the city needs to shake it loose, like how boiling water happens when it's too hot and it's trying to cool."

"You're telling me we're living on a giant brain. And this brain is a boiling pot of water?"

"I'm not telling you anything. I'm trying to explain what others have been telling me. If it's the global warming thing, well, we have our work cut out for us, but at least we'd know what to do. But if we're living on a brain, I don't know, maybe we need to pray to our brainy overlord. Some idiots think we're in purgatory and need to commit mass suicide to set ourselves free, and we need to stop those idiots from spreading their idiocy. There's also something about aluminum Christmas trees. I can't remember."

"Which one do you believe?"

"I don't know, that we're in a giant AI-powered simulation that's either glitching out or testing us. If so, doesn't matter; I'm just trying to keep our city under control. We've had to shut down the electricity in half the boroughs. The subways are shut down and so are the tunnels. We've had three dozen pileups from people trying to get off the island. A thirteen-year-old boy is trapped beneath a building. One guy's refrigerator exploded. No—wait—his house exploded, his refrigerator saved him. Half my staff are missing and the other half are in my bedroom. But we have power in the hospitals and a system for getting ambulances to those who need them, and we're just trying to get through to tomorrow, when everything will change again, and we'll have an entirely new set of problems to face."

"Understood."

The mayor leans against the bathroom wall and stares at the sink. There's grime around the drain. Who used this sink today? There are shells from Atlantic City on the counter, and cedar-scented moisturizer in a hand-pump jar. She touches the shells and brings them to her nose. For a brief moment, her headache dissipates. Then she remembers the president, still on the phone squished between her ear and her neck. He's droning on about how the Unmapping has already taken hold in small towns in upstate New York. "And, of course, that place in Wisconsin. Glowville or Glitterpop or whatever."

"I've heard the same."

"So it'll spread?"

She stares at herself in the mirror and holds back the urge to punch it, break the glass, and see what's on the other side. For a half moment she lets herself imagine a portal in the mirror through which she can jump and land above the clouds, riding the eye of the hurricane like she's riding a wild horse, barely holding on to the reins. "Probably, yes."

"Tell me what I can do to help."

So many people are telling her to tell them what to do. She wants to say, *You should know what to do! Just do something!* "Expediting disaster funding would be a good start. Getting FEMA out here, too."

"Great. I'll pass that on to my secretary."

The mayor touches the part of the mirror where she can cover up the bags beneath her eyes.

"Stay safe, Mayor. The world is watching."

Ready to watch her fail. If the public hasn't landed on this narrative yet, they will soon. They'll say she didn't see it coming. But who did? It seemed impossible. Why should the New York City mayor, in particular, out of all the mayors in the country, all the mayors in the world, have done something? Why did it happen to New York and not Atlantic City, for instance? Luck. People only think about the positive side of luck, but if you turn it upside down, for everyone that makes it big, there are a million unlucky losers. So no one's blaming the mayor of Atlantic City for sitting on his ass playing online Skee-Ball, when it could just as easily have happened to him. Months ago, the two of them had talked about it over slots together. Laughed about it. And then, later that night, had the best sex she's ever had. She'd screamed into her sheets.

The phone clicks out.

She wonders how long it will take anyone to realize the phone call has ended. Outside this door, there are dozens of people waiting for her. They talk too much. They need too much. It's too much for one brain to handle.

Her cell phone starts ringing. She sends it to voicemail. It starts ringing again, as does the landline, just as someone knocks on the door and as a text comes in:

NY Governor on the line. Emergency.

• • •

Esme isn't sure how long it takes Arjun to arrive after she calls him. Or how long she's been walking. All she knows is that it's late and that she's far from home and that she's still, somehow, walking. At the end of every block she thinks she won't be able to walk any more. And then she walks one more block. The rain comes and goes and comes again. Arjun has her phone location, so she can walk without worrying or thinking. Walking is the only thing that staves off the terrible truth that Marcus is gone.

When Arjun pulls up in his Emergency Management van, she does not cry. When she gets into the van and buckles her seat belt, she does not cry. When Arjun asks what's wrong, she bursts into tears.

Suddenly she's in his arms and that makes her cry harder. Hazily she sees herself leaning into him; she sees how she found his shoulder and let herself into it, let herself go. Somehow she is able to spit out the words she's been avoiding. Her fiancé is gone and she has no idea how to find him. Every word makes her cry harder. It is a pain she has known exactly once in her life, when her mother died unexpectedly, but Esme was young; she had forgotten. Now she remembers. The black hole of grief that nearly consumed her, it was there all along, hiding behind a thin curtain. Death is always there. At this point, there are only two possible answers. Marcus is lost, or Marcus is dead. The latter feels impossible. It just cannot be. As far as she knows, no one has died today. Not officially. The Unmapping has no body count yet. It's the missing that matter.

Some of these words must have made it out of her mouth, because Arjun says, "Let's check the registry to see if he's checked in." It's the first thing he's said other than "It's okay, it's okay," words that Esme doesn't believe but feel nice all the same. She wants him to stroke her hair and say it's okay; she wants to crawl into a mother's lap, any mother, or anyone who will hold her as they sway back and forth on a rocking chair. But now he's broken the dream with his words. She pulls herself back to sit up straight and looks out the window, ashamed. The tears are gone and they won't come back.

"What's his last name?" asks Arjun.

"Miller," Esme says quietly. "Marcus Michael Miller."

"Three M. Millers have signed in to shelters!" he says. "Let me see . . ."

Esme waits. Arjun clicks through a few screens and then puts down his phone, silent. Then he says: "I'm sure there's a backlog. You know how these things go. Every time I refresh, the website times out. There are so many technical failures today. What's one more?" He turns the key in the ignition. "Let's get you home."

"Okay."

They pull onto the road and, aside from giving Arjun her apartment building's GPS coordinates, Esme doesn't bother to look at the street signs or her map to try to put together where she is or where she ought to be. She feels the part of her that should ask these questions, somewhere inside her, and ignores it. Too tired. Yes, the fatigue comes now, after she's been awake for who knows how long, after a night of rough sleep, maybe even two nights, and she's at her limit. She closes her eyes. The rain pounding on the windshield begins to feel soft and dreamy.

"Sorry it took me so long to get here," says Arjun. "I had to drop someone off at a shelter. She was on her way to a date. In this rain!"

"Hmm." The heat blasting out of his van feels like a lullaby. Sleep is just there, on the other side of the vent, and she reaches for it. She rests her head against the window glass. It cools her cheek, which feels wonderful, like an ice cube, melting. Arjun is playing classical music on the radio. A flute sounds just like cool glass feels.

Suddenly the music has become surf rock and Arjun is saying, "We're here."

There it is. Gleamwood Gardens. "Ugliest building in the city," she says, waking from her half slumber. "Stupidest name, too." But now the name tickles something in her brain. Gleamwood City is the name of the Wisconsin town where it began. Ground zero for the Unmapping. That's half the reason why Marcus wanted to go, she remembers now. The matching names. He felt some cosmic connection. How could she not think of that? Maybe he doesn't want to go home. Maybe the name scares him—

"You don't have to go home," says Arjun. "We can drive all night to look for him. Whatever you want."

She glances at the dashboard. "You're almost out of gas."

"We'll drive until I run out."

"Then we'll be stranded."

"We'll get gas, then keep searching."

Esme yawns so intensely the music fades in her ears.

Arjun adds, "No, you need to sleep. Do you need anything else? Food, water? There's loads of extra in the back. Take what you want. I'll drop you off, get gas, and keep searching on my own."

"You will?"

"Yes. Show me his photo."

Esme opens the photos on her phone, then pauses. She looks at Arjun. "Why are you being so nice?"

"What kind of question is that?"

"You're not wearing your hat."

"I'm not."

"You always wear your hat."

"I lost it."

"I'm sorry."

"Why? You hated that hat."

"No, I didn't. Why would you say that?"

"The way you said, 'You're not wearing your hat.'" He smiles and his whole face brightens, even in the dim shadows in the van. His thick black hair is tangled in a way that makes her want to comb it with her hands. She does not want to leave this car. She doesn't want to go back to her apartment, where she'll be alone. Still no calls from Marcus. Nothing. All that awaits her is her empty bed.

Esme has a terrible thought. She can't remember the last time Marcus spontaneously did something nice for her. He loved her, yes, and she loved that he loved her; all she ever wanted from him was to be together and spend time together. But when was the last time he had so much as given her a card? He was anti-gift. He said they didn't need cards or presents to prove that they love each other. But this thought is surely coming from a place of sheer exhaustion. There must be real memories of spontaneous acts of kindness. She just can't reach them right now. They're hidden behind a curtain, crumpled in a pile underneath the bed. It's a feeling like when you know someone's name but it doesn't come. The tip of the tongue. Yes, it's under their bed, the one with warm flannel sheets and the smell of his deodorant. Even the thought of curling up on the floor makes her want to close her eyes. It seems she's experienced every emotion it is possible to feel, all in one day, and she's ready to collapse. There will be more she can do to find Marcus tomorrow, she tells herself. He's somewhere. She'll find him. If she believed in signs or magic or God, she'd send him a signal and wait for something in the world to respond. A mysterious tickle or a bird singing in the rain.

But Esme doesn't believe in any of those things. She believes in Marcus.

8

How do you know when night has become morning? The edge between them does not exist. And yet it does. No one ever seems alarmed when you tell them "good morning." Morning simply is, and they know it, and you do, too. And yet. At four a.m., everyone is sleeping, which means it is night. And yet the day begins, has already begun, which makes it morning. Or does it? On a day like today, a morning like this morning, a night like this night, the clouds are so dark the sun will be hidden long after it has risen, so there is nothing in the sky to say "Wake up, good morning." For hours after four, after the world shuffles yet again, creating new sets of problems and opportunities, it remains dark. Arjun stares at this darkness as if something in it will rearrange itself into an answer. He's been awake nearly the whole night, first lying in bed, awake, now sitting on the couch and looking out the windows, awake. It must be the adrenaline. Nerves coursing through him after a successful evening saving lives. After dropping off Esme, finding a nearby shelter, and waiting an hour to receive gas for his tank, he'd decided it was too late to search for Marcus, already two a.m., and he'd need to sleep to prepare for the next day, so he went home, to his father's quiet condo, which he tiptoed through to get to his room without waking him. His father is a little grumpy with Arjun. He's been a little grumpy for about two years. Ever since Arjun had to drop out of college and move back in. Was it because he dropped out of college one year before graduation? Or the fact that he had to move in? Or the fact that his father discovered his clonazepam? Yes. There are many things Arjun has done to disappoint him. There's also the general fact that he doesn't want to work in real estate or any other of his father's buy-and-sell businesses, and the philosophical differences underlying this difference: Whereas his father wants Arjun to care about money, Arjun just wants to help people. What do you need money for? "A place to live, for starters," said his father when Arjun made this exact point. "But that's what people have fathers for." He tries to make his father happy. Right now, that means not seeing him face-to-face. It means living lightly, as if he's already moved out. "Pretend I don't live here," he said during their last fight. "It's not like you talk to me anyway except to yell at me." But Arjun likes to remind his father that he does live here, and that in fact, when they're not arguing, he can be caring and useful. Late at night, while his father yells on the phone in his office with time zones from all over the world, Arjun empties the dishwasher and wipes down the sink. He tiptoes around the living room, picking up whatever books his father's left lying around, and puts them into neat piles. He prepares the ingredients for the next morning's chai so whoever wakes up first can simply turn on the burner. Then he goes to his bedroom—even as it fills up with various supplies and boxes meant for storage, his father's implied message being *If you are going to pretend you don't live here, I am, too*—and lies down happily, because even with all the supplies, it's a private room with a soft bed for him to sleep on, so when he gives the door a little slam, this is Arjun saying *I love you. Good night.*

But last night, Arjun returned home far too late for any of that. His father was asleep and certainly wouldn't want to be woken. So Arjun closed his door softly before a quick splash to the face and swish of the mouthwash in his private bathroom. Then he lay on the bed, squeezed his eyes shut, and commanded: *Sleep.* But sleep did not come. Instead, recent memories coursed through him, everything that had happened that day replaying itself behind his eyes, all the embarrassments and victories, and then, finally, guilt: when he realized he was still awake and could absolutely have searched for Marcus for at least another hour. But here he was on a too-soft feather bed, holding his phone screen to his face, looking at the GPS tag on Esme's phone. They'd shared their locations with one another so they could help each other out in case of emergency, which, you never know, might be now, so he checked. She didn't move. She was in the same place, and so was he, feeling guiltier and guiltier. And he couldn't decide if he should get out of bed and go look for Esme's fiancé or stay here to rest for a more productive day tomorrow, and every time he finally got up, he would be overcome with exhaustion and get back in bed, where energy coursed through every nerve in his body. And then he thought he may as well stay awake until four to see what happened, if the daily unmapping felt like an earthquake or stepping through a portal, but of course just before then was when his body decided to sleep. And maybe there was something about the shift at four that woke him up, because then it was 4:01 and he was awake again in a way that felt permanent, so he made himself chai and sat on the couch and waited for the sun to rise.

It didn't.

The sky went from dark-dark to less dark and that would have to be good enough given these clouds. His grandfather in Delhi told him to always stare at the sun for at least half an hour a day, either when it rises or before it sets. When he moved to America, he realized that staring at the sun like this was only possible due to the air pollution. In Delhi, at the end of the day, all the burned trash, sidewalk bonfires, thick sick car exhaust, and who knows what else, it all ends up hovering in the air, so many particles you can feel your throat grow three layers of sand. His grandfather, furthermore, smoked ten cigarettes a day as if to say, *You want my lungs? Take them.* There was an astrologist who sat on a mat just outside his temple who once told Arjun's grandfather he'd live to be a hundred. He was testing that limit every day, coughing his lungs out. The astrologist, his grandfather told Arjun, said that there are two things to know. Your birthday and your body. The astrologist wrote down his birthday and took precise measurements of his fingers, elbows, and toes and spent thirty minutes adding things and multiplying things and crossing them out and retrieving a result that he said would answer everything. The number five. This number times twenty would be the age of death and also show how many loves he would love, how many lives he would live. This number meant his eyes and ears would be in perfect health until his final breath, but made no promises about the quality of those breaths. So in Delhi, yes, you can stare at the sun through five hundred PPM, and it is beautiful. Here, if you look at it one minute after it rises, you'll burn your eyes to dust. That is, if you can see it. Which he can't right now, as it's somewhere behind the clouds, trailing the remnants of Tropical Storm Janus.

Today will be a good day. Yesterday turned around, didn't it? First, he saved that blonde girl, whose name he still can't remember. Then he saved Esme Green, whose name he'll never forget. Esme. The way she cried on his shoulder and pulled his arms around her. He was being very careful with his movements, so he knows. He knows it was Esme that touched him, not the other way around. It was a moment he'd been imagining for months, such a touch, her in his arms, needing to be held. And yet it was different when it happened. He didn't rejoice or tell himself *You did it.* He in fact nearly cried himself. And the reason he nearly cried was because he imagined what it would be like if Esme went missing, if he didn't know what had happened to her. He felt sadness for her and through her. Was that empathy? Level up for Arjun. He tried online dating but the people he dated all said he had no empathy. They literally all said that, in some shape or fashion, like they had a secret discussion with one another and agreed: no empathy. He was told he should feel more emotion when his dates would tell him things about getting a promotion or getting in a fight with their high school BFF. But in this line of work, empathy is hard. You can't feel the same feelings as every person that you evacuate from a flooded street or pull out of the rubble of a collapsed building. You can't feel empathy for the crashed subway car. Of course, Arjun tended to play up the dangers of this job when he was on dates. The job usually involved elementary school presentations and workplace preparedness lectures. But the days jumped from boring to insane and there was no in between. Who has time for empathy?

Today, there will be no time. He scrolls through social media to take in the devastation throughout the city. Devastation from the storm. Devastation from the Unmapping. Rivers in the subways. Flooding throughout Queens. Five row houses with missing walls on the verge of collapse. That thirteen-year-old boy is still trapped under a building in Hunts Point, theoretically, but where's that building now? The emergency is everywhere. Including here, on Staten Island. That's where he ended up this morning. He went to sleep in Brooklyn Heights and woke up in

Stapleton Heights. Mental note: Do the similarities of the neighborhood names mean anything? He posts this question to social
media. It receives no likes or comments.

He's on his fourth cup of chai when he hears his father shift
in his bedroom. Time for Arjun to go.

On his way to the van parked underground he texts Liz:
Reporting for duty, boss. It's all remote all the time from here
on out. She doesn't respond right away. He watches the city get
closer and closer as he lowers in a glass elevator. He imagines his
time will be devoted to the flooding today. He's on Staten Island
with a beach view—and floods. There's a little bit of flooding
everywhere but a lot of flooding here, the portable flood barriers and sandbags only doing so much, with so many buildings
newly placed on waterfronts that aren't meant for it, like on the
Long Island Sound and the Lower Bay and the East and Hudson
Rivers and the Narrows, and all along these waterfronts many of
the houses and apartment buildings and businesses are flooded
and more are at risk if the rains keep pouring over more dams
and barriers. There are shelters, but only one is on Staten Island
today, on the southern tip, fifteen miles away. There are many
problems this morning that will need people like Arjun on the
ground providing the solutions.

Right when he reaches the van, his phone dings. A long email
has just come in from Liz, detailing directives for the day. He
scans through it. Miles is still unaccounted for, and that's fine.
When they drive together, Miles makes them listen to terrible
audiobooks about business. Miles wants to be a businessman. So
Arjun will be on his own again, listening to whatever music he
wants, evacuating a street called Lamberts Lane, which, despite
being on the same Staten Island, is six whole miles away.

He phones Liz.

"Ms. Liz," he says.

"Mr. Arjun."

"This is great. I'm already on Staten Island."

"I know. We have the GPS coordinates of your van."

"Oh."

"Is that why you called?"

"No! I wanted to ask. I've never done an evacuation by myself before. Anything I should know?"

"You've done the training."

"Yes."

"You've teamed up with Miles for evacuations in the past."

"Yes."

"Then you know everything I do."

"Okay. Thank you for this assignment. I won't let you down."

He fastens his neon yellow *I'M HERE TO HELP* vest. He picked up five at the shelter the previous evening, after he dropped off the blonde woman. What was her name?

It takes three hours to drive six miles because of all the times he gets turned around from closed-down streets. FEMA vans and boats are out, doing whatever it is FEMA does. They tell him to go around the long way and he does, and so does everyone else who gets turned around, causing jams on every corner. By the time he reaches Lamberts Lane, not only has the sky lightened but the clouds have begun to dissipate and the rains have turned to mist.

Lamberts Lane. Why does that name sound so familiar? He drives by what used to be a fire hydrant but is now a geyser, and pulls over by an iron park bench. He grabs his clipboard, which he never uses but which looks official, and tightens his vest around his rain jacket. "I'm here to help," he reminds himself. He's written a little script of what to say, based on what he remembers from Miles. The street is flooded with about a foot of water. But he's prepared to walk through it in his waders. Arjun is ready.

The first house is ornate, with a frosted glass door. He rings the bell but no one answers. It occurs to him the electricity might be down, including for doorbells, so he lifts and lowers the brass door knocker. Still no response. He puts his ear against the door and hears some noises from within, so knocks again. A dog begins to bark, and a voice yells, "Quiet!" He knocks again. Still no answer.

Moving on.

The next house has a half dozen people sitting on the front porch watching the rain. The adults are sipping from mugs and the kids have juice boxes and their eyes are all on him. This will be a much easier sell. Arjun waves as he walks up and says, "Hi, I'm here to help."

"We can read," says the oldest man on the porch, who's sitting on a rocking chair with a cane on his lap.

"Pardon?"

"Your little shirt."

Arjun looks down at his vest, which states *I'M HERE TO HELP* in big black letters.

"How you gonna help us?" asks the old man. "Got a working phone?"

"Sort of." Arjun smiles. "I'm here to help you get to the closest shelter, where there will be food, water, phones, and charging stations."

"And where's that?" asks a middle-aged woman.

"Down by, um." Arjun checks his phone. "Conference House Park."

"Never heard of that," says the old man. "Stupid name."

"How far?" asks the woman, whose legs have become a jungle gym for two small toddlers.

"About eleven miles. Should be a quick drive, though!"

"Eleven miles? You're shitting me."

"Your street is flooded," says Arjun. "Your lives are at risk."

"Our house is fine. It's barely raining," says the woman, who picks up one of the toddlers now and pats her on the behind.

"It's true that it appears the rains may be letting up," says Arjun, "but that may just be temporary. These things come and go."

The clouds choose this moment to clear a hole in the sky. A lick of sun washes over the porch.

"Well, if you need anything, here's the emergency hotline." He hands them a flyer.

"With what phone?"

"Exactly! You can use a phone at the shelter."

"We're not leaving," says the old man. "Want to help? Bring us some beers."

Arjun laughs nervously and tells them to stay safe.

At the next house over, a group of college-aged boys are playing beer pong on the deck. They also refuse to leave, and try to keep Arjun from leaving, too, until he's bested them at pong. He wiggles out of there in a flash. At the next house, there's a young girl, alone. She barely says a word. At first, he takes her silence as encouragement to tell her all about the shelter and how they'll be able to help. But when he asks if she's ready to go, she shakes her head no.

"If I leave, I can't come back," she says.

"No, no, no, that's not true at all! Here, with this GPS device, if you turn it on and leave it here, you can program your phone to find it, no matter where it ends up."

"I don't have a phone like that."

"Oh. Well, you can ask someone else to put in the coordinates. You just have to take down the serial number . . ."

The girl looks terrified.

"Well, then. Maybe it makes sense for you to stay home. Do you want food? Water? Candy? Candy! You do want candy. Well, we don't actually have candy, but we do have granola bars. No? Okay. Call me if you need me." He hands her a flyer.

Some ask him questions, like "Why is this happening?" and "When will it end?" He has no answers. "You said you're here to help," they complain. "You can't help me understand?" And he responds that he is there to help people get to the closest shelter. "Will there be answers in the shelter? No?" Bye, then.

Not one single person agrees to be evacuated.

Arjun gets back into his van, turns on the radio, and pulls out his phone to check social media as the radio plays something poppy. There's a text from Liz. Don't forget to report back when the evacuation is complete.

Oh, he'll report back. He'll tell her everything. He texts her a long missive that takes up more words than his text drafts can contain, so he writes it in a note-taking app and sends it in chunks. He tells her everything about how difficult it is for these poor people who don't want to leave, and doesn't she have any empathy?

She texts him back: New assignment. Replenish supplies at Staten Island shelter.

Arjun turns the music down and calls Liz.

"Liz," he says.

"Arjun."

"I think you may have made a mistake in your text. There are still dozens of streets with people who will need to be evacuated today. Is that not the priority?"

"FEMA's come in to help with evacuations. We need your help with supplies."

"You're going to let FEMA come in and trample on our work? Do they know where the shelters are? Do they know our protocols?"

"Do *you* know our protocols?"

"I remembered what I could from Miles."

"Arjun, I don't have time for this. Do your job." Liz hangs up.

He sits there, stunned. The radio is still playing pop music, softly, something about being an independent woman. He feels like a failure.

Arjun calls her back.

"Yes?"

"Dear boss. Which supplies need restocking, and what do they need, and where do I retrieve the supplies?"

"Now those are the right questions to ask."

"And do these questions have answers?"

"Call the Staten Island shelter. They'll tell you what you need to know. I believe in you." Liz hangs up again.

The words feel hollow, but they repeat themselves in his brain. There is no time for wallowing. People need help. Remember the blonde woman who needed you. Who believes in you.

• ◆ •

The blonde woman lies on a hotel cot, massaging the crick in her neck. Sometime during the night, her pillow disappeared and her neck bent sideways. When she pulls herself up, something pulls back. She tries to look around, but that crick in her neck yanks on every muscle in her shoulder, upper back, and lower skull. Who even knew there were muscles in the skull? She has to rotate her whole torso to look around.

It's so bright. Bright, large, and crowded. She's in a huge conference room in a Holiday Inn that's been converted to a shelter with hundreds of cots, half of which are full, even though it's already nearly noon. The woman got in late last night, around midnight, and has been trying on and off to sleep, to little success. The cot hurts, the people are loud, and now, the lights are brighter than the sun. And it's hot. The air must be set to sauna-level heat, because she's sweating beneath her thin sheet.

Every time she falls asleep and wakes up again, it takes her a minute to remember why she's here. Date. Hurricane. Knives. Phone. Lost. And then the nice man in the emergency van. He could have kidnapped her or killed her but instead he took her here, to the Holiday Inn, where he had the keys to unlock the door. It was too late to check in, however, or maybe the check-in people were taking a break, because when they arrived, the front desk was empty. The nice man who picked her up and brought her here seemed equally confused at the lack of people. He walked with her until they found the door to the conference room with a sign that said *SLEEP HERE*, and helped her find an empty cot. The man whispered, "Get some rest. I'm sure someone will come by in the morning to help."

The morning has come and gone and no one has come to help. She lies on her cot for hours, in and out of sleep, listening to phone calls around her, people trying to reach their loved ones, to explain where they are: "There's a big building out there, you know, one of the big ones, I don't know, no, I don't see the Balto statue, goddamnit, let's try again tomorrow." She waits and waits for someone to come and help her, like the nice man said. Eventually, starving, she gets up and goes to the lobby, where there are now three official-looking people sitting at the front desk. They wear highlighter-yellow vests emblazoned with the words *I'M HERE TO HELP*. So the woman says hello, is there any breakfast for her to eat?

"Do you have ID?" asks the man on the left.

"No," says the woman. "I was robbed."

"Do you have a phone?"

"No," says the woman. "Like I said . . ."

"Sorry to hear that," the man in the vest says flatly. "Please fill out this form. If you can remember your driver's license number, that will help."

She doesn't remember. As she begins to fill out the form, the man hands her a bag of toiletries, a blanket, and meal tickets to be used for breakfast, lunch, and dinner.

She puts down the pen. "But there are only two meal tickets here."

"You've already missed breakfast."

"Can't I double up on lunch?"

The man in the vest hands her another ticket. He gives her a look that reminds her of her mother.

"Can I borrow your phone? I'd like to make a phone call, but I have no way . . ." Her request dies in her throat. The desire to call her parents is automatic.

"There are two community phones you may sign up for." The man pulls out a clipboard with a list. "Sixty people are on the waiting list to use them. You'll want to wait in that room across the hall."

"Are there any pay phones? I could call collect. Is that still a thing?"

"Most of the city's pay phones were removed last year. Only four remain, but we don't know where."

"Computer? Can I send an email?"

"Sign-up's at the end of that hall." There must be at least a hundred people waiting in that line. On the one hand, she should really contact her parents. They check in on her daily, ever since she moved out, sometimes calling her ten times in a row if she doesn't pick up. On the other hand, does she want that right now? They'll probably gloat that this happened. After years warning her of the dangers of the city, everything about the past twenty-four hours will prove them right. They'll force her to come home. There's no question about it. She can picture what they'll say. "You can find yourself right here in our kitchen once we get some healthy food in you. I bet you've gained weight out there." Maybe they won't say the last part, but they'll think it, without understanding that their version of "healthy" means unsatisfying fat-free garbage that only makes her want to eat more, while here on her own she lets herself enjoy what she eats and has actually lost a little weight.

"Never mind, then," she says, and begins to walk off.

But the man in the vest calls her back. "Ma'am, your form?"

"Oh, right." She isn't sure why, but something compels her to write down a fake name.

"Thank you, ma'am. Now I need to see your bag."

"Are you serious? I was already robbed."

"We need to check for weapons. Thank you for understanding."

She recalls the pepper spray in her purse and worries about what he'll think if he finds it. But he rifles through her bag quickly and hands it right back, leaving the pepper spray untouched.

"Doors lock at eight p.m.," he says, "to allow the workers to return home before curfew. Be sure to check in and out every time you leave and return. Next?"

The lunch line takes an hour and results in a single-serving box of granola with a foam bowl and plastic spoon. No milk. They don't accept her second lunch ticket, at least until after everyone's had their first serving. The woman takes her granola and bowl to an empty round table and eats two bites before someone else sits down across from her. "Nice dress," says a man in a leather jacket and ponytail, who smiles to reveal yellowed, crooked teeth. "Wonder what it'd look like on the floor."

The woman puts down her spoon. "Do people actually say that? Like in real life? Are you real?"

"Unless I'm the man of your dreams, baby."

"Come any closer and I'll scream."

"I'll be sitting right here, darling."

"Then I'll leave." The woman leaves her granola on the table and goes to the bathroom. There's no soap. She stares at her smudged eyeliner and mascara, thinking she looks a little whorish. No, those are her mother's words. She looks kind of sexy in a wild way. But that's not the look she's going for today, especially not with that creep out there, and whoever else might look at her and think something like that. So she scrubs off the makeup with water and paper towels. Then she opens the bag of toiletries she was given, finding a bottle of mouthwash and three small bottles of shampoo, and washes her hands with the shampoo while swishing the mouthwash. She puts on her rain jacket over her skimpy dress, zipped up to her neck. She gets acquainted with her naked face. She feels the urge to put on a little blush, but she didn't pack that in her makeup bag. Instead she pinches her cheeks and lips.

She leaves the bathroom to find the same creep standing in the hallway. She can pick out a creep with one half-glance. It's the way they look at your whole body with eyes that say: *You're meat.* And they're always the ugliest ones. So focused on women they forget about themselves. Her mom gives her grief for caring about her appearance. But she takes pride in looking nice. She enjoys her big body and how much space it takes up, enjoys even more having bright blonde hair and dramatic makeup. Here is my life, she's saying, and my life is beautiful. She can contour her face into anything she wants. Unlike this man. He probably hasn't looked at himself in years. Just pulls his long hair into a ponytail and doesn't even wash his face. His eyes are mud brown and his skin looks old and loose, like it was just stripped off a murder victim.

"You're disgusting," she says.

"You're a bitch!"

She rushes past him.

Down a hallway and to the left and then another left, she runs until she can't run anymore. She's at the end of a hallway with a dead end. She looks back, filled with adrenaline, but the hallway is empty. There's a door on the side that leads to a stairwell, which she rushes down, quickly reaching the emergency exit at the bottom. A paper handwritten sign says *CHECK OUT BEFORE LEAVING SHELTER* and a permanent metal sign says *ALARM WILL GO OFF* and defying both signs delights her as she pushes open the door.

It's cool out. Fresh and humid and dripping wet, with pools of standing water on every street and sidewalk. Alarm bells blare behind her. Storms have a way of opening up a world of smells. The flowers, the garbage, the secrets: suddenly you can see their aromas in the air. She's standing next to the West Side Highway. Across the street is a park and a pier. When there's a gap in traffic, she runs across. The light wind feels like nourishment. Bushes line the edge of the pier in pleasant winding spirals, their leaves glistening with water droplets. This place is nicely manicured, with equal-sized trees and identical shrubs. She likes that. "It's contoured," she jokes to herself. Everything is designed to lead you to the river. She follows the path, at the whim of her environment now. The Hudson River is her destination.

The water is rushing hard and fast, still high from the storm's rain. When she looks at it, she thinks: It's perfect. It doesn't want to explain anything. It has no urge to understand. It feels no shame and casts no judgment. Its movements are both knowable and somehow impossible. The woman tries to pick a spot on the river and watch as it flows, to see where it goes, but loses it in the churn. She instead lets her eyes unfocus, to take in everything at once, but finds herself drawn back to the specific movements of the river's flow. She spots the crest of a wave and watches it until it falls. An eddy forms and disappears. This moment. She wants to burn it into her brain. Then that one. Then the next.

She knows one thing, looking out at that water. She is not going back to that shelter.

◆ ◆ ◆

Arjun sets out on the long way from Staten Island to Manhattan, over the Verrazzano-Narrows Bridge to Brooklyn, and the Manhattan Bridge to Manhattan, because all the tunnels and ferries are closed. The trip is even longer than it should be from all the traffic and the fact that no one's allowed in the tunnels. Aren't people supposed to be home? Where are they all going? He crosses the Manhattan Bridge at the speed of a snail, watching the pigeons fly by. The music on the radio sings him through the ride, from '80s pop to '60s folk and back to Frank Sinatra, then to Jelly Roll Morton, with this radio station apparently going further back in time with every song, until they are finally at "Camptown Races" by the time he's returned to the Emergency Management building on the Upper West Side.

This building moved southward four miles on the first day of
the Unmapping, but back north four miles on the second, ending up near its initial position. Arjun wonders about this. He
posts the observation to social media. A perfect move, four
miles down and up each day, what does it mean? No one responds. He arrives in the basement parking lot to fill up his van.
After he tried calling the Staten Island shelter people and calling
them again when no one picked up, he eventually showed up and
they told him: "We need everything." So back at headquarters he
tells the storage room manager, "I need everything, but divided
up, so that one-eleventh of everything fits in every seat." They
show him to the stockpiles and let him do what he wants and
only later, almost at his destination, does he see the missed call
from Liz.

"Someone else restocked Staten Island," she tells him.

"Oh."

"Thanks anyways."

"But I filled my van. Anyone else need it?"

"Not right now. Stay on call."

"Okay. What can I do in the meantime?"

"Gather data," she says, harried. "We need data. Drive around
and report in when you see anything that doesn't belong. Don't
call me, though. Call the hotline."

"Anything that doesn't belong? Like what?"

"You'll know it when you see it." She hangs up.

Arjun half wonders if he should text Esme—her GPS tracker
shows that she's in the Emergency Management Department
building—but he already texted this morning, to make sure she's
okay, and she still hasn't responded. So he figures she needs some
space. Maybe she's angry because she watched his GPS tracker
and learned that he didn't try to find Marcus. But how would

she know? He continued driving for two hours, to the shelter for gas and then home. He's sure she would have fallen asleep immediately.

He feels useless. What can he do? He could search for things that don't belong. But nothing belongs. He could drive around until he finds someone in need . . . but his car is too stuffed full of things to accept any human being, unless they sit on his lap, which is not appropriate. Earlier, he worried the task of shuffling supplies around would feel like throwing a grain of sand into outer space with the goal of filling it up. Useless in the face of all the need. Now it feels like a boulder strapped to his back. The van feels heavy. It takes a deeper push on the gas pedal to get it going at every turn and stoplight.

Once he's on the West Side Highway, though, he feels fine. He can get the van up to a decent clip. Then he sees a girl walking up the sidewalk by the Hudson River Park.

It's the blonde woman from last night.

He pulls over and rolls down his window. "Hey!"

But she's off, walking more quickly through the park now.

He pulls out his megaphone. "Ma'am! Are you okay?" If only he knew her name! He looked up a list of all the names of people who checked in at the Holiday Inn last night and not a single name was familiar. He was sure that if he saw her name on the list, he'd remember it; the memory of her name was hidden just behind a corner. Something must have gone wrong. What are the odds he'd find and save the same woman two days in a row? And now she's running. Why is she running?

Arjun gets out of the van and jogs through the park after her, yelling through his megaphone. "Ma'am! How was your evening? I'm here to help!"

She runs to a public bathroom and disappears behind an

open door, pulling it shut. The door slams behind her, then opens wide again.

"Ma'am?" he calls through the open door.

"Please go away!" she says from inside one of the bathroom stalls.

"Are you okay? Did something go wrong at the shelter?"

"I have pepper spray!"

And now he sees himself in the cracked bathroom mirror. His hair is tangled and sticking straight up on the left side. He looks feral. He looks like a feral man harassing a nice woman in a bathroom, telling himself he's a hero. The image is broken in the middle. He feels himself spiral. He wants to sleep. He *needs* sleep. He wants to wake up and let this all be over. He'd have a much better time in dreams.

9

The storm has passed; the seas are rising; the taxi cabs have taken over the streets. And there is Esme, walking into the Emergency Management Department building, her church, her haven, her home away from home. She woke up this morning at 4:05, which is five minutes later than usual, but left her apartment at 4:10, which is five minutes earlier than usual, and arrived at work at 4:39, thanks to the taxi pulling up right outside. The four-to-five morning hour would turn out to be a fruitful time for cab drivers who would agree to drive and drive and drive until their rider found their destination, as the meter ticked up and up. But Esme knew where to go. Today, Gleamwood Gardens mapped itself just a half block east from where it was the day before, which was one half block east from where it was before that, and the Emergency Management Department was back where it was supposed to be, which would feel like some sort of sign if she believed in signs. She does not. She believes in data. She believes in fingers on the keyboard. She believes in the digital images on her screen, her eyes all over the city. What can one person do on their own? Nothing. What can they do with data? Everything. Here at Watch Command, she can monitor security camera footage and satellite video and news reports from every station. She can set up an alert to ding whenever a Marcus Michael Miller gets added to the missing person registry. She's here to work, yes. And she's here to find Marcus. There's no time to think about why or how, because every minute flows into the next, each one taking her further away from him.

But before she can reach her screens at desk sixteen, the interim supervisor tells her to go find Commander Cummings. "He's looking for you."

Esme feels a vague sense of guilt for skipping out on the task force yesterday. But they seem to have done all right without her. The electricity is on and the building is humming. No major disasters have appeared on the many television screens. She prepares her explanation for why she left. A family emergency. It was a family emergency. She's not in the mood to open up her heart and let him see the Marcus-sized hole, but she'll give him enough to bring on the pity. Maybe she'll echo Cummings's words: *I think we all agree these are extraordinary times.*

But when she finds him pacing the command center, yelling into the phone about how to find one's GPS coordinates, he doesn't mention it or ask why she was gone. He hangs up and says: "Esme. You're back."

She nods. "And ready to work. But you wanted to see me?"

"Yes. The electric grid task force is meeting in room 3B. Can you join them?"

She protests internally: *But I want to find Marcus.* Today she was feeling positive. She had planned to review the security camera footage around Gleamwood Gardens and the nearby streets. Then she'd follow where he ran until she couldn't follow any longer. Then she'd call every establishment that he passed by until someone confirmed that yes, they had taken him in and he was safe. If that failed, she'd monitor footage on the city's key running paths. She'd watch five screens at a time as they all fast-forwarded through the day. He has to be somewhere out there.

Commander Cummings, not noticing her hesitation, says, "Apparently, there have been five transformer fires in the past twenty minutes. On top of the downed poles from the storm. The incident map is just . . . unbelievable. The electric grid task force is the most important one, so thanks for joining. After the fires are out, take a look at the different operations units we've set up. We're moving a lot of people around and could use your input. I know this is all last minute. How can you plan for something like this?"

This seems to be something like an apology.

"Have you slept?" asks Esme.

He grimaces. "Who needs sleep when you have coffee? Go team."

She goes into a room she's never seen before on a floor she's never been to before to meet people she's never met before. They barely react when she walks in, all standing by a large screen with an outage map, talking over each other so loudly she can't make out anything. Once here, though, she's filled with the over-whelming desire to be helpful. She can be part of something bigger than her. If she can help this task force, maybe more people can help Marcus. She can do her part and save lives. The scent of coffee is strong.

"I'm Esme Green," she says to a woman on the side. "Commander Cummings asked me to join."

"Take a look at the latest written brief to get caught up," the woman responds, handing her a paper, which Esme scans quickly.

"This was written at three thirty. It says there are only five outages. But this map—"

"Shows the hundreds that have been reported since four,"

says the woman. "We know. We're trying to prioritize which areas to send the linemen to first. It looks like the biggest cluster is right here near Times Square, so that's a no-brainer, but the second biggest is on Staten Island, mostly a very suburban area."

"This is just a list of outages. Do we have data on how many people are affected by each one?"

"Not yet."

"And shouldn't we be thinking about what types of buildings to prioritize? Hospitals, maybe government buildings . . ."

"We can't know that. We don't have that information."

"We could glean the building size through the meter data, though. Not just as a straight scale, but we know that hospitals use electricity differently than most buildings, for instance—they run all night. And grocery stores go to a pretty consistent nighttime baseline with their freezer and refrigeration needs."

"That would take hours to figure out," someone complains. "We don't have time."

"Not if we model the data and run the right regressions. And—oh! I'm pretty sure all the building meters are connected to a database of addresses."

"Addresses don't matter here—"

"Yes they do, when you know what building they're supposed to be attached to."

The woman gets the others in the room to listen as Esme explains all the data they have access to. With that in hand they are able to delineate buildings by types, with each type mapping onto an index of priority—office buildings are the lowest, while hospitals are the highest and government buildings are somewhere in the middle, although most hospitals have backup generators, while government buildings without any backup supply have a more urgent need. The goal is to reconfigure the outage map into a heat map that combines proximity and priority, after pulling out and addressing separately anomalies like the Empire State Building on a tiny street. The mood is calmer once they have a plan. Esme is assigned to modeling and re-modeling the new outage map, while others are in charge of divvying up the resources, assigning site managers, finding site managers, mechanizing and maintaining the outage report line, and more details Esme can't keep in her head and doesn't need to—she has her task and so do the others. Hours pass in a flurry of activity. She understands now how everyone here seems wide awake despite a sleepless night. She herself only slept a couple of hours, yet wakefulness courses through her. Occasionally people leave to take short naps in various conference rooms. At some point lunch arrives, a multitude of frozen pizzas, baked one by one in the kitchen toaster oven.

Esme continues reviewing her work as she shovels a slice of mushroom into her mouth. But the woman she spoke to earlier—the head of the task force, whose name she now knows is Sian Kearney—gently suggests she take a break from the computer. "For your mental health." Esme obeys. She eats quietly as they chat around her, but small talk today means avoiding the weather—the storm has dissipated to cool mists, with another late-breaking heat wave coming soon—so they comment instead on how good the pizza is and how uncomfortable the nap room cots are.

A big man asks, "So who's on the task force to figure out why this is happening?"

The others laugh in agreement. For all their efforts to figure out the small things, there is still the underlying question of why. The big why.

"It's because of chaos theory," says a small man beside him.

"What's that?" asks the big man.

"Something about fractals."

"What's *that*?"

"The grid is a fractal."

"Your mom is a fractal."

"A fractal is a shape or pattern that looks the same at different scales," says Sian. "Like the Sierpinski triangle. Triangles within triangles. An infinitely repeating pattern."

"That doesn't sound very chaotic to me."

Esme gets up to go to the bathroom. This conversation brings her back to a dark period in her life. Chaos theory and fractals— this is a topic she once thought would be her calling. She was a sophomore in college taking senior-level math classes and doing rather well, but when her classmates started signing up for one-on-one research positions, she thought she should do the same. An old professor she'd never met posted a research request on fractals, and she signed up right away, talking up her good grades, although she knew nothing about fractals except for the most romantic ideas. Fractals describe the patterns behind how trees grow, coastlines form, rivers twist and turn. Fractals describe the shapes of clouds and seashells and even hurricanes. And fractals have something to do with chaos theory. Order and disorder coexisting. Predictability in unpredictability. Part of her thought studying fractals, and thereby chaos theory, could help her understand what happened to her mother, who simply died and no one could say why.

Through math, fourteen years after her mother's sudden death, Esme was finally ready to face the unknown head-on. Instead she found herself reading a foreign language without any usable translation. The first assignment her professor gave her was to read a book that she found completely nonsensical. Barely readable English led to blocks of dense equations, with variables that came out of nowhere and operators that combined in ways she'd never known possible. It seemed both extremely rigid and hopelessly boundless. Strict equations somehow led to endless noise. She'd hoped to get swept up in the art of it, to lose herself in that noise and come out on the other side understanding the world better. Yet her eyes scanned over the text, taking in nothing. The second assignment, presumably, drew upon the lessons of this book, asking her to tackle equations with an even more nonsensical computer program. She never even attempted it, and in her shame, instead typed and printed out a letter explaining why she had to stop working for the professor. They met in a garden in the middle of campus, where she handed him the letter without looking at him. She remembers the garden being very green. It wasn't even cold enough for the trees to turn colors. He walked with a cane and had a big white beard and didn't say a word as she handed him her letter. She walked away before he could finish reading it.

Then came a weeklong period of almost total despair, during which she thought for certain she'd need to drop out, that she was a failure, that she could never let herself be seen by that professor again, that she didn't deserve to be a student anymore. She hid this despair from Marcus, whom she'd been dating for a year at that point, but mentioned offhand that she was thinking of switching majors, that she wanted something a little more concrete than mathematics, something she could touch with her hands, and he said, "How about premed?" and this depressed her even further until he then suggested, "How about statistics?" And that was that and he was right. This was a major in which you didn't have to know the "why" behind the equations; you just figured out how to use them to study data in the real world.

At times, Esme's studies were still edged with despair, once she discovered in higher-level courses how easily data can be sliced, diced, and interpreted to mean anything you want. It seemed to suggest that there is no true answer except the one you create. This thought depressed her. But at least she could finish the homework, which came in two flavors: There were the problem sets that merely required memorization and application of the right formula in the right place, and there were the open-ended assignments asking her to study certain data sets and come to some conclusion, where it didn't matter what the conclusion was as long as you had followed the steps correctly. She got through her courses with top grades.

Still, something about the topic bothered her. When she and Marcus were discussing life after college, she finally told him. Rather, she couldn't contain her frustration around him any longer. "Statistics aren't real!" she said after reading a job description, slamming her laptop closed. He asked her to tell him more. "Every job is just, basically, help us prove this or that. Not study this or that. They have an agenda and they want someone who knows the right formulas to prove them right. Remember how everyone used to hate fat and love sugar? And now it's the opposite? Statistics. Statisticians did that."

As she spoke, it looked as if each word was taking Marcus farther away, and by the time she finished, he was staring at her from a great distance, eyes fuzzy and unfocused.

Esme waited for him to speak. She felt like she had just gone through confession and was waiting for instructions on how to right her wrongs.

For a full minute, he said nothing, continuing to look as if he had reached the precipice of a cliff and was trying to figure out his way down. Distant and afraid.

Then he said, "Why didn't you tell me?"

"I'm telling you now."

"Why didn't you tell me they were teaching you how to lie?"

"I don't mean . . ." But that's exactly what she meant. She just wouldn't put it in those terms. In that moment, and many times after, she appreciated his honesty. He made her look at things differently. But . . . "I still think statistics are useful, right? They have to be. I just haven't figured it out. I haven't found the right job."

"You don't have to get a job in statistics." An undergraduate degree never really mattered for an entry-level job, he said— all she needed was a diploma. And he was right about that, too. And somehow she knew that if she ended up getting a job using statistics, he'd be disappointed in her. He would never say anything outright like that, but he made his preferences known, and his preferences had a tendency to be correct, and so she respected them, and wanted to respect herself through his eyes. So she stopped browsing statistician jobs and instead scanned through lackluster postings for customer service, administrative work, volunteer teaching, real estate assistance, social media management. And when Marcus got his dream job in New York and wanted her to move with him, she found the opening at the Emergency Management Department, and it was the first one she liked that accepted her.

It was perfect.

So much of her life has revolved around Marcus.

How could she lose him?

Yesterday, she walked for ten hours in the rain. Ten hours that were completely wasted. At the end of it, all she accomplished was discovering her own smallness. She did the calculations and realized that she'd covered about one-third of one percent of the city's sidewalks. What was she thinking? He'd be walking on the street, waiting for her to find him? In a storm? No. He'd have found somewhere to take shelter, somewhere behind closed doors. And eventually she was crying in Arjun's arms, so tired and grief-stricken she felt drunk. She was weak.

But Marcus needs her to be strong. Today she can work hard. If she works hard, so will the others. Hundreds of colleagues are searching for people like Marcus. She can do her part, too.

What would Marcus do? He would want to learn everything he could. When he heard about the Unmapping, he wanted to see it in person. But that's because there was nothing to read about it. First he would read. He would read whatever he could find about Gleamwood City. Then he would put it all together and try to understand.

Esme pulls up her phone to see what she can learn.

◆　◆　◆

The *Gleamwood City Weekly* is on hiatus. Not by choice. The newsman's printing room, on the third floor of the factory complex, is blocked off with caution tape. "Problem with the printer," says a man he doesn't recognize wearing a black suit and sunglasses. Sunglasses? Indoors? "What, too bright?" asks the newsman. The newsman had emailed a copy of the latest weekly to the printer but received an unintelligible error message, so came to check it out, only to learn that, according to this sunglasses man, he wouldn't be printing anything in the near future, because the printer was broken beyond repair. How? Why? "Its time was up," says the man. "We're shipping in a new system from Santa Rosa. Should be here in a few weeks."

That's fine with the newsman. The latest edition is bunk anyway. He finished it two days ago and so much has changed since then, he was planning to throw it out and rewrite it from scratch. He just wanted to print one copy of what would have been, for posterity's sake. Maybe one day it would be pinned up in a museum.

He wouldn't have known what was happening around the country if not for the hundreds of phone calls he received. He usually doesn't read the news of the world out there. But the world, it seems, is trying to get in here. Through his phone. Since yesterday, it's been ringing nonstop. The *Times*, the *Post*, and every dang *Journal* has been trying to get hold of him. So have reporters from dozens of TV and radio stations. All the people who laughed at him earlier. He lets them all go to voicemail and doesn't worry when that inbox gets full.

But when he sees the word *Bluzz* on caller ID, he picks up right away.

"Marcus?" He remembers that reporter who came to visit three months ago. The tall one in the blue jacket who sat on his porch and drank his light beers. The only one who believed him.

"No. My name's Rick," says a deep, wonderful voice. "But Marcus told me all about you. I want you to write for us. Everything you know."

"What's there to know?" asks the newsman. "You have the video. You have your little article."

"We need to go back. We need to go way, way back. We need to know about *you*."

"About me?" The newsman's heart skips a beat. The headlines of his disgraced history go pop-pop through his brain. "Nothing to know about me."

"About your town. About Gleamwood City."

"Why do you want to know all that? It has nothing to do with this."

"Because why did it start there? What makes Gleamwood City special? There's almost nothing I can find about it online. What's the history?"

"I could fax you a few copies of the *Gleamwood City Weekly*. Each issue provides a snapshot of current events and a recap of some important moment in its history."

"Who has a fax anymore? You could just tell me what I should know. Pertinent facts. An overview. When was it founded?"

"I still don't see how that's relevant. It's just a random city. It just happened to start here."

"You never know with these things, my man. You give us the bits and pieces, we put them together. We're looking for the crumbs. Can't have a cake without crumbs."

"But where would I begin?"

"Try the beginning."

Of course the newsman knows about the founding of Gleamwood City. Everybody here does, but the newsman, in particular, has been tasked over the years with writing stories about the city's history. The founder of the town, Hans Gleason, died before the newsman moved here, and the founder's son Franz is a recluse, but there are still a couple members in Management who knew them both, from their beginning until, well, now.

It starts with Hans's childhood in the woods, a love of trees, and a deep distaste for his father's profession in the paper industry. He grew up in Manitowoc, where his father managed a paper factory a stone's throw from Door County. Every summer, they'd drive through the wilderness to the tip of the county, where the thumbnail of Wisconsin pokes into Lake Michigan, where Green Bay washes out into Greatness. Paradise. The tip of the land is one mile wide, so you could take a short walk from the bay to the lake without breaking a sweat. But take one step inside the forest and you'd see nothing but trees. Beech, basswood, sycamore, sugar maple, red maple, silver maple, every kind of maple. Six kinds of oak and five kinds of fir. Hans loved these trees. He knew the best ones for climbing and eventually taught himself to jump from branch to branch, traversing the land fifty feet aboveground. While his father fished and his mother plucked wildflowers, he learned the names of every tree. Some of the trees, he discovered, were three hundred years old. He hugged them tightly and said, "I want to be just like you." He cried after a storm when a tree got blown over, but rejoiced to see the fallen log turn into a new home for a million different creatures. Frogs and insects and even a fox and her kits. He'd climb over and through hollow logs in a self-created obstacle course, timing himself and pushing himself to do better every year.

It took him a heck of a lot longer than it should have to discover how paper is made, and even longer to make the connection that would break his little heart. One year, on their way home from Door County, his father decided to detour through Benderville to check on a subcontractor. There, Hans saw thousands of acres of clear-cut devastation. Barren land, without even a peep of a bird, a trill of a grasshopper. Not a single fallen log: Every dead tree had disappeared, like they'd been sucked up by aliens, just to become pulp for someone's forgotten grocery list. The sky was green and clouded. He wished it would break open and strike whoever did this with lightning right there. But it was his father. His father did this.

Hans kept his mouth shut and stayed polite and obedient throughout his childhood, quietly promising himself to live a better life instead. He'd been a rationalist ever since he figured out how to fit a triangular toy block into a square hole. Sometimes you have to think one thing and say another. The effort paid off, as his father eventually provided him a lump sum to start his own business.

So Hans packed everything he had into a rickety old truck and drove to the edge of Door County, where sandy bluffs melded with trees and cliffs overlooked Green Bay. Where green life flourished. Where his life would begin. He cleared an area by the shore—after reseeding the clear-cut lot in Benderville, to ease his conscience—to build his aluminum tree factory. Aluminum was a hot business in the area and aluminum trees were the ideal solution to the Christmas tree conundrum. With mass proliferation of aluminum trees, there would be no more clear-cutting of old growth forests only to replace them with massive monocultural tree plantations, stripping the soil of nutrients and flooding the waters with pesticides and killing every bird and bee in sight just for a little holiday decoration. Instead, aluminum Christmas trees would sprout here like a forest and be shipped off to the world to provide a permanent Christmas fixture, no cutting required. And it would be more than the factory. He would create an entire community around it that furthered his ideals. A way of life with as little impact on the land as possible, populated by people who appreciated nature and simplicity. He named it Gleamwood City.

His time as head of Gleamwood City was cut short, however. Only two years after snipping the ribbon, he was taken by a bout of whooping cough. On his deathbed, he said he wanted his body left to rot in the woods like an old fallen tree, a postmortem habitat. He also said he wanted to become a whooping crane, and that doughnuts were the devil. He said a lot of things in his final days that were ignored. He was buried in the center of town, beneath the spot where the factory's largest aluminum tree stood guard year-round.

The founder left a young son, borne by a prostitute who lived and died in Manitowoc. And so little Franz Gleason, barely old enough to know his times tables, with bones still loose and growing, obtained more than fifty percent of the voting shares of the company. While technically too young to be named CEO, he was in charge of the selection of CEOs and could fire them at will and therefore was, in all but name, now the chief executive of Gleamwood City at seven years old.

But the head of Gleamwood City had no interest in running Gleamwood City. Franz was a tiny speck of a boy with blue eyes that watered at the edges. His diminutive nature increased as he grew in age. When he gave annual speeches to the workers of Gleamwood City on Christmas Day, the child wore platform shoes and padded his clothing, particularly around the belly and chest, to reassure everyone he was well fed despite his seeming inability to keep on weight. He always wore a red boilersuit, supposedly in solidarity with those who worked the most difficult jobs at the factory complex in the foundry—the ones who oversaw the pots where aluminum oxide was dissolved in molten cryolite, and, later, the ones who mixed wood shavings with oil resin for the TruTrees, which had the unfortunate tendency to burst into flames. But maybe Franz just wore this red boilersuit because it took very well to being stuffed. As he grew in age, he continued to diminish in size, so he padded his clothing more and more, with cotton and fine down torn from his pillows, and his platform shoes grew in height until they were practically stilts.

It's said all the energy in his body went to the madness in his head. Maybe it was because he was always surrounded by people who treated him like royalty, or like a prisoner, or both. Maybe it was because his father named him after Franz Ferdinand, the man who was assassinated before he could inherit his kingdom, which little Franz took as a horrible prophecy. Luckily, the management team Franz selected did a fine job running the place on their own. They adjusted nimbly with the industry even after Charlie Brown killed the aluminum tree, adding a plastic tree department and later a TruTree department, all while keeping up with the founder's legacy of morning songs, evening hugs, and weekly affirmations. They maintained a community no one would want to leave—not least because turnover was inefficient— with scheduled activities like hiking, sailing, hunting, and fishing, and workshops like canning, dancing, and lucid dreaming, something to satisfy every sensibility (minus those of a religious, sexual, or drug-focused nature), and everyone was happy.

Except, apparently, little Franz. He escaped as often as he could on the company sailboat. He often sailed back and forth through the Porte des Morts, the area between the tip of the county and the island beyond, where dozens of boats had crashed to their death. He would never set foot in a car or plane or anything powered by gas, but he sailed that boat like a dog in a truck, tongue wagging out the side of his mouth. On his eighteenth birthday, his first day of true freedom, he packed his sailboat with enough money and provisions to last him a year and took off on a trip to circumnavigate the globe.

Six years passed without any word. Franz was presumed dead and a mournful service was held in his honor on Christmas Day at the foot of the town's prized aluminum tree, where Franz's father had been buried. Just as they were wrapping up the service, Franz showed up wearing the same red boilersuit and walked through the crowd to the podium at the tree, where he said "Merry Christmas" and walked away, leaving the others to discuss the miracle they'd just witnessed.

Skinnier, quieter, and stranger than ever, Franz locked himself away in the master bedroom in the tower on top of the factory complex, and no one hears from him or sees him except on Christmas Day. Despite his strangeness, or perhaps because of it, Franz is well loved in Gleamwood City. The fact that he wears a red boilersuit to show solidarity with the hardest workers inspires others to do the same. Red boilersuits have been popping up like spring tulips, no matter one's physique, position, or predilection. They get custom-made by the factory seamstress, with fits adjusted year after year. Sometimes the waistband is high and tight, other times low and loose. Some wear red hats to match the suits, and others pick up the trend. It's all for Franz.

And then there are his Christmas words.

It's been five decades since Franz's return and he still leaves his room just once a year: Christmas Day. There's no religion in Gleamwood City except the religion of Christmas and the aluminum tree. On this day, Franz runs as fast as he can to the giant Christmas tree at the center of town. There he shouts something either completely nonsensical or utterly profound, depending on your mood. "Seek truth in dreams." "Infinity is boundless and bright." "We are all one person." "Timelessness can be found between the hours of midnight and four." Then he returns to his room, where he waits another year before showing his face again. Just like the Christmas tree, Franz has become a nostalgic tradition—or decoration—of life in Gleamwood City.

Yet none can deny that Franz's Christmas words have veered lately toward incomprehensibility. "Some live to escape, others escape to live, others escape to escape." "A river begins but never ends, except when you wake up." "Everything comes from something else. It goes all the way down." The most recent quote is "Always remember to look at your hands."

The newsman knows all this like he knows his own name. He's written about the city's history countless times for the weekly hagiography, zeroing in on and repeating certain events with the seasons, like the time Franz capsized at the Porte des Morts, and the time his Christmas words correctly predicted an April blizzard.

But the newsman feels a little paranoid about sharing all this with Rick. He's been feeling a little paranoid ever since Marcus posted that video. Especially given that earlier today, a set of janitors showed up at his doorstep, offering to clean the whole house for free. He told them he could clean it fine by himself but they insisted, saying it was a gift from Management.

So he drives to Manitowoc to find a café with internet to write and send his missive in anonymity.

At the end of the email he writes, Any of this helpful?

He gets an email back from Rick right away.

Good god, yes.

•   •   •

- *Did Gleamwood City scientists MANUFACTURE the Unmapping? Source says mysterious factory is closed off to outsiders. Theories suggest wild experiments.*
- *An investigation into manufactured "TruTrees." Can SMELLING them give you CANCER?*
- *No drugs, no booze, but yes to LUCID DREAMING? A deep dive into the Unmapping's GROUND ZERO.*
- *Gleamwood City founder contracted DISEASE in TIBET. Is Unmapping a PANDEMIC that CITIES catch?*

- *Throw away your red clothing—so you don't join a CULT!*
- *LOCAL PROPHET predicted blizzards and murders. Did he predict the UNMAPPING?*
- *Unmapping city FOUNDER only talks on CHRISTMAS? Is that when this will END?*
- *Missing the forest for the TruTrees: These people want to replace the world's REAL trees with ALUMINUM.*
- *A mysterious shrinking disease: This retirement community has been growing SHORTER every month. Are we next?*

Esme skims dozens of articles Bluzz has published about Gleamwood City's connection to the Unmapping. It's possible Bluzz is playing up this connection because they're the ones who first broke the story from Gleamwood City itself. Marcus broke it three months ago, when he went to Gleamwood City and broadcast the Unmapping for the world to see. No one believed it. Now Bluzz must be reveling in the attention. Each article has thousands of comments. But who's writing? Some articles are posted with bylines she doesn't recognize, but most are unattributed.

When she pulls her attention from her phone, she realizes the electric grid task force is wrapping up. Pizzas are eaten, water glasses are emptied, bladders are relieved, and people are nearly falling asleep at the table. They've been here all night, Esme remembers. "Good work, everyone," says Sian, yawning. "We have a plan for at least the next twenty-four hours, scheduled by division. Have we notified the branch directors? Wait, yes—yes we have. Good. Let's circle back tomorrow."

After receiving brief personal thanks from Sian, Esme returns to desk sixteen at Watch Command.

Now, finally, she can review yesterday's security footage of Gleamwood Gardens.

But she quickly finds she is unable to access the archive of data. She has the ability to tap into any security footage in the city recorded that day, but at night, the data is compressed and stored under the jurisdiction of the police. Esme's only option is to submit a request for the data she seeks.

As soon as she hits Submit, her stomach sinks. She immediately realizes the futility of this effort. Her aim is to figure out what time he left the building. Yet he could have gone out the back door or down the stairwell, both of which are monitored by privately owned cameras that do not transmit to the city. But even if she successfully learned what time he left, what then? She theoretically would want to pick up the footage from nearby buildings at around that time.

But she doesn't know what those buildings are.

Yesterday she could have written them down.

Now it's a whole new world.

She'd have better luck bringing up a series of live feeds from random spots around the city. Even this would be a crapshoot. Only slightly more efficient than going out herself to search block by block. Yesterday's search now makes Esme cringe with guilt. What a waste of time, when she could have stayed here, reviewed the day's footage, had an actual chance of finding him. But she had to leave; she needed to go home to see if he was there. And when he wasn't, what else was she to do?

Dueling emotions of meaninglessness and guilt battle in her mind; she feels completely ineffectual yet somehow entirely at fault for Marcus's disappearance. Here comes a list of things she could have done differently. She could have called her landlord from the office and urged him to knock on their door. She could have gone home right away. She could have stayed home! She could have listened better when Marcus first told her about the Unmapping so they could have made a plan. Why didn't she listen? If she had been paying attention when she first stepped outside . . . She feels the black hole of despair in her chest threatening to overtake her. The weakness of fatigue. But no. She won't let herself fall back to tears or sleep. That would be even more of a waste.

She stares at the video feeds in front of her. A park in Brooklyn, a library by the Hudson, a mob of porta-potties in Hell's Kitchen. There is nothing useful in any of those videos. Nor will there ever be.

But wait—there is something.

On a few different screens, she's noticed a splotch of lemon yellow. She zooms in to find a flyer with the face of a young boy playing with a train set. Someone's son is missing and these flyers are intended to spread the word. *If you see him, call . . .* Whoever created these flyers has been busy. They show up on nearly every screen in Hunts Point.

This gives Esme an idea.

She creates her own flyer in record time, a crummy thing in Word, but at least it has his photo, her phone number, his name. Ideally she could print on yellow paper, something bright and eye-catching, or perhaps a blue to match Marcus's jacket, or something big and loud. Ideally she could book a jet and have it write her message in the clouds. But for now, there's no way to change paper color in the settings, and the skywriters are all at home, so plain white will have to do. With bright red letters. She schedules two hundred copies to be printed, then heads to the copy room on the fifth floor. The printer is chirring with activity when she gets in. She reviews the first papers coming out of the printer and is pleased with the results. Now there is something physically in her hands that will bring her closer to Marcus. The red lettering will catch an eye or two.

"Esme."

She whirls around to find Commander Cummings, standing with his arms crossed around his chest.

"Do you need something?"

"You. I emailed you. Haven't heard back. I went to the grid task force, but Kearney said you went back to your desk. I went to your desk and saw the print job underway."

"Oh."

"The grid task force gave rave reviews about your work. Now we could use you in shelter supply. Seems there has been some miscommunication there. You don't look tired, but if you are, take a fifteen-minute nap. Do it the Thomas Edison way. Hold a spoon in your hand and when it falls, you'll wake up feeling refreshed. Works like a charm. I've never felt better!"

"Right now? I'm a little busy."

He glances at the flyers.

"Who's Marcus Michael Miller?"

"My fiancé."

"Oh." He uncrosses and recrosses his arms. "Sorry to hear this."

"Thanks."

"You know, you can talk to me. I know you don't know me well, but."

"Thanks."

He's still standing there, pulling on his purple tie. "And if there's anything you'd like to ask me. You know. You can. This has been hard on everyone. My wife, she's a mess."

"I'm fine." She wonders if she should try to smile. If it would look as false as it would feel. Instead she lets her eyes glaze until his face blurs.

He clears his throat. "Thanks, Esme."

"I'm happy to help."

She isn't sure if that's a lie or the truth. Maybe she is actually happy to be part of something bigger, which, as she reminds herself, could indirectly help Marcus.

Or maybe she'll lie until she believes it.

10

Arjun, we need to talk.

It's Liz. It's a text on his phone. Arjun knows he's in trouble before he knows. He has a way of knowing things, and sometimes he listens to this knowledge, and sometimes he doesn't. Like the way he knew it was a bad idea to chase after that blonde woman yesterday, but he did it anyway, because there was something else telling him to. There's a heart thing and a brain thing and sometimes there's a disconnect.

Brain: Stop running!

Heart: But I must save her!

Brain: From what? From you? Look at you. Not even wearing your cool hat. Just a creep.

Heart: Not a creep. Never a creep. A good person. A hero.

Brain: A creepy hero.

Heart: AKA a human. And what else can I be?

And now he knows that something about his failures yesterday is connected to the text on his phone from Liz, who "needs" to "talk." Does she really *need* to talk? Is she bleeding and at risk of dying if she doesn't get to speak to Arjun one last time? And what is "talk"? She needs to lecture.

He was sitting in his van with the key in the ignition because he was just about to head to work, like he was on automatic pilot, when he remembered he didn't know where to go today, so he drummed his fingers on the steering wheel, then scrolled through his email and saw no instructions, so he texted Liz: Reporting for duty. Then she texted back with the worst possible reply.

Brain: Get it over with. Do what you need to do.

Heart: Never! Throw your phone into a river!

Arjun calls Liz.

"Arjun."

"Ms. Liz."

"This is not the sort of question I tend to ask, but are you on social media?"

"A little bit, I guess. On the various occasion. Almost never, but sometimes."

"Have you been on it lately?"

"Sure, I guess." When he first woke up, after he took his morning clonazepam, he checked his texts to see if there was anything from Esme, but there wasn't, and this wiggling wanting feeling brought him to social media. He can't remember a thing from it now but he'd spent at least two hours scrolling, with everything historic and monumental and also somehow hilarious, but none of them stuck with him except one video, for some reason, of a lemon doing the cha-cha.

"So you've seen your video," says Liz.

"What?" Putting his phone on speaker, he opens social media and scrolls through frantic news reports of more cities unmapping—Ocean City, Virginia Beach, San Antonio—interspersed between jokes and reactions and photos and scores of bots all saying versions of the same thing over and over: DON'T FORGET TO LOOK AT YOUR HANDS LOOK AT YOUR HANDS LOOK AT YOUR HANDS LOOK AT YOUR HANDS . . .

He scrolled to his own feed to see if there was a video he'd posted without realizing, but there was nothing since Mental note: Do the similarities of the neighborhood names mean anything? and, later, A perfect move, four miles down and up each day, what does it mean? Both of these posts seem nonsensical now, and they've gotten no interaction except for several responses from the LOOK AT YOUR HANDS bots, so he deletes them. "Ms. Liz, what are you talking about?"

"Search for the hashtag 'emergencycreep.' One word."

"Okay . . ."

He sees himself. He sees himself running in his yellow *I'M HERE TO HELP* vest with a megaphone in one hand and a GPS device in the other, although the device looks like it could be anything, really, and he's chasing a blonde woman through Hudson River Park. It's hard to see the expression on her face but you can only imagine her terror. And the running man, Arjun himself, has a feral look.

"You see it?" asks Liz.

"Yes."

"It's gone viral."

"Not really. Only if you search for it."

"It's in the process, then. It's not a good look. Chasing down some poor woman."

"I apologize. I was trying to help."

"We're getting a lot of phone calls about this calling for us to fire you."

"Oh."

"I don't want to fire you."

"Thank you."

"I do want you to take the day off."

"But I don't want to take the day off."

"This is not optional."

"Okay."

"Get some rest. We all could use some rest."

"But I still have the van."

"That's right."

"Should I bring it back to the office?"

"Not necessary. In fact, please don't drive it today. If you do leave the house, don't wear your work clothes, or anything identifying you as an Emergency Management worker. But there's still a stay-at-home order. So technically you should stay home."

"You got it, boss." He hears the disappointment in his voice, despite his effort to sound friendly. He adds, to fix his mistake, "Boss knows best," but this comes out sounding spiteful.

"Look," says Liz. "I appreciate your effort. I know what happened was an innocent mistake. But sometimes we have to do things just because we have to. We'll get you back to work in no time."

"Tomorrow?"

"Maybe. Gotta go."

Arjun hangs up the phone. He removes the key from the ignition. He takes off his vest. He's still wearing his polo, but it's hidden underneath his jacket. He wishes he had a hat. Any hat. His father has a few up in the condo but he doesn't want to face his father right now.

It doesn't make a difference that the fight is entirely one sided. Arjun's father wants him to either move out, or toss out his clonazepam. "You don't have to leave but I won't have a druggie live here," his father says. Arjun has agreed to move out but it's been difficult to find a place that meets his standards, and how could he possibly move at a time like this? And whenever they get into this argument, Arjun tends to ask why his father had to leave Arjun's mother anyway? And why can't he let Arjun be Arjun? And his father would say, "You are you without the drugs! The drugs make you not you anymore!"

So Arjun lives lightly, as if he doesn't exist, as his father puts increasingly ridiculous objects in Arjun's bedroom, using it as storage for his business ideas, because why not, if Arjun isn't living there? Real estate isn't enough; his father is always on the hunt for the next object that will change the world—which he defines as getting a lot of sales. When they were on good terms, his father would ask Arjun to keep him in the loop on the hip young trends, and by trends, he meant merchandise, and Arjun was happy to oblige, as he himself was always fascinated by what people purchased and why. Fidget spinners, sunset lamps, squishable pillows, bucket hats, snow globes, and fashionable brass knuckles. The snow globes are a personal favorite of Arjun's. He'd never seen one before moving to America, and then one day he popped into a tourist shop to send a gift to his mother and was surprised to find a snow globe of the Taj Mahal on sale. He shook it up to watch the white flecks fall and tried to imagine what it would really be like if it snowed in Agra, a city that only ever went from hot to less hot. So he sent one to his mother and kept one for himself in his backpack as a good luck charm, though he often forgot about it.

Now that they're not on good terms, Arjun has stopped giving his father advice, and he has no clue what the objects in his room are for. On the first day of the Unmapping he came home to find his room filled with massive jugs of water. On the second day there were dozens of big boxes labeled *MICROWIND* in black marker, and a utility-sized battery looming in place of a bedside table, huge and white and humming. Seemingly overnight a crop of fur coats had sprouted by the window.

Now Arjun has three options. Option one: Go upstairs and admit his failure to his father, after which they'll inevitably get in a fight.

Option two: Stay in this van, scrolling on social media, where, it seems, someone has found out his name, and therefore his social media account, and now his private messages are filling up with strange hateful comments and cryptic lyrics by the Police.

Option three: Go on a walk. Understand this new city. And if someone happens to need help, he'll be there. A rogue helper. The Best Samaritan. Imagine someone choking with no one around. And there's Arjun, ready to save the day.

Heart and brain agree: Go walk.

Outside, he discovers he's in a neighborhood that his map calls Claremont Village in the Bronx and that somehow feels very much like Harlem, with brownstones and bodegas on every corner. If not for the power outages, the empty sidewalks, closed-down stores, and that one glassy high-rise towering over everything else, it would feel perfectly normal. The day is sunny and bright, almost too warm for his jacket. He adjusts his backpack straps and starts walking.

His backpack is heavy. Alongside his regular items—his wallet, keys, pills, and Taj Mahal snow globe—he stuffed in rations from the van: granola bars, bottled water, GPS trackers, and portable chargers. If anyone is in need, he'll be ready. But the heavy water bottles make the backpack dig into his shoulders. He tells himself that's fine, that he could use the exercise, but the weight pulls and digs until he worries his shoulders will be sliced open. After five blocks of struggling, his shoulders are spent. He takes off the backpack and removes half the bottles, promising himself he'll pick them back up on the way home, but if in the meantime someone else takes them, then that person probably needs them. Feeling great about this decision, he puts one bottle of water at the end of every block he walks, assuming someone will find it and celebrate their luck. In this way he unloads every bottled water except two, one for himself and one for a stranger he may happen upon in terrible need. So far he's seen no one.

In fact, it is a glorious day and Arjun tells himself this is a blessing, that Liz is right: He needs to rest, and this is restful. But there is something antsy pulling at his neck, even more so now that his shoulders have been released of their burden. Purpose. What is his purpose? The feeling makes him want to take another clonazepam, although that will have to wait until evening. It makes him want to check social media so he can drown this crinkly feeling in cat videos. But he doesn't want to see that awful video of himself. So he keeps walking and tells himself he'll smile at every person he sees. There's no one walking on the streets except him. He tries and fails to catch the eye of the passing drivers. The streets get more inhospitable as the river gets closer; he has to cross under a highway three times.

Three granola bars and twenty blocks later, he sees a group of people congregating in a street, sitting on the ground and at folding tables. Behind them is a small grassy park with a view of the Bronx River. They've set up barriers and cones at either end of the block. Arjun gets closer. They're painting something on the pavement; images of roses are scattered on the ground. Arjun steps around the cones and sees the words: *Free Antony*.

◆ ◆ ◆

It's day three of being trapped underground, which the kid knows by two things. First, the clock on his flip phone. Second, the ceiling of his hideaway. Each morning he wakes up and it's different. The walls and the ground of this little enclosure he's in stay the same: dirt ground, concrete walls, and wooden planks above his head beneath the ceiling that confines him. On the first day, when he heard footsteps faintly, coming from somewhere to the left, he decided he was next to a building basement. Unless they were not footsteps but drums or thunderstrikes or the beating of the heart of a demon getting ready to eat him up like candy. The second day, he heard no footsteps, no nothing, and the ceiling was cold and made of metal. Now, day three, it's silent again and the ceiling is reinforced concrete. He goes through a period of waking and sleeping and reading his comic books with his flashlight. He's read each book ten times by now. He knows every word and can recite them to himself when he wakes up but doesn't want to be awake yet. He wants to sleep until someone can save him. In another life, he ran and ran. He thought he'd run away forever. Then he got startled by a gunshot and a cop and he ended up here, in his hideaway, his prison, and the lid of the world closed in.

The first thing he did when he got here, two days ago now, was call his mom. He called her three times before she woke up. It was four fifteen in the morning.

"Who's this?" Her voice was angry.

Of course she wouldn't have his number saved from this brand-new flip phone, the gift from his brother.

"It's me, Mama."

"Baby? Where are you? Why are you calling? Why aren't you in bed? You in trouble?"

He told her he was trapped but he didn't know where. The words felt funny to him. He knew the situation was not good. But on the other hand, a second ago he was running from a mean-sounding cop. Now he was safe. He had a backpack full of candy, water, and comic books. He had all the time in the world. He told her he was fine. He was safe and had food and water. But he was also trapped underground.

"So that's it, huh?"

"Yeah."

"You're just gonna call me and tell me you're trapped underground and you don't know where and that's that? That's all you can tell me?"

"Maybe you should call 911."

"Fuck me if I'm calling 911!" There was commotion behind the phone as she muffled the mic and yelled at someone else.

His brother's voice came on the line. "Antony? The fuck are you?"

"Trapped underground somewhere. I don't know. I was running and I got confused—and—I don't know." It was almost funny to him. Scratch that, it was funny. He couldn't stop laughing.

"Okay. Okay. We'll find you. Tell us everything you know."

The kid told his brother and mother about his plan to find the spot in the abandoned house by the Chinese restaurant. He left out the part about planning to leave home forever. Just a nice hang spot with good free food. He kept talking before they could ask any questions about that. He told them how when he was running, he heard a gunshot and got scared. He didn't know where it came from, whether it was from the police that were out that night, or that man he saw running, but he went the other way, and then he got lost, and then he found a hiding spot, so he crawled down. And then something trapped him down there.

"Crawled down where?" asked his brother. "Where did you hide?"

"It was an empty building, like a construction site. There was a wooden wall with good handholds down and around the side of it. I think I'm somewhere to the side of what was going to be a basement. I wish we had a basement. I want a basement with a Ping-Pong table."

"Shut up about Ping-Pong. Where exactly was this construction site?"

"I'm not sure. Somewhere near the river, I'd bet." He worried he was saying the wrong thing. In his head, as he ran, his mental map got all screwy. It's possible he ran in the opposite direction.

"That's good," said his brother. "Real good. We can work with that. We'll find every construction site by the river and then we'll bust you free. We'll get everyone in UNCUT on it. We'll get you in no time."

"What if you can't find me?"

"Then we'll call 911. They'll find you. Someone will find you, no problem. You're not packing, are you?"

"Huh?"

"Not carrying anything for UNCUT you don't want to be found?"

"No!"

"We'll figure something out. Trust me, Brother."

He did. At the time, the kid believed him.

But that was two days ago.

Nobody's coming to save him.

• ◆ •

Free Antony. Arjun is familiar with this name and this phrase by now, as it's popped up a few times on social media. It's about that kid who's still stuck beneath a building in Hunts Point. Arjun checks his phone. He's here. Hunts Point. It's the ground beneath his feet. Is the kid down there somewhere? Antony.

Arjun sidles up toward the group of around twenty people painting on the pavement. The words *Free Antony* are surrounded by dozens of flowers, which themselves are speckled in little black polka dots. He hides his eyes with his hands, pretending to block out the sun, really hoping they won't recognize him from his viral video. He takes a photo for social media. Then he remembers: He's currently hated on social media. So he decides to post it under a fake account. He thinks about his name. It should be something very American. Bob Johnson. But no, no one is named Bob anymore. John Bobson. Much better. John Bobson posts the photo.

So Powerful. #FreeAntony

One person notices the new arrival. A short Black woman with green hair and a huge smile calls out, "Hey, you! Want to help paint?"

He puts his phone in his pocket. "Really?"

"If you want. You have that look. Like you want to help."

"Yes, absolutely." How did she know? He isn't even wearing his *I'M HERE TO HELP* vest. Arjun pauses for a moment, scoping out the roses being painted on the street. They're creating a flower mural that extends outward and outward. There are roses and tulips and big white flowers he can't name. Geraniums? Gardenias? "But I'm no artist."

"That's fine. You can paint the little ants on the flowers that have already dried. It's super easy."

"Oh." He can see them now, the six-legged insects crawling on the stems and petals. "Ant for Antony?"

"You got it. Also because ants are fucking great."

"Don't ants eat flowers?"

"Ants help flowers! They aerate the soil and help spread their seeds. And they're a collective. They're in this thing together."

"My father says ants are invaders from the underworld. But he refuses to kill them himself, so he always makes me smush them with Windex and a paper towel."

"Who's doing the invading? They were here first." She hands him a paintbrush.

Arjun imagines Antony, somewhere beneath the ground. He must be around here somewhere. What will this painting do? Maybe the kid will smell the paint fumes. This street, it seems, hasn't moved. None of the streets have. Just everything around them.

Arjun examines the other painters for a minute, admiring the differences in their techniques. One paints three round circles and then the legs. Another paints each set of legs on each round circle before moving to the next. Some ants have bodies with skinny parts, some round. He decides to paint an ant with a triangular head, skinny middle section, and round rump. His first ant has a pair of antlers—is that the right word?—that are far too long, but his second ant looks just about right, and his third ant is even better.

The other painters are solemn, nothing like the cheerfulness of the green-haired woman. He wants to ask why they're doing this, but the answer seems clear: to commemorate Antony. He assumes they assume he has already died.

"Let's take a break. It's sandwich time." A friendly male voice comes from behind Arjun, who turns around to see a young Black man holding four big paper bags, dripping with grease, with the word *UNCUT* written on them in black marker. The man has an easy smile and Arjun can feel everyone else relaxing around him, except for one old woman who says, "I'm still painting!" and another old woman who says, "Where'd you get those sandwiches, JR?"

"I know a guy. After lunch, you can keep painting, and who-ever else wants can go help me find my brother."

His brother.

"And who's this, baby?" JR nods at Arjun but looks at the green-haired woman.

"Our newest recruit," she says.

"Somehow I doubt that," says JR, "but all are welcome."

"He's been painting like crazy. Like, so concentrated."

"I can be a recruit," says Arjun. "What am I a recruit for?"

"Let's start by getting you a sandwich," says JR. "What do you want?"

"I'm okay. You didn't get one for me."

"We always get extra, otherwise Uncle Joe complains, he's always hungry. But he can take a day off his million-calorie diet."

"I don't want to take Uncle Joe's extra sandwich."

"Take it," says a large man, who has already opened the bag and unwrapped a sandwich. "It's vegetarian."

Arjun accepts the food.

"What's your name?" asks JR.

"Arjun."

"That's cool. Cool name."

"Really?"

"How'd you find us?"

"I was just walking. Then there you were."

"So you didn't see us on social media?"

Arjun shook his head. "I suppose I saw the hashtags. Free Antony."

"That's good. But not enough. That's why we're here. That's exactly why. It's one thing to say something online. It's another to be here in physicality. You know? Flesh and bones. My mom, she didn't even want to call 911. She said she'd just post it to social media and people would step up to help. How could they help if they ended up on the other side of the city? We've been lucky. We've been able to get most of our family here." Arjun looks around. Most people here are Black, but many don't look related, and a couple look Middle Eastern.

"You're all family?"

"We got our family-family, our extended family, our extended-extended family, and our found family."

Arjun thinks about what JR said. Antony's mom didn't call 911. "Are you saying the authorities don't know about this? I know there might be some difficulties, but I do believe . . ."

"Nah, we called 911 eventually. Of course we did. Of course. Fuck all that did us. Course, it didn't help that my mom was hysterical. But still. She was like, my son is fucking trapped underneath a fucking building, and they were like, lady, you're crazy."

"They really said that?"

"Maybe not in those words, but yeah, pretty much. They were like, where is he? And she didn't know. And they were like, we can't help you if we don't know. And she was like, I don't know! He's trapped underground, somewhere in Hunts Point, and that's all I know. And they were like, where are *you*? And she wasn't going to fucking tell them her own fucking address, are you kidding me? So they could just send some social worker to arrest her and take her away from her son? So she wouldn't tell them, but they wouldn't do anything unless she told them her address, which she didn't, and so eventually they hung up."

"I'm so sorry," he says, then wonders why he's apologizing, then remembers he works in the same building as the 911 call center, so perhaps he feels some sense of shared blame.

"I know, I know. Since then we've been spreading the word. We're posting to socials, we're calling the mayor's office, like, nonstop, and we're here, because this is the closest we can get to little Ant. We're putting up posters and knocking on doors to ask people to check their basements. But most people don't trust us and won't let us in and don't understand why we're asking them to look in their basements. Like, for what? It's hard to explain how they can help find Antony. Like, I don't know, knock some Morse code on your floor, dig a hole in it or something. Anything! And they slam the door in our faces." JR's face grows worried. "My brother, man. He's still down there. He told us on the phone that first day that he had a lot of water. But how much? Now he's not picking up. We gotta do something. I don't know what will work, but we gotta do something. We gotta do everything. Everything we can."

The others have stopped eating to listen as JR speaks. His voice carries in the calm and sunlit wind. JR now looks up at everyone around him. "The fact that you're all here today," he says, and doesn't finish his sentence before he looks away and shakes his head. "It's so fucking hard," he whispers.

The woman with the green hair finishes for him. "The fact that you're all here today," she says, "even those of you who didn't know Antony, is so important." She looks at each one of them, holding their attention. "No matter what happens, we have to stick together and keep fighting to free Antony. Free Antony!"

"*Free Antony!*" they start chanting. "*Free Antony! Free Antony!*" Arjun joins in. He feels his voice join with the others tentatively, then louder. He hears himself singularly, his voice higher pitched than most of the men's and lower than most of the women's, a melody in a chorus. The voices swell. "*Free Antony! Free Antony! Free Antony!*" He wonders how long the chanting will continue. Is this a protest? Arjun has never been in a protest. Someone unveils a speaker and starts playing funk music. The green-haired girl starts dancing, which embarrasses Arjun on her behalf, until others join in, until he feels embarrassed for himself, being the only one not dancing. *"Free Antony! Free Antony!"* Do people typically dance at protests, or has this shifted into something else? Arjun pounds his fist in the air, which feels enough like a dance movement. Others nearby him do the same. JR's girlfriend takes Arjun's hand and holds it up high. Arjun smiles and shakes his hand in the air, exulting, then pulls out his phone to take a video. Everyone displayed on his screen turns up their dance for the camera.

The music gets louder. Soon, others poke their heads out of the windows of nearby houses and apartment buildings. Everyone is stuck at home, presumably bored out of their minds, or, based on Arjun's brief time in the field, either hungover or still drinking. A group of middle-aged mothers comes out to see what's happening and they stand there awkwardly for a while until one of them joins the dancing. Then the others join. More start leaving their houses to mill around the street—preteens, elderly, people in pajamas, people in business suits. They join the dancing. And more join. There are a hundred people now. Two hundred. More music speakers have appeared on the street and the songs clash with one another but everywhere there is dancing.

It feels all wrong. They are supposed to be mourning. He wants people to know why this is happening. He taps a young mother on the shoulder and tells her about Antony. He sees her face struggle with grief. Satisfied, he continues going through the crowd, spotting the people taking a break from dancing, to tell them about Antony. The looks on these people's faces. The music continues. Now it feels correct. There is joy and sadness properly mingled. All these strangers, they don't know Antony, but each of them has their own private grief based on the past half week. Grief for the future. Grief for what has been lost. Grief that no one wants to admit: that their lives, as they know it, are gone.

Something is happening. Arjun can sense it. It stirs beneath the streets. *Through* the streets. This flower-painted pavement. He spent fifteen years of his life in Delhi, half of which was spent outside in the streets, playing hide-and-seek in the park, playing gully cricket in the gutters, exchanging empty glass bottles for candies at the markets in the alley. It was hot outside, but hotter inside, and there was always something to do out there. Delhi was a city that lived in the streets. They laughed and danced and ran in the streets. Monsoon season was the best, because the air was clear and the puddles stretched for miles. Once you were soaked past the point of no return, you could stay out there for hours, feeling invincible. Surrounded by people. People who would never harm him. People who knew him. Somehow in a city of sixteen million, he always saw someone he knew. An uncle or a classmate or one of the many, many cousins keeping tabs on him. He could never feel lost or alone in the city. They knew who to trust. They knew how to trust.

What about here? What happens when you put five boroughs through a blender and tell them to stay home? They won't stay home, not for long. New York has logic and structure. Or so he thought. Now Arjun senses the grief and fear in this city. There is only so much one human can bear, let alone eight million. All these people dancing, it stems from this fear. They dance because there is nothing else they can do. Logic has forgotten itself. All it takes to save a boy is to paint. All it takes to spark a movement is to dance. It feels like driving from place to place with no memory of the road, hoping you'll turn up in heaven. He doesn't know what will happen next, or how. But there is chaos, yes. Chaos stirs in these broken neighborhoods. There is madness behind the windowpanes. It's only a matter of time until someone cracks it open.

PART TWO

11

Days pass in a new rhythm. Just before four, everything that can shut down does shut down. Water, electricity, gas, everything. Hospitals and government buildings switch to their backup generators. Apartment buildings turn on their old, mildewing rooftop water towers, freshly outfitted with new filters. Then the world turns. Then the work begins, and Esme watches a city come back to life. It starts with a complicated series of digital examinations to study the new positioning of pipes and wires that run beneath the city. They test for voltage, breakage, and failures, and if the tests return satisfactory results, they turn on the electricity block by block, then switch to water, section by section—many of the water valves are themselves electric, making this order of operations essential—and finally, once the electric and water utilities are confirmed to be working smoothly citywide, they do the same checks for gas. If there's any indication of failure, they send out their crews to review and fix it in person. Failures might lead to brief electric overloads or minor floods or gas leaks but those can be handled one by one. At the same time, on an individual basis, building residents, owners, and managers are expected to check their own properties' connections. It is a slow process and many neighborhoods never get their electricity or water for the day, and gas often never gets turned on at all, so people who cook or heat their homes with gas are left in the cold. The city prioritizes areas with shelters, hospitals, grocery stores, and government functions—what become known as touchpoints—so said buildings can plug back into the grid and save their backup power, and those fortunate enough to be mapped near the touchpoints see their luck increase and can have something like a normal day, with toilets that flush and computers that charge, and they can work and study and play games and bake bread and whatever else it is that they do to occupy themselves in these long, lonely days at home. Those without such luck have to trek to the nearest shelter for food, water, and toilets, which often requires motorized transportation, which, these days, means taking a cab. It's not lost on anyone that the houses farthest away from the shelters with gas, food, and charging are the ones who need these services most, and the burden of finding and paying for a taxi adds up, especially day in and day out, even with subsidized rides, so the city begins prioritizing the neighborhoods farthest away from the touchpoints after the touchpoints themselves. After this, the neighborhoods that are halfway between the touchpoints and the farthest away become the unlucky ones, unlucky for simply being caught in between the fortunate and unfortunate. But there's nothing to be done about this, so the city focuses on rigorous outreach, directing people to the nearest grocery stores and shelters, all of which are marked with GPS tags and posted on a website, but they can't count on people checking the internet every day, or even receiving mass text transmissions, especially if they've had no power, so they urge anyone who does receive the map to spread the word to their neighbors. This directive confuses many, because it seems to directly contradict the stay-at-home order, which is still in effect but doesn't apply to people who can prove they are going to or from a shelter or are government workers or volunteers or anyone tasked with keeping the city afloat. But also, people are allowed to try to find their homes. Most businesses have been forced to close their doors—if their workers could even find them—but groceries are supposed to stay open. What about their workers? They stay at the stores now, living large, eating freezer sheet cake and cooking eggs in microwaves.

There are many conflicting directives. Don't panic buy. Do prepare. Sleep well. Wake at four. Use spare bottled water for your toilet tank. Don't even think about wasting it that way. When the water is on, stock up, and also, share. Don't trust strangers. But listen to the volunteers telling you where to find shelters. For the love of all that is good in this world, please don't kill yourself. Stay off social media. But stay on to receive the city's important updates. If you have no water and the situation is dire, you may relieve yourself in the shower, but only number one. Otherwise use one of the thousands of portable toilets placed on sidewalks throughout the city, but don't worry that these portable toilets tend to disappear and show up in one borough at a time.

It's not possible to understand everything in the universe, but Esme is giving it her best effort. She arrives at her desk at 3:55 to be the first to discover the day's new world. Then she flits between task forces like a bee in a flower field, learning just enough to give her input before moving on to the next one—she learns, she explains, she leaves, in a give-and-take that feels harmonious to her. And when there is nothing to be done with the task forces, she studies. Esme is becoming friends with numbers again. On the first day, a row house collapsed from a missing support wall. Since then, Esme has pulled the blueprints of every row house she can to test for similar vulnerabilities, concluding that the first collapse was an anomaly. She studies where water stocks have been sent and which water lines have constant issues, which buildings have never had their water turned on at all, usually in certain sub-neighborhoods, or owned by certain landlords. For fun she maps noise complaints and realizes that partiers are getting rowdier and more dangerous, leading two people to fall drunkenly from rooftops to their deaths. She is concerned to learn about the uptick in disaster tourism helicopters but pleased that they tend to hover in the wrong locations, where nothing exciting happens. She studies which shops have been broken into and where—break-ins have increased of late, especially at night, particularly just before the clock turns at four, when a thief can be helpfully transported in a building to a different neighborhood, far from cops and suspicious neighbors. She has been studying the location patterns of her favorite buildings—the Empire State Building, the One World Trade Center, the Whitney Museum, 30 Rockefeller Plaza, Grand Central Terminal, the Belvedere Castle, and the Emergency Management Department building. And every single lighthouse. There are thirteen lighthouses in New York City, if you include the Statue of Liberty, and they always have their lights on. Most of the lighthouses were already equipped with their own private power stations and automatic switches—unconnected to the grid. The ones that weren't are now. The Statue of Liberty was equipped with a solar panel on day two of the Unmapping, because everyone needs a beacon of hope. And so Esme finds the lighthouses. She finds them easily with satellite footage, thirteen beacons in a dark and jumbled city. She keeps track of their coordinates on a yellow notepad and sometimes stares at the numbers, hoping they'll sort themselves out. She runs the numbers through the computer, too, but there is no discernible pattern. When that's finished, she writes down the location of Gleamwood Gardens, too, because if nothing else, she wants to know where it is, in case this is the day she finally decides to stop sleeping at the office and go back home.

It's been one week.

The flyers were a failure. The stapler she borrowed from the office was broken, and the blue tape she tried using was equally useless on sodden trees and slick metal poles. On a normal day, she'd be able to pilfer duct tape from storage, but the field team was monitoring supplies like guard dogs. She tried to tape up exactly one flyer before giving up. Even when she tried wrapping the blue tape all the way around a stoplight pole, it kept falling. After that, her hands simply stopped trying to make it work, because they understood before she did: This was pointless. It felt like a prank she'd pulled on herself. She could not imagine a world in which someone saw one of these flyers, then saw Marcus, then had the recall to remember the phone number on the flyer, or the volition to take a photo of it, amid all the other things there were to think about and worry about. Or a world in which Marcus, wandering one of the city's twelve thousand miles of sidewalks, would happen upon it. No. As she stood there in the middle of the sidewalk, staring at the flyer that had fallen from the pole into a puddle, where a pigeon was now pecking at its sodden pulp, she knew this was a fool's errand. Esme alone can't save Marcus. Her individual efforts are useless. But plugged into a greater system, she can do something. The most effective use of her time is to be the best worker she can possibly be and make the department as effective as possible, because the system will, eventually, work. And there is some use for the flyers, she realizes: If she drops them around the office, they will be picked up by people with the eyes to the city. People in every task force in every division will know his face and be ready for it.

So she's volunteered to take on double and triple shifts, working until she's too tired to think, then she splashes water on her face, rinses with mouthwash, and takes a cot in the overnight room. The beds are uncomfortable but she's so exhausted by the time she allows herself to sleep it doesn't matter; four hours pass in a blink (which she has decided is more than enough). Then she wakes up and does it all over again.

Patience. She needs patience. Marcus is out there and she just needs to keep working until he turns up. She's aware of the disorganization at the shelters. It's just a matter of time until they catalog everyone correctly and update their records. This is not their first priority. Their first priorities are food, water, and health. Not names. So she will wait. She is good at waiting. She's been waiting for four years to get married. What's another day? What's another week?

When she can't think any longer, she flips through her notebook of GPS coordinates for her favorite buildings: her own personal touchpoints. She read more about the "spoon nap" that Cummings had mentioned; apparently Thomas Edison would hold a metal ball in his hand as he dropped into sleep, so that when his hand released it, at the first moment of dreaming, he'd be woken by the metal clang—and get right to work. Salvador Dalí did the same, she learned, with spoons. There was something about the space between wakefulness and sleep that turbocharged creativity and provided the answers. So she lets her eyes drift over the shape of her handwritten eight, the sharpness of the four, and the way no twos ever look alike, hoping an answer will position itself in the pages.

The Empire State Building. Grand Central. Belvedere Castle. Gleamwood Gardens. The lighthouse. The other lighthouse. She needs these personal touchpoints. Without them, she's losing all sense of time and space. She floats from room to room to computer to sleep in an order that changes every day. She barely remembers her conversations. She knows she's doing good work—the best work of her life—but it's the only thing she can do.

She needs to understand. There are infinite ways to examine any one thing but she wants to find out the truth. She needs the nonsensical to make sense. And if she can't understand everything, at least she can gather a list of things she doesn't understand, to put them all in one place.

For instance, the house with the lights.

There's one house that always has its lights on, no matter the time of day. Even as the rest of the grid shuts down. She learned its registered address from a nearby security camera and cross-checked it with old Street View photos. Now she takes on the daily challenge of finding the nearest camera through which to watch. It's a tan building with pink shutters and a wrap-around porch. She aches for a porch as big as this one, rather than their tiny two-person balcony. But what draws her to the house is the roof with the light. Through the dormer windows in a mansard roof, there's a spotlight that shines nearly as bright as the lighthouses. It shines out into the sky and is so bright it makes the nearby security camera blur. Esme doesn't know why, but it makes her feel safe. Here is something dependable. No matter what happens to the city, this house keeps its light on. Esme doesn't know how. But the consistency of it warms her. She imagines a big family with five kids that eat waffles in the morning and spaghetti at night and end each day reading books in front of the fireplace.

There would be no fights in this household.

Every time she pictures her own apartment, the one she shares with Marcus, all she can think about is the fight. Their final night. It was the worst fight they'd ever had. All through-out dinner—she'd made mushroom marsala—he seemed giddy but distracted, giving one-word answers to her questions as he shoveled food into his mouth. How was your day? Great. How was work? Busy. Good busy or bad busy? Good. How's the food? Amazing. But it's cold. S'okay. He'd gotten home late and, imme-diately when he was finished, said it was time for him to go. After just ten minutes. When he put on his jacket, Esme walked to the front door of their apartment. "Wait."

"What?"

"We need to talk."

"No, we don't," said Marcus. "I know exactly what you plan to say, and you know exactly how I'll respond, so we could either get each other worked up before I leave, or I can just leave now." He reached for the doorknob behind her.

"If it's so predictable, why can't we fix it?" She pressed her body against the door, blocking his hand. "We can't keep doing this. We can't keep having the same fight over and over. This is something we need to work through."

"We have worked this through," said Marcus, pulling his hand back. "And every time we do, we come to the conclusion that you're overreacting and you apologize and I forgive you. So, Esme. Let's get to the ending. I forgive you. I agree we can't keep doing this. So let's stop. Now please move."

"I spent an hour cooking for you."

"Do you want me to cook? I can cook. You know what time I get home, though. You know I can't cook until seven and that doesn't work with your schedule. I can pick up takeout. You can pick up takeout. Whatever you want. Now will you please move?"

"You always have to leave. You always work late, come home late, and then go back to work. You're throwing your whole life away for this clickbait website. Are you going to work for Bluzz forever? Is that the most you're going to do with your life, publishing headlines like *This Deodorant Could Give You Cancer*?"

"Esme," Marcus warned. "That was low. You know I love this job. You know that it's important to me. But you're upset. So I'll let it go." He spoke as slowly and patiently as a teacher dealing with a petulant child.

"So it's this, forever? Never seeing each other. You blow in and blow out as if I'm hardly even here."

"I'm here all morning. You're the one on the morning shift. Are you also, to quote you, 'throwing your whole life away'?"

"I picked this job for you!" cried Esme. "I moved here for you. And you can't even stay home when I ask you to."

"You can't ask me to stay home. I just got a huge tip on something I've been working on for months."

"Tonight it's a tip. Tomorrow it's something else. The next day? And the next? What's the tip, anyway?"

"It's hard to explain."

"Try!"

"There are layers to this story."

"Well, then, peel them open."

He sighed. "Four hundred aluminum Christmas trees were just delivered to Gracie Mansion. They're sitting in the mayor's driveway."

"Okay . . ."

"*Four hundred.* What do they need all those for? Gracie Mansion is usually decorated with exactly fifty Christmas trees, and usually, they're Norway pine. I think there's some backroom deal, a promise to buy more than enough aluminum Christmas trees in exchange for . . . something. I'm going to scope it out and see if I catch anyone walking in or out. If nothing else,

I'll post a photo of the trees and let my followers do their own questioning."

Esme didn't know what to say to that. "Aluminum trees? This is something you've been working on for months?"

"The question of where power lies in the New York mayor's department, yes. How do decisions get made? Who says they have funds to build a new luxurious park in midtown Manhattan, while construction projects in Queens have been languishing for years? There are mountains of dirt sitting next to people's homes, unused cranes blocking their roads. So yes, I've been tracking the mayor's relationships for months. Maybe years. I'm waiting to break the news that she's sleeping with the mayor of Atlantic City. Once I have a little more proof."

"Who . . . cares?" She tried to say this delicately, but it came out sarcastic.

He stepped closer to her then, towering over her as she was backed against the door. "Who cares? You don't care who's in charge of your life? Eight million people live and die in this city. Their lives are at the whims of the elites. If I can't change that, I can at least expose what's happening. And if you can't under-stand why that matters to me, that's your problem."

"My problem," she said to his chest, "is that I'm sick of fall-ing asleep alone. I barely feel like I have a boyfriend, let alone a fiancé. And a husband? Will my husband ever be home? At what point do I say enough?"

Marcus grew quiet. "What do you mean?"

"At what point do I admit to myself that we'll never get married?"

Shaking his head, he walked to the kitchen table and sat down. "Not fucking this again." He put his head in his hands.

"Yes fucking this again." Esme walked over and stood behind

him. "I need you to tell me you want to marry me," she said to his back. "I need us to make a plan. We can go to City Hall tomorrow."

"You can't just go to City Hall and get married. You have to make an appointment."

"So let's make one now. Open up the website."

"Great. We're going to make an appointment right now just to solve a stupid fight. Is that how you pictured the most important day of your life?"

"I pictured it happening, period!"

"It will."

"Really?"

Marcus stood up and took Esme in his arms. She still burned with anger, but she let herself melt into his strong shoulders as she cried. He squeezed her tight, a silent answer. *Patience*, his body seemed to say. He would marry her. He would.

Then he left without saying goodbye.

There's another strange thing about the tan-and-pink house with the bright light. Every day so far, this house showed up right next to the Empire State Building. It's something that would make her believe in signs if she believed in signs. No, she simply likes it for a reason she can't explain. It feels right. She writes down its coordinates and stares at the numbers until her eyes hurt. She finds the house with the light, and when she sees it, she feels hope.

◆　◆　◆

The wife in the house with the lights has never felt so hopeless.

Every day her husband leaves to search for their car so they can finally escape to a cabin with a cache in a forest filled with waterfalls and eagles and salmon and life, real life, life the way it was meant to be, the only thing she has ever wanted, this life with her husband and their future children.

Yet her husband is gone.

Not gone-gone, but good as. Every day he searches for their car. Every day he comes back empty-handed and exhausted. The first day he reached their old address to discover that their detached garage had been replaced by a post office, so their car is somewhere, anywhere, nowhere. He searches for it all day, leaving his wife alone for nearly every waking hour. During this time, while normally she would bake or clean or weed the garden or make progress on the many home improvement projects she has going on at one time—sanding down and repainting the cabinets, refinishing the bedroom dresser—now she can't bear to think of anything but him. As if thinking about anything else will take him further away. Instead she sits, waiting by the window, playing white noise and soft music, tying and untying her hair in increasingly complicated French braids as she peeks through the wooden planks he put up the first day on the first-floor windows, and she prays for his safe return.

The first few minutes after he gets home make it all worth it. When she sees him and he sees her, nothing else matters. He comes inside and they make love with a vengeance, an explosive desire, like today is the last day in the world. They grip each other in need, but it is not just her own need. He needs her. She has never felt so important. Like the beacon to his life, just as he is to hers.

Then she massages his feet and feels the energy seep out of him like air from a punctured tire, and he's left spent until the following morning, when, just after four a.m., he gets up to leave again.

In some ways, it already feels like the world has ended. People on the street look lost and confused. There are blackouts on her block nearly every day, which she can tell from the darkened streetlights and sad open windows. There is less violence than she might have predicted with the collapse of civilization. But she knows violence is often unseen. Behind closed doors. Many are drawn to her spotlight, still shining from the dormer window in the mansard roof, and knock on her door, hoping for an answer, how she has retained electricity while the rest of them have not. But her husband has warned her about this. She knows better than to invite in a stranger who may very well take everything she has, and may very well take her, too.

Until the woman in red.

This woman has knocked on her door every day at eight in the morning. The wife doesn't answer but peers through the boarded-up windows to spy on the strangest-looking woman she's ever seen. She is six feet tall but has the face of a child, as if someone created a larger-than-life doll. She wears a red long-sleeved jumpsuit that looks like it belongs in a factory, a matching red headscarf covering up her hair. Her entire being is lost in this red, except her face, pale and blank, with thin lips and eyebrows so light they blend into her skin. But the strangest thing of all is how this otherworldly woman arrives every day at the same time. How is she able to find her?

The wife half fears she's going mad.

So on the third day, she decides she must respond. To make sure this woman is real.

"What do you want?" the wife asks through boarded-up windows.

"To make a friend," says the woman in a voice that is a little too thin for her liking.

"You don't have friends?"

"I have many friends," says the woman. "Do you?"

The wife scarcely remembers the waitressing friends she had before she met her husband; they fell away like autumn leaves. And she'd never been interested in getting to know her husband's friends or their spouses: All were people they would soon leave behind, once they made their way up north. She imagined her old friends who used to laugh at her husband would beg for help now. How to generate your own electricity and grow your own garden. She was glad they were gone.

"No friends," the wife says, surprised at her own blatant honesty. "Just my husband."

She does not want to invite this mysterious woman inside her house but decides she can at least allow her to sit on the rocking chair on the porch while they talk through the boarded window. "Take a seat. I'll be right back." She gets herself a bottle of water from the basement cache. On second thought, she gets two, because despite everything, she still has her manners, and this strange, dollish woman has an innocent face. And why not pour the water into her nice crystal cups, squeeze some lemon juice into it, and grind up a sprig of lavender from the herb garden in their window? And how about a packet of freezer biscuits, too? They have plenty to spare. She heats them up and puts them on a tray with the herbed water and pushes the whole thing through the front door quickly, then shuts and locks it so they can speak through the window.

The woman in red asks question after question about how the wife has spent these last few days, then further back, about her life, her husband, their dreams. The answers pour out of her like rain, and suddenly it's hours later. How did that happen? And when did she invite this woman to join her on the couch in the living room? Perhaps it's the fact that the woman's voice is quiet—not thin, she realizes, but deep and low, once you draw her out. Perhaps it's her face. Now that she's inside, and the wife has had a chance to study her, she discovers the woman is beautiful. Everything about her has simple symmetry. Her face's blankness, which she mistook as childlike, now seems something more ethereal. Eternal. The wife feels a connection for the first time since she met her husband—she can sense this woman's strong purpose, something in the way she holds herself, and the wife wants to understand why, what her secret is, but every time she asks a question, the woman just turns it around to her, so without realizing it she is sharing more than she has in a very long time. Perhaps it's simply that she needs to talk to someone, anyone, and this woman happens to be here. Eventually, after two trays of biscuits have been eaten, she checks her watch and sees with alarm how soon her husband will be home. She doesn't know how to remove this woman from her house, but when she checks her watch for the fifth time, the woman in red understands, with grace, that she should leave. So she does. Afterward, the wife realizes she knows almost nothing about this woman, including her name.

That's the first thing the wife asks when the woman comes back the next day.

"Call me Serafina."

The wife finds herself looking forward to these visits. She still doesn't understand how this Serafina woman is able to find her at the same time every morning, but she's stopped wondering. Serafina simply shows up and the wife gets swept up in deep talk and, for a long time, feels calm, undistracted, and present. Although afterward she feels strangely guilty, like she said too much, even as she can hardly remember what, exactly, they spoke about. There are so many different topics of conversation that they all blend together. Whatever it is, it makes her feel raw. She makes up for it by being extra loving to her husband when he gets home at the end of each day, with extra-attentive foot rubs and back rubs and fingers pressed to his temples. He doesn't suspect a thing. Not that there's anything to suspect.

On the seventh day, at the end of their conversation, Serafina asks a new kind of question.

"Did you know your home always appears next door to the Empire State Building?"

"Really?"

"You didn't know? Every day it's been this way."

"I haven't seen it."

"You should come outside."

"My husband could be back anytime now. I can't leave."

"But you can. In fact, you must."

And the wife feels the necessity of this. She must. For days now—a week? More? She has been glued to her couch inside the house because, at any moment, her husband could return. She hasn't stepped a foot outside, unless you count the screened-in porch. So today, she readies to leave the house for the first time, checking the thermometer and barometer: It's a warm day for mid-November, so she puts on a light jacket, although as soon as she steps outside, a breeze makes her shiver. "Here," says Serafina, handing her a red scarf that matches the one Serafina wears around her own head.

"Thank you." She wraps it around her shoulders.

"Do you see it?"

Yes, there it is. The Empire State Building. On the same side of the street as her house and towering above everything else. The clouds are moving swiftly above, so that it looks as if it's falling. The wife gets dizzy and closes her eyes. "My god."

"Yes," says Serafina.

"The tallest building in the city, and I've missed it this whole time." She feels a twinge of anger at her husband, who must see it every day but has said nothing about it.

"Not the tallest," Serafina corrects. "Not anymore."

"Oh. But it should be."

"We agree."

"We?"

"You'll see." She holds out her hand and together they walk. Even though it is next door, the entrance is several hundred feet away. She can identify its general vicinity, though, by the huge crowd gathered, extending all the way across the street and down the sidewalk, with everyone staring up in one general direction.

"What are all these people doing here?" asks the wife.

Serafina doesn't answer. But when they approach and push through toward the front of the crowd, the wife thinks she understands. As she peers between the heads of strangers, the entrance slips into focus. It is a garish combination of old-fashioned and modern, with normal-sized glass doors in a black granite setting. Above that, three copper tablets stretch high and are crisscrossed with metal, and beyond this are glassy windows in a gray stone setting that repeat and repeat and repeat until they become sky. The windows are somehow bluer than the sky; it looks not so much a reflection as a magnification. The wife has never been inside this building before. Why spend money to look at a city she's lived in her whole life? But now she decides it's the grandest thing she's ever seen. The infinite windows. The now-cloudless sky is stark behind and within it. An impossible blue. It looks like it could create its own weather, reach its own universe, capture the moon.

"We feel this building is drawn to your light," says Serafina softly in her ear. Her face is so close her lips almost kiss her cheek. After spending several days with this woman in the privacy of her home, the wife feels proud to be with her in public, in this crowd of a hundred. She feels chosen. "We saw the light from the window," says Serafina. "So I wanted to meet you and then I discovered: The light comes from you. You have a light, my lovely friend."

It sounds like a secret. Serafina strokes the stray hairs out of the wife's face, tucking them back into her French braid. Her scalp tingles underneath Serafina's fingernails and she reaches up to touch them. Then she realizes Serafina tied the red scarf around her head.

"It's just a simple spotlight," says the wife, patting the scarf down at her neck. "My husband built it himself out of an aluminum parabolic mirror. Around this we have about a dozen lamps and flashlights. Any light that shines into it gets concentrated and beamed out to one point."

"Everything you've told me about him makes him sound like a smart man."

"He's incredible."

"But what about you?"

"What about me?"

"You've told me nothing about you."

"I've told you everything."

"Only about the past seven years. About the time since you met him. About how you've positioned your life around his. And why is he never home?"

"I've told you why."

"Does he know how lonely you are?"

The wife turns away. "I'm not lonely."

"You are," says Serafina.

The wife longs for her husband's better days. He has so many personalities it feels like she has a whole family in one person. He can be serious, make her laugh, make her think, make her cry. She dreams of the day when they can live by Salmon River Falls, just the two of them, and be happy. But lately he's been leaving her behind, and at the end of each day, he's barely there. She worries now, is this what it will be like upstate? So busy keeping their lives together he'll have no time left to enjoy it? No time for her?

Serafina commands, "Come inside."

"Is that allowed?"

There's a metal barrier at the edge of the crowd, and beyond that, a row of men standing guard at the doors. The guards all wear black bandanas wrapped around their faces and all-black mismatched outfits, looking like they scoured through the nearest laundry pile. Three of them are holding rifles on straps around their necks, and two have pistols on their hips.

Serafina smiles and slips her hand in the wife's. She brings her through the crowd to a quieter entrance on the side with a much smaller crowd. This entrance is similarly guarded, with a row of men with bandanas and mismatched guns. They nod in approval and let Serafina and the wife inside.

Behind them, people call out angrily. "Why them? Why not me?" "My office is up there!" The guards tighten their rank around the doors and call out a warning for the crowd to not come any closer. "Stay where you are and stay calm." "Stay calm? You're calm!" One of the guards shoots a rifle into the air. The wife watches this from inside the building doors, tones muted, like a movie on low. Serafina puts a hand on her back to hurry her away.

The first floor is empty, except for the half dozen guards

monitoring the exits and elevators. Serafina leads her hand in hand to the central elevators, which are mirrored metal with a cloudy outline of the building itself. The wife sees herself in the mirrored doors only briefly before they open, her image getting split down the middle until it disappears. The inside of the elevator is all ornate marble and gold. Before they step in, Serafina takes off her shoes, revealing the softest-looking feet. The wife does the same. Her own feet are puckered and small.

"Are we going to the top?" says the wife. "I've never been to the top before. I've never been inside. What can you see from up there? Is it everything everyone says it is? How far can you see? I can't believe I've never been here before. Can you see beyond the city? Can you see the ocean?"

"Not to the top," says Serafina. "Not yet." She swipes a key card and clicks a series of buttons. "When these doors open again, I must ask you to be silent." The wife closes her eyes, as if practicing being quiet, as she waits for what's to come. The carriage jolts quietly—they're heading down.

The elevator opens to darkness. Serafina turns on a flashlight to guide their way through the pitch-black basement. The only thing she can see is the ruddy red tiles, but she gathers that the room is very large. Even though they're underground, it feels almost like they've gone outside, with featherlight air, and the noise—what is that noise? It sounds like something imitating the ocean. Like the air is breathing. She imagines it's an expensive air-conditioning system. They walk a winding path and she can't say why but she feels confident that Serafina knows where they're going. She feels she's in a submarine going along the bottom of the ocean, and Serafina is her captain. Their hands are gripped tightly together.

Then Serafina opens a door. She hears it unlatch and sees the light behind it creep through the gap. Briefly, bright fluorescents shed light into the dark room behind them.

That's when she sees the bodies.

A dozen or so women are curled up in the fetal position on the floor, covered in red blankets and wearing red scarves around their heads. The noise that sounded so much like the ocean is instead the susurrating gasp of sleep.

"Come in quickly," Serafina whispers, pulling her into the room and closing the door behind them. On the table is an opulent spread of pickled fish, fresh fruit and vegetables, cheese, and an electric kettle, which is already turned on, with water boiling. But the wife has lost her hunger. She is staring instead at the wall, where a poster of an elderly man with watery blue eyes and red coveralls is pinned.

"Are you hungry?" says Serafina. "Feel free to eat. As much as you like." She pours the boiling water into a teapot with green leaves in the strainer, then pours two mugs, one for herself and one for the wife. Serafina blows on her own mug.

"Eat?" the wife says, suddenly crying. "You're telling me to eat? What's happening out there? Why did you bring me here?" She peers at the tea, a grayish green that smells like mint and dirt. "Are they on drugs? I don't do drugs. I won't do drugs. Is this food drugged? Are you going to rape me? What's in this tea?" She wonders, if she tried to leave, whether she'd be able to find her way. Those men with guns guarding the entrance, are there more of them inside? Are they meant to keep people out, or in? She is shocked to discover that Serafina is hugging her and stroking away her tears, and equally shocked to discover that she leans into the hug, that this woman smells like mint and feels like home.

"Shh," says Serafina, stroking the wife's cheek. "I didn't mean to give you a shock," she says softly, like a lullaby. "It's mugwort tea. Calming. Good for mood, digestion, and menstruation. There are no drugs here except the power of our minds. Those women are all completely fine. Nothing bad will happen to you. There is no reason for fear. You can leave anytime. But I ask you to let me explain first."

"Now. I'd like to leave now. What possible explanation—"

"They're sleeping."

"Everyone at once? In the middle of the afternoon?"

"They're in a state of lucid dreaming. Think of it as meditation."

A big body wave of relief. She trusts this woman; she might love this woman. Her words are a better salve than any tea. "Lucid dreaming?" she says, hiccuping. "The dreams where you can fly?"

"Flying is just the beginning. They are creating their own worlds."

"Their own worlds?"

Serafina explains, and as she does, the wife feels as if she already knows what will be said, that rather than learning new information, she is being reminded of something she was told long ago.

They were taught to dream by the man in the photo— Serafina says—the elderly one with watery blue eyes. His name is Franz. ("Franz?" the wife asks. "Franz who? What's his last name?" But Serafina doesn't know.) Franz came to them more than a year ago as a guest teacher at their Tibetan yoga studio on the twenty-fifth floor of the Empire State Building, offering a weekend intensive workshop to all the building's office workers for free. The focus of this weekend was lucid dreaming. They were unsure of this strange man at first. He was small, shorter than any of them, had a high-pitched voice, and wore a bright

red boilersuit, with an extra pinned to the front of the room. It
would all make sense, he promised, seeing the skeptical looks on
their faces. He spoke calmly, but he had so much to say you could
feel the freneticism behind his words; he didn't talk quickly but
he talked avidly, unendingly, making them laugh, making them
listen. Serafina doesn't remember the specifics; even that weekend, and shortly after, she had a hard time remembering the par-
ticulars. But she remembers he told them to look at their hands.
He set a repeating timer for thirty seconds, a calm chime that
was memorable enough to remember in a dream yet startling
enough to wake you up. Each time it went off, he instructed them
to look at their hands. He was talking and then, *chime*, everyone
had to look at their hands, and he'd keep going as if nothing had
happened, *chime*, unless someone forgot. This was practice for
the dreams, because in dreams, hands tend to be liquid, unsolid,
many-fingered, diaphanous, wrong. In dreams, *chime*, you can
take one finger and put it through the palm of the other. Once
they could do this, he said, *chime*, the first task would be to put
on the red jumpsuit, which, by now, was seared into their brains.
He said they wouldn't need to work to put it on; they could simply blink and look down and there it would be, a clear marker
that the lucid dream was working.

On the first day, he taught them how to prepare their minds
for lucid dreaming. On the second day, he showed them how to
take control of their dreams. On the third day, he taught them
how to take control of their lives.

It was a rigorous and exhausting schedule with very little
true sleep. But they found it unbelievably empowering. By the
end of the weekend, one woman realized she had the power to
end her abusive marriage. Another practiced cello in her dreams
until she could gain the confidence to pick up her old instrument

and perform again. Another was able to quit her addiction to painkillers. "And you?" the wife asks Serafina, but she continues her story as if she didn't hear.

All of them could fly.

The weekend ended with a warning. The world is just as moldable as dreams, he told them in a voice that had transformed from grating to soothing as they sat in a semicircle. He had practice, this was clear. He said a great transition was coming, something impossible to explain but that they'd recognize when it came. (Serafina, of course, recognized the Unmapping immediately as what had been forewarned.) He told them how important it would be to practice the dreaming, so when the great day came, they'd be ready. "Ready for what?" they asked, transfixed.

"Ready to take life in your own hands."

To take life in their own hands. What did that mean? But he wouldn't elaborate. It was clear the women needed to figure this out for themselves. Over the following year, it was discussed for a long, long time, as the women, now inextricably bonded, continued to meet week after week. It had something to do with the idea of a malleable reality, some said. The dream world jutting into the real world. Some believed in the possibility of a great rapture, and they could either dream it away or dream it into being. Some noticed how intensely Franz hated the fake Christmas trees that decorated their building lobby, something called TruTrees, and wondered if the rapture would have anything to do with that. This was no more than a small thought that strengthened the more it was repeated, because yes, now they all remembered how much he hated the TruTrees, because, he said, they made it impossible to tell the difference between dreaming and reality. And then they remembered one particularly strange dream about TruTrees, which they'd blocked from their minds, a bizarre plot that, he'd hinted earlier, was a test that would truly showcase their abilities. ("What was the dream?" the wife asks. But Serafina tells her to have patience.)

He had disappeared at the end of the workshop while they were in this final dream. They woke to a blaring alarm and he was gone. The surprise of his disappearance made them briefly forget the dream, despite its vividness. They still had so many questions! So the women searched the rest of the building, but he was nowhere to be found. They decided they must invite him back for another weekend, but he hadn't provided any contact information.

That was a year ago. Since then, they've been waiting. They've been practicing. They've been finalizing their plan.

So they will teach the wife how to dream. It will begin with a visualization. The photo of the elderly man with watery blue eyes will be seared into the backs of her eyelids. In a guided meditation, this old man will be her chaperone, welcoming her to the Empire State Building from behind the concierge desk and walking with her to the elevator, which, he will explain, leads to floors that each contain a different dream. The first floor is empty. But not the same way an unoccupied office is empty. The first floor is an abyss, with the emptiness of space before time. The second floor is filled with colorful shops selling doughnuts so warm they melt in your mouth. On the fourth floor, you can spin on the tips of your toes in an endless pirouette. On the ninth, you can paint a beautiful mural like Michelangelo. On the thirteenth, you meet and dine with the president of the United States. The twentieth transports you to the top of Mount Everest. The fiftieth brings you to the moon. The sixtieth allows you to walk on ceilings. The seventieth allows you to slow down time until it stops. They will teach her to understand the difference between dreaming and reality, warning her to never try to read or look in a mirror—both will disturb her into wakefulness. They will tell her to never close her eyes. To always keep them open. This is the most important directive. Be open to the light. What does that mean? On each floor, the light gets brighter and brighter. On the eighty-sixth floor, she will be able to fly. On the hundredth floor, she will reach a new reality.

But that will come later.

Now, as the wife takes a small sip of her tea, followed by a longer, deeper draft, Serafina says, "Let us teach you to take life in your own hands."

◆　◆　◆

"Esme." A flashlight shines in her eyes, waking her up.

She fell asleep in the cot room for a ten-minute nap between her morning and afternoon shifts and must have overslept her alarm and then some, because it feels like she just slept through the afternoon. The flashlight moves from her eyes to the floor, leaving a burning afterimage. She blinks at her watch until it settles into focus. The time is noon. The next day. She slept twenty straight hours.

"Commander Cummings," she mumbles.

"It's time to wake up."

He hands her a cup of coffee. She sits up and takes a sip. It tastes like sour almonds. She takes another, gulping it down. So much time she wasted while asleep. Now she needs to make up for it. How many emergencies has she already missed? "Follow me," Commander Cummings says quietly.

"Which task force do you want me on today? I feel like the grid team is in a good place at the moment but the food stocks have been all over the place. The shelter task force hasn't been listening to my recommendations. It's so obvious we need to direct the shipments straight to the shelters and move as needed, rather than bring them here first to a central repository."

"Hmm" is all he says in response as they walk through the halls and take the elevator down to the second floor, where he leads her to an oval conference room surrounded on all sides by glass windows. There he sits at the head of the table. She feels proud to be in a one-on-one meeting with Cummings, spotlighted, seeable by everyone else, like she is being awarded a prize. This is her moment to be recognized.

"Take a seat."

"I'd rather stand, if that's okay. My legs are sore."

"Then I'll stand, too." Cummings stands up and crosses his arms over his chest, then uncrosses them and puts his hands on his hips, then clasps his hands in fists, then unclasps and puts them back on his hips. Finally he sits back down and grips the table. "Tully and I were talking about your work ethic."

"I'm sorry I slept for so long," Esme says quickly, feeling awake in every particle of her body. "I didn't realize how tired I was. I've been working really hard—"

"We know, Esme. No need to apologize."

"Okay. Thank you." Esme regrets her choice not to sit. The room pulses and makes her feel woozy. It's too warm in here. Stuffy. Like she's in an airlock, breathing in her own carbon dioxide.

"Your work has been extremely valuable."

"Thank you."

"It's clear to everyone here that you could use a break."

"Yeah. I really needed that sleep."

"I mean a bigger break." He clears his throat. "I hear you've been working two and a half shifts daily for a week straight. According to federal regulations—"

"I know it's overtime. Think of it as volunteer work."

"We've received reports from several of your coworkers. You're . . ." He clears his throat again, but there's nothing in it— just the weight of unspoken words. "People have heard you crying at your desk. And in the bathroom. And in the cot room."

"Oh." This is not going to be a meeting of two minds or a moment of recognition. This is a reprimand. Now the floor-to-ceiling windows make her feel exposed. When people walk by, she can tell they peer in, curious, but avert their gaze when she turns to look. She feels she's in a zoo. But do the others think of her as an angry gorilla? Or as a wounded, pathetic bird? Esme struggles to keep her face calm. "I'm sorry, I—"

"And the flyers. There are reports that you keep leaving flyers around the office. It's a distraction and it's making people uncomfortable. It's rather sad, you know. A big hit to morale. And that's hard enough to find these days. Morale. We have to keep up the team spirit."

"Team spirit?" Her emotions betray her. Angry tears spring to her eyes. "My flyers about my missing fiancé are making people uncomfortable?"

"We were thinking you might want to take some time off work. Spend some time at home."

"I can't go home."

"I was worried about that. So I contacted your building manager at Gleamwood Gardens. He provided the coordinates."

That's not what she meant. "Oh."

"Lana gathered your things and put them by the front desk. There's usually a few cabs on deck out there. You'll be able to get home without a problem."

"We're in a crisis. And you're turning me away?"

"As I said, your work has been extremely valuable. But we've reached something of an equilibrium. Things are under control."

"No they're not! There is so much more we need to understand—"

"We've figured out how to offload your work. Everyone is willing to take on a little more if it means you get to recover."

"Everyone? Who's everyone? Who exactly was in charge of this decision?"

"Go home and rest up somewhere more comfortable than an office cot."

"I don't need to be comfortable. I'd prefer to keep working." Traitor tears keep springing up in the corners of her eyes. She blinks and a handful of them fall from her eyes at once. "Have I broken any rules?"

"Esme."

"Commander Cummings?"

"This is not a request."

12

On the one hand, it's a step up. After just one driftless day, Arjun was asked to help man the phones on the 911 dispatch team, a difficult role that usually requires months of training, whereas he was given two hours to read both the training manual and the special emergency addendum, and at the end of the two hours he was assigned a call station, clapped on the shoulder, and told to do his best. He considered the position to be a great challenge, one that warranted respect and was luxurious in its own way, sitting on your bum all day, passing on people's problems to somebody else and, with the click of a button, sending out ambulances or police officers or otherwise telling important people what to do. Who polices the police officers? Arjun. Who commands the commanders? Arjun. Well, maybe it doesn't go that far, but still, it feels like a step above his role on the field team, which was, essentially, chauffeur.

On the other hand it's a step down. Arjun was clearly offered this role out of desperation as the dispatch team quickly dwindled—moving away or running away or dealing with "family issues" at home—while the emergency calls increased. Callers had been waiting on hold for an average of thirty minutes. Managers who had never picked up a phone in their lives are now helping out with the dispatchers when they have a free minute. But the managers have more important things to do. Not so with Arjun.

On the other-other hand, this job is the most stressful thing Arjun has ever done in his life. Within the span of a minute or less, he talks people through the worst moments they will ever experience and he, alone, is tasked with making the correct decision, and when the phone clicks away, he has to hope for the best, monitoring the situation as well as he can, but ultimately having no way of knowing what happens to most of the voices on the other end of the line. They call him and tell him, calmly, they think they're dying, possibly from a heart attack or maybe a stroke, or they can't remember who they are. They inform him that kids in bandanas are smashing the windows of the coffee shop across the street, and are they coming for me next? They tell him their stove is on fire, their bathroom is on fire, their entire guest bedroom is on fire and they have no extinguisher. Fires have cropped up like weeds. All these burning candles. Don't people know how to blow out a candle? They call him to complain about the loud neighbors partying until four in the morning, about the various cults that are seeming to crop up, those women in red, the men in blue, the people camping in tents on the street; they worry about their missing dogs and cats, their missing mothers; they tell him they don't want to live anymore, ask him if he thinks this is real or a mass hallucination; they see aliens in the sky; they feel their skin turning to computer parts. The calls are getting stranger and more frantic. It's one thing to have one irrationally bad day. It's another for these days to pile up on top of each other until they collapse like the Tower of Babel. They wonder if there's something to the idea of suicide as freedom that's been rolling around online. The rumors and ideas are flying faster than the winds of a hurricane.

The red-suited women are going to leap off the Empire State Building. The blue-jacket men are building jetpacks to build a city in the sky. The true answer is to build a new city underground. Some have figured out that 911 services' location triangulation is all out of joint, meaning Arjun can't send police cars to every single caller, so they've begun calling just to hear themselves talk. And if he says he's hanging up, they threaten to kill themselves and so Arjun transfers them to the suicide hotline and hopes, and hopes, and hopes, squeezing his fingers into a ball until he thinks they might break.

For the past few days they've put him on the afternoon shift, from one till nine p.m., but he often stays later when the night team doesn't show. Meanwhile, Esme is in the office, too, but he's barely spoken to her at all. First of all, she keeps working through lunch. Second of all, she's been attending all these meetings in various rooms on various floors, so she has been hard to find. Third of all, whenever he catches her in a hallway or the vending machine room, she seems like she's only half there. She appears to be sleeping in the office, because he's seen her come out of the shower rooms with wet hair and she's worn a version of the same outfit every day, cycling through Emergency Management polos that are too big for her.

On the fourth day of phone work, he arrives early to catch her during lunch break. But of course she's eating at her desk in Watch Command, as he sees from the lunchroom, with a bag of nuts open while her head is hunched toward her computer screen. He walks over.

"Esme."

"Arjun."

"How are you?"

"Good, you?" She doesn't look up from her screen, which

shows various security streams from a dozen streets Arjun wouldn't be able to recognize if he tried.

"Good." He waits to see if she'll say anything else. Her long, curly hair is pulled into a frizzy ponytail, free from a face that is pale and sunken.

"Is that really your lunch?" he says, pointing at the nuts on her desk.

"Yep." She types furiously on her keyboard, seemingly forgetting his presence.

"Just so happens I have an extra bagel and cream cheese, though," he says. "I bought too many at the grocery." He removes his lunch from his backpack and puts it on a paper plate. She looks at it like he's given her a piece of radioactive waste.

"I'm okay," she says. "Hunters and gatherers, and all that."

"Right." He knows what she means. She's eating like a caveman. They used to make fun of people who were on the caveman diet: nuts and fruits and misery. A life without cheese? Despicable. They used to talk about everything.

"Suppose I should have brought you a dead rabbit instead."

"Good idea." She nods, leaving the bagel untouched. Did she even hear what he said?

"Hey, Esme?"

"Yeah."

"I just want you to know you can talk to me," he says. "If you need to talk. Whenever you need." Six short days ago, she cried in his arms. He remembers how she pulled him close, her fingers clasped around his shoulder. Her hair, long and loose, spilling over her face. That feels like a different person than this woman who stares at her screens with eyes so wide they might fall out of her head. "I'm working afternoons now, but I can always come in early, like we used to. When is your lunch break?"

"Arjun, I don't have time for this."

"Oh." It feels like he's been slapped. "Sorry for interrupting."

She doesn't acknowledge his apology. He stands there for a few more seconds, trying to think of something to say. Then he walks away with his bagel. He wishes it were time for clonazepam. There are still eight stressful hours to go.

How extremely his mood has shifted in three days. When he was walking here on the first day of the phones, he was so excited he accidentally kicked off his left sneaker. Three days later and his feet dragged the whole way from the condo to the van and from the van to the building's elevators. Now he has an hour to kill before his shift begins, and he's lonelier than ever. Hundreds of people are waiting to talk to him and he has no energy for it. He goes outside and nearly steps on a massive anthill. There are thousands of little ants swarming around the dirt pile in between two concrete slabs, running around like their lives depend on it, completely unaware of the massive being with a sneaker that could easily smash their home to smithereens. What kind of ants are stupid enough to build a home in the middle of the sidewalk in downtown Manhattan? He thinks about stomping on it just for some relief. But he crouches down instead and watches the ants work. He admires their delicate walk up the steepest slopes and the way that when he puts a finger in their path they change course immediately around it. How did they survive the storm? Arjun imagines their home must have been washed away with the rains, if not blown off in the winds. And now look: Just one week later, their home is as big as ever.

Arjun's phone dings. It's a notification from social media. His pseudonymous John Bobson account has been growing steadily in recent days as he's posted about the #FreeAntony campaign. It started with that photo of the mural. Since then, he's been reposting everything he can, about #FreeAntony and other things, with a few words of commentary. How stupid he was for not realizing this before: There is no need for him to be smart or funny; he can simply borrow the smart and funny things that already exist. Sometimes, he accidentally reposts fake stories or images, like a photo of the president holding a #FreeAntony sign, or a story about how aluminum trees are causing the Unmapping—but what if they were true? Still useful. Still interesting. Still getting him lots of likes and new followers. Not all of them are successful—some of the posts get exactly one like, from the person he reposted, but every so often one of them blows up and he can't say why. He just keeps posting without worrying, even if only one out of every twenty do well. It's been a little ding of happiness these past few awful days. But now he silences his phone so he can study the ants until it's time to head back to work. For once he doesn't daydream about anything; he simply watches the ants move tiny pieces of dirt from one side of the hill to the other. There's nothing more to it than that. There is no secret and no story. No dreaming. Just ants.

Arjun realizes he doesn't need to return to work. He could say there was some family emergency. But then what?

He could stay outside, go on a walk, pretend he got lost, maybe.

He could take a plane to Delhi to see his mother and grandfather, joining the ranks of the others who've fled the city.

He could go home and take a nap amid the stacks of boxes of fur coats and "microwind." Curious, he'd opened one of the boxes, because they were about five feet tall—which didn't seem very "micro"—to find a dozen strange metal contraptions that looked like flowers in frames. A marble of red surrounded by five blades enveloped in a black metal circle. He wondered if his father was investing in art, until he later saw one of these contraptions pinned to the outside of the living room window, hooked up to a cable leading to a human-sized battery. On the battery was a console with numbers dialing upward, so Arjun decided it must be some sort of tiny wind energy system. "Oh," he said to himself. "Microwind." But if he went home now, that would surely lead to some interaction with either his father or the poor souls he hired to move all these goods in and out.

Or Arjun could just sit right here and no one would tell him not to.

But an ambulance goes by, the siren breaking Arjun's rebellious state of mind. The reality right now is that Arjun is needed. He's not exactly in the mood to hear someone's worries about their dog's neon shit or listen to their final breaths. The calls are banal or extreme with nothing in between. Time expands with boredom and adrenaline. Every moment is eternal. You could rearrange a whole new city with all the time you have in a job like this. But still. A job is a job and he can be a hero.

At his desk, the first three calls are pranks. The fourth is an accident and the fifth is a report of gunshots. Then a mobile number shows up on the call screen. Right away he knows this will be a difficult one. It's an old-fashioned phone with no GPS capabilities. When he gets a landline, he can send a car over right away. When he gets a new cell phone, he can narrow down the location to a three-block radius. Then there are the old, dumb phones, which are nearly impossible to find with triangulation, what with the cell towers placed wherever they please. He picks up the call.

"Nine one one, what's your emergency?"

A small voice says, "I'm trapped and I'm scared and I need help."

"Where are you? What's your name?"

"I don't know. My name is Antony."

• • •

The kid is thirsty. That's the first thing he thinks when he wakes up, the last thing before he falls asleep, and everything in between. The constant, ever-present thing. He brought five bottled waters and has been going through them as slowly as possible. Only when he thinks he can't bear another moment without a drink does he allow himself a gulp. And it's the most perfect and beautiful thing that's ever existed, water, sitting in his mouth, like the longer it stays unswallowed, the more he has to drink. He pictures his entire body submerged in a pool. Floating in the river, letting it take him away. He dreams of ice cream and wakes up satisfied, with the taste of mint chip on his tongue.

There are other thoughts, too, and sometimes he is able to think them. Like when's the last time he peed. Like the comic books he has memorized by now and recites to himself and laughs at each time.

Like the idea that if he dies this way, he'll be happy.

He wanted freedom and, in a way, he got it.

Then there's the part that reminds him, No. Try calling 911. Every day since day one, he's tried to make a call, but it hasn't gone through. No service, no service, no service. He hates himself for not doing more that first day, when, for twenty-four hours, he could use the phone to talk to his mother and brother. Who else could he have called? Everyone. But then he waited for them to show up and then the ceiling of his hideaway changed to something bigger, thicker, of pure concrete, so he couldn't make any calls at all.

Until today. The seventh day.

His flashlight has dimmed to a weak pulse and he doesn't know how much is left on the portable phone charger. He's been using the phone as little as possible. Just once a day, attempting a phone call.

Today, the dispatcher connects him to someone else, who connects him to someone else, and the kid sits there and waits, and each time, when it's someone new, he says, "It's Antony," and they pass him on to someone else, who says, "Please stay on the line," until it goes to someone else, and he says, "Please." He says, "I'm trapped and I'm low on water and I'm scared," until it clicks out. The kid thinks he should cry, but he doesn't. Sometimes crying helps people listen; sometimes it turns them away. He tries dialing 911 again, but before he can finish, his phone rings in his hands. He puts it on speaker. He hears a room full of voices, some crying out with disbelief, "He's alive!" The voices settle to quiet and someone says, with an echoing nasally voice: "Tell us everything you can."

"No," says a deeper voice from someone else, "we need to be more specific. Tell us everything you can about where you are right at this moment."

"I don't know," says the kid. "Underground."

"How much room do you have?" asks the deep voice. "Can you walk around? There must be a way out. *How else is he still able to breathe?*" This last sentence is asked to the group.

"Kid, can you breathe?" says the nasally voice. Someone else tells him to shut up.

"I'm in a space between things," he says. "It's like a hallway but there are beams of wood going through it, kind of like the red laser lights in heist movies protecting all the diamonds. I can crawl around them in this hallway thing, this space between things, but I can't stand up. I can crawl in a circle around something large, I think a building, and get back to where I started."

"What's the ground made of? What are the walls? What is the ceiling? What else do you see?"

"The walls are cement or something hard," says the kid. "The ceiling is some kind of thin metal. There are little holes in the metal. The ground is dirt and there are pipes running through it."

"What kind of pipes?"

"I don't know." He coughs. "Black."

"And those pipes go through the walls?"

He checks. "Yeah."

"Is there any space around the pipes? Reach in and down."

The boy sticks his hand through the gaps around the pipes that run through the damp dirt from one wall to another. The first one closes and makes his fingers pinch. The second one opens up.

"Put your ear up close. Do you hear running water?"

The kid obliges, putting his ear on the dirty plastic. "Yeah. I think so."

"This pipe should extend beyond the outer concrete wall and drop down. Reach all the way around it. Dig underneath it a little, and down under the wall."

The boy digs his hands underneath the water pipe, down by where it disappears into the outer wall. The ground is loose and loamy. It falls away easily, opening up even farther into the ground. He pushes the dirt around. The opening keeps opening. It scares him. Will he fall? He repositions himself to lie flat and keeps digging. There is an opening. It's loose and large. He turns on the flashlight and peers into the void.

"There's a big area behind the pipe," he says. "Maybe I could let myself down into it."

Someone shouts out, "Yes!"

"This is good," says the man on the phone. "We may be able to get you out."

◆ ◆ ◆

Arjun has been preparing for this. In addition to the training manual there is an online document with additional instructions special to the Unmapping. With every shift change, a new version of the PDF is sent to the team, each with different kinds of typos. The focus of this document is helping dispatchers find their callers' locations. If GPS coordinates are unavailable, the caller is asked to look out their window and identify nearby landmarks: lighthouses, iconic skyscrapers, monuments and statues and public parks. It also provides sample scripts to explain why someone's water or electricity might be down, along with instructions on finding the nearest shelter, which, it is important to assure the caller, receives tons of supplies every day. It also includes several specific instructions for various edge cases. One of those cases is for people who claim to be trapped underground, and if such a person should call 911, they should immediately be transferred to Bill Cummings. But here is this kid. Here is Antony. On the phone with Arjun. Arjun hears the kid's dry, scratchy breaths and wants to say something, anything, to make him feel better, to make him feel less alone. He wants to tell him about the people painting his name on the ground, putting up flyers, carrying out a great effort to find him. But that is not in the instruction addendum.

Arjun transfers the call.

And what happens next? An hour passes with minor fires, major injuries, car crashes, break-ins, and suicidal ruminations.

Then another, and another. Yet Arjun can't stop thinking about the kid, the way his voice sounded so dry, his little cough, his quiet words, like he couldn't expend any energy to be louder. And an admission: *I'm scared.*

When he gets an evening break, he scans the 911 public call log on his phone. There, in the public records, he can read the AI-generated transcript.

But after Arjun transferred the call, the transcript is blank.

Arjun logs back in to his computer to pull up the audio file from the call. He hears the boy, as he's transferred from department to department, and the way the phone call clicks out.

They didn't provide him any help whatsoever.

Arjun returns to the 911 dispatch room and finds the boss of the day. It has changed every day since he began. His boss tonight is a man not much older than himself with a name tag that says *Clarence.* Arjun met him when his shift began earlier today, but didn't get a chance to learn anything other than his name before he was shepherded to the phones. Now Clarence is typing something on his laptop with an open bag of Fritos and five bottles of 5-Hour Energy.

"Mr. Clarence," says Arjun.

"Call me Clarry," Arjun's boss says with nervous energy, clapping his laptop closed. "And your name is . . ."

"Arjun Varma."

"Right. What can I do for you, Arjun?"

"What happened to the call with Antony Reed?"

"What do you mean, Arjun?"

"Emergency instructions required me to transfer the call to Commander Cummings. But according to the records, he never got that far. The call was transferred to Commander Cummings's secretary, who transferred it to someone else, and this happened about five times, and then the call dropped. Did anyone call him back? I tried to follow up on the case file but it disappeared."

"Ah. Well. Let me see."

He reopens his laptop and clicks around a bit. "Apologies, Arjun, but I don't think I can help you."

"Apologies, Clarry, but is there anything you can tell me?"

"I'm sorry, Arjun." Clarence shows him his screen. He's pulled up the same thing Arjun has. The case file is blank after Arjun transfers the call. Clarence brings his laptop back to his lap and eats a fistful of Fritos.

"Could you please speak to Commander Cummings about this?"

Clarence stares at Arjun as he chews.

"It's my duty to follow up on my calls."

"Sure."

Clarence types something on his computer, then looks surprised to see Arjun still standing there.

"It'll be a bit before I get a response, I imagine. But hey, I'll let you know as soon as I do."

"Thank you. I appreciate it."

"Of course. And hey, I appreciate you! This is a tough gig." Clarence pulls another 5-Hour Energy from a drawer. "Want a pick-me-up?"

Arjun declines. He heads back to his seat, where three calls are waiting for him. The first needs to be transferred to the EMT, the second is about a false fire alarm that keeps getting pulled, and the third is some old lady trying to have phone sex, but she's calling from a landline, so he sends one cop car to get her on indecency and misuse of emergency services. On his cell phone, simultaneously, Arjun searches social media for any new mentions of #FreeAntony. His feed is flooded with photos of the boy's face, from when he was a baby until most recently, aged thirteen, tying up a new pair of sneakers and smiling wildly. On the headset, on his screens, there are ten things happening at any given moment. Are the responders and respondees talking to each other? And what happened with the fire on former Flatbush Avenue and what about that huge pothole that cars keep crashing into? And yet somehow he needs to speak on the phone with a voice that is cool, calm, and collected, as people scream. The boy. Antony. Little Ant. There are a billion ants in New York City. More than there are people in this bottomless maw of a country.

People need and need and need and Arjun thought he wanted to be needed, but now he doesn't know what he wants. There is too much need and not enough Arjun, and whenever Arjun tries, he fails. Arjun's father calls ants invaders from the underworld. Arjun pictures ants making tunnels all the way underneath the river, leading from Times Square to the Atlantic Ocean. Swimming on little ant surfboards of grass and leaves. He wants to know how ants survive a hurricane. If the water doesn't drown a colony, the winds would sweep it away. Already he knows the answer has to do with being underground. He pictures their little tunnels underground, with so many branching paths they can trap the rain and redirect it to a well, leaving the rest of their homes safe and dry. They're down there waiting for the rain to stop and then they reemerge with a vengeance.

All Arjun wants to do is help. And yet they removed him from his post and put him on these phones and now the phone calls don't matter anyway. He doesn't know what to do. Except one thing.

Arjun downloads the recording of the failed 911 phone call and prepares a social media post. He finds the most heartbreaking photo he can find on the internet, one from when Antony was about five years old and wearing tennis shoes that were ten sizes too big. This will be the image behind the recording. *I'm scared. I need help.*

And *click.*

13

Esme has been awake since four a.m. Her body knows when the day begins. Not when the sun unveils itself. Not when the clocks ring. It's when the idea of night has become untenable. It doesn't matter how late she stayed up the night before. Always at four, she wakes. Her eyes snap open. The dark world settles into focus. Shapes solidify. A new dawn spills out into the sky.

And yet.

She would prefer to make time stop. To turn a moment into a universe and walk around until she finds him. Or turn it around so she can go back. Or to make it simply cease, so nothing has been or ever will be. Her first day at home she spends horizontal, getting up only to check the door or grab one of Marcus's protein bars and eat it back in bed. The second morning, it's the same: waiting for time to pass until she gets called back to work or Marcus comes home. The third morning, she understands no one will call her in and Marcus is not coming, so she gets out of bed.

It's not that she's found energy. More that her body is revolting against the idea of sleep. Or it's the fact that she's completely lost her blanket; somehow, despite her barely moving an inch, it's fallen off the side and gotten stuck underneath the bed, and the window is open, letting in a chill breeze.

She's supposed to be taking time off. To spend time at home. To relax.

Her apartment is a mess.

When she got home three nights ago, she was half hoping she'd find Marcus waiting for her. Waking up from a nap or perhaps lounging in the bathtub. Maybe he would have even cleaned the whole apartment to prepare it for her return. But no. It was just as much of a disaster as when she left it. Scattered books. Upturned drawers. The entire contents of the portable wardrobe on the ground. And there was more. A small barrage of flyers had been dispatched underneath her door, saying things like *mutual aid* and *community building*. Apparently, Esme could have signed up to receive free lasagna from her neighbors. Or signed up as a volunteer to make and distribute said lasagna. She returned to the hall to find even more notes posted there, which she hadn't noticed in her rush to get in. Advertisements for a community gathering on the rooftop, dog-walking services, and marijuana deliveries. On the ground outside her door were stale cookies in a small paper bag with a smiley face drawn on.

Esme doesn't want cookies or drugs or lasagna. She wants Marcus.

Now, once she finally forces herself to get out of bed, she cleans because there's nothing else to do. The clothes on the floor all get neatly folded and put back in their drawers and compartments. Old leftovers are thrown in the trash. She picks up all the books scattered around the studio and organizes them by color on the bookshelf. Then she decides to organize them by author. Then she decides to put all Marcus's on one bookshelf and Esme's on another, lingering over the ones from her mother, the old romances that Esme secretly stole when she found them in the basement amid the piles of her mother's things that Esme's father could never throw away. She tosses all the nearly empty candle jars and lights the one full one that remains, then blows it out. She starts scrubbing old stains out of the sofa, then, failing at that, covers the stains with pillows. She showers and scrubs every crevice in her body. Two hours later, everything is clean. Except Marcus's travesty of a desk.

A child's scream sounds from upstairs. The apartment building is waking up, and the children are already angry at the world, complaining about their strawberries and Cheerios. Esme vaguely recalls that she's been hearing these kids for the past two days, all stuck at home attempting virtual school. But the noises of her building, often rambunctious, have all been ignored, save for anything that might, theoretically, be a sign of Marcus's return. Every time someone knocked on the door, she walked to it with trepidation, knowing without knowing that it wouldn't be him. It wasn't.

At least this mess on his desk is not her doing. It's all Marcus and only Marcus. He works here late at night sometimes after getting back from evening interviews that require an immediate write-up. Then he'd be off in the morning, leaving piles of notes and papers scattered around the floor. The mess bothered Esme, but whenever she tried to clean up for him, he'd complain that he couldn't find what he was looking for, so she bought movable wall panels to block his desk from view, so he could be as messy as he wanted and she didn't have to see it. But she needs to see it now. Even though it's still only six a.m., there is this cleaning energy that wants to continue now that the rest of the place is neat. So she steps behind the wall panels and goes to his desk to sort through the trash. There are a dozen piles of handwritten notes from interviews, printouts of scientific articles from various journals, and multiple drawers full of empty protein bar wrappers. There are photos of his interviewees—Esme recognizes the CEO of a vita-min company—and dozens of yellow legal pads filled in with hur-ried handwriting. Tucked in between the notepads are flyers from various events, including one that catches her eye, advertising a hundred-year anniversary at some church. She picks it up. She recognizes the drawing of the church. It's a small brick building with three colorful stained glass windows, each adorned with an eight-pointed star. It's where she went for a baptism. The Pathway Pilgrim Church. Where was that again? She reads it through, sur-prised to learn the celebration will be held on December 25, yet there's no mention of Christmas. There is also no location listed on the flyer. Only the directions to look up the location by click-ing through a QR code. Marcus never told her he was working on a story about any church. But he sometimes doesn't tell her about his stories until they're over. "Too many layers," he often says when she asks. "Too much still unknown. You'll read it when it's ready." Hidden behind the stack of papers is a small framed photo of the two of them. The frame has fallen backward and cracked. The lower drawers of his desk are the worst, colonized by a huge tangle of cords and pens, some of which are leaking. Her hand gets covered in black ink. She rushes to the sink to wash it off. Then she returns to the desk area, which finally looks agreeable. There, taking a step back, she sees something strange.

There's no laptop.

There was always a laptop somewhere in that pile. But now? It's an empty desk.

Perhaps he has it with him?

Don't be silly.

A dog barks from the apartment below.

Marcus must have brought it to the office before the Unmapping. That's the only explanation.

It occurs to Esme that she hasn't been in touch with anyone he works with. She doesn't know them at all. A couple of times, Marcus asked her to meet them, urging her to join him at one of their frequent happy hours. But she didn't fit in. She tried, twice, and both times felt so awkward she didn't say more than two words. They had their own inside jokes, their own stories, their own universe, and Esme was outside it. She especially wanted to meet Rick, Marcus's boss, whom Marcus idolizes. But Esme was surprised to feel an intense jealousy when she met him. This is the one whom Marcus calls his biggest champion. His biggest supporter. Why not Esme? And so, even though Rick seemed genuinely nice, she was glad that whenever he tried to ask her questions, someone else would inevitably interrupt them before Esme could answer, because in fact Rick's kindness made her despise him more, which only made her despise herself. Because this was Marcus's mentor and she wanted to love him like he did. But she couldn't.

Yet now she regrets not getting their contact information. Esme opens her phone to look through the Bluzz website for phone numbers. There are none listed. But there is an email address for news tips, so she opens her email and writes a message. This is Esme, Marcus Miller's fiancée. I'm sure you're aware that he's missing. Please call me with any information. Equal parts frustrated with herself for not doing this earlier and pleased for doing it now, she scans the email. It feels like a positive step forward. Maybe they can put their best investigative reporter on the task. Or second best, after Marcus. Why not? She adds: I hope you can do what you can to help. She hits Send.

A reply comes right away. But it's just an autoreply from a generic email account: Thanks for reaching out. We do our best to read every email, but we are currently receiving thousands of tips a day, so if we don't respond within 90 days, please assume that we're not interested.

Esme puts her phone away and goes to the tiny balcony. Today there's a view of the East River. The building sways. It's a windy day, and the building tilts forward. The sway of the building frightened Esme at first. She'd only noticed it after they moved in, when their boxes were piled up in the middle of the room and they were taking a break on their little balcony together, admiring their own lives, when the building lurched in much the same way. She almost asked Marcus if they should move. But he predicted her question and told her he'd already talked to the landlord, who'd assured him that the building could withstand hurricane-force winds and that it would sway and that was fine— in fact, it would be able to sway forty feet in either direction safely, due to something about vertical columns and horizontal girders, and Marcus had even done his own research to confirm this, so they were safe. She feels safe now, in this memory, when he put his arms around her and swayed her back and forth, gripping her tightly all the while, to prove that one could, in fact, sway and be safe. One could fall sideways but if you had the right support system, you would be secure. He was that for her. He was her anchor, her girder, her foundation.

Is. She tells herself to stop thinking of him in the past tense.

No use staying in the apartment, where memories of Marcus lurk around every corner. Esme takes the elevator down and heads out for a walk. The weather is too warm for her turtleneck sweater, but she doesn't want to go back. Her immediate neighborhood is inhospitable. Highways and high-rises. The East River should be right behind her but the view is now blocked by a steel warehouse. She walks west through downtown to the Hudson River, where she reaches a park with a view of Hoboken.

Esme can't remember if Hoboken has unmapped or not. But she doesn't know it well; she wouldn't know the difference.

She walks to the edge of the pier. Then she pulls out her phone to check her time and location and confirm that it's seven a.m. and she's in Hudson River Park. There's a photo of Marcus on her phone lock screen, a selfie of the two of them, the closest thing they have to an engagement photo: After Marcus gave her the ring, he took a selfie in bed, with her hand on his face, showing off the humble ring, and her hair taking over their pillow. She'd just been woken up by Marcus, who got home late and said, "Quick, wake up, it's important," and she was worried and said, "What? What?" and that's when he showed her the ring. She cried with joy into her blue flannel pillow. Same bed, different state. This was when they lived in Washington, DC, just before college graduation, after Marcus had gotten the job at Bluzz. What proceeded was a whirlwind of packing, preparing, unpacking, cleaning, arranging, and rearranging, until suddenly they had settled into a routine in New York City. Like stepping into a dream. It was perfect. She worked the morning shift, he worked afternoons, and they came together for dinner, but first, she had hours to herself in the afternoon and came to love them. New York is the best place to be a lonely person. Esme spent those afternoons going to museums or galleries or free concerts or record stores where you could play whatever you liked on the spinner. Sometimes she'd just walk for hours, through parks and neighborhoods and shopping districts, over bridges and along the river, until her feet hurt, and then she'd either take a break or buy new shoes and then keep walking.

Marcus was right to bring them here. He was right about everything. She'd positioned her life around his rightness. Even before they really knew each other. She was the lonely girl no one spoke to after her mother died, for fear of being infected by her grief. And he was the boy everyone talked to. The only Black kid in a rural town in southwest Virginia, an oddity to be examined, and then, as he proved himself to be friendly and funny and smart and athletic, admired. And he basked in their glow. Esme, too, admired him from afar. She was simply happy for him and she couldn't say why. When they were paired as biology partners together in high school, she felt this glow briefly turned toward her. He had chosen her to be his biology partner. He had chosen her. She assumed he had chosen her because she had the highest grades in class and he wanted an easy semester. But he was as curious and hardworking as she was. They never spent any time together outside the classroom, but for an hour a day, he would talk with her, laugh with her. He opened her up as easily as he sliced through their dead frogs. And yet she felt alive. She liked to hear him breathe as he examined pond matter through the microscope. His resting breath was loud and rhythmic. He sucked in deeply through his nose, over and over, as if the energy he burned through required three times more oxygen than the average human being. He was exceptional in every way.

It was the first time Esme had been interested in another person's body. She'd spent her lonely childhood getting lost in other people's minds, through books and more books, but with Marcus, his mind and body were connected. Every movement of his felt intentional, the way he could handle a microscope with delicacy, then explode with energy into a sprint as soon as he hit the track. Sometimes she watched him at track practice, doing her homework on the bleachers. She didn't care if he saw. He didn't mention it in biology class. But he knew she loved him, and he handled this love delicately. He didn't flaunt his many high school girlfriends around her. When he walked through the halls, holding hands with one girl or another, he smiled and waved at Esme. And then, when they went to college, when suddenly he wasn't the most amazing person in the room, when there were thousands of equally attractive, funny, and smart young men, he saw Esme, who always admired him, who made him feel singular and special, and decided that he would love her back.

Esme stands on the edge of the pier and looks down, hoping to see her reflection. Perhaps River-Esme would have the answers? But the river is churning and the water is cloudy. She half wonders, with detachment, what it would be like to let herself drop into the river. Simply to let it wash her away into the harbor, where she could disintegrate into sand.

Esme thought she was good at being alone. She's spent years of her life being alone, practicing for this.

She's miserable.

But she's not alone. Never alone, not in this city. Not even now at—she checks her watch—seven fifteen.

To her right, there are a couple of people pasting up a poster that says *Free Antony*.

Before her, a gaggle of seagulls wrestles over a small silver fish.

Behind her, on the street, a group of what looks like protesters marches by, walking casually and holding cardboard signs to their chests.

To the left, a woman with knotty blonde hair is sitting at the edge of the pier, dangling her feet down, looking as if she, too, might jump in and wash away.

On a different day, a better day, Esme might look at all these people and feel some sense of solidarity. That they are all in this together. That they can hold each other by the elbows and fight for what they believe in, whatever that is. That Esme can find Marcus and those poster people can free Antony and the protesters will get what they want and that blonde woman can figure out what it is that brought her to the river.

Now all Esme can think is: I'm too tired.

• • •

The blonde woman's hair has gotten tangled past the point of no return. She's discovered two large tangles at the nape of her neck that are turning into knots, and the rest is on its way. She peers over the waters of the Hudson River, hoping to see her reflection, and the water is thick and churning, but yes, she sees.

She sees herself, restless and churning.

She sees herself moving, always moving, quickly from one place to the next, yet staying in the same place.

She sees a body of water. The beginning of life itself.

It's been several days of living on the streets since leaving the shelter; she's lost track. At least a week, a week and a half. And she loves it. Maybe this means she's crazy, but for whatever reason, she loves it. She lives it. She lives! She has no parents sending passive-aggressive texts or begging for her to stay on hour-long phone calls or showing up at her door with trays of low-fat stevia sugar cookies. She has hours to herself. It's not always easy, no, now that the simple facts of life have become difficult questions: What will I eat today? How will I eat today? Will there be water? Will I make it through the day? Will I make it through the night? And answering these questions takes a lot of time and energy. When it rains, she finds an awning to hide under. When it's cold, she wraps her shelter blanket over her head and shoulders and brings her rain jacket around everything and breathes hotly until she's warm. She sleeps hard and fast at night, hidden in the bushes at Hudson River Park, and languid and slow by day on whatever bench looks most inviting. She hides from cops that make their curfew rounds. She keeps her pepper spray close to her chest, and when she finds a knife in the confiscation bin outside a shelter, she swipes that, too. The spray has only so much pepper, while a knife is forever.

All this takes time and energy. And yet there is still time after that. There are hours every day for the woman to walk and think and walk and think. She had never had so much time to think. At her copyediting job, thinking was not the goal. It was to follow the formulas on commas and participles. Then she'd go home and be shuttled from one thing to the next—phone calls from her parents, cooking, eating, working out, scrolling through dating apps, wondering when her waist would ever decrease in size.

These thoughts go through her mind out here, too, but eventually she gets tired of them, or they get tired of her, and she's left with nothingness.

Holy moly, what beauty.

In this clearing, she can see which thoughts are worth addressing and which should be shucked away. Old desires to watch video tutorials on exciting new workout routines are replaced by a prolonged wonderment over the idea of eternity. Where did it begin and where does it end? If there is no beginning, what then? But there is, there must be; everyone talks about that Big Bang, but where did it come from? The universe is expanding. The future is the present. A quote pops into her head. *Never let the future disturb you. You will meet it with the same tools that arm you against the present.* Is that right? Who said it? Doesn't matter, names don't matter—

What a life she'd been ignoring.

The future and present, both. They've been drowned out by the past and by the stories the past contains. An overbearing father and picky mother. Everything they ever said or would ever say. She positioned her life around what would make them happy. Now she saw that was a mistake. They don't exist. There is only this.

It's the river. She asked, when she first walked here, what answer the river could bring. Well, with patience, she found it. Purpose. It has a clear purpose. It knows what it is and where it's going. The piers around it might change, but the piers are still piers, as if the river causes them to settle. The river watches the sun set every day.

But she's getting hungry and this curly-haired woman on the pier nearby is crying noisily, so it's time to leave the river, come back later. Her stomach rumbles. The dinner at the shelter last night was white bread with plasticky cheese. So tasteless and nutritionless she lost the desire to eat and threw it away. Now she is hungrier than she's been in days. That's okay. She'll just walk around until she finds a shelter. She has a trick for finding shelters. Simply follow someone until you get there. Not stalking, or anything like that. She walks a block or two behind them. Whenever she tries to find a shelter on her own, she ends up somehow walking in circles. But if she follows someone, anyone, wherever they're going, regardless of where they're going, she ends up at a shelter. Then at the shelter she gives some fake name, gets some food and maybe a nap, then leaves and keeps walking, eventually finding her way back home. To the river. The place she currently calls home. No matter where she ends up, if she follows the river, she can find her way back.

The blonde woman hurries off the pier, away from the crying woman. She's not sure why this woman's sobs make her feel so uneasy. It's not just that it's a nuisance. Maybe she's running because this woman seems like a previous version of herself.

Someone who would cry openly and loudly, half hoping someone would notice her and comfort her. So she walks east into downtown Manhattan until she finds a group of people worth following. They look about her age, thoroughly mid-twenties, each carrying several full grocery bags. They're moving so slowly she nearly walks into them without thinking about it, so she pauses to pretend to check something in her bag until a safe distance grows between them. She tries not to listen to their conversation, but she can't help it. One of them, a woman with a buzz cut, is complaining about how heavy the sweet potatoes are, but the complaints are jokey and exaggerated. "I'm dying!" Another, a man with a huge Afro, boasts that he's carrying all the milk and could probably carry the woman with her sweet potatoes, too. A different woman pulls a marshmallow out of her grocery bag and throws it at the milk-carrying man. He berates her, indignantly, about what a waste of precious comestibles that is. Something about the way they talk to each other, so casual and comfortable, makes the blonde woman hungrier than before—hungry for conversation. Like the first nibble of restaurant rolls that puts your stomach into overdrive. She planned to follow this group until she found a shelter but now she just wants to hear them talk. What is it about these people in particular? They look perfectly average, wearing jeans and army jackets. She's followed dozens of people over the past week, including a witchy-looking elderly woman through Chinatown, a businessman pacing quickly through Battery Park, a group of teenagers dancing through the streets of Harlem, a parade of Lululemons speed walking over the Brooklyn Bridge. None of them made her react this way. Perhaps she's simply ready to come out of hibernation.

She follows the group of people carrying groceries for several blocks until they disappear down a set of stairs.

They've gone into a subway station.

She follows them down, though she can't say why. Just like she can't say why she walks anywhere. She could try, after the fact, to come up with a reason why but has decided that most decisions are instinctual and that the explanations come afterward from a brain trying too hard to make sense of things. The stairwell is papered with posters showcasing an ant-covered geranium flower with words in the flower petals: *Free Antony*. The posters grow in number and diversity of color and style as she walks down the stairs. There are no lights here; she walks in near darkness, trusting the voices of the group ahead of her to guide her. Laughter bounces through the halls, punctuating their murmured conversation. Finally, around the corner, there is light.

Down in the subway station, there is a new, sleeping city.

Hundreds of colorful sleeping bags skirt the walls, filled with people dreaming and snoring and muttering in their sleep. The mood is quiet and the light is dim, with the occasional electric lantern providing the only source of shadow. It's still early, she realizes, which is easy to forget when you wake before sunrise and hours pass before the rest of the world wakes. The group she followed to get here has fallen silent, in respect for the dreamers. They head to the middle of the station, where long, clean folding tables are set up, surrounding a few people who are sitting in a mountain of boxes and appliances, playing rock paper scissors. Upon seeing the new group, one of them checks his watch, then picks up a music triangle and strikes it, filling the room with a tinkling noise that bounces off the empty train tracks and abandoned subway cars.

"Housekeeping," he yells lacklusterly as he continues to chime the triangle. A morning wake-up call. Many of the people in sleeping bags stir. Some sit up, yawn, talk to each other; others pull their bags over their ears. Overhead lights turn on; appliances are plugged in; bacon is laid out on a griddle; smells and sounds crackle the world awake. There's a large fan running by the stairs. A towering pile of cardboard boxes.

And there is . . .

"Rick?"

She gasps the word aloud to herself. Her date from the night of the storm. Over the past week, she's nearly forgotten his existence. Except she hasn't. His words have been there, in the back of her head, saying: *I'm enamored by you.* As she was enamored by the world. The beauty of the words fits perfectly. *I'm enamored.* And there he is, walking down the same set of stairs she just entered through.

Without thinking, she leaps behind a pillar. She's terrified that Rick won't recognize her—or that if he does, he won't like what he sees. Her hair is a mess and her face is makeup-free. She quickly opens her mirror and considers putting on eyeliner and mascara. But no—if he doesn't like what she looks like first thing in the morning, then he may as well know now. At least she's still wearing her favorite dress, underneath the long rain jacket. She washed it in a single-stall bathroom just yesterday, closing the door and taking it off to wash it in the sink, naked, and, for a brief moment, took in her body, feeling nothing whatsoever about it. Now she removes her rain jacket, then puts it back on, but leaves it open so that her dress can be seen. She emerges from her hiding spot behind the pillar. He's deep in conversation with the marshmallow woman, with a pen in one hand and a notebook in the other. But she walks over with her head held high. He notices her before she reaches him, and excuses himself from his conversation. "Are you . . ."

"Yes," she says.

He takes her head in his hands and kisses her full on the mouth.

"Wow," she says.

"Is that okay?"

"God, yes." He kisses her again, with big, full lips, and a hard, closed mouth.

"Are you okay?" he asks her. "I've been worried. When you didn't show up that night . . ." That low, smooth voice is even better in person. And his eyes: dark brown, the darkest she has seen. His beard blended into his skin on video but now there is a world between the scruffy hair and the smoothest brown skin. He makes her feel jittery and nervous and seen.

"Never better."

"Really?" He looks skeptical.

"Well, maybe by some measures. I could really use a haircut. And a new change of clothes."

He looks at her dress. "Wow."

All the blushing she's ever done in her life happens right now.

"What's going on down here?" she asks, quelling the urge to close her jacket.

"Down here? What happened with *you*?"

"I asked you first."

"Fair, fair." He laughs. "Let's try something. You're like me. You're coming down here for the first time because someone sent you a tip. *'Go down into the subways.'* You walk down and see this. What would you think?"

"Oh, I don't know. I'm out of the habit of asking questions. I would just come down here and take it all in."

"What exactly would you take in?"

"Well . . . all the sleeping bags, obviously."

"Obviously. What else?"

"It's very . . . clean." The tables are completely clear and, beyond the sleeping bags, the train tracks are pristine. No trash, no rats, no dirty puddles of water. "I've never seen a subway station so clean."

"You say that like it's a bad thing."

"It's just a little jarring. It sort of clashes with the subway station aesthetic."

"Aesthetic? Oh no. Am I dating a photographer?"

"Maybe it's something about the lighting. Are those the usual fluorescents?"

"And now she's talking about lighting, everybody. Definitely a photographer." He laughs. "Fine, pretend you're me, then, not you. You-as-me walk down here, trying to figure out what's going on. What do you think?"

"First thought would be, where'd my old body go?"

"Ha ha."

"Second thought would be, I guess, maybe homeless people moved down here because police have been harassing them after curfew."

"Sure."

"But these people don't look homeless."

"You're right—most are not homeless."

"Now I'm stuck. Tell me."

"Yes, here you get stuck. So you ask someone, what are you doing down here? And at first no one wants to talk. But you realize that's because they don't know what to say. So instead you start asking them other questions about their life. And then you start to put something together."

"What is it? And wait—why wouldn't the police come down here and kick everyone out?"

"At first, they did. But people just kept coming. More than what was worth dealing with. The police had other things on their mind."

"Yeah." She pauses. "Like what? And who's Antony?"

"Like what? Where have you *been*, woman?"

"I've been sleeping in Hudson River Park. Someone stole my phone. I lost my apartment." Just saying the words aloud makes them real. She feels like a wire hook is tugging at the back of her eyes, making them sting.

"Oh, girl."

"It's okay."

"Is it?"

"I don't know." The sting in her eyes worsens.

Someone rings a metal bell from the center of the station. "That's breakfast," says Rick. "You want?"

"God, yes."

She eats the best meal of her life, buttery eggs and greasy bacon, and toast to soak up the drippings, then goes back for a second serving after everyone else gets their first. As she and Rick eat, sitting on the ground, he cross-legged and she with her legs tucked beneath her, she tells him everything that's happened to her since that first night. And he tells her about Antony. The boy that everyone's thinking about. And what's happening here, underground.

"It's the real thing," he says. "The revolution."

She has to hold in a laugh. But he looks so earnest it makes the laughter die in her throat. He's looking at her like a child looks out a window in daydream. Like he's hardly there. Yet his body is very much there. Their knees are nearly touching and she feels his skin emanate heat. She leans slightly forward until they touch. It seems the physical contact brings him back to his body.

To her body. He touches her knee in an act that's so seductive it thrusts fantasies rudely to the forefront of her mind. She can visualize the entire three-act play of lovemaking as stills from a movie. The buildup. The climax. The denouement. It brings her back to that first night, when she went out in a storm because she was ready for his body. A week and a half later, they are touching knee to knee. Yes, he kissed her today, when he first saw her, but that felt like an act of surprise more than seduction.

"What was I talking about?"

"The revolution?"

"Right." He pulls his hand back. "The question starts, why won't city officials save this boy? Like, even if they're doing anything about it, anything at all, they've made no sign of it. They haven't mentioned it. They refuse to answer any questions about it. It's like they want to pretend it's not happening. Then the question becomes, what else are they ignoring? Who gets their water turned on first, and who hasn't had clean water since this began? You know the answer. It's always the poorest families that face the impacts first and worst. Even now, even when everything's supposed to be all mixed up, the poor somehow still get the worst of it. So everyone who comes down here, they know something's wrong. Everyone knows. And I'm not just talking about the past week. There's something deeper. Something stranger going on. Then we got the Unmapping and everything cracked open. But still they didn't know what to do. Then they learned about Antony. There's our moment. People are paying attention to this. It's an opportunity."

"An opportunity for what?"

He leans in and lowers his voice. "People will not be the same. We all understand that the city won't save us. If they can't save one person, one boy, how can they save all of us? So they're discovering a new sort of power. That's how we'll create a new paradigm. We get to choose what that is."

"So what is it?"

"Don't know yet," he admits, bringing his voice back to a natural register. "I'm not the one with the vision. I just try to keep track of what's happening. There are a lot of competing ideas about who gets to be in charge and what that means. Everyone agrees that the current bureaucracy is fucked, but some people say that means all bureaucracies are inherently fucked, while others think we just need to restructure them. I mean, you need structure. Like, the way we feed people. This communal meal situation takes a lot of planning. There are people who take care of the logistics and other people who think about, well, what does it mean that we're feeding the people, who's feeding them and where is it coming from, and how can this be scaled? Food doesn't just appear. People are making it happen. If they can do this, what else can they do?"

She looks over at the hub where food was cooked and served, finding all the appliances shut down and put away, being replaced by protest signs, masks, and safety goggles, as a dozen people wipe down and fold up the tables, sweep and carry out the trash, check on the battery-powered power stations, everyone appearing to have a task and know what to do.

"I'm not here just to write stories about group meals. But my writing about them helps bring attention, public support, and funding. I understand my own power. Most journalists don't. Or they pretend not to. They pretend they're disinterested third parties. They pretend they don't understand the consequences of what they report on. We know the truth. All of us, we're discovering what power is. And right now, the power is down here. I can feel it. You can feel it, right?"

"I guess so." She looks around and tries to understand what Rick is talking about. Then she thinks it might be better not to understand. After all, something brought her down here. She can't put a name on what it is, other than a . . . something. Something magnetic.

"But what's the goal?"

"A lot of people have a lot of goals. A lot of ideas. A lot of people agree on the what—better public education, affordable housing, mental health services, things like that—but they disagree on the how. Should we bring back popular assemblies? Should we all get to vote on individual budget proposals? Should we dismantle the city government and replace it with citizens' panels, the same way we form juries? And the big question is, do they have the time and wherewithal to come to a decision and stick to it? And who will be in power after?"

The breakfast bell rings again. "Circle up!" a woman calls. All around them, people start getting up and heading to the piles of painted signs, shields, and goggles.

"What's happening?" she asks.

But Rick sidesteps the question as he sees his friend, a good-looking Black man, tall and lean, with a short, bushy beard and a plain black baseball cap. Rick slaps the man on the shoulder and pulls him in.

"What do you want, boss?" says the tall man.

"Marcus—I mean Michael," says Rick. "What's the plan?"

◆ ◆ ◆

Good, sweet Arjun always has a plan. Whenever Esme has a problem, Arjun is happy to help. If they're eating lunch at the Emergency Management Department, and she sighs because she doesn't know what to do with her time that afternoon, he looks up a dozen free shows and events for her to choose from. Whenever she complains about her trouble falling back asleep after waking in the middle of the night, he provides relaxation techniques. Whenever she's unsatisfied by her lunch, he always has an extra snack. Sitting on the pier, more depressed than she's ever been, Esme decides to call Arjun. She doesn't know how he'll help pull her out of this great black pit of despair. She doesn't know how to say *Make me feel better*. She doesn't even know if he'll pick up the phone.

He picks up right away.

"Esme!" He yells her name. She's so relieved to hear his voice she nearly cries.

"Arjun," she says. "I was thinking about what you said."

"Esme, wait!" The background noise is loud with people yelling and chanting something she can't make out. "Hang on!" After a minute the background noise quiets to a low buzz. "Okay, go!"

"Where are you?"

"Don't know!" he says happily. "I'm in a protest. It started in Times Square. We marched north, I think. No, wait. South. Oh, we're headed for the Lincoln Tunnel?"

"Is this a bad time?"

"No!" he yells. "What is it?"

"I was thinking about what you said the other day."

"What did I say?"

"You said, 'If you need to talk, let me know.'"

"Hang on. What?" It seems like the phone clicks out, but the call is still going; he's put her on mute. She watches a pigeon pick at an old french fry.

His voice comes back. "Sorry. Continue!"

"Never mind. You said you're at the Lincoln Tunnel?"

Esme finds the group of protesters within fifteen minutes. She hears them first. It starts with the drummers. Then the tubas. Then the chanting, with so many different chants from different areas she can't tell one from another. There are hundreds of people here, marching down the street. Most look happy. There's a good beat. A good mood pervading the area. The day has grown hotter and the sun has reached the point in the sky where its rays sneak between the skyscrapers and beat down ruthlessly on everyone around. Esme feels sweat spring up beneath her turtleneck.

She pushes through the crowd, looking for Arjun, until she discovers him standing on the sidelines, waiting for her. He is glowing in the sun, wearing a plain white T-shirt. She rushes over and hugs him. There's not a lick of perspiration on his body. He smells like sugar. His arms reach tentatively around her to return the hug.

"What's happening?" she asks, but he doesn't seem to hear and she doesn't really need an answer. "One second!" he calls out. "I'll be right back." He's waving down someone with a television camera, telling him that he's available for interviews, and "Would you like to interview one of the protesters who's been here since the beginning, aka me, Arjun?" The beginning of what? Esme wonders. She is generally aware that people have been protesting. People are always protesting. But protests are not for Esme. Protests are for people with friends, who come with their signs and take their selfies, or they are for people who are angry, who've been slighted by the world, and Esme is neither. Marcus used to go to protests for work and he'd ask her to come with but why? So she could sit with him on the sidelines while he interviewed angry college kids? It's not that she doesn't care about the various causes that have come up; she just knows, statistically, that one more body makes zero difference. But she's feeling good about being here; she even accepts a painted cardboard sign from someone that doesn't have any words but is a picture of an ant atop a flower. She heads into the rush of people and lifts her sign. Maybe it's the fact that she hasn't seen another soul for days. Maybe it's the drumbeat, the music. For a moment she thinks she sees a flash of blue jacket, or Marcus's head, but no. She's just been thinking about Marcus and seeing him everywhere. Every single person she sees could be him. That man in blue could be him. That other man—no, that's a woman. That one is the right height; that one has the correct head and hair. Arjun's voice is in her ear now, saying, "Esme! Follow me! We're going into the tunnel." He grabs her hand.

They turn left, away from the main thrust of the crowd, and he pulls her delicately but surely. He swims through the crowd and she lets herself be pulled. His hand is smooth and strong and holds hers with firm tenderness, and she wonders how it can be so soft and sweat-free. She's missed the experience of feeling a body. Now she's surrounded. She wants to lick the shoulder of someone, anyone, to taste the trueness of this sweat. She is ready to take her sweater off, to wear only her sports bra; she wouldn't be the only one. She laughs at the thought, then laughs even harder. They are marching with a new and smaller crowd now, squeezing Arjun and Esme. Esme and Arjun. They are in this together, going into the Lincoln Tunnel. Is she really about to take over a tunnel? And then what?

And then:

She sees Marcus.

It's him. She knows it's him. There are a dozen people between them, and this man has a beard and a black baseball cap, but it's him. And he sees her. He catches her eye and looks like he's seen a ghost. His mouth opens slightly.

It's just a flicker. Then he's off.

It was him.

He's running away from the tunnel now, as she's getting pulled in. She releases Arjun's hand. Still the thrust of the crowd is headed tunnelward. They push against her as she squeezes through them. Sweaty, stinking bodies, and anger in the air. Their chants are loud and echoey in the tunnel. *"Free Antony. No justice."* The chants clash with one another. *"The power of the—" "No peace—" "One, we are the people—" "the power of—" "no justice—" "Antony—" "Show me what—" "Show me—"* They are yelling in her ears and Marcus is getting away. Getting away? What's happening? She keeps pushing, gets back to the main area. Is that a blue windbreaker, just around the corner? There's a flash of blue everywhere she looks. She runs and runs even though there's no way she can catch him. Catch him. Catch Marcus? He's alive, and he's running. Why is he running? He's alive. Yet he doesn't want her to know it. He's running. And she's running, too. Her lungs scream with the effort. She keeps running. She keeps running until she loses him again. She loses him again and again and she will keep losing him until he's gone.

14

Arjun has lost Esme. But he doesn't care. He feels like his smile might lift him through the tunnel's roof into the sky. She hugged him. Then she let him hold her hand. She hugged him, and then he held her hand, and for two full minutes, he had her fingers in his. She is nearly as tall as he is, and when they hug, their bodies fit together. They fit together well. They can talk about this and that and anything else. He pictures them getting married and sitting at the same table, eye to eye. He can do the cooking. She can just do the eating. She can watch him, admiring his spice technique, thanking him for being so generous and kind. He's very good at cleaning, too.

It's not that he doesn't want her to find Marcus. He does. He wants her to find him and then break up with him. Who's Marcus anyway? Over the years, she rarely spoke about him, as if he didn't exist. But he also knows that when someone goes missing, if you don't find them within a week, it usually means one thing. Death. And she knows it, too. They work in a field of harsh realities. She must know. And maybe she's grieving. And maybe she can grieve with Arjun. He'll be there by her side. Whatever it takes, he'll be there.

Except right now, he's in the middle of the Lincoln Tunnel,

which is dark with the lights turned off except for the flashlights that others have brought, strobing onto the ceiling. Everything that's happening is real. It makes everything else outside this tunnel feel unreal. The past days. The past week. The past two years. They are out of his head. Now there are people pushing up beside him and chanting everything under the sun, and so is Arjun, picking up whatever chant feels right, yelling until his throat grows hoarse. He wishes he had a megaphone. The chants echo and the ground shakes. They have succeeded in taking over the central tunnel. The space was already emptied of cars, sure, and blocked with pitiful orange-and-white barricades, as were all the tunnels going in and out of the city, with not enough electricity to keep the ventilation going, a necessity given all the car exhaust on the average day; but now it has become a tunnel for people, as have the two outer tunnels, as well as every other tunnel and bridge in and out of Manhattan, to hold the city hostage until the mayor Does Something About All This.

What is All This and what can the mayor Do? Arjun isn't exactly sure, but whatever it is, he believes in it. They want the mayor to find and free Antony. They want more food and water. The city wants this, too. Arjun knows this. And yet they're doing terribly, and he knows this, too. They need to do better and he's standing in a tunnel underneath the Hudson River hoping that if he yells his head off here, someone will listen. The people here want many specific things. Food and water and safety and also the revolution. He learned all this as he spent more and more time with JR and his friends, helping them prepare. Arjun wants one vague thing. For the Emergency Management Department to manage itself better! They finally need him and instead of being useful he's been shuffled around from boss to boss in increasingly useless jobs. He's been moved from the phones back to the supplies and now to a new job as front desk night shift at a nearby shelter, with a different boss who doesn't even bother to learn his name.

"No! Justice! No! Peace!" Arjun chants until his throat hurts, then stops. The others around him also begin to quiet, presumably from their own sore throats, and so he realizes this is not the time to preserve one's voice; this is his moment to step up. There is always someone random starting and leading a chant. Arjun can be that random someone. "Free Antony!" he calls out hoarsely. "Free Antony! Free Antony! Free Antony!" An old man grabs Arjun's arm and puts a finger to his puckered old lips. Arjun is the only one chanting. The people have quieted. The flashlights have turned off. The old man says they're doing a moment of silence. "For what?" asks Arjun. A hundred people shush him. The rest of the flashlights turn off. He takes out his phone and records the scene. The recording shows blackness and silence. It's perfect. He posts it to social media. Then a dozen lights turn on. Flashlights, pointed toward a woman lifted on someone else's shoulders with a megaphone at her mouth. She has a buzz cut and is beautiful and embarks on a speech about inequality. Arjun's barely listening to the words; he's taken by the mood and her voice and everything around him. He lifts his phone to record it live for social media. So do dozens of others. This is a beautiful moment and he is there to capture it. To pull open this moment and make it a bigger moment, a forever moment, a multiverse moment. This is a moment that people will cut open and use and reuse until it becomes hyperreal. This is Arjun's moment, full of beautiful anger, to share with the world, and reshape it.

•   •   •

Anger is trending at the mayor's mansion. The mayor is furious but her press secretary is even angrier, and don't try talking to the social media manager today. Even the smiling photographs on the walls take on a menacing look. As she predicted, the mayor is being blamed for everything. It's part of the job. Scapegoat. But for this? For this kid? Antony? What did they expect? That she'd bring in the National Guard to blow up every basement in the Bronx until they find him? How much do they want her to do for one boy, when there are millions of other New Yorkers to care about?

How much is one life worth?

How about a million lives?

"They've taken the Lincoln Tunnel," her social media manager screeches, just as the mayor receives a text from the Atlantic City mayor on her personal phone.

JOHNNIE: Are You Okay Love?

The mayor begins to type back, but the social media manager's voice is so very loud. "And they've already blocked every other bridge and tunnel in and out of Manhattan," she says.

"The tunnel was already closed," says her press secretary. "What's the point?"

"They're declaring victory!" says the social media manager.

"That's the final hole," says her scheduling assistant, who has her by the elbow to make sure she gets to her next meeting. The mayor can't remember for the life of her what's next on her schedule, so she puts up with this twerp's elbow grab. Silvered aluminum Christmas trees line every corridor, but they're undecorated, menacing, glinting light from the ceiling. "Unless we can force them off the bridges or leave by helicopter," says her scheduling assistant, "we're trapped in Manhattan."

"We're not leaving Manhattan," says the mayor. "We're setting up a citywide quarantine."

"Huh?" says the social media manager, who's barely keeping up with the group as she types furiously on her phone. This is a girl who looks barely old enough to work and is always trying to position the mayor in a candid photo for the feed. The mayor finds her unbearable, but her communications director has insisted the girl be involved in everything to do with the Unmapping. He claims it's because social media is a more effective way of disseminating important information immediately without needing to go through so many channels of approval. Grocery store GPS coordinates, food repository updates. The mayor thinks it might have to do with the communications director wanting to stay home with his family, rather than bunk in the basement with a hundred other bureaucrats.

"That's brilliant," says her press secretary. "They think they're fighting us? They're helping us. No one leaves this city. Mayor's orders."

"Yes, and a quarantine could also help lessen the projected migration outward," adds her scheduling assistant.

"What do you know about that?" the mayor snaps.

"I was at your meeting with the Economic Development Corporation earlier this morning."

"Right." What a waste of time that was. Fat men in identical blue button-downs with no ties, telling her she needed to worry about the city's tax revenue while more than a thousand people were still missing. *We're in a state of emergency and you're worried about the fiscal impact analysis?* she almost yelled.

They pass by a bathroom.

"I need a toilet break," the mayor lies.

She walks inside and sits on the toilet with her tights pulled down to text Johnnie back. Not gonna lie. Not great. Protests taking over the city. Everyone mad at me. I like a good protest, gives them something to do. Gives us cover to do something interesting. But this? What can we do? How can they not see we're already trying? Because Antony. Because we've had to keep our efforts around saving the kid under wraps. For reasons. PR team told me why but already forgot. What a mess. I need a drink.

JOHNNIE: Sorry, Love. Want A Dick Pic?

She says sure.

The second-worst part about fucking the mayor of Atlantic City is that he capitalizes every word in his texts, making it feel like she's reading a news headline. The worst part about fucking the mayor of Atlantic City is that she loves him and he loves her but he won't leave his wife. Otherwise, he's the only salve she's had in all this. When she can't handle the present moment, she pictures her shack on the ocean, the little blue house she bought just outside Atlantic City, in which she spends two weeks of the year with Johnnie, loving and living and taking hot baths. These two perfect weeks are enough to get her through the other fifty. Sometimes, his young son comes along. Little Angelo, named after Johnnie's father. The mayor adores Angelo, calls him her little angel, with his shiny blonde curls that look like Shirley Temple's, and the feeling is returned. Whenever she asks him for a hug, he jumps up into her arms and nearly bowls her over. How long until he's too old to do that? Will she still be in his life? When will Johnnie ever leave his wife? Everyone knows about their relationship except, somehow, the press. He needs to keep up appearances, and she supposes she does, too. She agrees publicizing the scandal isn't worth the risk to their careers. But one day she plans to leave it all behind. Yes, one day. But when? This past week she's been texting him every spare moment, even calling him once or twice. Of course, she can usually only get in a few words before someone more important calls her back.

She gives up on trying to pee—she's severely dehydrated. Also underfed and undercaffeinated. Magically, her chronic headaches have disappeared. Turns out severe stress is a good replacement for caffeine addiction. Anytime she thinks she's tired, someone wakes her up with worse and worse news. Unfortunately, it's been accompanied by chronic anger and shortness of breath. She breathes in deeply now, imagining her house on the shore.

If only their entire cities would switch spots. Then she could wake up on the ocean.

A photo text comes in from the Atlantic City mayor. She hides the notification. She's not in the mood to look at a photo of his genitals wearing a miniature swimsuit, but the text still makes her happy. This text means *I trust you*. It means *I love you*.

Of course, Atlantic City has unmapped, too. But no one seems to care. Everyone lives in the casinos at this time of year anyway, and there haven't been any major problems with the grid or water. Their city is simpler. It's a problem of size and scale. In New York, everything is hanging by a thread. Some of the underground water mains are covered in rust, making them impossible to turn on and off. If one of those breaks, the impact of the failure would be astronomical. That used to be her greatest fear. Now there are a million other fears on top of that one. What happens when New York City and Jersey City combine? Will there be such a thing as a city anymore? Or a country? It's already spread to Mexico, after a border town in Texas unmapped with its Mexican neighbor. El Paso and Ciudad Juárez used to be one. Now they are one again. Unmapping with each other like kissing cousins. Will everyone lose what they thought of as home?

The mayor's home is hardly her own right now. It's become the new hub of governmental activity. Everyone comes here to ask her what to do. Then they stay here. But not for real sleep. No one truly sleeps. People nap all over. All the guest bedrooms and couches are public napping property. There are sleeping bags in the office basement. The air-conditioning is on blast. The lights are bright all night.

The mayor puts her hand on the knob of the bathroom door. Then she takes it off. These few moments of peace in the bathroom are all she has. Her little temple of cedar-scented moisturizer and shells from Atlantic City. She picks up a shell from the counter and holds it to her ear to hear the ocean. She holds up another shell to her other ear. Then she leans against the wall and closes her eyes, letting herself drift away in the breeze of the waves. There's no ocean here, except the one raging inside her. The darkness feels good beneath closed eyes. She could fall asleep right here.

The darkness becomes darker, truer darkness.

She opens her eyes.

It's pitch black.

"Motherfucker!" she yells, flicking the light switch uselessly. "Where's Dean?" she yells out. She opens the bathroom door and yells it again. "Where's Dean?" Her press secretary is right there, with her phone's glow lighting up her face.

"Calling him right now," says the press secretary.

"Dean!" yells the mayor into the phone as she walks into an aluminum tree and kicks it, grateful no one saw her do that.

"Ms. Mayor."

"How quickly can you fix this outage?"

"I don't know."

"That is the wrong thing to say right now."

"I don't know," he says again. "We don't know what happened. We're looking into it now."

"Obviously," says the mayor. "At least turn on the backup generator."

"We can't," he says.

"Wrong."

"I'm sorry, but we can't. It's supposed to be on already. It's not. We're—"

"Looking into it. Great. Look harder. Call me when you find out." She hangs up the phone and mutters, "I'm surrounded by incompetence."

Someone yanks the phone from her hand.

"Sorry," says the press secretary. "I really need that back."

The mayor takes her own personal phone out of her pocket. There's a new notification of another photo message from the mayor of Atlantic City. She swipes left to dismiss it and turns on her flashlight to walk through the hallway down to the kitchen, swerving to avoid the aluminum trees. Why are some of them in the middle of the hallway? Maybe others got frustrated and kicked them, like her. One is lying on the ground and nearly makes her trip. She kicks it to the side. She's starving. A blackout would be a good excuse for a snack. She hasn't had time to eat all day.

"We're now fifteen minutes late for the meeting with the governor's scientific advisory board," says her scheduling assistant, grabbing her by the shoulder.

"I'd think they would understand, given the circumstances—"

"They're in the ballroom basement with a lantern."

"Great."

Her assistant guides them to the ballroom basement by the light of his phone. With the elevator out, they go down two flights of stairs. "I can walk down stairs by myself," she says. "You're going to pull me over." At the bottom of the stairs she walks into another aluminum tree and pushes it over with a crash, uncaring. She finds the group of scientists surrounding a white globe of light. They've positioned three cell phones so their flashlights beam onto folded-up pieces of white paper, which reflect and diffuse the light like a lantern. The mayor doesn't have time to be impressed by the ingenuity; she's still fuming at the Christmas trees as she takes in a dozen half-lit faces, wondering which ones she's supposed to recognize. They're quiet as she takes her seat. Her scheduling assistant breaks the ice by requesting a round of "reintroductions." So yes, she's supposed to recognize at least some of them, but their names bounce off her like light off a mirror. She finishes the circle by saying, "And I'm the mayor of New York City," to appreciative chuckles. "Now let's get down to business. What's happening and how are we going to stop this thing?"

"Well." One of them starts to speak. In the shadowy lantern light his many wrinkles make him look like a zebra. "We may have gone past a global warming tipping point," he says carefully.

"What else is new?"

The scientists are quiet.

"You know that people will be angry with us if that's all we have to say. Global warming? What the hell does global warming have to do with what's happening right now? How can you prove it, and even if you can, who cares? What we need right now are short-term fixes, not pie-in-the-sky claims. There's a boy trapped underground and you're talking about global warming?" The mayor's scheduling assistant coughs, a subtle jab to get her to stop talking. "This is the populace speaking, not me. But I have the same questions, to be honest. I want answers. When will they turn on that goddamn backup generator?"

"The point is," says the elderly scientist, "we need to switch to renewable power as quickly as possible—"

"Again, what else is new?"

"I'm just saying—"

"We need hammers," says a younger scientist. "We need hammers and nails and wood—"

"That's neither here nor there—" says someone else.

"We need hammers!" he says again.

"Let him speak," the mayor says.

The young scientist tells her about the idea to connect buildings by force. His team at Columbia University has been studying which buildings stay together and which do not. Some row houses that share a wall have been split apart. But most stay together. The row houses sided with vinyl or engineered wood seem to break apart. "But the houses made of brick and wood, well, we need to do more testing, but so far we've gotten positive signs that these might stay together—"

"Good. More of that."

Someone else protests: "Completely ridiculous. Those experiments have never been replicated—"

"So replicate it. Prove it. I came here for solutions. Anyone else have something useful to say?"

The table is silent.

"Miss Mayor," her scheduling assistant says quietly, "I've just gotten word that the backup generator for the mansion is broken. Someone smashed it and left a poster that says 'Free Antony.'"

"Now that is the *wrong* answer." The day is November 16 and the boy has been underground for eleven days. And they are trying. They are working. She's been told they are, at least. She doesn't know the details. But supposedly they got hold of him and were able to lead him down underground to walk along the pipes and tunnels, and at that point they lost touch with him. But they're still looking for him. While they're working on a million other things. Fixing broken pipes and replacing burst transformers. They've put out several press releases alluding to their efforts without being specific, because specificity is dangerous. And yet those all go ignored. The protesters leap on one little phone call that accidentally got dropped, ignoring the fact that the city called him back. They want to be angry and nothing will quell that. She knows it won't. She's not in control of what grows on social media and what doesn't. She's not in control of the protests, no. The city is turning into a zoo, and she's trapped in the basement with a dozen dying zebras.

The mayor gets up and starts for the stairs again. Her scheduling assistant leaps up beside her and grabs her elbow. She shakes him free and walks into the dark. A thump strikes her stomach; she's walked into a filing cabinet.

She dreams of the day Johnnie steps down as mayor. She would step down right after him and they would be together. He would cut off his white mustache and be a new man. She would let her hair grow natural and be a new woman. Here it's slicked in a tight bun behind her head. The easiest way to maintain it every morning. And severe makeup, for the constant cameras. Out there, no makeup, no bun, natural hair and a loose sundress. Two weeks out of every year. Her favorite is winter, when the boardwalk is cold and empty. Inside the casinos, there are no seasons. But on the beach, the sand is chilled and the only sounds are from birds and waves.

That feels a world away.

There's too much and it never ends.

The mayor pulls out her phone for its flashlight.

JOHNNIE: Did You Receive The Photo?

The mayor responds with a heart-eyes emoji.

JOHNNIE: When Can I See You Next?

The mayor types a response into her phone: I DON'T KNOW!!!!! Then she deletes it and writes: Leave your wife and move in here.

JOHNNIE: Ha Ha.

"Mayor," someone says, but she can't see who. "Mayor," someone else says. "What should we do?"

Everywhere she turns, someone's asking her what to do; someone shines a light in her eyes, temporarily blinding her.

"About what now?" she asks into the blindness.

"The protesters blocking the way in and out of Manhattan. We have a supply of water due in from Jersey City."

The mayor turns around. Her hand hits someone's shoulder. She feels a palm on her elbow. Her scheduling assistant is back, like glue.

"What should we do?" asks the voice, the many voices, possibly even the voices in her head.

"Shut them down. Shut it all down."

•   •   •

It starts with an itch in the eye. A tickle in the throat. Then there's coughing from nearby. It echoes throughout the tunnel. More people cough. It comes in waves. "Tear gas!" someone cries. Arjun can't see it in this dim light, but he can feel it now. "Cover your nose and mouth," someone calls out. "Don't touch your eyes." With one hand, Arjun pulls his white T-shirt over his nose, while the other maintains an iron grip on his phone, still recording live. His eyes start burning. The majority of the coughing is coming from the direction of the New York entrance. Where

Esme ran off. But now everyone is running away from it. They're running to the Jersey exit, pushing Arjun into the flow. "Stay calm!" Arjun yells, letting himself go with the crowd's current. "Stop running!" His vision goes blurry. There's so little room to get around here he fears a stampede. But he lets himself go with it. Walking quickly among the crowd. His lungs seize. Is there enough air down here? Down deeper into the tunnel. And deeper. Then the surging crowd slows to a stop. He leaps up to see why. The effort makes his chest hurt. It's dark and his eyes are watering uncontrollably, so it's difficult to see, like looking through the surface of a swimming pool, but he hears a voice through a speaker:

"*This is the police. Everyone in this tunnel is under arrest.*"

People run from the voices, farther into the tunnel. Arjun runs with them. Then the people in front of him stop moving. There's nowhere to go. They're at a standstill. *"Cooperate and you'll all be fine. This is your final warning."* Arjun checks his phone. The live video has stopped. He lost service. But he has Verizon! But it's still recording, even if it's not airing live, so he's getting everything on video. He pushes back through the crowd, back to where he stood earlier, when he had four beautiful bars that allowed him to live stream a beautiful video. They are all pushing away from the New York entrance but he is heading toward it. He tries to swim through the many sweaty bodies. How did so many get in here? "They kettled us in," someone cries out, in answer. He's coughing and can hardly see. The tear gas gets worse the closer he runs to the entrance.

Someone knocks his phone from his hand.

"No!"

Arjun pushes forward to where he thought he saw the phone fly, accidentally elbowing someone in the stomach. "Hey!" they yell at him and push him back. "I'm sorry I'm sorry I'm sorry," he says, now crouching on the ground and searching for his phone, eyes streaming with tears. It burns. He rubs his eyes and they burn worse. "Honest mistake," he says, "I need to find my phone!" But the person he elbowed is long gone, having run away from the tear gas. More people run past him. Then they are gone and the ground is clear and he rubs his hand on the pavement to find it—there! He finds his phone, with a thick, deep crack down the center of the screen, but with the video still recording. And the live video is back. It stopped temporarily but now it's back. He lifts it up and films the group of police officers in thick black riot gear, silhouetted by bright lights. They are marching toward him, releasing more tear gas. Arjun stands strong and captures the video. They look like aliens walking on a misty moon, with their head-to-toe riot gear and massive shields, surrounded by gas and backlit by red flashing lights. He's coughing so hard he feels knives in his chest. This is gold. This is the best video he has ever taken and will ever take. "I'm getting arrested now," he narrates. "See you on the other side." And he takes one last panoramic sweep, surrounded by police, before he turns off the recording and puts it in his pocket. They push him forward roughly out of the tunnel, then pull him backward to yank his hands behind his back. Arjun laughs, then coughs. His phone is already buzzing. The notifications are coming in like mad. As they bind his hands with zip ties and take him away, he counts the buzzes. A hundred in a minute. Two hundred. If this keeps up, there will soon be a thousand. Thousands. Hundreds of thousands.

One million.

15

Marcus is alive.

He saw Esme and ran.

Marcus is alive, and he saw Esme and ran.

Esme is standing somewhere in Manhattan with no idea where she is or what to do or even what it was that made her stop running. There's a parade of police cars and there are sirens everywhere and there are voices and yelling and nothing is familiar, nothing feels grounded; she could be on the other side of the planet, or transported to an alien world, where they built a new city only pretending to be New York. A bodega with its windows smashed, a blank skyscraper, an abandoned brick house, graffiti on the street. A painting of an ant eating a tulip, tearing it apart, on the ground beneath her feet. Everything is upside down. She's sweating and her legs are burning and her feet are blistered in her leather flats but she feels the need to keep running but she doesn't know where but she can't stay still but she certainly can't go on. One deep breath, now, standing wherever she's standing. Then another. The smell of rotten asparagus. Marcus is alive. She's been waiting for an answer, and now she got one, clear as the sun. His jacket, his height, his head. His face and none other, even if now adorned in a short, fuzzy beard. The beautiful structure of his cheekbones. And those eyes. Those eyes that saw hers. Then looked away. And then he disappeared.

Now she's sitting. When did she sit? She feels she's in a dream, in disconnected scenes, not knowing how she got from one to the other. But her seat is on the pavement and her back is against a glassy window. A dirty flyer breezes by and gets caught on her knees. People walk by without looking at her. She wonders what it would be like to be an ant, looking up at giants, hoping you don't get crushed.

Ants don't betray one another.

Marcus betrayed her.

After all she's done for him.

She did everything right.

Everything he wanted.

She picks up her phone. His face is on the lock screen. She resists the urge to smash it. The coward! If he wanted to leave her, why couldn't he just leave? Why go through all this? She opens the phone to delete his photograph. And every other photo of him she has. That's ninety percent of her photos. It's easier to mass delete everything. So she does. She goes to her contact list. She has three numbers saved. Marcus, Arjun, and her father. She deletes Marcus's number. She tries calling Arjun, but it goes straight to voicemail. She calls her father, expecting the voicemail.

But a woman answers the phone.

◆　◆　◆

Her name is Patricia Lynn, but she goes by Pat. She has big arms and bigger blonde poufed hair, and she's in love with Esme's father.

Pat tells this to Esme—the famed Esme, the beautiful and talented daughter—on the phone. Pat met Esme's father at the Roanoke city council building, where she works as a receptionist and sees him every day. Pat knows everyone in the building, and everyone knows her, because anyone who comes in through that front door is subject to Pat's scrutiny. What are you here for? Where are you going? What's your name, love, and do you want a cookie? She's determined to make everyone her friend, because everyone here is worth loving. Because everyone here shows up. If you show up, you get love. Her ex-husband left her while she was in the delivery room. She was screaming his name, wondering where he went, why his quick bathroom break was taking so long. He'd gone pale, watching what was going on down there, then given her a quick nod and said he'd be right back. That bastard. They got married as soon as she found out she was pregnant, which was a total shock, with her being forty-five years old. He wanted her to get rid of it but of course she wouldn't, this possibly being her last chance at having a child. So he puffed out his chest and said he'd marry her instead. She'd agreed. The idiot.

Now here was a city government with councilmembers that showed up every day and all their staff showed up, too, and every time they showed up, it was a celebration in Pat's mind. These were people that didn't run when things got tough. And things do get tough. The work is grueling and thankless. At least that's what Pat gathers from asking people questions. Some days, the Roanoke city councilmembers walk in and give her a look that says, *Help me.* They tell her about the bills they are trying to pass, about school funding and real estate taxes and zoning reforms, and all the people pulling them in different ways. They also complain about their wives and in-laws and whatever else is on their mind. They're far more open with her than they should be, but she's not one to complain about that. Blame it on the power of her extra-butter sugar cookies. Everyone likes talking to Pat.

Except for Esme's father, who, for a long time, was never un-friendly, but always quiet, saying no more than "Hello" in the morning when he walked by her desk. And at lunch, as workers from all over took their seats in the courtyard to joke and debate and laugh, he always sat alone in a far corner by a lemon tree. She had a view of the courtyard through the glass walls by her desk and she'd watch him eat without doing anything else. He didn't read; he didn't scroll on his phone; he didn't look sad or happy or anything. He looked like he was lost in a memory somewhere far away.

She was determined to make him her friend, so one day, she went up to him during lunch. "Anyone sitting here?" He shook his head no. "Can I join you, then?" And he nodded his head yes. And she pulled out her own sandwich and a Tupperware of cookies. "I know you always say no when I offer a cookie. But don't you think you might want one over lunch? It could go real well with that sandwich of yours." And he smiled and nodded a yes and held out his hand for a cookie. And she told him about the funny thing her daughter had done that morning, the way she'd peered at the cookie Pat had given her for breakfast, and thrown it on the floor. "She said, 'No more cookies!' like it was her life on the line. I was like, what? My own daughter doesn't like cookies? Did I really give birth to this thing? And she was like, 'Ms. Anna said sugar cookies will kill you!' and I was like, goddamn, that's a thing to say to a little kid! And then she went over to the cookie box and picked it up like she meant to dump the whole thing on the ground and I was like, 'Hey! Darling, you don't have to eat a cookie if you don't want to, but you can't just throw every cookie you see on the ground. Sometimes it's okay for others to eat cookies.' And she was like, 'No more cookies for mama!' And I was like, that's fine, I won't eat them. I had to promise her ten times that I would just bring these all to work and give them away. Apparently my three-year-old has put me on a no-sugar diet." Esme's father laughed at that. "I suppose I should warn you, these cookies might kill you. Or you might become addicted. If you do, there are plenty more." She waited for him to say something in response. He didn't, but he also didn't seem to be annoyed by her presence either. He'd eaten the whole cookie in four bites. She asked him, "So do you have any children?" And he said yes.

"Her name is Esme."

It was the most she'd ever heard him say.

Of course, it took just a couple of sentences after that to understand why he didn't like to talk. That stutter. She'd never heard a worse one. But it wasn't a stutter like she knew from the movies. He didn't trip on his words like a broken record. No—it was like someone put their hand on the record, stifling its movements to a full stop. His words would be trapped in his mouth, held back by some force she couldn't see, and she'd have to wait for him to work out the mechanics of setting them free. This wait could take up to a full minute. Yet he could say "Her name is Esme" and when he spoke about his daughter, the pauses between words decreased in frequency and length. When the hour was up, and Pat had to get back to work, she asked, "Is it okay if I eat with you again tomorrow?" And he nodded.

It took a long time to get to know him, given how difficult it was for him to talk. But Pat was happy to do most of the talking, as was her daughter, Tina, when the two of them finally met. Over lunch, and over dinner, and over weekend breakfasts, he told her his story slowly, in fragments. And once Pat put it all together, once she knew who he was, she fell in love. Or maybe it was the act of putting it together that made her fall in love, piece by piece. Pulling him apart and putting him back together, with a little more information, a picture more in focus. Either way, she was there.

● ◆ ●

Esme blinks away the tears. She hangs up the phone. This woman on the phone is nice. She is kind. She is friendly. Esme barely had to say two words and the woman narrated her life's story. Esme understands why her father likes her.

This makes her unbearably angry.

Another man keeping a big secret from Esme.

Not just one secret. Two. Two women in his life now. This woman. And her daughter. This woman in her father's house, answering his phone as if she lives there. If she reached voicemail, would it still say "You've reached the Green Machine"? Or would this woman have changed that, too? Esme's tempted to call back and check, but that would just lead to that woman picking up the phone again, and for what? So Esme can cry on the phone and make her feel terrible? It's not this woman's fault, her father's secrecy. His lies. She and her father had a system that she thought was working. They didn't talk much but when they did, they were open with each other. But now this. What other secrets has he kept from her? How many other women?

Another blink, another spate of tears. This is not about her father. She blinks and her eyes blur. This is about Marcus. This is about how she knew he was falling away from her. Nothing materially had changed about their lives but she could feel him slipping away and she denied it, and he did, too, and so they fought about things that didn't matter while avoiding the only thing that did. She closes her eyes until the tears stop, then opens them and feels empty. A dirty flyer is crumpled by her feet. She is an ant without a home. She blinks and there's someone there. A face. A man. Crouching down, watching her. He has wrinkles on wrinkles and white frizzy hair and a silver beard streaked with ginger.

"Are you okay?" he asks.

Esme shakes her head no.

"I shouldn't have asked that question. Let me try this again. Can I help you?"

She peers at his black clerical collar, the large silver cross around the neck. Esme doesn't know what to say. Can he help her? Can he tell her why her fiancé left her in the worst possible way? Can he show her the way? Maybe he could convince God to make Marcus come back. Or maybe if she becomes a nun, she won't care about Marcus.

"Did you get tear-gassed? Are you hurt?"

Esme shakes her head no.

"Would you like a bagel?" he asks. "Maybe some coffee?"

She nods.

"Follow me."

He leads her on a walk away from the protest toward his church, and on the way, he tells her he noticed her running off and was concerned. He shows her his small cardboard sign that says *Pastors for Peace*. He came to the protest to tell as many people as he could about the shelter at his church, where anyone was welcome for food, rest, and prayer. "No need to pray," he says when he sees the look on her face. "We have plenty of food. Not enough prayers, but plenty of food." The reverend leads her past an auto repair shop with broken glass windows, urging her to be careful where she steps. They walk in the gutter of the street to avoid a block with trash bags piled up. He apologizes for the rough walk. "City services have been a little busy," he explains, which she already knows. Finally, in between a series of row houses, they arrive at a brick church with three colorful stained glass windows adorned with eight-pointed stars, and a wooden sign: *Pathway Pilgrim Church.*

"I've been here before," she says quietly, realizing. "I came to a baptism."

"Oh? For whom?"

"I don't remember." She never got their names.

He opens the church doors, which are covered in flyers. Inside, the church is painfully undecorated. There are tall white walls and gray carpeted floors and several rows of light pine pews lined with pink cushions. There's nothing on the walls but a single icon above the altar, the outlines of an eight-pointed star.

There is murmuring throughout the room and it doesn't change when Esme or the reverend walk in. A handful of people are sitting on the pews, reading books of hymns or prayers or Bibles, Esme can't tell. Some of them have their eyes closed and are muttering to themselves. She wonders what they're praying for. When she came those years ago, she didn't understand what was happening with the baptism. Their prayers made her feel unhinged and confused. But it was a nice thing, sitting in these pews. The wood was exceptionally smooth and the air was refreshing on a hot day. Now, still, the air-conditioning is on blast and makes Esme shiver. But it's invigorating. Like she's coming back to life. She catches a whiff of cinnamon and butter, striking up a hunger that makes her feel faint. "Bagels are in the courtyard," the reverend says quietly, "but if you'd like to explore the nave after, let me know."

He leads her around the edge of the nave to a hallway that passes by several conference rooms, which are filled with cots and sleeping bags. Then they reach the courtyard out back, where long folding tables are set up and at least three dozen people are eating from paper plates. Near Esme is a table that has a pot of coffee and a few scraps of fried vegetables but is otherwise empty.

"Looks like Michael already put the food away," the reverend whispers. There is a quiet mood in the air. The others speak with the politeness of strangers. This is not their home and these people are not their family. Yet they smile at one another and laugh quietly at some private joke. She tries not to catch anyone's gaze as she eyes their food. "Bagels" was an understatement. Their paper plates are filled with scrambled eggs, roasted carrots, bacon, and the softest-looking cinnamon sugar cookies she's ever seen. "But we can go into the kitchen. Follow me."

There is another table near the entrance to the courtyard, filled with flyers and pamphlets. Something makes her pause. It's a flyer announcing the one-hundredth-anniversary celebration coming up on Christmas Day, a month and a half away. The same flyer she found on Marcus's desk. She stops to examine it. The image is unsettling, though she can't say why. The drawing of the church with the stained glass windows, simple and elegant. The eight-pointed stars. It's just as she remembers. The fact of this is what makes her uneasy. Somehow, she would feel better if it had changed in some way.

The reverend has already left the courtyard. The air is still and heavy. She goes through the door back into the church, down the hallway, and into the nave, where she finds him pacing the pews.

"I worried you got lost," he jokes. Then he notices the flyer in her hand. "You're welcome to join," he says. "If you sign up for our emails, we'll send out the coordinates the morning of the celebration."

"A hundred years," says Esme.

"And many hundreds more, one hopes."

The flyer was among the hundreds of papers she'd found in Marcus's space. Yet this one wasn't crumpled up like the others. It was pressed flat between two legal notepads, as if being pre-served like a dried rose. She'd picked it up and studied it. She'd wondered why Marcus cared.

They walk to the end of another hallway to an exit door, then step outside briefly, and in through another door to the adjacent row house. Here is an airy kitchen painted white with big open windows. On the stove are several glass trays half filled with hot food covered in plastic wrap. He unwraps the trays, gives her a paper plate, and tells her to dig in. She spoons roasted vegetables and cheesy scrambled eggs onto her plate and eats it all quickly. He laughs. "You must have been hungry." He scrapes cream cheese onto a bagel and wraps this up in a paper towel. "Take this one for the road," he says. "I need to get ready for the evening prayer meeting."

He opens the door for them to take a step outside before re-entering the church.

"This house is connected to your church," says Esme.

"Yes."

"Has it been that way every day?"

He nods.

"Before the Unmapping?"

"Of course. This is where I live, and where my father lived."

And now, as if the two thoughts were connected, she thinks of the flyer in her pocket. "You seem really well prepared. This flyer doesn't say the location of the anniversary celebration."

"Why would it say the location if our location moves each day?"

"Exactly." But the flyer on Marcus's desk had been put there before the Unmapping. Did that have the location? She'd have to check later. "What's the story?"

"Pardon?"

"My fiancé had this flyer. My ex-fiancé." She looks down and realizes she's still wearing her engagement ring, which she covers up with her other hand. "I saw one of these flyers on his work desk, but he's not religious at all. He's a reporter. So he must be writing a story about you? Maybe about the hundred-year anniversary? Do you know Marcus? Marcus Miller, of Bluzz?"

The reverend gives her a blank stare.

"Bluzz—it's a news website. Kind of fringe."

The reverend keeps looking at Esme. She grows self-conscious of the sweatpants she's wearing with her turtleneck sweater. Is it sacrilegious to wear sweatpants inside a church?

"I do not know a Marcus," he finally says. "It's time for the evening prayer meeting. Do you need directions to a nearby shelter?"

"But I thought you said this church was a shelter?"

"We're at capacity for overnights, unfortunately."

The reverend hands her a cup of coffee and begins talking to her about how religion can be a shining light in times of upheaval, how faith is the best way forward. As he speaks, she realizes he is walking her toward the front door, shepherding her gently with little waves and steps. Is he trying to convert her? Or make her go away? They're at the front door and she has the wrapped bagel in one hand and the coffee in the other. "How can I sign up for that email list?" Esme asks. But he pretends not to hear, just keeps talking about some verse from Timothy or Titus or both. "Maybe

I'll come back for the one-hundredth-anniversary celebration," she says. "Can you tell me more about that?"

"Apologies, I have to get ready for evening devotions."

"But how do I sign up?"

"This celebration is really for members of the church."

"I could be a member."

"I don't know," he says. "I don't know if this place is for you, Esme."

"You don't want to convert me?"

"We welcome all to the faith who seek to find the truth," he says.

"Of course I want the truth," she says.

"There is the truth you want, and the truth you don't want," he says. "The truth you don't want is oftentimes even truer."

Esme is now far past confused. She wonders if this is what it's like to go to church on a regular basis. Get lost in a sea of confusion, then look to the man at the front of the room who somehow has the answers. She wonders when she told him her name.

Three ambulances drive by, followed by a fire truck.

"Be well," he says. "I hope you find peace."

16

The pain is in Arjun's throat, lungs, eyes, neck, hands, and ankles. The tear gas has a heatless burn. Prickles and ash. He feels he's becoming dust from the inside out. Cleaned out. Emptied. He's already vomited twice and there's nothing left to release. There's nothing left to feel but happiness. Yes. Now he's sitting on a school bus with his hands in a zip tie behind his back, face pressed against the cool glass of the window, eyes streaming. Blurry. He's here and he's so happy he could vomit again. And again.

His time at the police station is long, then brief. First he gets told to sit on the floor in a large bright room, surrounded by hundreds of moaning people. Hours pass as the others get called up to a desk one by one, to answer questions and then be shepherded into a different room, from which they don't return. Finally someone in an official-looking outfit taps Arjun's shoulder roughly. When he reaches the desk, Arjun tells them that this was all a big mistake, that he works for the city and was passing through on his way to his job, at Emergency Management, saving lives, a job that he needs to get to now, quickly, remember, to save lives. He urges them to look through his backpack so they can find the navy-blue Emergency Management polo shirt, and the lanyard with the security card, which they do, and they make a phone call to someone, asking to confirm his profession, and then they hang up and let him out without being charged. Really? Arjun is amazed that this works. They cut off his zip tie and hand him his backpack and tell him to find somewhere with a shower and a laundry so he can wash the tear gas remnants off his skin and clothes. Before he leaves, one cop leads him to a single-occupancy restroom to rinse out his eyes in the sink. "You got it bad," the officer says. "What kind of idiot heads straight for the tear gas canister?"

A social media star, Arjun thinks, splashing water on his eyes. His video already has three million views, and his private messages are filling up with businesses asking for him to sponsor health supplements, first-aid kits, and sparkly rope. Worth it for the cause. He's proud of what he's done. The city's turmoil is now international news. He scrolls through notifications filled with languages he doesn't recognize, with reposts from people all over the world. His video was posted by an account called Azeri TV with a caption translated back to English as *New York Burying Citizens Under Buildings*. Fine. Yes. #FreeAntony is trending, and with it are photos of the boy, photos of ants, and even the photo Arjun took the first day he met Antony's brother, when he created his John Bobson account. The photo itself is not very good; it's hard to tell what's going on—just a dozen or so people painting a mural on the ground. But others have provided the needed context: This is the day the movement began, and the people who started it. This is the beginning of something big. John Bobson already has twenty thousand followers, and the number is going up quickly. His video is picked up in Hindi now, too. Maybe his mother and grandfather will see the world from his eyes, if the video gets picked up by the local TV news in Delhi. They will watch it and understand him. They will see the video from the pseudonymous account and know it's Arjun. "That's my John Bobson!" his mother will say. "So brave. A true American." And his grandfather will cough and say, "The kid's an idiot, no respect for anything," but Arjun doesn't care what his grandfather thinks; he cares about his mother, who will understand that the world is a dark place, and that not only is Arjun unafraid of this darkness, it is his duty to face it head-on. His mother will watch as he runs right toward the tear gas canister as the police release shadows and smoke. Evil is a cloud. It obscures and hides. Goodness is the light. Like this brightly lit bathroom in the police station, where Arjun is washing his hands. The light exposes everything, all the graffiti on the wall that's only half rubbed clean, every glistening pore on Arjun's face. He looks at himself in the mirror. His eyes are redder than they've ever been and his hair is disheveled— badges of honor from a rough arrest—but otherwise he looks truly happy. Dare he say it? He looks good. Adrenaline and success look good on Arjun. He's breathless.

Before he leaves the bathroom, he checks his phone. His work shift was supposed to start an hour ago. But he feels he has a good excuse to stay home. He needs to shower and change his clothes, like the policeman said. He's washed off his hands, arms, and face, but his neck burns and his ankles burn and he needs a good hot bath. His GPS tracker reminds him that his father's apartment is in deep Queens, as it was this morning. It was a slow taxi ride to get into Manhattan over the long and winding Robert F. Kennedy Bridge, which would probably be impossible to cross now, given the protests. He'll have to wait until the bridges reopen to get back to his father's apartment. Not that he wants to. He could go to work. Not that he wants to do that either. He checks his map to find Esme's location. She's not far. He texts her.

ARJUN: You home? You ok? I just got out of jail. Tear-gassed. Intense!

ESME: Yeah I'm home.

He's disappointed she doesn't react to the news of his tear-gassing. Just a few hours earlier, she hugged him and he held her hand. Now there is a period at the end of her text. It didn't take long for him to learn when he first moved here that a period at the end of a text meant seriousness. Meant anger.

ARJUN: Can I come over? Could really use a friend right now

He winces at his own text and wishes he could undo it immediately. But she texts back right away.

ESME: Yes. Me, too. Please come

This response soothes every part of him, like a high-dosage clonazepam.

Arjun finds the building easily. Esme has complained about its ugliness, saying it looks like a concrete beehive. Arjun wouldn't call it a beehive, more of a termite mound, with all those balconies dotting a mass of concrete, which he wouldn't call ugly unless he had a particular fear of termites, but for him it's the fact that the building is so huge, so very tall, that makes it look unnatural. After a building reaches a certain height, there are no reference points for measuring it. Nothing to compare it to. It would not be possible for Arjun to know that, for instance, it is about half as tall as the Empire State Building, or the fact that it's the height of twenty tall tamarind trees stacked atop each other, like the ones outside his grandfather's apartment. Tall is tall and the top is in the sky. It's the only skyscraper in a three-block radius.

Arjun finds Esme's name on the electronic touchpad and presses the button for her to buzz him up, but the screen fills with a single word scrolling across it, repeating over and over: *ERROR ERROR ERROR.* Is it just Arjun or are the spaces between the words decreasing? It looks like one word now and the letters in fact are jumbling together. *ERRORORERRERRORORORORREEER.* He texts Esme and she doesn't respond but a buzzer sounds and the front door releases. He's in! Inside everything is all shiny metal, including the empty concierge desk, including the floors, which are covered by a lemon-yellow carpet. So very different from the concrete exterior. He feels like he stepped from one planet to another, from the desert to outer space. He gets into the elevator and clicks the button for the forty-third floor. Forty-three floors! And that's not even the top. The doors close. He's in a box, metal on all sides, shiny metal that distorts his haggard reflection. He blinks ten times to clear the red out of his eyes and tries to comb back his hair with his fingers but that just makes it stick up straighter. The elevator heaves and shakes itself free, then finds a steady rhythm back and forth as it ascends. He wonders how often this building has lost power and how many people would not be able to survive the stairs. What if someone tried but had a heart attack on floor forty-two? The thought makes him sweaty. He sucks in his breath and coughs out phlegm. Each cough is painful and brings him closer to Esme. To her apartment. The elevator is past the tenth floor now. He is going to her apartment, where she lives, to sit on her couch and possibly step out onto one of those tiny concrete balconies. Twentieth floor. Does she have a nice couch? He imagines it is a mustard-yellow fabric, a little frayed at the edges, but comfortable. Thirtieth floor now. He wishes he'd brought some wine. *Please come.* She wants him here. He said he needs a friend and she said, *Me, too.* Or perhaps some groceries so he could make dinner. Thirty-fifth floor. Perhaps a bag of chips? He didn't even bring a bag of chips. He has an excuse—he was tear-gassed. He's ill. He needs a shower and a nap and a friend. Esme. Forty-first floor now. Did that elevator screen skip forty? Forty-two. Forty-three.

The elevator doors open.

Esme's apartment is right there.

He knocks on her door.

She opens the door.

"Thanks for coming," she says. "I'm moving home tomorrow. You can help me pack."

◆ ◆ ◆

The mayor's kitchen is empty. The mayor's bathroom is empty. All the mayor's usual hiding spots are empty. Even the bedroom. Except for one thing. In the unlit room, in a tin bedside a trash can, the cell phone she left behind is seizuring with texts and calls. Her ringtone barely gets a chance to take a breath before it starts up again. The ringtone was supposed to sound calm, all tinkling bells, but when it's interrupted by beeping notifications, it sounds ominous. Like a warning.

The bedroom door bursts open and six people file in. "Is she in here?" asks the social media manager. They heard the phone's ringtone from the hallway but they can't see anything, partially because the electricity is still out, hours later, and partially because there's nothing to see.

"Use your phone flashlight," says the press secretary.

"I'm busy," says the social media manager, her delicate face lit by her phone's glow as she scrolls through the angry comments to her latest social media post on behalf of the mayor. We hear you. We feel you. We just want everyone to be safe.

"That's a no," says the press secretary, who walks around the room with her phone flashlight, poring over the ground as if she were Sherlock Holmes. "She's not here."

"She's not here?" says the secretary of environment.

"Where is she?" asks the secretary of finance.

"Where, indeed?" The press secretary turns to the scheduling assistant, who himself is still searching for the mayor in the bedroom, throwing back all the covers. She pokes him on the shoulder. "That question is for you."

"I don't know!" he cries. The press secretary gives the scheduling assistant her meanest look, which he can't see in the dark but can feel anyway. "I only went to the bathroom for thirty seconds!"

The mayor of New York City is gone.

And yet her cell phone is still ringing.

The voicemails are filling up the mayor's cell phone inbox, but they won't be accessed for another two weeks, after a time of deep confusion, because there is no process for a missing mayor, but when the mayor's replacement steps in, they will be able to unlock her phone and review all the messages, too late to matter.

VOICEMAIL TRANSCRIPTION: Bridges cleared and the tunnels cleared, but imagine we don't want to open the tunnels back up again to traffic, right? Has that changed? What's the procedure here? We'll return the barriers and keep an eye on it.

VOICEMAIL TRANSCRIPTION: Take that back. There's a new wave of protesters blocking the Willis Avenue Bridge and Third Avenue Bridge. Unless you say otherwise, we'll clear them now.

"Shit," says the social media manager. "My phone died. Anyone have a portable charger?" No one responds. There's the sound of running in the hallway. The scheduling assistant picks up the landline. There is no dial tone.

"Fix this," says the press secretary with her hand on the shoulder of the scheduling assistant. The gesture is meant to indicate that she is speaking to him in the dark, not that she's carrying out a physical threat, but if the meaning is misconstrued, that's not her problem.

"Where is her driver?" asks the scheduling assistant. "Maybe he'll know."

"Good question. Call him."

The phone goes straight to voicemail.

VOICEMAIL TRANSCRIPTION: Madison Avenue Bridge now taken, too. We've processed two hundred arrests so far. What's the plot? Appear to be converging around the areas that block the way between Manhattan and the Bronx. We're going in over 145th Street to take them from the other side.

"Call the mayor of Atlantic City," says the press secretary.

"Why would I do that?"

"Just call him."

"My phone just died."

"Use my portable charger."

"Hey!" says the social media manager. "I thought you said you didn't have one."

"I didn't say anything. I'll be back."

VOICEMAIL TRANSCRIPTION: Mayor, we're getting reports of vandals in Hunts Point covering their faces in bandanas and forcing themselves into strangers' homes with power drills and jackhammers, pounding on the basement walls, then leaving with everything intact. Where are they getting all those jackhammers?

An hour passes in a moment. The press secretary returns to the bedroom. "Any word?"

"No," says the scheduling assistant.

"I leave you for an hour and there's nothing? Who else can you call? Think of a hundred people you can call, add ten more names, and call them."

"A hundred and ten phone calls . . . sure. Can you help?"

"I'm *thinking!*"

VOICEMAIL TRANSCRIPTION: The vandals are also tying rope from one house to another, all still in Hunts Point. We're considering this an insurrection, so bringing all our forces there. If you disagree, say so in the next five minutes.

Everyone leaves the bedroom. The phone keeps ringing. Thousands of missed calls. The text inbox is full. The voicemails are saved in an empty space that will be called and retrieved and transcribed by a terrified intern.

VOICEMAIL TRANSCRIPTION: We're hearing someone found the kid. Antony. A goddamn relief. Now we can get the protesters to shut down. Get your team to disseminate this information immediately. Send it through the mass alert system. We need them to stand down.

The sun sets. Someone returns to the bedroom to retrieve the mayor's cell phone.

VOICEMAIL TRANSCRIPTION: Mayor, we've been attempting to alert the protesters that Antony has been found. No one believes us. Need assistance now. How can we disseminate this information? Need a voice of trust. Need you. Mayor, we are doing our best here, but really need some guidance.

The mayor's cell phone dies.

• • •

Esme's apartment is filled with dozens of boxes. The boxes advertise mattresses, appliances, and wholesale fruits. But they all say one thing: *I'm leaving you.*

"You're moving?" Arjun can barely say the words. He doesn't want them to be true.

Esme nods. "Leaving tomorrow. Going home."

"To Virginia?"

"Yes. If I can get out of the city."

"And if not?" He lets himself imagine the tunnels and bridges locked down for another day, even as he knows that's not possible, with swarms of protesters getting arrested, and even when a new swarm appears to block a bridge, it's only so long before they're taken away, too. Maybe they'll find some other way to block the exits. Maybe they'll cover the roads in glue, or buy a massive boat and put it in the middle of the road. Maybe they'll bomb the bridges. That's not a good thing to hope for. But Esme doesn't seem to notice his question. She's packing a pile of plates into a salad spinner box.

"How did you get all these boxes?" Really? That's all he can think to ask right now?

"There are loads in the basement trash room."

"Oh."

She picks up a mug with the Bluzz logo and tagline: *I told you so.*

"I found Marcus," says Esme.

"Oh." This news makes his stomach sink although he knows he should be happier. "Good. That's good!" His skin burns around his neck and chest. His eyes still tingle with heat. He walks to the kitchen sink and splashes water on his face to wash out the tear gas and to do something with his hands. "So you found him," he says, in between splashes, "and you're moving

away together"—*splash*—"and you'll be very happy together."
He fills his hands with cool water and presses his face into his
palms, then stays there, hands clutching skin, bent over in the
sink. He wants to ask her, why am I helping you, then? Where
is Marcus, then? For years she's rarely spoken of him and when
she did, it was only to complain, and even though she pretended
to be lighthearted about it, Arjun could hear the bitterness in
her voice. Marcus was never there for Esme. Just like now. She's
packing up her apartment and where is he?

"He's not moving with me."

"Oh."

"He left me. He was never missing. He just . . . left."

Oh. Arjun's stomach leaps into his throat. He turns the
phrase around in his head. Marcus left. He left Esme. He didn't
die; he left her. Esme is no longer engaged. "I'm sorry?"

She moves her head, somewhere between a nod and a shake.

"But also, he's alive? Are you glad?"

She snaps, "Of course I'm glad."

"Want to . . . talk about it?"

"I want to pack. Then I want to leave and forget I ever lived
here." The words feel like a slap. Not just because of the information they contain. But because she doesn't seem to realize whatsoever the effect her words are having on Arjun. She's his closest
friend in this city, ever since his college friends moved away, or
maybe even before that, ever since he dropped out of college and
they stopped having reasons to hang out with him. Then he got
the job at the Emergency Management Department as a driver,
one of the only jobs he liked that didn't require a college degree,
and met Esme, and everything turned around. Now she's leaving
and, besides that, she doesn't care what will happen to him.

Arjun reminds himself: It's not about me. He's here to help

Esme. She's been through a lot. Esme lost her fiancé, probably
giving him up for dead. Then, from the grave, she was betrayed.

Arjun says, "Tell me what to do."

She tells him to pack up Marcus's things in trash bags so she
can throw them out. "I don't want to touch them," she says. "Just
bring them straight down to the dumpster." He starts with the
contents of Marcus's desk, which is mostly filled with trash anyway. He holds back the urge to examine the documents, to try
to make this mysterious man a little less mysterious. But that's
not why he's here. It all goes in a trash bag. Then he heads to
the bedroom, which is quite small. Esme had told Arjun that
their bedroom is technically a walk-in closet, attached to a studio apartment, but they use the main room as a living room and
the closet as a bedroom, and in said closet, a double bed barely
fits between two dressers. He opens the one on the right to un-
load Marcus's clothes. There's hardly anything inside. He doesn't
mention this to Esme. Marcus must have removed his clothes
himself, but he left a couple pieces behind in the drawers to not
raise suspicion. Most of what's in here is old and full of holes.
But a couple of the items are nice and soft. It would be a shame
to throw them away. Arjun peels off his own plain white T-shirt
so he can put on one of Marcus's ribbed V-neck T-shirts. At that
moment, when his head is in the shirt and his arms are struggling to find their holes, Esme walks into the bedroom.

"Sorry," she says.

"Sorry!" he says, shirtless.

"What are you doing?"

"The police officer told me to wash the tear gas out of my
clothes," he says, pulling the shirt the rest of the way on to cover
up his lanky lack of muscles. "He also told me to take a shower to
help stop the burning on my skin, but. Haven't had a free moment

yet. I'll just wash my shirt and put it back on. Okay if I borrow this shirt in the meantime? And maybe a pair of pants? Where is the laundry? Should I use a sink?"

"God, I'm so self-absorbed," says Esme. "Forget about the laundry. Keep the clothes. I completely forgot about what happened earlier. Are you okay?"

Arjun smiles. Then he removes the smile from his face. "Yeah. I mean, it was tough. Second-most-painful experience in my life."

"Your car crash," says Esme. "That'd be the first-most-painful, right?"

"You remember?"

"Of course I do." She sits cross-legged on the bed, smoothing down the blue flannel sheets. Above her hover several floating shelves, now emptied of books and framed photographs. "You told me about your car crash the first day we met."

"And you remember that?" He leans awkwardly against the dresser, with a floating bookshelf pressing into his back.

"Do I remember? 'Hi, I'm Arjun. Almost died in a car crash. What's your name?' It's hard to forget."

"I don't imagine it went quite like that."

Esme laughs. "I liked it. You had a story to tell and you weren't waiting around to tell it."

"It was my first day. I was so excited to save lives. Ever since I almost died."

"I know. That's what you said the day we first met."

"Right."

"And then I asked, 'What do you mean you almost died?' And you said there was a terrible car crash."

"So you asked me about the car crash, and I had to answer."

"But you can't say something like 'I almost died' and not

expect someone to ask you how. Also, you didn't really tell me what happened with the crash."

"I almost died. And then I was saved."

"Yes, you told me that part. But what's the whole story? Why'd you crash? Or who crashed into you? What happened?"

Arjun squeezes his hands together. "It's kind of embarrassing."

"Now you have to tell!"

He loves to see her smile. He keeps his own smile off his face. "No, I don't."

"Yes, you do! Do you want me to beg?"

"Maybe."

"Okay, Arjun." She gets on her knees and clasps her hands in prayer. "Please, please, please tell me about your car crash. I'll do anything you want." She jumps up and grabs his shoulders. "Please, Arjun. I'll die if you don't tell me. I'll just die."

"Okay!" He pushes her away and she lets herself fall dramatically back to the bed. "The thing is . . . ah . . ."

She lifts up her head. "Yes?"

"I stole the car from my father."

"Now this is a story. Why?"

"I mean, I had access to it. But I didn't have my driver's license. I didn't care. I was so angry at him for making me move to New York City and leave my mother behind." He tells Esme how his mother never really wanted to leave India, but pretended she did, nodding along as Arjun's father gathered them together to spin his ridiculous dreams, which all varied wildly but had one commonality: moving to America. His father wanted to own every high-rise in New York City, start a candy factory in Jersey City, and rebuild the Port Authority. He wanted to play Ping-Pong with the US president. Arjun didn't want to leave at first—his biggest dream was to buy a moped and drive quickly

through the alleyways, with cows and downed cables as his obstacle course. But his dad made America sound wonderful, and
when he bought a television that wouldn't hook up to cable but
did play a scant few videotapes of noir movies and *Miami Vice*,
Arjun was hooked. He began helping his father at his various
ventures—it started with selling candy at a candy shop, then
graduated to working in a tourism office where his father had a
second job, and then his father lucked into inheriting the candy
shop from the kind old childless owner, which he immediately
sold, and then had the funds to purchase the tourism office, with
enough profit to finance the purchase of an apartment building, which, after raising enough from rents, he sold so he could
purchase an even bigger apartment building, and so on, always
buying and selling and buying and selling and somehow making
this work until he was running a fruitful real estate business out
of his bedroom and overseeing various shops on the side, with
enough in the bank to give it a go in the States.

But by then Arjun's maternal grandfather's health had severely declined, and so, a day before they were supposed to leave,
his mother claimed she had to stay back and take care of her father through his final days. She said it would be temporary and
that she would talk to them both on the phone often and join
them soon. These days became years and, although she kept her
promise about the frequent phone calls, she never came. Arjun
was excited about the prospect of moving to America but never
pictured living here without his mother, especially because without her, his father got harsh, sometimes a little mean. So Arjun
was alone with his father in the city, living in increasingly large
and tasteless apartments in buildings owned by his father, never
staying put in one neighborhood long enough for him to get to
know anyone. Not that anyone wanted to know young Arjun,

with his thick accent and funny fedora. He had a lot of time stewing alone at home, and, sick of movies, sick of television, he would borrow his father's luxury cars. "It's not like he even hid the keys," says Arjun. "It felt like he wanted me to take them. I think he knew." His father cycled through cars even more quickly than he cycled through apartments and condos. They were usually bright colors: lime green, magenta, electric blue. Arjun's favorites were the white ones, though. It didn't matter what type of car it was; if it was white, he was in it. Especially the Ferrari. The white Ferrari that reminded him of *Miami Vice*, of his younger, hopeful self. It was impeccably clean, no matter how many times his father drove it.

So Arjun took it.

When his father was away on an overnight trip in Toronto, Arjun took the car up north to the Saw Mill River Parkway. He drove carefully to get there, then let loose. "It was this twenty-nine-mile stretch that snaked along a river, and I would just go down and back, down and back, as fast as I could, until my brain got so tired I was ready to go home." At one point, though, a cop car appeared behind him. "Whether he was hidden in the trees, or someone called him on me, I don't know." But Arjun didn't slow. He put the gas pedal to the floor, and went faster and faster, up to 130, 150, 160, 170 . . . "And I lost him. I beat him. I won. I never felt so powerful." He felt he had a special connection to the steering wheel, and to the trees around him, to the earth and sky. A deep concentration flooded through him and made him feel like he could control the world. He could lift up the car to fly. But this fantasy caused a half-moment's lapse in concentration, and so he missed a slight bend in the road. When he hit the rumble strip on the right, he panicked and twisted the wheel left, straight into the concrete road barrier. "I flipped over the barrier and into the other side of the highway, and flipped again past the shoulder. Two and a half rotations. Nine hundred degrees." There his car landed in a row of trees, which was lucky, because if not for those trees, he'd have landed upside down in a freezing river. "I don't remember much about what happened next, but I was told that the cop caught up to me pretty quickly, and the ambulances came not long after, and they had to free me from the car. I was dangling upside down by my seat belt with a broken pelvic bone. Then it was all the things you hear about in movies. Bright lights, fading nurses, waking up in a room with my body in bandages. And a whole lot of charges. Speeding, of course. Also reckless driving. Fleeing a cop. Stealing a car."

"Stealing a car? But it was your father's."

"Without that charge, my father might have been charged for child endangerment and sent back to India. This is before we were citizens. I told the cops I stole the keys out of my father's jeans. I lied to help him. And yet he's still never forgiven me."

This last part isn't exactly true. His father was angry, yes, but Arjun expected this, would have been disturbed if it hadn't been so. His prized Ferrari was smashed to bits. But when Arjun apologized about the car, his father got even angrier. "You think I care about that car? I nearly lost my son!" No, something else is driving a wedge between them now. But Esme doesn't need to know all that. He looks at her, wondering what she'll say. Are those tears in her eyes?

"Wow," she says.

Arjun feels uncomfortable under her gaze. "Embarrassing, right?"

She shakes her head. "So that was the most painful thing that's ever happened to you."

"I suppose the event itself wasn't that painful, given that I was unconscious during most of the painful parts. It was healing that was painful. I wasn't allowed to move, but I hated that. I don't know if you know this about me, but I don't like to stay still."

Esme points at his fingers, which are currently drumming on Marcus's dresser. "No way."

"When they finally took off my casts, everything hurt. They told me it was because my bones had stitched themselves back together too quickly, too well, and they were sort of stuck. Something about cartilage? So when I would bend in any direction, I got the most painful feeling in my pelvis even after it had completely healed. Yeah. That hurt. I healed too hard. But still. If I had to rank the events themselves, as opposed to the aftereffects, getting tear-gassed might have been more painful. The cops said I 'got it bad.' Want to see the video?"

"Yes! But didn't you say you need to shower? I've been making you stand there."

"Doesn't bother me." But now that he's thinking about it, the tickling, burning feeling has come back to his skin. "Yes, I suppose I could shower."

"Let me show you."

For years he's been dreaming of something like this. He's not only in her apartment, but in her bathroom. They're in it together. Every word feels charged with meaning. Every movement. The way she looks at him with concern. The way she gives him her best towel, a fluffy gray thing, and shows him her shampoos and conditioners and asks what else he needs. Does he need lotion or aloe vera? Should it be cold water, to help the burn? She says she's not used to healing someone from tear gas and doesn't know what's right or wrong, but neither does he, so he says yes to everything she suggests. Esme turns on the tap after wrestling with the knob and turns the dial all the way down. He tests the water with his hand. The freezing water is a shock on his skin. But that's not why he's shivering.

17

Bluzz mug? Toss. Framed photo of the Empire State Building? Toss. Painted teapot? Toss. Esme's life, piece by piece, is re-examined, sorted, then put away or thrown away. How did they get so many things? Even in just the kitchen. Why did they accumulate so many mismatched bowls? And these shot glasses? She has never used a shot glass. She spent years putting the apartment together, building her dream life with Marcus, a dream now as shattered as a broken glass. Toss.

The fridge, at least, is nearly empty, since Esme has already thrown out all the leftovers. The only things left are two half-empty bottles of mustard and five teal cans of beer, neatly tucked into the back of the bottom shelf.

Esme usually doesn't drink. She's never been drunk; she doesn't like the idea of losing control. She's seen what it does to people. In college in DC, Marcus would sometimes walk down the U Street bar strip late on Friday nights to witness the drunken girls teetering in tiny outfits that were more straps than dresses, men standing on strangers' cars, and clashing club music pumping from every corner. He said it was like going to the zoo. She joined him once and was horrified. But then, after they moved to New York, Marcus himself once drank too much at a Bluzz holiday party, which she learned because when he came home, he crashed into the bed while giggling madly, waking her up. She asked him what was so funny and he just kept laughing harder, shaking his head, tears streaming down his face; he lifted her hand to his cheeks as proof to feel the wetness. "I'm crying," he laughed. "I'm crying." The more he laughed, the more annoyed Esme got, because he wouldn't tell her what it was, and because when she insisted and he tried to tell her, he just laughed even harder, heaving now, able to say, "Will"—*gasp*—"tell"—*gasp*—"you"—*gasp*—"later!" And then he ran to the toilet and, with the bathroom door wide open, vomited until the laughter stopped. She saw him drunk only that one time; otherwise he, too, liked to stay in control, although he had the occasional beer or two with dinner. Now she stares at the five beers in the fridge, in jeweled blue cans, and thinks, why not? If nothing else, this is a special occasion.

Arjun's in the shower, and Esme's going home.

On her way from the church back to Gleamwood Gardens, Esme received a text from her father urging her to check her email. She then opened a blank email with a file attached, a ten-page Word document apologizing for not telling her about Pat. He wanted to be sure they were a real thing first, that there wouldn't be another mother added to her life, only to be subtracted again. But now he's sure. After two years, he's sure. Two years? Esme thought with anger. Esme had come home for Christmas each year, plenty of time for her father to reveal his secret, and he had said nothing. But he hopes to propose, he wrote, and he wants Esme to meet Pat and her five-year-old daughter, Tina, first, before Christmas, so they can have Christmas all together, as a new family. You'll love Tina, her father said in his letter. She loves math and reading, like you. Esme doubts she'll think of Pat as a mother, but she's excited about the idea of having a sister, someone she can help with math homework and to whom she can recommend her favorite books. So Esme messaged back asking if she could come home the next day, and stay there for a while, without explaining why, and her father said yes right away.

She won't stay in Coal Hollow forever, of course, just long enough to figure things out. She misses the quiet of the woods behind her father's house. Not the muffled half quiet of her apartment building, where you can hear each neighbor cook and fight and watch their shows, but something larger, more expansive. Certainly nothing like the office at the Emergency Management Department, where a constant drumbeat of anxiety runs through everything. She loves working there, yes, the feeling of her brain at top gear, moving quickly and subconsciously while she monitors five videos and at least two text feeds, while responding to the messages that come in from her boss at the same time. She works so fast that if she stops to really think about it, she gets paralyzed. It's like typing on a keyboard. She can type a hundred words per minute by just letting the words flow to her fingers. But if she ever stops to think, How am I doing this? Which letter is where and what comes next? her fingers get sluggish and trip on one another, not only making simple spelling errors but fully substituting the wrong words, with "not" becoming "rot" and "now" becoming "then." But while there is no need to think about the "why" of typing, she would like to think about the big "why" in her life. Why am I doing this? Why am I here? For the past four years, she's been putting out fires at a job she picked because it was the first one that picked her, and the "why" has fallen to the wayside. She's beginning to think she's never made a single decision in her life.

She's ready for the "why."

Esme opens a beer.

When her mother died, there was no reason, and no matter how many times she asked why, why, why, there was no answer other than that, sometimes, there is no reason. Sometimes things just happen. And she spent her life trying to prove this wrong, to study cause and effect, to focus on things that made sense, and anytime something didn't, she would move on. Why bother if there is no why? Why did Marcus choose her? Don't ask the question. Why would he ever leave? He wouldn't. Moving on. Why did she work at a job that made her wake up at ungodly hours in the morning? Why, indeed. It's easy enough to come up with answers and repeat them until you believe. It's not that she didn't believe her work was important. It's that she believed it was *too* important. That it was the only thing that mattered, because she didn't think to question it. If you see a fire, put it out. But how many fires do you have to put out before you stop to look around and see the man pouring gas on the tinder?

She'll go home and think about the "why" and the "how" and the "what next" all together. Yes, with time and space and a new job search. There must be something. She scrolls through the open job listings that have "unmapping" in the description. Hundreds of new jobs have been posted with this keyword in the past few days, most of which seem to be unrelated to the topic, but many are frantically seeking people to help deal with it all.

The night is cool on her tiny balcony and the beer tastes better than she expected. She peers at the can. It's an IPA, which she thought she hated, but the can says *wet hops* and maybe that's the difference. The air feels wobbly. A gentle wind makes the building sway. Or maybe it's Esme swaying, with her beer half drunk already. She closes her eyes and feels her body tilt back and forth. She breathes. She pulses. Her body readjusts itself to the gentle sways of balance. Something is always readjusting, re-finding the center. Life is churning. The river is flowing. Her thirst is increasing with every sip. She finishes the beer and goes in for another.

Arjun's in the kitchen, brewing a pot of coffee. His hair is wet and he's wearing Marcus's clothes: black jeans and a red V-neck T-shirt. The colors are flattering on him, if the hems are a bit long.

"There you are," he says. "Couldn't find you. I wanted to ask if it's okay for me to make coffee."

"I was on the balcony."

"Then I decided to claim it as payment for moving help."

"Of course," she says, "and do you want a beer, too?"

"I'm good with coffee. You want?"

"At this hour?"

"The night is young and we have more packing to do."

"God, you're so good."

"Yes. I'm an excellent packer."

The red V-neck shows off a smooth, dark chest. The pants, though too long at the ankles, otherwise fit him just right. Marcus is slender from years of running. Arjun is slender naturally. His skin looks smooth. It glistens from the memory of water. His wet hair is slicked back away from his face, except for a single lock on his forehead. Esme resists the urge to tuck it behind his ear. "Let's take a break. You've already done a lot."

"Of course."

"Come join me on the balcony. I'll bring the beers, in case you change your mind."

"Then I'll bring two mugs of coffee, in case you do." She leads him to and through the balcony doorway, watching her reflection ripple on the glass like sunlight on a swimming pool.

"A little cramped out here," he says, setting one of the coffee mugs between his feet.

"Our balcony is so popular it's standing room only," says Esme. "That's what Marcus used to say."

She regrets saying his name.

"I knew he was alive this whole time," she says quietly. "I can't say how, but I just knew it. And yet, seeing him in person, I could hardly believe my eyes."

Arjun says, "Hmm," an encouragement for her to keep talking. She sips her beer. This one tastes better than the first. She checks the can to confirm it's the same beer. It is.

"It was like I saw him for the very first time. And I didn't like what I saw. A coward. He ran from me. He actually ran away. Like I'm some sort of monster." She turns the beer can around in her hands, letting her vision unfocus. "The look in his eyes made me see myself, too. This sad, stupid woman. She's pathetic. She's so pathetic her boyfriend can't even break up with her without breaking her."

"Is that what you think?" asks Arjun. "Do you feel . . . broken?"

"No. But for a long time I thought I would be. I couldn't imagine a life without him. I didn't need to. Or I just didn't want to."

"And what do you imagine now?" he asks.

"I don't know." Esme's hand subconsciously touches the pocket where she usually keeps her phone. "I mean, earlier today I was sort of excited about all the possibilities. There are tons of remote jobs. I could find work anywhere. I could move to, I don't know, South America. I could move to Peru. Maybe I could move to Gleamwood City, to see where it all began."

"But you're moving to Virginia."

"For now. Who knows what after that. A lot of jobs are based in DC, which isn't too far from my dad's house, just a three-hour drive. There are a hundred think tanks and political action campaigns and congressional working groups and things like that. I didn't mind living there in college. In fact, some of the best years of my life were in DC. It felt like everybody moved there because they wanted to change the world in some way. Not just respond to it."

"You want to change the world?"

"I don't know. I just wish I'd asked myself these questions earlier. I spent four years here in limbo. What a waste."

Arjun swallows a big gulp of coffee. Esme follows suit, draining the rest of her beer. She opens a third.

"I just wish I knew why he did it."

"Well," says Arjun. "I think you do know. You said so earlier. He didn't want to hurt you."

"I mean why did he dump me? Why did he get tired of me? Why didn't he just talk to me?"

"Why does anyone get broken up with? Why does anyone like one person and not another? I don't like a lot of people."

"Really? I thought you liked everyone. You're so friendly."

"No, I'm not."

"You were friendly right away when you met me."

"Because I liked you, stupid."

"I liked you, too," says Esme. When this new recruit showed up and started talking to her, he was so energetic it was hard not to like him. But she would have been just fine continuing to eat lunch on her own every day. Then he kept showing up, and she kept enjoying the conversation, and eventually, yes, she had begun to look forward to it, a constancy to her day, where she could reflect about her morning and whatever else was on her mind. While Marcus was complex in ways that drove her crazy with admiration or frustration, Arjun was a pure source of joy that filled a gap she didn't know existed.

Arjun says, "The other day, I got a Snapple cap that said,

'Think the best of people.' It was the first day they put me on the 911 phone lines."

"You were on the 911 phone lines?"

"I'm sure I told you that. It's when we overlapped in the office, days four through seven, before they put me back in the field." Esme tries to remember, but it feels like she just woke up from a deep sleep; those days are a blur. "Well, I was," he continues. "The first day on the phones, I got that Snapple from the vending machine. It was like it was a test. Think the best of people. That day I got maybe fifty calls that were a complete waste of my time, and I couldn't understand how people don't realize when they waste my time, they're hurting the people who need me more. Don't they understand that calling me to tell me about their day is going to make it take that much longer for me to send an ambulance to the guy with a heart attack?" He catches his breath. "But every time I got frustrated, I thought about Snapple. I tried to think the best of the people calling me. They were scared and didn't know what was happening. Do you understand why I'm telling you this?"

"Kind of."

"Maybe you should try thinking the best of Marcus."

"Why? Marcus knew what he was doing. He knew what was coming. He planned it. What else could explain his missing laptop? His missing wallet? I feel like such an idiot. Everything important was already gone. Somehow he knew it was coming and he planned the whole thing."

"Still. Perhaps he thought you would be better off not knowing what happened to him. That makes it a tragedy. You're Juliet of Romeo and Juliet. You're Ilsa of Rick and Ilsa. You're Mia of Brian and Mia."

"Brian and Mia?"

"*Fast and Furious.*"

"Oh. Didn't they end up together in the end?"

"Yes, but Paul Walker died. The point is, a tragic story is a lot better than getting dumped. Now you can say, 'Listen to this crazy story that nearly killed me but here I am.' A missing fiancé, never found. It's like you have one foot in the land beyond."

"You're putting a lot of words into his mouth and you don't even know him."

"Do any of them ring true?"

Esme shrugs. "Sometimes I think I didn't know him at all." This feeling has long been with her. The complete otherness of Marcus. He was always knee-deep in some new idea she only half understood. It excited her as she tried to catch up. But it meant she was blind to his running away. "I'd rather not think the best of him. I'd rather not think of him at all. I'd rather be happy. Like now. This is nice, being here with you."

"Really?"

"Yes. This is nice. I'm having a good time." Saying the words makes them true. She's feeling rather wonderful. Two years of sharing a lunch table with Arjun and this is the first time she really feels like she's talking to him. But he was always easy to talk to, to laugh with about this and that. And he always radiated friendliness and kindness.

Perhaps there's something more, too. Yes—the way he looks in that V-neck T-shirt, in the dim moon on the balcony, she finds herself woozy with the realization: She's attracted to him. His body gives off a warm radiation. His eyelashes are long and thick and his skin is soft and his lips look softer and tonight, she's opened up and let him in.

He notices her staring at him, then looks away, as if caught. She takes a half step closer to him. "It's beautiful, right?" says

Esme. "We have a river view." They're in Manhattan on a small plaza east of FDR Drive, right next to the East River, and on the other side, where Queens meets Brooklyn, a row of short buildings stands before a line of skyscrapers, a counterfeit skyline. The small buildings are lit up, but the skyscrapers are dark, their glassy windows turned into mirrors for the stars. "This is the first time I've had a river view. Thank god the rivers don't move. Did you know the East River isn't really a river?"

"I did not know that."

"It's a tidal strait."

"What's the difference?"

"I don't know!"

"I'll look it up." Arjun pulls out his phone.

"Before the Unmapping," says Esme, feeling dreamy, "we were a block away from the Hudson. Every day since, we've turned up half a block closer to the East River. A half block farther east each day, easter and easter. Like Easter! We rise again."

Arjun looks wary and puts his phone away. "But there's nowhere farther east to go."

"I imagine we'll jump across the river to Brooklyn next. I've always wanted to be cool enough to live in Brooklyn." She takes a sip of beer. "I'm on my way with this IPA. I used to think they were gross. I thought that's what made them popular. Like hazing. It gets you into the cool club. Hey, it's hazy!" She laughs, feeling light and lifted. "Am I cool enough for Brooklyn yet?"

"How far exactly has the building moved each day?"

"Half a block east. Just about."

"So in one more day, that would bring us to the center of the East River."

"It doesn't work like that. Everything tends to map to where it fits. Piers map onto piers. Sidewalks to sidewalks. Foundations to foundations. So like I said, it'll bring us to Brooklyn. That is, if this pattern holds. I'm sure it's just random. Everything is random! There's no meaning to anything!"

He says something mumbled—Esme catches the words "tends to"—and grabs the second coffee mug, which is shaped like a disco ball and glints in the light. A gift Marcus brought home from some crackpot convention called Cosmic Summit. Arjun drinks deeply.

"I just have to tell you," she says, "I feel absolutely wonderful right now. My life may be ruined, but I feel amazing. Why is that? Why am I so happy?" There is a joy running through her like lightning through a wire. It makes her feet feel light. It makes her hands feel like dancing. She wishes she had some music.

"Maybe it's the river view," he says quietly. "Maybe it's the beer."

"Yeah." She takes a step closer to him, still looking out at the river. "Maybe. Or maybe it's something else." She turns her gaze to him. He doesn't meet her eyes.

"What?"

"You've opened me up," she says. "You've cracked me open."

He still doesn't meet her gaze. She wants him to kiss her but he doesn't. She hears him breathing heavily as he stares at the river in concentration, his fingers dancing wildly on his coffee cup. She looks out at the river and takes another step closer. She wants nothing more at that moment than to feel his lips on hers, to discover their softness. His hand on her waist. Around her waist. Those fingers going wild on his mug. What else could they do? She imagines his fingers on her body. Imagines them down there. She has slept with only one man. These memories need to be replaced with something new. Someone new. His eyes look so serious. He still hasn't kissed her.

"Can I just . . ." she says, not knowing what to say next.

But her body knows; it brings her forward to kiss him, softly on the lips, which remain closed for a moment, then open, then he puts a hand on the back of her neck and brings her in, her mouth with his, his tongue dripping with bitter coffee, and his lips exploring every part of hers, discovering, and for a minute, she is not herself, she has lost herself, and she doesn't care.

◆ ◆ ◆

Is the newsman a newsman anymore? The *Gleamwood City Weekly* is on hiatus. First there were issues with the printer, and then issues with the software, and now everything is on hold. So who's writing the news? And who is he without it? But the news in Gleamwood City has never been that new. Always he's been churning out more of the same. Another lost cat. Another update from Management. Another testimonial about the monthly open mic. And now there is real news. Scientists have been coming from all over the world to study the Unmapping. They've been trying to track the movements of the city's buildings. Their efforts, so far, have been a total failure. The scientists tried pinning up color-coded signs on each house, but the company sent a strongly worded email suggesting that all workers should take them down if they'd like to keep their jobs and homes. Then the scientists tried taking fingerprints of the roofs, but the satellite footage was always somehow blurry. Management made clear that they couldn't kick the scientists out, but they could make their jobs as challenging as possible. Most scientists ended up leaving in frustration. But a few stayed.

The newsman asks them questions. Mostly they complain about how frustrating it is to work here. ("Don't they realize

that the more they shut us out, the longer we'll need to stay?")
The newsman asks why they care, when there are so many other
unmapped cities they could study. "Gleamwood City is ground
zero," they say. "If this is where it all began, this might be where
it ends." He asks them what they've found so far, and the scientists are cagey, until finally they make an admission: not much.
The roadblocks thrown up by management have made it difficult to gather data, and the paltry information they've been able
to glean has either contradicted itself or shown no pattern no
matter how many different ways it's sliced and diced. But the
scientists have noticed a few odd things. The trees in the forest
seem a little funny. It's something they can't explain. Something
about the smell, maybe. Or the way they stand so utterly still,
no matter the breeze. One scientist has bored a core sample
to find that it has no rings. "A tree with no rings? Why would
that be?" the scientist asks the newsman. "And why is everyone
wearing red coveralls?"

Why, indeed. The founder's son, Franz, has worn a red boilersuit since the day he learned he could dress himself. When he
was little, he said he liked the color; when he was older, it became an act of solidarity with the metalworkers. So what if he
inspired others to also wear them? These boilersuits are good all
year round. Breathable and layerable. The newsman tried one on
once. But he decided red wasn't his color. It brought out the red
in his nose and made him feel like a reindeer.

"I'm the one asking questions," says the newsman. "You
tell me."

But the scientist persists. "Why do the people in red sleep in
tents at night? I thought everyone here has a house built to their
desires?"

That's new, since the Unmapping. Or did it start earlier?

He can't remember. All sorts of people like camping in various places. It's not his concern. "Why do you sleep in a trailer?"

"And why do they sleep at the foot of the town Christmas tree at noon every day? And why do they walk everywhere holding hands?"

"They what?" The newsman isn't aware of this. He's usually waking up from his late-morning nap at noon, and lately, he's been staying at his house nearly the whole day through.

"You know, the famous aluminum tree in the center of town, where the CEO gives a speech every year, or a sermon, or whatever. The Christmas tree that's up all year round."

"Of course I know that tree." But he didn't know people are napping there. Or that they're holding hands. That's not in any of the city rituals. "Who cares about a nap? Maybe you need a nap."

"And are they connected to the 'Red Cloak' cults springing up around the country? Were they the first? Do they think the TruTrees caused the Unmapping, and if so, why?"

The newsman brushes him off and returns home. He types *red cloak cult* into his browser but nothing comes up in the search results. He assumes the scientist was making something up to jar him. But why? But he drives into his favorite café in Manitowoc and searches on the internet there. A thousand results show. All these cities are complaining about people disappearing from home to join the ranks of those in red.

A story is here. A real story. He spends the drive home thinking of all the questions he'll ask, all the ways he'll interview the so-called Red Cloaks, the big story he'll break.

But when he arrives home, he forgets all about it.

His house is surrounded by cars from Management. Three people stand by the front door, holding clipboards, while a dozen or more are inside, carrying items out to the curb.

"What's the meaning of this?" he asks.

They tell him they're shutting his paper down for good. The newsman needs to leave.

"Go where?" he asks.

Not their problem.

Two decades now he's lived in Gleamwood City, loved Gleamwood City, found freedom in Gleamwood City. And he fought hard to get here, with ten sets of interviews. Even after interviewing, most people had to wait several years before a spot opened up. The newsman got lucky. He applied just when they were starting their own weekly newspaper and needed a man at the helm.

And now he has to leave.

"But my car," he says, watching someone from Management drive off with it. "How do you expect me to get anywhere?"

Not their problem. It's a company car. He's had it so long he forgot. It's the same with many of his belongings. The television, hunting rifle, computer, phone, and rocking chair. All technically borrowed until the end of his time here, which never bothered him, because he thought he'd die here. They'd told him he'd be able to retire with a great pension and endless free time. Not that he wants to. The day he stops writing will be the day he's ready to take his final breath.

Not yet.

So he puts some clothes and a spare notebook and pen into a backpack and begins walking.

It's a five-hour walk to the nearest town, and the newsman is fine with that. It's a lovely day, too warm for November, but that's been the norm these days, and a balmy fifty degrees allows him to walk without a jacket. It feels like spring. The birds are singing, ducks quacking, finches fucking. Even the owls that should be sleeping are hooting out their joy. He isn't that mad to be leaving. It always felt like he lucked into living here, like it was better than he deserved. After a world of turmoil he wanted stability, and in his twenty years in Gleamwood City, not one thing changed. At least before the Unmapping. But now he thinks there might be something strange about it. For instance, why does no one have children? As far as the newsman knows, the founder's son was the first and only child ever to set foot in Gleamwood City. Just as quick, he answers his question: Children mean change, and the whole idea of this place is to keep things the same. Gleamwood City was founded to keep trees in the ground. Or the idea of them. While Franz was off sailing the world, or holed up in his bedroom, the management team pushed forward with new ideas to keep up with the times but from the same heart, replacing the aluminum trees with plastic, and plastic with the immortal TruTree.

But change is inevitable.

When you don't have children, you die, and who's left?

They bring in more workers. Always there are more people who want to come. Yet the town never builds new homes. What happens to the old? What happens when people retire? He was told they would treat him well in retirement, but there was nothing in the paperwork. He never got to know anyone well enough to wonder, well enough to say goodbye. Everyone's congenial, but no one sticks around long enough for a real conversation before their next activity. Again, that was always fine for the newsman, who was happy to jump from story to story, along with his first and closest companion: the Truth.

At least, one little piece of Truth.

Sure, you can't know everything about everything. Anyone who thinks they do—unless their name is Albert H. Einstein—is delusional. He's been happy enough knowing a little bit about a little bit and keeping his head down for the rest of it.

But there certainly are a lot of strange things happening lately, now that he's thinking about it.

Like the aluminum tree outside his house.

Not bought, not brought, but sprouted that morning. He tried pulling it out and a whole array of aluminum roots came up. A practical joke. A strange send-off.

But who put it there? He'll never know. Because he's leaving forever, walking along the spiral road out of town, to get to the main thoroughfare, where perhaps a kind driver will offer him a hitch. He's on his own, if you don't count the breeze that carries an owl's hoots through the trees.

He's nearly reached the city boundary now. He pauses before he gets any closer. It looks like a tollbooth, only instead of asking for money they ask for information as they check you in and out of the city.

"You don't want to leave," says a high-pitched voice from behind a tree somewhere.

The newsman nearly jumps out of his skin. He looks around and sees a boy sitting cross-legged on the ground, half hidden in the underbrush.

Not a boy. A very short old man. The man is dressed from head to toe in the red boilersuit that Franz made popular, and his face is covered by a fisher's hat with a neck flap and nylon face covering. But he can see the eyes, which are old and wrinkled.

It almost looks like . . .

"Franz?"

The son of the founder of Gleamwood City nods. "The one and only," he says in a lower voice, one that the newsman recognizes from his yearly jaunts to the town Christmas tree. Hearing it now, it seems fake. Franz seems to confirm this by returning to his higher register when he says, "Unless I'm just someone who looks like Franz. How would you know the difference?"

"No one else is nearly as short as you. No offense."

"Wait a moment," says Franz. He puts on precarious-looking platform shoes and unrolls his pants to reach the ground, and when he stands up straight, he's the newsman's height. "See? I'm not short."

"I'm not joining," says the newsman.

"What do you mean?" asks Franz.

"I'm not joining your cult. Or whatever it is."

"Cult?"

"Your red people sleeping at the foot of the tree. I heard about you. I don't know what you're selling, but I'm not interested."

"I'm not selling anything."

"Then what do you want?"

"I want to know why you're leaving."

"Why I'm leaving?"

"Yes."

The newsman sighs and sits down. "I wish I knew." And just like that he's telling the old man everything. He's often been on the other side of this equation; he knows how easy it can be to get someone to open up. All you have to do is ask them question after question, getting deeper into the things that make them smile, and then, when you're in deep, weave in the questions you're looking for, so gently they don't realize they've begun telling you their deepest secrets. Don't worry about why I'm here. Just tell me where you grew up. Did you like it? Do you like it now? What's it like? He could always feel when the moment presented itself for a real question, a real answer. It's something he could never explain, but when it happened, he knew. And now he is fully aware that he's on the other side of things, telling this old man more than he'd care to, but he finds himself enjoying it. It's nice. For twenty years, he's only asked questions. He hasn't done much talking. After an hour of talking, maybe more, the newsman feels energized. But he's also hungry. He pauses to retrieve a piece of beef jerky from his backpack.

"Lunchtime," he announces. "Want some?"

"No, thank you. There's a good hot meal waiting for me back in town. Cream of tomato soup and freshly baked rosemary bread."

The newsman takes a bite of beef jerky. It's drier than he thought it would be, and he's already drained his water. "That sounds good."

"Would you like to join us?"

"Who's this 'us'?"

"I believe you know."

"Your little red cult."

"Some have called it that. I just call them my friends."

"The answer is no."

"How about this. You're a journalist, right? Why don't I tell you everything I know about Gleamwood City and my friends."

"Really? Everything you know?"

"Everything I know."

"How will I know what you're saying is true?"

"How do you ever know?"

"I'm kicked out of Gleamwood City. I'm not supposed to be here."

"I have a plan for that."

Franz instructs the newsman to walk through the checkpoint, give them his name, then turn right when he can't see it any longer and circle back through the woods. "Easy," Franz says.

"Once you're in the system as gone, they won't care about you. They'll forget about you."

The newsman does as directed, with fear in his throat as he speaks as casually as he can with the tollbooth woman. But she looks completely unflustered, even when the newsman briefly forgets his name. "I'm not coming back," he says. "This is it for me." The tollbooth worker nods and waves him off with a smile. When he's made it around a bend, he says to nobody, "Think I'll take a quick piss," and goes into the woods.

He finds Franz just where he left him, sitting on the ground and picking his fingernails. "Well?"

"Easy as blueberry pie."

Franz springs up to stand. "Off we go, then."

"Go where?"

"Anywhere. I talk better while I walk. Isn't it beautiful here? I know you agree." They start weaving along an overgrown trail.

"So let's hear it," says the newsman.

"Where do you want me to start?"

"Try the beginning."

Franz tells the newsman that he hated growing up here. He hated that he was expected to be grateful for the world he'd inherited—along with the fact that he was discouraged from making any changes or any decisions whatsoever. "They told me it was a utopia," he says. "It was my father's dream and he made it a reality. I remember being disconcerted when they said that. *My father's dream.* This was all supposed to be my father's vision. Not mine. Not anyone else's. And yet they all acted like it was the most natural thing. To live in someone else's dream. But that's the problem with dreams. Only the dream's dreamer can truly understand it. Have you ever had a nightmare?"

"I don't dream."

Franz laughs. "Right."

"I mean it. Maybe when I was a kid. Maybe."

"Well. We'll have to get back to that. The point is, Management distorted my father's dream. For instance, I don't think he would have meant for me to be trapped here while I was growing up. But I was. The trustee wouldn't let me go anywhere, and whenever I tried to run off, security caught me. I learned they'd let me sail within eyeshot of Gleamwood City, but any farther and they'd send out their motorboats. I wasn't just trapped. I had no power. I was completely at the whim of the trustee. And that's just one way they compromised my father's vision."

"I always heard you called the shots. That you controlled the CEO."

"That's what they wanted you to think. It's a much better story, a much more fun story—little kid CEO!—than the truth: They'd been trying to control me since the day my dad died. Because, yes, I still technically owned half the shares—at least, the trustee did. And everyone was terrified about what I'd do with the company when I turned eighteen and could finally access my inheritance. I kept telling them I didn't want to control the company; I never wanted it—and they'd just tighten their control, imagining some secret plot. I can't say why they acted the way they did. Only that their actions only ever put us increasingly at odds."

The newsman wasn't sure what this had to do with anything, but sometimes you had to let your interviewee just talk until you got there. Franz pushed through a bush and held the branches back for the newsman. "Careful here—these branches are prickly. There. What was I saying?"

"You versus Management."

"Right. The point was—the dream. My father's dream. He

loved trees, nature, the simplicities of life. Let's start with simplicity. Management took that word to mean that everything should be the same, so they built every house the same and hired every worker to be the same. You can kind of understand their logic. The opposite of simplicity is complexity. The opposite of complexity is homogeneity. But in this case, *a* does not equal *c*. I don't believe sameness is what my father wanted. The woods are the opposite of homogeneous. Look down at your feet. What do you see?"

"Some grass. Shrubs. And that's a fern, right?"

"Yes it's a fern. What kind?"

"I'm more of a tree guy."

"Do you know how many kinds of fern are in this forest? How many different shrubs? That right there is a maidenhair fern, and right next to it is the Christmas fern. My favorite, if we see it, is the interrupted fern. Wait—just behind that shrub!" Franz leaps into the bushes and calls out, "You coming?" The newsman follows—walking through a spiderweb—to see Franz caressing a junglelike plant that's just as tall as he is. "You understand why it's called the 'interrupted fern'?"

Sure enough, halfway down each frond, the leaflets disappear and are replaced by brown wormlike things.

"It's interrupted by that ugly grub."

"This is the most important part of the fern! These are the spore-bearing leaflets. This is its future, 'ugly' as it may be—this is everything it has been working for."

The newsman feels embarrassed.

"The point is, there is no sameness in nature. And everything they've been doing has taken us down the wrong path from the beginning. Such sameness can make a man go mad. It's no wonder they broke reality."

They broke reality? But Franz doesn't follow up on that; he stops talking and heads back to the main trail. The newsman follows silently, knowing he's about to learn everything. That old man is working himself up to it. The newsman knows how to wait. He finds himself wishing he had a recording device. Then realizes that, no, what matters most is the Truth, no matter who else hears it.

"It's the trees," says Franz.

"The trees," says the newsman.

"It's the TruTrees. You know how they're made? They're made out of actual wood pulp. And oil resin and a whole lot of other stuff, chemicals that I can't pronounce, but I do know the jury's still out on whether they cause cancer. But that's beside the point. They're made out of real trees! I can't tell you how I've complained about this. The whole point is to preserve trees. Not cut them down and put them in a blender with cancer-causing chemicals! But Management says everything they produce takes materials, and the TruTrees are still immortal, therefore in line with my father's vision of reducing clear-cutting. 'Immortal.' You hear that? Immortal! They think they're gods. The more we try to simulate nature, to print it in a factory, the further away we get." Franz stops walking, crouches down, and picks up a handful of soil, uncovering a warren of worms. "To immortalize a tree is to blaspheme it. That's what it is. I don't believe in God but I do believe in Nature, like my father, and we've blasphemed. We created something we shouldn't have. Something that defies the laws of nature. And now here we are. One thing leads to another. Nature's laws have been broken. We created something terrible, and now there's chaos in every major city in America. Soon, the world."

"That's a rather simple thing to say," says the newsman,

though in truth, he is a little confused. "So the TruTrees caused the Unmapping?"

"For a long time," Franz says, walking again, "I thought there was something very wrong with this place. But I couldn't say what. Only that I was miserable. My sole respite was sleep. It was my dreams. No matter how boring the day might be, the dreams were always exciting. I even liked the nightmares. They felt like a test of character. But usually, they were wonderful. I won't bore you with the details. But I was obsessed with writing down my dreams. I'd wake up in the middle of the night three times and write them down. I lived many lives in my head while I was trapped in my room with my trustee growling down my neck. I didn't realize, but I was teaching myself to lucid dream. It was all I had."

"Until you turned eighteen."

"Pardon?"

"Then you got everything. Right? Your inheritance."

"Yes. I told you I didn't want it, though. I took out enough money to fund my sailing trip and I left as soon as I could. My god, the things I saw. I wanted to see how other people lived. I went to Russia to live in the snow. I went to India to live in a slum. I went to Vanuatu to live in a forest. When I went to Tibet and stayed with Buddhist monks, they taught me about lucid dreaming. That was my place. I stayed there for years. It's where I recognized what I already knew."

"What did you already know?"

"That reality is a dream, and at the same time, your dreams spill over into reality. Like, for example, in my lucid dreams, I would practice sailing, and I truly felt myself improve. In dreams, I practiced sailing through rogue waves and hellish winds. And when I took to the waters, the real waters in waking life, my body knew what to do." Franz stops walking. "Dreaming helped me live. Dreaming helped me see."

"See what?"

"How to fix Gleamwood City." Franz's eyes are fixated on some point in the middle distance, as if the answer can be found beneath a bush or under the wings of a moth.

"Right."

"But by the time I returned, it was too late. The management team had bought me out. The trustee claimed he'd gotten word that I died, and he sold my shares to Management. They pretended it was all a misunderstanding and that I would have standing on the board, and they threw me a huge party to celebrate my return; they pretended to love me. But that's the thing about pretending. We can pretend our TruTrees are real trees. They can pretend to love me. But I can tell the difference. You can always tell."

"Aren't you pretending in those lucid dreams of yours? They're not real."

"Lucid dreaming is the most honest thing you can do. When you dream, you can't help but face all the things you hide from yourself. The question is, are you prepared to face them? To best them? What are you hiding?"

"Me?" says the newsman.

"Yes, you," says Franz. "Who else would I be talking to?"

"Nothing. You know about my past."

"But what are you hiding from now? When you have nightmares, what are they about?" Franz stares at him with intensity. The newsman feels like he's pinned to a wall with a thumbtack so he can be better examined.

"I just told you. I never remember my dreams."

"So you say. You have this entire world inside you that you're ignoring."

"I like reality just fine."

"Do you? In reality, Gleamwood City has been spinning out of control. All starting with those fake trees pretending to be real. Those blasphemous TruTrees. I started to see them in the forest. I started to see them everywhere. I *smelled* them everywhere. I picked a couple pine needles and smelled them and the scent was correct but too strong. They smelled so . . . much. Like this smell was hiding something. Or attacking something. I took a core sample and found no tree rings. And on top of that, the hole I'd made in the tree disappeared the next day. I thought maybe I'd dreamed it. So I tied a ribbon around the tree's lowest branch and looked at it hard and blinked five times and said, 'Remember this. I am awake.' And yet the next day, that was gone, too. Fine, I thought, some animal took it, or maybe a hiker who wanted a clear view free of human influence. But I found that same ribbon on a different tree on the other side of town. And elsewhere, a tree with a round hole from an increment borer, and when I sampled it, I again saw no rings." When he finishes, he takes a deep breath, as if he'd just emerged from underwater.

"A little strange, but what's that got to do with anything?"

"Everything! Aren't you listening?"

"I'm doing my best."

Franz takes a deep breath, as if preparing his voice for the final note of a song. "Our TruTrees started replacing the real trees in the woods, and then they started replacing each other. They were so interchangeable, they became unidentifiable. They lost all sense of distinctiveness. Even their location. The location didn't matter anymore. They would switch one with the other, like they were jumping between worlds. I did more tests to confirm this. More ribbons. And notches in the tree trunks. I tied my shoelaces to the top of a tree. I trimmed the branches into patterns. I sculpted my father's face into the wood. Anything I could. And it kept getting worse. Then the same thing started happening with our houses. You know all the houses we built here are identical, right? Not just that they were built from the same blueprint. Everything about them is completely identical. The paint colors. The accessories. The decorative duck-themed throw pillows—"

"I picked out those pillows—"

"No, you didn't. The people who come here all have the same taste. That's the trick. They know what you'll want, and they show you the plan, and then they show you the crappy alternatives, and you pick the one they want you to pick. It didn't bother me when I slept in the tower. But when I started making friends again, I'd go to their houses and get completely lost. They didn't seem to realize anything was off until I told them. Then they noticed it, too. It started to drive me crazy. So I left. I took off by boat and got out of here."

"You mean when you were eighteen and sailed the world?"

"No. I mean, yes, I did that. But more recently, too. I sailed to Manitowoc because it was the first place I could escape to. But while I was there, I noticed our TruTrees in every shop window. It would come for them soon, I knew it. So I warned them. Then I sailed to every city on the shore of Lake Michigan, all our best clients, warning them, too. I sailed through each of the Great Lakes, all the way to the Atlantic. There I turned south and went down the East Coast, to New York City, Ocean City, and all the way down to Mexico. I've been helping people prepare. I knew what would happen. And I know how to stop it."

There is an energy to this little old man that the newsman hasn't felt in a long time. Still. The newsman doesn't believe a single word this man has said. "Oh yeah? Prepare how? How exactly does one prepare for this?"

"It's complicated."

"Sure. Of course it is. Are you telling everyone to take a bunch of naps? That's the only thing I know about your red-cloaked friends."

"They're taking their lives into their own hands."

"By sleeping?"

"That's just one side of it."

"Sounds like you've been busy."

"Sure have."

"But now you're back."

"Now I'm back."

"And you know how to end the Unmapping."

Franz says yes casually, as if he were being asked whether or not he ate breakfast that morning.

"I suppose you want me to ask you how," says the newsman.

"Not really. I know you won't believe me."

"You're right. See, here's where your story falls apart. You're telling me you sailed to Manitowoc, to every city you could reach on Lake Michigan, to New York City, and down the East Coast. And, presumably, you returned from this trip. All in the past three and a half months? Sorry, bud, but it doesn't hold up."

"I left after what you call 'the Unmapping' first came for our houses. This was nearly two years ago."

"Two years? It's been three months!"

"Three months since you've seen it, then. I'll give my father something. He built a resilient town. It can handle mixing up without seeming like anything is wrong at all."

"And I saw you last Christmas!"

"Are you sure? Or did you see another old man in a red suit? Tell me, was he wearing a hat? Could you see his face?"

"This just can't be true. For the past two years, minus the

past three months, my house has been sitting exactly where it should. I remember exactly the day it happened. It was the day after I met with a neighbor named Joe. I was interviewing him about our new gutter-cleaning system. And he told me about the trees that dropped big, thick walnuts into his downspout, which confused him, because there were no walnut trees around. I went to check my own gutters and found them stuffed with helicopter seeds from my maples. But the next day, it was different. My maples had been replaced with sycamores. Then I realized it wasn't the trees that moved, but my house. I drove that spiral road and got to the edge quicker than I should have. That was the first day something was wrong. That was the first day anything changed."

"Well." Franz thinks for a moment about this. "This was the day after your interview with Joe?"

"Yes. And haven't you been locked in your bedroom for years? You're telling me you're out and talking to all these people, you're sailing to the ocean and back? You only leave your room on Christmas Day."

"So the story goes," he laughs, coming back to himself. "Which Management has fed you well."

"I—"

"Always felt like you were making your own decisions and writing your own stories, didn't you? Tell me, am I currently locked in my bedroom?"

"Well—"

"Would you believe Management always mocked up what the next week's paper should cover, and they were right every time?"

"I—"

"You only ever got information they wanted you to have."

"Maybe it was predictable because this is a predictable town."

"Nothing's perfectly predictable. Not like that. And what

happened when you started sharing real news? Once you started investigating? They shut you down."

"They let me write about the Unmapping in the *Gleamwood City Weekly*, though."

"Did they?"

"Well, I wrote about it when it first happened without any consequences or anything like that."

"Sure, but wouldn't you say it had a certain tone? A jokey, everything's fine sort of tone, in line with their vision. What if you tried pushing the envelope? What if you tried to break the mold?"

"I—"

"You were hired because you never questioned anything. You think of yourself as some great seeker of truth. You're deluded. You thought you were above it all back at the *Post* when you got that assignment you didn't believe in. But you did it anyway. Then you blamed your editor when it was all you. Are you going to listen to what people tell you your whole life? Or are you ever going to make a decision for yourself?"

The newsman doesn't know how to answer that.

"I don't know about you," says Franz, "but I got tired of trying to fit into some rigid vision. I wanted to go undercover. To pretend I was someone else. Then, at least, I wouldn't be doing what they predict. Pretty easy, with these outfits we give to the workers down in smelting. It was years ago, now, when I first went undercover. Before I thought anything was wrong. In fact, I finally learned to love this city before I realized anything was wrong. You have to really look at a place, for a long time, to see it clear."

"I guess."

"I know the opposite is also true. I'm guessing it's that way with you. You loved this place so hard you turned blind."

The newsman looks around now, through the eye opening

in Franz's fisher hat, as if he will somehow see what he is talking about. Blind? He can see just fine. He knows these trees well. Sugar maple, basswood, paper birch.

They walk in silence until their meandering path leads to a clearing. There Franz grabs the newsman's arm, gesturing for him to stop. The newsman looks out to see a cliffside campsite. There's a great bonfire surrounded by two dozen people in red suits. Their own hats have been pulled up to their hairlines as they eat from bowls in their laps.

"So this is it," says the newsman. "This is you asking me to join you."

"Yes."

"Isn't it ironic that you're telling me to listen to myself, but also telling me to listen to you?"

"Yes. Yes it is. But at least I'm giving you a choice. Or clarifying that you always had one. You could always say no. You've lived your life never saying no."

He recognizes the others. He doesn't know them well but he's sure he's seen them around town before. They look happy in a way he's not used to. Not the placid contentment of life in Gleamwood City. Like something bigger is moving them. They are eating with a ravenous hunger, laughing and joking with equal fervor.

"I can say no to you. I can walk away and never come back."

"Yes, you can. But will you?"

Franz holds out a red suit.

◆   ◆   ◆

Esme and Arjun are kissing on the side of the two-person balcony. She pushes her chest into his, and he wraps his arms tightly around her. She can feel how much he wants her and that makes her want him more. She hasn't kissed anyone like this in all her life. Needing to push herself all the way inside him. Like her body will meld with his . . .

"Stop pushing!" he cries out suddenly.

She pulls back. "Was I pushing?"

"I could have fallen!"

"I'm the one closer to the edge of the balcony."

"I could have fallen sideways! I hate it out here!"

"Okay! I'm sorry. Really? You hate it?"

"I feel like this building keeps moving. It doesn't want to stay still."

"It does that. It's very tall. But sturdy, I promise. A building this tall, you need it to be able to move with the wind. See? Like this." Esme sways her hips back and forth, making her realize how very drunk she is. She laughs, then leans in to kiss him again. He pulls away.

"Can we go inside?"

"Of course." She grabs her beer, but it's empty already. When did that happen? She slides open the balcony door, walks into the living room, and collapses on the couch. "Come sit on the couch with me."

He sits as far as he can on the other side of the couch with his coffee cup gripped tightly in his hands.

"Are you okay?" she asks.

"Yes. Fine. Just a little freaked out, I guess."

"By me?"

"No. Yes. No, definitely not. By the height. I get vertigo."

"I didn't know." Esme moves closer to him on the couch. "Are you okay now?"

"Yes," he says without looking.

She puts her hand on his cheek and tilts his head toward her. "How about now?"

"Yes," he says. She kisses him again. He eases into it, pulling his left arm around her, and up into her hair. It makes her want to put her own hands all over him, on his shirt, up inside it, nails digging into his back. Her hand skims over his pants and briefly she feels his stiffness. "You know," she whispers, "I've only ever been with one person. I've always wondered—"

"No." He pushes her away. He's still holding his empty disco ball mug of coffee.

"What's wrong?"

"I don't know."

Esme sits up and crosses her arms on her chest. "I thought you wanted this. Do you want this?"

"I did! I do. I just . . ." He stands up. His hands are shaking, holding that empty mug. "I drank too much coffee. I don't know what's wrong."

"Do you want a beer? Would that help?"

"Why are you doing this?"

"Why?" She doesn't know how to answer that. "Because I'm having a good time. Because I like you. I thought you liked me, too."

"Of course I like you, Esme. I love you."

The words sit in the air like a storm cloud.

"What?" she says softly, although she heard every word.

"And now you're using me," he adds. "And tomorrow you're leaving me."

"Love?" she says. The word feels strange coming from her mouth, as if, like water vapor hanging in the air on a cold day, she can see it before her, a diaphanous cloud.

"Yes! Has it not been obvious for the past two years?"

Esme doesn't respond.

"And I thought I meant something to you, too," he continues. "And now you're telling me all your time here was a complete waste. That's what you said. A waste."

"I didn't mean *you*—"

"Right. You didn't think about me once."

Esme stands up now. Her brain takes a moment to catch up. The world spins and settles back into place. She repeats everything he just said in her head, then realizes: She's angry. "I'm sorry that you were in love with someone with a fiancé. What did you think would happen? That I was going to leave someone I had committed to for life, just because we had a few fun lunchtime conversations?"

"It was more than a few lunchtime conversations. It was every single day I was in the office."

"I mean, god, Arjun, we've hardly had a real conversation until tonight. We talked about fun stuff. Light stuff. And I enjoyed it. I also enjoyed getting deep into things tonight. But I'm sorry you were apparently imagining me in love with you all this time, without actually trying to get to know me. Fuck. I'm so drunk." And dizzy. The world spins before her eyes.

"What's a 'real' conversation? You're saying all our conversations have been fake?"

"Not fake. Just . . . light."

"I tried asking tough questions. What's going on with Marcus? What's going on with your father? You skirted around the questions, and not once did you ask them of me. But I learned about you either way. I learned your moods and all the things you like and don't like. I learned how to read between the edges. It's all I had. And it was enough."

Esme softens. "I'm sorry. I guess I just . . . I had Marcus." She leans against the wall.

"Please don't say that name." Arjun picks up a couch cushion and hugs it to his chest.

"I'm sorry," Esme says again, stumbling to the floor. The world is turning, and with it, memories from the past two years with Arjun come circling in. She closes her eyes. Did she know it this whole time? Does he really love her? How is that possible? Why is the world still turning? Oh, that's why. Her stomach wants to leap through her throat. But not from love. She tastes her dinner mixed with acid on the back of her tongue. She tastes three hoppy beers. Esme runs for the bathroom to let herself go.

18

Arjun's hands won't stop shaking. Esme is vomiting in the bathroom and his hands won't stop shaking. He tells them to stop and they don't stop. He grips them one in the other and then he's just shaking his own hand. Where is that clonazepam? He searches through his backpack, opening it zigzaggedly. There's his blue work polo. His water bottle. His wallet. His Taj Mahal snow globe. His granola bars that have melted stickiness through a rip in the packaging. The pills aren't there. He empties his backpack onto the floor and sorts through everything, shaking it out and putting it back. The pills are gone.

It's long past the time for his evening pill and they're gone. And he drank two strong cups of coffee. Stupid, stupid. The first cup made him feel great. The first half of the second cup made him feel even greater. The second half of the second cup made him feel like his head might explode. Glumly he gives his snow globe a shake, but his eyes are moving too fast to watch the flakes calmly drift down. He puts everything away.

The problem is they are up so very high. Standing on that balcony earlier with Esme, he had imagined himself falling into the river, over and over, and each time he imagined it, it became more real, until it felt almost like an inevitability, something he

should just get over with so he wouldn't keep torturing himself—
no. Even now, while he's safely sprawled on the couch, gripping
its fabric, he feels as if he's barely hanging on. When Esme tried
to comfort him about the building's sway, it didn't help. When he
remembers what she said about the building's trajectory, a cold
feeling seizes his chest. He could see himself fall. He is high. Too
high.

And yet he feels so low. Two years of pining after Esme and
when something finally happens between them, it's all wrong.
Worse than wrong. It's a disaster. First, she confirms that she
hardly thought of him, that she never even wondered about him,
that he means nothing to her. Then she kisses him to get over
Marcus. Then she pukes from drunkenness. Yes, the kiss was
nice at first, but it was a drunken kiss, nothing real. Little Arjun,
getting kissed by drunken Esme, who then ran off to puke her
guts out, who probably won't remember in the morning, who will
forget him fully like he never existed.

Arjun needs to do something with this feral energy that's
now spread from his fingers to his legs, so he continues packing
up her apartment. He half notices as she crawls from the bathroom to the bedroom and moans. Let her moan. Three beers?
Three beers and this happens? He goes into the kitchen and examines the cans. They are nine percent alcohol. Still. He considers opening a can for himself but thinks better of it, then thinks
better of thinking better of it and cracks open a can, tips his chin
back, and lets the golden liquid flow down his throat. He wills
his body to calm. That doesn't happen with the first sip. Nor the
second. Now the beer is gone, minus the three drops dripping
down his chin, and he's woozy as he puts ceramic bowls in an
air purifier box, letting them clang all over each other, half hoping one will break. He unfolds a different box, which advertises a

lawn mower. In go the pots, metal on metal. *Bam bam bam.* He needs his clonazepam. His precious little pill. Where is it? Gone! Probably flushed down the toilet. Or stolen by the cops for a little cop party. His father has already tried flushing it away. When that happened, Arjun just got a refill from his doctor, although it took more than a little begging, both of his father and of the doctor, because the doctor needed the father to go on record about his wastefulness. "What have I done wrong?" his father asks. "How have I failed you? First the car, which I can understand. Boys will be boys, and boys love cars. But this? This? Am I so terrible that you need drugs to live with me?" Arjun's father is a man of thinning hair that he keeps trimmed and combed back, but an imposing and handsome face. He wears expensive suits with colorful ties, often purple or lime green, something to be remembered. Arjun wishes his father would be either taller than him or shorter, so Arjun could avoid his gaze, but they are of equal height, their eyes so close together when his father yells, face-to-face, that he thinks their eyelashes might brush one another's. Arjun started taking clonazepam during college, prescribed in his second year after his fifth anxiety attack. "What is your body telling you?" asks his father, whenever they have this fight, which is often. "Why don't you listen? Why smother it with drugs?"

"It's telling me that I need to stop having anxiety attacks!" Arjun yells back.

"Talk to me. Talk to yourself! Come to my yoga class."

"You think a little pranayama is going to save me?"

"How do you know if you don't try? You become a druggie and you think there's no other option?"

"I'm no druggie. I just want to get through the day."

"Sounds like a druggie to me!"

His mother is not much better. After his father first found out

about the clonazepam, she called Arjun on the phone to express
her disappointment. She even started crying. "We've failed you,"
she said. "We have one son and we failed him." Then his grandfather came on the phone to whisper, "You couldn't even hide
it? All you had to do was hide it." "We failed him," his mother
moaned again. "Where did we go wrong?"

When you separated us, Arjun thought. When you changed
your mind and decided I wasn't worth it. "You've been perfect,"
Arjun said to his mother. "Sometimes brains go a little haywire.
My therapist tells me that's what happened to me. It might be
connected to the car crash, it might not. Probably not. Sometimes
these things just happen." He could never explain why he would
start panicking in the middle of a biology exam, why he needed
to leave, why he didn't even make it to the door before he passed
out. He wanted to be an EMT. He wanted to save lives. "It might
be the stress of the career," he said to his father, "or the classes."
"So pick a different career," his father retorted. "Take different
classes. If your body is rejecting this idea, why not listen?" When
Arjun learned that stealing a car disqualified him from the EMT
profession for life, the panic attacks increased—and so did the
dosage of clonazepam. Even so, even while the physical symp-
toms of his panic attacks were suppressed, he continued to feel a
debilitating sense of dread—his heart would not pound and his
chest would not tighten but he'd feel himself screaming, muffled
beneath a blanket—until he dropped out of school.

Since then he'd gotten into a steady rhythm and it worked for
him. There was a part of the day, usually between two p.m. and
five p.m., between his morning pill and his evening pill, when his
hands would shake and he'd feel a familiar tightness in his chest,
but these feelings became part of him, as natural as breathing.

But now the tightness constricts his lungs and his hands are shaking intensely as he holds—and drops—an empty metal pot. It clangs loudly on the linoleum floor. Esme moans from the bedroom. He picks it back up and puts it in a box and folds the flaps into one another. The kitchen is all packed now, so he finds a sponge and a rag and wipes everything clean. Every little speck on the inside of the refrigerator: gone. The crusties inside the microwave: scrubbed. He removes each stove coil and scours them clean. Then the oven racks, one by one. He cleans the living room with equal vigor but, unable to find a vacuum, finds some packing tape instead, shapes a piece into a circle with the stickiness on the outside, and presses it on the couch and rug to collect the dust and hairs.

Now it's just the bedroom left, where Esme is sleeping, so he goes in there, trying to hold himself as quietly as he can, to empty what's left in the dressers and portable closet. At least clothing is silent when it falls from his hands. But there are dozens of metal hangers, the last items to be packed, and the idea of dropping them so close to a now-sleeping Esme terrifies him. She's lying on top of the blankets, curled up in the fetal position. He feels such anger that it overwhelms the pity. Mostly he's angry at himself for letting himself get swept away in fantasy. A fool. And where's the clonazepam? He should have looked through his backpack right away. Stupid Arjun. He pulls a blanket to cover Esme, trying hard to let it down without his hands shaking, then leaves her, leaves the metal hangers where they are, turns off the bedroom light, and returns to the kitchen to get another beer. At the first sip, his stomach twists. Is he also going to vomit? What a pair of stupid fools, equally pathetic. At least Esme was, at one point, engaged to a fiancé. At least she used to have something real. What does Arjun have? A solid stomach, it seems, because the twisting feeling goes away, but it is replaced by a deep chill in every inch of his body. He goes to the living room and sits on the couch with his knees to his chest, rocking back and forth, wondering how he got here, how all of this came to be, and he swears he feels the building sway; it lurches three inches forward, and the chill overtakes him in waves, pulls him up, his legs shuddering, his pelvis shuddering, his stomach, chest, neck, and it's getting higher, up to the chin, crawling up his teeth, ears, nose, and behind the back of his head, and he tries to squeeze his eyes shut to make it all go away, he knows once it takes the eyes, this icy feeling, once it takes over he'll be gone, and yet it comes, the wave, the shudder, pulling him up, taking over—and he's gone—he's gone—

◆ ◆ ◆

Arjun is watching Arjun. He is hovering above the couch, looking down on a version of himself who has his knees to his chest and is gripping his hands so tightly together it looks as if his fingers might break. Arjun is at the ceiling now, pushing to get through. It hurts his shoulders. He's caught by an invisible barrier, pushing him against the ceiling, harder and harder, squeezing him two-dimensional, losing his body but feeling it all the same, the pain. His skull is the last thing to be squeezed flat. And then his entire body bursts through the ceiling, a move so painful it finds the limit of pain and goes one toestep beyond, to the apartment above, pitch black but full of people, with ten kids and cousins sleeping in sleeping bags on the floor as a crib rocks slowly in a dim wind washed by moonlight; then he's pulled again to the ceiling of this apartment, and this time, the break through the barrier hurts less; he's in a messy two-bedroom where a couple still awake from a fight is making love on the kitchen counter to get through it and forget it; up now, to the next floor, and the next, faster, too quickly to get anything more than a quick flash, a heart-shaped bathroom night-light, an empty bottle of Grey Goose, a chicken running loose, a cat in the apartment above chasing its squawks, and up he continues until he's on the roof, soaring past the water tower surrounded by a dozen humming cooling towers, where there are people on lawn chairs with beers, waiting for the night to pass; higher now, the city stretches out before him, bright lights getting smaller, sirens no longer audible; higher, to the thin clouds, where the sucking feeling is pulling at his chest, even though his body hardly exists, it's a piece of paper, and there's a vacuum tube lifting him up and—it stops. His body stops but the world moves. The city is a map before him, a detailed painting on a thin piece of paper, and this paper is now growing larger, but he is not falling; the world is coming to him. The world is flat and it is coming. This city, or this paper that looks like a city, rising up to greet him, as if he were falling, but he's not; he's in the air perfectly still, stapled to the sky, as the buildings rush up at him. But he's not scared; it's just a photograph, one piece of glossy paper rising up to the clouds. A rough wind comes and bends the photograph; he can see its edges, its flatness, how it moves and swirls. The wind grows harder now, in all directions, and the photograph bends and rips in two. It rips again and again until the photograph is a million different photos, each building in the city on its own piece of paper that shudders and swirls with the others like fake snow in a snow globe. The pieces begin to fall, one by one. When they land, it is quiet. He watches where they go. He's forgotten all pain or sense of feeling; now his mind is in the ripped pieces of photo paper as they scatter through the air, feeling a softness when each one settles into a new and perfect place, like a crick in the neck being sorted out. Twisted muscles untwist. A knot unknots. Then there is just one fragment of paper left, a perfect square, with a still photograph of Gleamwood Gardens, its residents drinking beers on the roof and standing at the edge to watch the stars turn on one by one. And he can see where it should land, a blank space in the city, right where it came from, and this feels correct, the two fit together, they are perfect, and he sighs—but his sigh creates a wind that takes the paper at the last second, blowing it into the East River, where it gets swept up in spiraling currents, this photograph of Gleamwood Gardens, churning in the froth until it disappears beneath the surface.

· · ·

"Esme, wake up." Arjun turns on the bedroom light. She doesn't move. For a half moment Arjun fears she's dead. She's been sleeping for four hours without making a sound. But he shakes her shoulder and she moans, pulling the blanket over her head. He pulls the blanket down. "Esme. It's important. Wake up now."

"Hmm?" She looks at first like she doesn't recognize him, but after a moment, her eyes settle. "Oh, Arjun." Her brow furrows with remembering. "Oh, god, Arjun. I'm so sorry, I ruined everything."

"Esme. Be quiet and listen. This building is going to go into the river."

When he returned to his body, from whatever that was, a meltdown or panic attack or something completely new, he knew it to be true. Arjun had come back to himself slowly and painfully, like waking from a deep sleep, his body paralyzed, and then he breathed into it, slowly, breathing life into his toes and his fingers until, digit by digit, he came back to life. He felt cleaned out. Calm. His hands had stopped shaking. He felt the gentle sway of the world. Everything is always moving but it can be contained and calm. The movement in the world, somehow he felt he understood it better. He also recognized that he might be going crazy.

"What do you mean, the building is going into the river?"

"It's just like you said. The building has a trajectory. Remember?" He lifts up the notepad that he found on Esme's side table with the GPS coordinates of Gleamwood Gardens. "You found out it's been moving a half block eastward every day. The next stop is the East River. We have to evacuate. We have to leave now."

"No," she murmurs. "It doesn't work like that . . ." She pulls the blanket back over her head.

"Who are you to say how things work? We are in a world where impossible things are happening. Wake up and let's go." He resists the urge to pull the blanket back again, instead sitting down on the edge of the bed, trying not to touch her.

"No . . ." she says, yawning.

"Esme." He stares at the wall, keeping calm, pretending he is talking to a six-year-old in his kindergarten presentation. "Let's say it's probably not going to happen. Let's say there's only a one percent chance. That means we have a one percent chance of transporting inside a building that lands in the river. Where it is definitely not meant to be. Where it would almost certainly collapse. Wouldn't you rather leave, just in case? Call it my craziness. Do something nice for my craziness. My craziness is telling me this will happen, but maybe it's wrong. If it's wrong, then we go outside, we wait till four, until the building unmaps somewhere completely reasonable, and then we find the GPS tracker, I pay for the taxi, you laugh at me, and we live another day. Or I'm right and we go outside, wait till four, and stand safely on the street as the building collapses. Which it will. You found the pattern yourself."

"It was a fluke," she murmurs. "Noise. It won't last."

"But what if it will?"

Esme sits up and rubs her eyes.

"The building would collapse."

"Yes."

"I mean, we don't know if it would collapse." Her voice sounds clearer now. "But it would be in the middle of a river. It would at least flood. The water would find its way in and flood the basement, and maybe the bottom three stories. How deep is the East River?"

Arjun shakes his head.

"The building could land somewhere flat. It could push the ground down until it forms a new and solid foundation under and around it." She's talking slowly, pausing between each sentence, as if each one requires her to stop and visualize the words she just said. "But we couldn't count on this. It would be sitting on the bottom of an unstable river. Not even a river. What's the bottom like? It can't be level. All those rocks. And then everything that sinks to the middle. Didn't someone find the ruins of an old building down there?"

"I thought it was a dead giraffe."

"Maybe there's a building foundation down there. Something that feels like it fits." She grabs the notepad from Arjun's hands and stares at the numbers. She seems fully awake now. "Maybe Gleamwood Gardens is running away from Gleamwood!"

Arjun doesn't know what to say to that. Esme is writing on the notepad, crossing numbers out and rewriting the same ones.

"It would lean. It would fall. It would fall into the river."

"Yes."

"So we would need to leave."

"Yes."

"But what about everyone else?"

Arjun waits for her to draw her own conclusion.

"We can't just leave. We'd need to evacuate the whole building."

"I know," he says.

"How much time do we have?"

"A little over two hours."

"Shit." She puts the notepad down on her lap. "There are about two thousand people in this building. We couldn't evacuate everyone ourselves. We'd need to call into the department and convince them. Who's in charge right now? Not Commissioner Tully . . . Not important. Whoever it is would need to send a mass text to evacuate everyone in this building, but it would be imprecise, it might reach our neighboring buildings . . . so we'd have to specify Gleamwood Gardens. Only people from Gleamwood Gardens need to evacuate. But people would sleep through their texts. We'd need to run through the hallways and wake people up. Bang on every door and scream, what? What could we say? There's a bomb? There's a fire? Maybe that's it. That's the whole thing. You and I could pull all the fire alarms and get everyone to leave. Keep it simple. I've never pulled a fire alarm before, but one time, when I was young, I touched one and imagined what it would be like to pull it. I remember it was very cold."

"So you agree?"

"No." She waves him away and stands up, pressing her fingers to her temple. "If we pulled the alarms, then the fire trucks would come, too, and they'd want to go inside, and if they did, they'd see there's no fire, but would want to check it out anyway, and how could we keep them from heading in and doing their jobs? No, yes, we can pull the alarms, but we'll still need our bosses on board. You know these things take time. The process. But we could try to jump through the process. Call in a favor. Who would do me a favor? This is not about favors. We'd have to reach the right person to just pull the trigger without going through the hoops. Maybe Willy. Willy will listen to anything you say if you say it right, like if you say it's all a dream. We could tell him he's in a dream and in this dream he should send a mass text evacuating Gleamwood Gardens or else Satan will rise up from the deep."

"We could theoretically do that, yes."

"Even after all that, many would refuse to leave. We'd have to force evacuations. Maybe the firefighters would be helpful for that. We'd have to carry people out of their beds. Tell them to stop packing all their framed photographs. They can bring their pets, though. How will we fit all these cats in an elevator? They'd get loose and run through the halls. They'd start fighting. We have to evacuate and you're asking me to break up a catfight?"

Who is she talking to now?

"You have one minute to grab everything you can, and then leave the rest behind. Everything else will become rubble. The photographs, the coffee mugs, the books. The books! Oh, god, these books have been with me for as long as I can remember, and now I'm going to leave them? Some of them were my mother's!"

She gets up and rips open one of the boxes that Arjun taped shut, tearing the lid in her impatience. Unsatisfied, she opens another box, this one with books. She glances at one, then tosses it aside.

"Esme."

"You're right," she says, as she upturns the rest of the books. "It's not about the books. There are more books. If we are really doing this, if this is happening, it needs to be now. But how do you know? How?" She turns to him now, imploring.

Arjun, sitting with his hands trapped beneath his thighs, stays quiet.

Esme sits on the bed beside him. "Why are you so certain that this will happen?"

"I just am."

"But why?"

"I can't explain it."

"Can you try?"

There are many reasons, each of them insufficient, yet each of them is enough. It's in his body. It's in his fingers. He saw it in a vision. He still sees it. The numbers on the notepad don't mean much to him. He can't keep them still when he looks at them. He sees the people instead. People in the street. Two thousand angry, sleepy people at two in the morning, then three, then four, and then . . .

"They'd be angry," says Esme, echoing Arjun's thoughts. "We'd wake up two thousand people for something we're not sure about, force them to get out of bed, and scare them into evacuating, without enough time to sort through their things, to just get outside, and wait around on the streets until, what? What would they do out there? How many streets would they fill up? How many more people would we wake? There would be cops who probably wouldn't know about the evacuation and someone would have to explain but we'd be busy inside and no one else would really know what's going on. We'd have to hope no one gets sick of waiting and goes back inside, we'd have to hope that the building really will crash into the river, to make all of this worth it, because if it didn't, there would be two thousand sleep-deprived people on the streets, angry and possibly ready

to follow suit if someone starts to protest, or smash windows, or
. . . no. No, I don't think that would happen, I think they would
be pissed, but nothing like that. They'll just want to go back to
sleep."

"Everyone has been through a lot."

"And if the building does land in the river, as you say—"

"As you predicted."

"As one potential outlier set of data suggests." She stands up
but seems unsure of where to go, so sits back down. "If it does
happen, it will be big. This will change things. The city will suddenly seem a thousand times more dangerous. If one building
falls, what's to stop another? People will run away. They'll move
away. Some for good. And I don't blame them. I mean, I'm already planning to leave. But if I weren't? And this happened? I'd
definitely think about it. You might want to, also. But where will
you go? Where will everyone go?"

There are many places Arjun could go, but he does not think
she wants an answer.

"And what about people who stay? What everyone has been
through . . . Like you said. It's been relentless. There's only so
much we can take. Every day a new emergency, but somehow we
believed we were handling it. It's already hard to know what to
believe. Who to believe. We've had to ask everyone to forget what
they thought they knew. To trust us. And now this." She picks up
a book that she flung onto the bed and caresses its cover. *Hiking
the Adirondacks.* "Even if we save every single person who lives
in Gleamwood Gardens, we might still lose them. And others,
too. It might be too late. They might get swept away somewhere
. . . somewhere we wouldn't be able to reach them. They'd be lost.
They'd be lost in a place where they couldn't find their way back."

Arjun knows better than to ask what she means.

"We'll stand on the side of the river and watch. We'll blink and the building will be in the river. Just there"—she stands up and points to the empty wall, presumably toward a location somewhere in the river—"it will land just right there. And for a few moments, maybe five minutes, it will look stable. It will look like a miracle. There will be this massive building jutting out of the water, like a new world escaping the old one. I'll wish briefly I could have stayed in the building, on the roof, so I might be transported into this new world, too. But only for a moment. I'll come back to myself, remember this is not a miracle but a disaster. You'll be standing there, too. I might want to hold your hand, because my life is disappearing and I want something solid to hold. Can I hold your hand?"

Arjun nods. But she continues standing in the center of the room, holding the book to her chest.

"But the miracle won't last. The building will wobble. We won't be sure where it will go. It might lean toward the shore. Toward the shore! We'll need to evacuate not just this building, but every building nearby . . . Wait. There will be new buildings there. We'll have to hope it falls sideways into the water and that the only damage is to the building itself. We could do more than hope—we could call in a helicopter with a wrecking ball . . . yes. That will help push it in one direction. But it might not be enough. We'll still have to make sure no one is near the shore. Including us. We won't be able to watch at all! This is all wrong. We won't be able to see anything. We'll have to evacuate somewhere at least three blocks inward. Is that right? Our building is fifty stories tall, and if each story is fourteen feet high . . ." She closes her eyes and mouths numbers silently, adding and subtracting and mumbling, until she seems satisfied. "Yes, three blocks would be more than enough. But I could try to get updates. I'd stay on the phone with the division head or the dispatcher. No—that'd be a waste of their time. We could tune into the dispatch channel to hear them talk to each other. But I think I wouldn't want that either. I'd rather wait there with you, until it's all over. What's the point of knowing if there's nothing we can do? I'll live in these moments as if they're the only ones that matter. Someone nearby will try to pass the time with music or the news. Most others will ask them to turn it off. Like me, they'll want to wait in silence. With respect. Like at a funeral. All of us in our own private world between worlds. Time will stop. We won't be sure it will ever start again. Have you ever seen two thousand silent people? It won't feel real. And it will feel more real than reality. A reality we can't escape no matter how we try.

"At some point, it will become clear that it is four o'clock. Someone will check their watch and whisper the time to their husband. The whispers will go through the crowd like a wave, cutting through the silence. Then it will be 4:01. Then 4:02. The others will grip each other's hands and hold each other close. Shut their eyes and count to ten. Then twenty. Then thirty. No one has told us what happened. Where is Gleamwood Gardens? Is it in the river? Or is it safe? Nothing matters until we know. Before four, the wait was slow and full of grief. After four, it is infinitely painful. I squeeze your hand so hard you get bruises. The need to know is overwhelming. It feels like a pot of water about to boil. It breaks the silence.

"And then we forget the very idea of silence. The crash. We only hear the crash. It's very loud for a very long time. What is time anymore? The water—the water! It hits the shore in waves. Maybe ten feet tall. We're still safe three blocks inland; we may see the water dribble up the streets to our feet. For some people, that's the breaking point. How can we live in a world where this happens, if it's not due to the wrath of God or the collapse of reality? They'll scream with grief. But we'll all be grieving. Most of us will be okay, even in our grief. There's something I've come to appreciate about grief. The way it can feel just the same as love. And when you don't grieve anymore, you grieve the loss of grief. It's the last thing you have that feels real. I loved my life here. I love that I'm so sad to leave it behind."

Tears are shining on her cheeks. "But the water," she continues as if she isn't crying. "The water on the street. It doesn't concern you or me. Because we know what it means. It means we succeeded. It means we were right." There's a woozy clarity in her eyes. "And then we'll fix it. Let's go."

19

Four a.m., Christmas Day. Seven weeks after the Unmapping began, five and a half weeks after the Gleamwood Gardens Catastrophe. These are the anchors to life now. Two dates that separate "before" and "after." Esme wakes in her childhood bed. An owl hoots softly from a sycamore hollow. The window, cracked open, lets in a few flecks of snow and a breathing wind, but Esme is warm beneath her sheets. She's in Coal Hollow, Virginia, where, theoretically, everything is where it's supposed to be. Their maps stay put. Yet even after more than a month in Coal Hollow, her body hasn't shaken the habit of waking at four a.m., nor the habit of walking to the window as soon as she gets out of bed to see where she is and what surrounds her.

She was worried about moving back. She was looking forward to it, yes, to spending time with her father and getting to know Pat and Tina and exploring the woods, but she also worried she would feel stifled and stuck, or that it would feel like going backward in life, retreating to her childhood self. When she was young, she had been happy spending an entire weekend reading books on her bed or collecting caterpillars in the woods behind her house, completely unconcerned with the happenings of the world. But New York changed her. Marcus changed her.

He opened her up and made her curious, made her want to be involved. So she couldn't fight the feeling that moving to Coal Hollow would feel like giving up on the world.

But she needn't have worried. She discovered a new universe of things to do online. Along with applying for jobs, she's been working on dozens of remote freelance gigs helping cities around the world manage their own Unmapping responses. An online data marketplace has sprung up for people like her, with various requests for analysis. Sometimes she puts together digital maps of grocery stores, schools, or public transportation routes; she's figured out how to program a map that updates daily with given inputs from various GPS devices on free, open source software that anyone can use. She spends a lot of unpaid time in online forums debating various ideas and answering questions like, Why do the trees never move? Esme conjectures that it's because they are alive and already moving every minute of the day. What about the rivers? Not alive, but still always on the move. What about the pavement on the streets, then—why do the streets stay put while the sidewalks move? The streets, some posit, are already connected with one another and so there is simply no other configuration in the world where they would fit, whereas sidewalk panels are unconnected and therefore swappable. When new cities become unmapped, they turn to the online data marketplace for help. And she's glad to help. She doesn't take on every request, like the ones hoping to predict the next day's map or the Unmapping's intercity spread—that's beyond her skill level—but she spends some of her free time playing around with such data on her own, comparing the work produced by different statistical programs and equations. She ends up taking multiple requests from a professor at Columbia University who is studying different techniques to reaffix buildings to their surroundings and to each other, and eventually, this professor offers her a permanent position, based in their observatory in the Palisades, to study the Unmapping's underlying causes. Esme's surprised a university would hire anyone without a PhD, let alone without a master's degree, but the professor, Dr. Sonia Sokolov, tells her that's not needed for the research associate position. Besides, Esme's college transcript shows top grades, and wasn't she the one to predict—and help save thousands of people from—the Gleamwood Gardens Catastrophe? Esme doesn't mention the fact that it was sheer luck and Arjun's persistence that led to the evacuation, not her. She wants the job. And she gets it. It will begin on January 2.

As far as she can tell from the news, things have been getting better. Much of life has transitioned to the online world, and as far as the rest goes, people have figured out the new daily rhythm of discovering where they are and where they need to go. And there is a flurry of creative research on the ground in New York and elsewhere. Yes, there was a brief panic after Gleamwood Gardens crashed into the East River. Even though no one was killed or even injured, many fled the city. Those who stayed typically did so because they had no choice. Esme won't deny that it feels a little like purgatory. Like the world is in between things. Waiting for what's next. For many people, life has been put on hold. Businesses have permanently shut down. Evictions have been paused, as have utility shutoffs. Those who aren't making money also aren't paying their bills, and there's nothing anyone can do about that. She worries about the suicides reported on the news, about the random shootings, about mysterious cults forming, about people who've gone past their breaking point. On the one hand, people have been learning how to adapt. On the other, how do you adapt to a reality that doesn't make sense?

Every resident in New York City still wakes up every day with no idea where they are.

But here in Coal Hollow, every day provides the same view: a forest, with a path through the woods that leads to a clearing filled with clover underneath the snow.

This morning, from her window, the forest is still a forest. But something is different.

There are voices coming from the living room.

For twenty years, Christmas was a lonely time in Esme's life. Even more so in recent years, when she and her father stopped exchanging gifts, ever since she explained to him the inefficiencies of gift giving. Billions of dollars are wasted each year, Esme explained, when people spend too much money on gifts they're not sure the recipient will like, whereas the recipients can get more value out of spending that same amount of money on themselves. Marcus had explained this to Esme, and it made sense, so she carried it on. Marcus and Esme would instead pick out gifts together, or agree upon a special date, like a Broadway show. Esme and her father decided that instead of purchasing each other gifts, they would each spend a hundred dollars on themselves instead. But her father would put off spending it, so Esme did the same. There were no gifts, and never a Christmas tree—he never found the need, when they had so many trees right in their backyard, which Esme's mother used to decorate with tinsel and ornaments, a tradition kept up by her father. Still, for a week at Christmas, she would come to Coal Hollow to read, cook, read some more, and walk through their tinseled trees, while Marcus would spend the week in Atlanta with his grandparents. It was always a quiet time, if a little lonely.

Not anymore. Now there are two new people in the Green house alongside Esme and her father. Pat and her daughter, Tina, have filled the place with noise. Tina's always screaming over some toy or watching a video on her tablet or begging Pat or Esme or Esme's father for attention so they can watch her sing a new song or do a backward somersault.

But at four a.m.?

Esme walks to the living room to find an aluminum tree and a floor full of presents. Tina is already digging in, removing the wrapping paper delicately from a large rectangular box, which is as tall as Esme but much skinnier, while Pat sits on a rocking chair drinking a mug of coffee.

"Should have warned you," says Pat. "On Christmas, this is about as late as she can stand waiting. But now that you're up, why don't you look around that tree yourself?"

Esme explicitly told Pat she didn't want anything for Christmas, and Pat explicitly told Esme that she'd ignore this directive.

"I'll wait until my dad wakes up," says Esme, and she grabs a cup of coffee, meaning to head back to her bedroom, until Tina cries, "Esme!"

"Yeah?"

"Not you, Esme. Other Esme." Tina has just opened her first present: a cardboard cutout of Esme.

"What is *that*?"

It's from a photo Pat took when the four of them went to visit Washington, DC, so Esme could see her old favorite restaurants, Pat could see the First Ladies dresses at the National Museum of American History, and Tina could see the pandas. Pat had insisted on asking tourists to take group photos of the four of them whenever they saw something interesting like a protest or a politician, even though the politician was often long gone by the time they got their photo taken, and might not have been a politician at all, just a man in a fancy suit. Esme recognizes the cardboard cutout from the photo they took underneath a restaurant sign that said *Left Wing, Right Wing, Chicken Wings.*

"She's already worried about missing you when you move away," explains Pat. "This way she can stop whining to me about it. And she can talk to Paper-Esme whenever she's bored. It's a win-win."

"So what's mine? A cardboard cutout of Tina?"

Pat blushes.

"Which is exactly what I wanted!" As much as Esme tries, it still feels awkward between them. Pat is great at keeping up a conversation but sometimes there's a pause and Esme doesn't know what to say. With Tina, it's much easier to get along, but almost too easy—Tina gets exhausting. Five-year-old Tina likes knock-knock jokes, fart noises, and the killer-hug game, where Esme pretends Esme's hugs are deadly, and when she catches Tina, Esme says, "You're dead now, you're dying and you're dead," and Tina squeals with laughter, delighted to be dead, testing how long she can go limp. It was fun the first five times, but how about fifty? How about a hundred? At least Tina has Christmas presents to keep her occupied today. Esme will be glad to be leaving. It's been pleasant but strange, living in this house that is not her home any longer, but some other family's home, a family with an aluminum tree.

Pat grew up with an aluminum tree, she explained to Esme. She grew up right after the aluminum tree market crashed, so even though they were poor, her parents were able to buy one for a quarter. They didn't have the time or tools to chop down a tree and didn't have the money to buy one; they often didn't have any presents other than a home-baked Christmas cake. But they always had their aluminum tree.

Esme nestles into the couch and stares at the tree, colorful with light. Pat set up the display, with green, pink, and blue lights arranged around the tree, rotating to cast a shifting spotlight onto the silvered branches. There's something uneasy about it, the way it shimmers too brightly, with its branches reflecting more light than they take in. Or maybe it's the way the rotating lights make it look like the branches are moving, yet always staying still, like they are melding into and moving through each other—

◆   ◆   ◆

The Christmas tree at Rockefeller Center in midtown Manhattan is fake this year. The city officials responsible for locating and retrieving a live Norway spruce from a nearby forest forgot about this minor responsibility until it was too late and it was two weeks past time for the tree-lighting ceremony. So the owners came upon an advertisement for a good deal on the Gleamwood City Special, a fake tree called "TruTree" that looked just like the real thing and could be delivered in forty-eight hours. Then the mayor's replacement forgot to show up to the tree-lighting ceremony, because the first thing he did when he inherited the role was to fire the scheduling assistant because "I'm in charge of my own damn time," so the tree-lighting ceremony happened without him, and when he saw the articles that didn't include him pop up on social media, he got angry and called the Rockefeller Center managers, demanding they put out the lights and reschedule the ceremony for the next week, which he then forgot again, so the same thing happened, until it was Christmas morning and he could put it off no longer.

Still no one notices the difference, it seems to Gina Brown, the missing mayor of New York—yes, she has a name besides "Mayor," which nobody calls her anymore. Rockefeller Center is as crowded as ever, perhaps more so, despite the city's population dwindling; hundreds of thousands of people have fled after the Gleamwood Gardens Catastrophe. It's lucky that no one was killed when the skyscraper fell into the East River, or else there might not be any people left in the city anymore. It's even luckier that the city media team decided to spin this catastrophe as a great success. They were able to predict and prevent a disaster! And now they had the tools to study every other major building's patterns, to make sure this wouldn't happen again! It wasn't clear how accurate that was, but there were dozens of stories detailing the effort they were putting in. Still, though, not a bad idea to have an evacuation plan and a life jacket. Despite this, the city seems to be doing well. People have learned to adapt, even without a competent mayor. Now each department is carrying out its own business. The Human Resources Administration keeps shelters stocked with food and water while the Department of Small Business Services provides grants to bodegas and grocery stores. On the other hand, the lack of communication sometimes leads to breakdowns. Like when the Department of Buildings ordered row houses to be condemned while the Department of Housing Preservation and Development began working to preserve these same buildings. And with the TruTree. Besides all this, there is apparently a mental health crisis, with suicides and robberies and cult activities continuing on an alarming upswing. But what is one to do about that?

Gina learned this at her little beach house outside Atlantic City, where she read the morning news headlines, then turned off her phone, put on her wetsuit, and headed to the shore. When she first came here, she imagined a permanent vacation, where she would relax with her feet in the sand by day, getting up only to meander the beach and search for seashells, then retire to the house, where, in the evenings, Mayor Johnnie and his son, Angelo, would come for dinner and bubble baths. But the days were long and there were only so many seashells that could fit in one bathroom, so she soon grew restless and tried to pick up a hobby instead. She tried knitting, embroidering, and baking bread. She even briefly toyed with the idea of turning the detached garage into a blacksmith studio. Then one morning she saw the surfers. At first, when she saw people swimming out there, she nearly called 911—it was a dim and frigid morning, far too cold to swim, and they weren't getting any closer to shore. But she put off making the call, for fear of having her identity uncovered. She wore her hair natural and loose and took her makeup off, but still, she imagined the 911 responders would want to know her name. She knows this can't last, this life unknown, but wants to extend it as long as possible before she's found out and her reputation comes crashing down. Or she'll come up with some excuse, some tragic story about how she was lost and couldn't find her way home. In the meantime, she watched the swimmers. Three silhouettes, bobbing up and down in the waves. And then she saw them stand on water, all at once. As if Jesus Christ had split into a trinity, and each facet was coming for her, to make her answer for her sins. Sleeping with a married man. Yelling at her interns. Abandoning her duties during the height of crisis. But they didn't come for her. They fell off their surfboards and tried again. And when they finally came to shore, tearing their wetsuit caps off to release salty golden hair, she asked them if they could give her a lesson. They didn't seem interested until she opened her wallet and showed them the stack of hundred-dollar bills.

Still, despite vivid days in the ocean and muted nights with

Johnnie and Angelo, she found herself missing the city, especially as Christmas neared. It seemed totally reasonable that she could walk around Rockefeller Plaza to see the famous Christmas tree, and pretend she had cut the ribbon herself, yes, that she created this or had a hand in some way. It used to be her favorite part of the job, seeing the joy on people's faces, and on Christmas, everyone is happy.

So she puts on her sunglasses and tells Johnnie to do the same and even buys a pair for little Angelo, too, and together they drive into midtown Manhattan, to hold hands around the Christmas tree, which has a little sign with a QR code leading to a website where people can guess what species of tree it is. The website doesn't have the answer, just a poll. Spruce or pine? Gina knows. She read the articles about its origins. It's neither. It's a TruTree. Yet it smells real and feels real. Everything about this moment is perfect. Too perfect. This perfection feels simulated, like she's stepped into a play where she's only pretending to be the missing mayor of New York, and she doesn't know the next lines. But what's the difference? She picks off a handful of pine needles and folds them in half until they break, then sniffs, and the aroma fills her with pleasure. Instrumental holiday songs play from tiny speakers at the base of the tree, wordlessly glorifying snow and presents and fire-roasted pies. She tells little Angelo to smell the pine needles in her hand. "What does this smell like to you?" she asks.

"Your bathroom soap!" he says back.

"Let me smell," says Johnnie, who takes the missing mayor's hand and sniffs it. "Ah, yes. I smell your skin. Delicious." He pretends to take a bite.

From the speakers, a woman starts singing along with the tune. "Silent night. Holy night." This is a shift. They usually only have instrumental music. Too many complaints about the lyrics, which are either too religious or too sacrilegious. The missing mayor closes her eyes and lets herself enjoy this moment. "Sleep in heavenly peace. Sleep in heavenly peace."

Then the music stops, although the voice continues.

"We intend no harm," says the voice, unaccompanied. The music behind it picks back up again, louder, an instrumental "Jingle Bells."

Gina's skin prickles. "Let's get going."

"What is it?" asks Johnnie.

"I don't know," she says. "Nothing good." The voice continues, *"You have ten minutes to clear a fifty-foot radius around the tree. We intend no harm."*

She's holding Angelo's hand and trying to pull him away, but he wants to grab more needles from the tree. Johnnie picks up his child in his arms and starts walking quickly north.

"Our car is the other way!" says the missing mayor.

"We'll get it later," he says, jogging now. She runs to keep up. The voice continues. *"The time to access the next world is now—"*

"Someone needs to get them away from the tree!" the missing mayor says, looking back to see, amid the people fleeing the square, many are staying, and some are inching closer—

•   •   •

Rick holds Darla's shoulders as they watch the tree at Rockefeller Center, waiting for something to happen. They're a safe distance away, watching from a rooftop bar, with Rick having gotten a tip about this, whatever "this" is. She shrugs his hands off her shoulders. "You're distracting me." Underneath her short-cropped bleached blonde hair, a large digital SLR camera hangs around her neck, with a brand-new long-range zoom lens, and she takes test photos of the tree, fiddling with her settings. But it's hard to get the lighting right from this far away: There is a mismatch between the picture she imagines and what shows up on her camera; there is something about the scope of the city she wants to capture, the true magnificence of everything surrounding this one little tree, which in reality is a big tree, but it looks so small and isn't that the point? But through her viewfinder she sees that yes, yes, something seems to be happening, although she can't say what, as people start running away, and others hold hands, so she zooms in all the way and captures their faces, sees their fear, and wonders if Rick sees it, too, but he's not looking; he's checking the messages on his phone, with a tip about a boy, missing once again—

◆　◆　◆

Antony is running, the running feels good, it's finally cold and so he can run as fast as he wants, and this time he knows where he's going, he's leaving this wild town, the town that can't keep still, because he wants to be somewhere still so he can run, and up north he goes, to the woods, where he could eat mushrooms and spear rabbits and be a wild man forever. It's been weeks and weeks of being trapped, stuck at home, at a virtual school that's worse than real school, because he can't concentrate on the tiny screen on his phone—the only thing he can use when his brother hogs the computer, especially while his mother hovers over him. He's not even allowed to run anymore, his only freedom from the tiny room in his house being when his mom makes him go to church, any church, whatever church happens to be nearby that day, because he can't go to school but he can go to church, but this is not a freedom as much as it is another form of imprisonment, with priests and reverends telling him what to say and do, but it's Christmas today and so every church will be packed, they won't be looking at any little kid, it's the prime moment to run, so the boy runs with his flip phone and a bag that will last him a month, and now he hears all the sirens from cops from all over and doesn't care, on he goes to freedom, wherever it may be, because, yes, these sirens aren't for him, these are sirens of freedom—

◆　◆　◆

Sirens surround the Gleamwood City aluminum Christmas tree as a handful of officers in heavy duty bomb gear examine the ground at the foot of the tree and a dozen Wisconsin state troopers stand guard. Roger the newsman takes off his hat, pulls his notebook and pen out of his pack, and walks up to them.

"This is a controlled area," shouts a mean-looking cop with a long and skinny neck. "Stay back."

"Fine, I'll stay right here," says Roger, holding up his hands innocently. "I just want to ask a few questions. I'm a journalist."

"What's your outlet?" says the long-necked cop.

Roger peers into the deep valleys of his neck between the tendons. "Formerly the *Gleamwood City Weekly*. Now I'm independent."

A chubby cop with red cheeks responds, "We got a tip of a bomb about to go off right at this tree. Apparently, the 'Red Cloaks' are targeting manufactured Christmas trees all over the country. A bunch just went off at noon on the East Coast. Here's the biggest one in the Midwest. Although, most of the trees they're targeting are those fake ones that look real. TruTrees?

This one's a nice and shiny aluminum. Still, though, we gotta be here. It's almost noon. We're also looking for Franz. You know Franz?"

"Shut up," says the long-necked cop.

"Sergeant, why not question him? He's in a red suit after all. I'm sure he knows Franz. What's your name, buddy?"

"Roger," he says.

"Mr. Roger, Franz usually shows up at this tree at noon on Christmas Day, is that right?"

"Yes, that's right."

"Good detective skills," says long-neck.

One man in a bomb squad outfit calls out, "We're clear." He walks up to the officers. "Nothing to concern us here."

"What about that sparkly stuff on the ground?" asks the red-cheeked cop.

"Just pine needles," says the bomb squad cop. "Nothing to worry about."

"Then why do they sparkle?"

"It's a trick of the eye. It's the sun."

"You're very brave," says Roger to long-neck, looking for a name tag. He doesn't find one but does see the word "Sergeant" embroidered on his chest pocket. "Sergeant, is it? Do you go by Sergeant? Is that what your mom named you, fresh out of the womb?"

The cop refuses to catch Roger's gaze. He growls, "Do you want to be charged for obstruction of justice? Go away so we can do our jobs."

"Here you are, right in the middle of the action, where you believe a bomb will go off. Very risky."

"I agree!" says red-cheeks. "It's my first bomb threat."

"Shut up," says long-neck.

"But don't you think you might be forgetting something?" says Roger.

"If you say one more word—"

"What are we forgetting?" asks red-cheeks.

"You said the bombers are targeting TruTrees. Where are all the TruTrees in Gleamwood City?"

The long-necked cop opens his mouth, then closes it. He turns around to look at the factory, where smoke is filling the horizon. "Shit." And the cops start running toward the factory, and when they are gone, the people in red walk in, hand in hand, and light the tinder of needles sprinkled with aluminum dust, and the kindling goes up in flame, the hottest heat, so the aluminum tree is enveloped in fire, burning without burning, every single one of its silver branches shining, absolutely beautiful, while soon, beyond the tree line, as Roger knows, the factory will explode—

•   •   •

The wife watches the fires on three different screens. The Rockefeller Center TruTree fire replays on the left laptop, the Gleamwood City factory explosion is on the right, and a running feed of many others scrolls through the middle.

Just for a moment, though. Just for long enough to show her husband what's happening.

Sirens sound outside.

The wife turns off the screens.

"So this was you, Rosemary?" her husband says. "You did this?"

"In a way, yes. In another way, no. I knew it was going to happen. I did not stop it."

She has a hard time explaining the past several weeks to her husband. What she remembers best are the dreams. These memories are largely unspecific, but certain vivid moments stand out. Like the first time she discovered she could swim without losing her breath. Flying was easy, yes, but swimming? Unbelievable. She swam beyond the waves, her arms stroking the cool water as dolphins surrounded her, and then as she left the surface and went down, as the water darkened and darkened, she couldn't see anything at all, but she felt completely safe as she glided through the embryonic waters, buoyant and warm. On she continued, into the darkness, until she discovered what was on the other side: light. There were massive sea creatures glowing red, purple, blue. There were colors and clear sounds of bubbles that popped and sparked.

She also remembers one terrible morning, where she was half awake and half in a dream, and in this dream, her body was face down in the water, and she could not breathe; she could not move or escape. The others noticed her struggle, her eyes moving in fear as her body was captured by sleep paralysis, and they massaged her feet and fingers until the feeling returned to her body and she gasped in glorious air-conditioned air. "They saved me," she said. "They saved me from drowning."

"But you weren't drowning. You were sleeping."

"Yes."

She also remembers the dreams of the forest on fire. There were trees that would burst into flames if you breathed on them the wrong way, but they would not burn her. She could walk through them and feel no more than a slight tickle. This was a favored dream that made her feel powerful.

And then she dreamed she was pregnant.

This one was real.

She knew it by the soreness of her breasts, so painful it woke her from sleep and kept her awake for hours, during which time she tried to count the days since she'd arrived and utterly couldn't remember, but she did remember that on the day Serafina brought her to the Empire State Building, it had been just under a month since her last period. Before being taken in by the women in red, she had tracked her cycles diligently, checking her basal body temperature and cervical mucus to test for ovulation in hopes of conception. After she joined the women in red, her dreams of being a mother were forgotten and replaced by dreams of water, lights, and a forest on fire.

But her body didn't forget.

"Our baby brought me back," she says to her husband as he rubs her shoulders. When he reaches for her feet, to take out the glass and clean the wounds, she kicks him away in pain.

The dream of being pregnant: That's when she knew she had to leave. But she didn't know how. She dreamed she was leaving a hundred times, only to find herself up on the hundredth floor, surrounded by sleeping others. She dreamed she went to a doctor, who told her she was wrong, that there was never any baby. But eventually she recognized this dream for what it was, and she told him: "You're wrong. There is a baby in me. There always has been and always will be. We've already named her."

When she woke from that dream, she vomited on the floor, then cried with relief—her real body was reacting to the real pregnancy. Everything was real. So much was uncertain, and she was willing to put her life at stake for answers. But not the life of her baby. The baby reminded her of a deeper, stronger dream. One of Rosemary with her husband in a cabin by the river where she'd grow vegetables and he'd howl at the moon and the baby would learn how to crawl through the trees.

So she ran.

That was this morning.

She hardly remembers how she escaped; she must have taken the stairs, unable to use the elevators herself—what floor was she on, and did she go up or down?—and found her old clothes, or someone's clothes, to shuck off the red scatter-shot outfit they'd given her on the first day. But when did she change? And where were her shoes? And the guards, were they still there? They must have been—all she knew was that suddenly she was sitting on her screened-in porch, where her husband had been sitting, waiting for her. Her feet were bloody. She didn't know where the cuts came from, but her husband saw the broken glass.

"You said your life was at stake?" he says. "What do you mean?"

"Did I say that? I don't know . . ." She squeezes her eyes to try to remember.

The sirens grow louder. Three police cars drive by.

Her eyes grow wide. "They'll be too late."

"Who? Late for what?"

"We need to get out of here. Now."

"After you rest—"

"No. Now."

"And go where?"

"Anywhere. I want to be far away when it happens."

"When what happens?"

"The women, they'll—I can't—"

A fire truck joins the others just down the street.

Her husband says, "I know where to go."

◆　◆　◆

Today is the day of the one-hundredth-anniversary celebration at the Pathway Pilgrim Church. It also happens to be Christmas. But that's irrelevant here. The reverend's great-grandfather founded this church for those interested in the word of God alone. If it's not in the Bible, it's not worth thinking about. This sometimes causes anger on Christmas Day, when people stumble into his church expecting a Christmas service. There is never a Christmas service. Today, not even a prayer meeting is scheduled, just a celebration in the courtyard over food and drink. The stragglers will be confused and they will ask him, *Why do we not talk about the birth of Christ? Why not honor this most holy of days?* And he will answer, *You may do as you wish.* And some of them will sputter: *Filthy Calvinist. Heretic.* And he will again say, *You may do as you wish, but this is a joyous occasion, so please carry your anger elsewhere.* And he will think but not say, *I'm not Calvinist. Do your research.*

The reverend will understand their anger and confusion. It comes with the territory in such a church, where everyone is told to find their own path to God, and yet there are rules—for example, no Christmas and no Easter, but yes to Sunday services. When he was young, he asked his father, then reverend of this same church, "Why do we have to attend services on Sundays, then? Why read the Bible at all?" And his reverend father, after years of stern warnings, finally gave up and said, "You think you're smart for asking these questions. Go, do what you like. Skip services. Then you'll lose the faith and I'll lose you." He wanted to prove his father wrong. He set out to be the most religious nonreligious man that ever lived. He left New York, buying a half-broken Toyota and driving it all the way to San Francisco. There he could love with God's love and live in God's love. He found freedom and decided that this was the same as finding faith. In freedom, God's wind, he moved about the city, where each waking breath was a prayer, a devotion. He felt free to love bodies like his own, taut and lean, all V-lines and limbs, and felt love for bodies unlike his, strong and full. He prayed in strokes and touches, in sweet words and charms, in dark corners of lowly bars. With these men, he spoke of the Holy Spirit until the small hours of morning. He wore a large silver cross proudly around his neck.

Then his father died of heart failure. It shouldn't have been a shock, but it was. It was far too soon. Yet his father was just shy of seventy years old, and he himself was nearly fifty. How had that happened?

So he returned to New York to inherit the role of reverend. There he discovered a freedom that was internal and could be found anywhere. And beauty. The green-and-red stained glass windows with the odd eight-pointed star he never understood. The weekly and daily space to pray and think. Here he would put on the mantle of his father, who wore that of his own father, and so on, back to the great-grandfather who founded this place. And who will inherit it after he's gone?

He has no son of his own.

But now he has Michael.

This beautiful man walked into the church nearly five months ago, back when he was named Marcus and needed so very much. "I need a tether," he said ambiguously, and the reverend believed he knew what he meant. He asked to become confirmed, to rename himself after Saint Michael, and afterward, Michael quickly became his most devoted—and spirited—congregant. He always offers to lead Thursday evening Bible groups, and whether or not he's leading, he's always ready to ask questions and debate the meaning of various passages. He owns five different Bible translations to compare each verse. Sometimes Michael's intense line of questioning frustrates the reverend, who just wants to receive the Bible's lessons without worrying about the implications of the different translations. But ultimately he believes Michael is doing good work. Michael devotes every part of himself to being here. To learning the word of God and truly understanding it. Asking question after question until he's satisfied. If anyone could make God answer his questions directly, it would be Michael.

It was Michael who convinced the reverend that his one-hundredth-anniversary celebration would be successful, even post-Unmapping. He helped him set up QR codes on flyers that he taped up throughout the city and prepared enough food to feed a hundred. "A hundred people for the hundredth anniversary," he told the reverend. "We'll do it." Michael purchased all the food and paper plates and plastic cutlery, set up the tables and chairs, and found an old stereo system to play music. The reverend is grateful that Michael did so much, because he's been too busy worrying to do anything useful. He's envisioned this day for months. A joyous culmination of everything he put into the church since his father's passing. The vigorous and spirited Bible study group members would come, he thought, as would the many parishioners who'd sat in these pews over the years. He sent multiple emails asking for RSVPs, and although none responded, he was sure they'd show up.

Now he's not so sure. The party was supposed to begin an hour ago. He refreshes his email in his private office, sitting with the door open wide so he can see the pews, but no new emails come in.

Of course, there are challenges. Starting with the perpetual challenge of how one finds a church in an unmapped city.

Even though most are familiar with guiding themselves with GPS coordinates by now, it still would be a pain to get here, in midtown Manhattan, especially if they woke up somewhere like Staten Island, especially for something as frivolous as a party. Then there's the fact that so many have fled the city. Ever since the Gleamwood Gardens Catastrophe, that horrid building that smashed into the river. By God's grace, it was empty, but it put a fear in people that can't easily be erased.

Even the church's recent residents have begun to drain out. The reverend knows he should be grateful that his parishioners' absence likely means that they are safe. And the fact that shelters like his are emptying of people means they have somewhere more permanent to sleep at night. The church's role as homeless shelter was only ever meant to be temporary.

Still, Michael was convinced the anniversary would be successful.

So why is no one here?

"Today's not a great day for a party," Michael says, walking into the reverend's office, holding out his phone. "City just sent out an emergency text. The stay-at-home order is back."

"Why? What happened?"

Michael puts his phone in his pocket. "Nothing much. Don't worry. We're safe here."

"Will you have to leave and write about it?"

"Not today. Today is for celebrating. Even if it's just us."

Michael gestures through the open door to the five permanent inhabitants who've been sleeping here each night, currently playing hearts on the floor by the altar. They don't talk much and don't seem religious. The reverend wishes he could get to know them. Most of them hardly say anything, except for one, who says the same thing over and over—"Look at your hands"—no matter what anyone else says to him. The youngest looks barely over eighteen. This one came in wearing a brown fedora hat with a big cast around his left arm and shoulder, which he later sawed off with a knife from the kitchen. The reverend often finds this boy in the pews, silent as they hold services and Bible meetings. The few times the reverend tried to talk to him, however, the boy smiled and walked away.

After the fourth time that happened, Michael told the reverend that the kid was deaf, or nearly so. "He can't hear you." The reverend felt foolish when he learned this. "How'd you find out?" "Simple: He told me." Michael explained to the reverend, as they set up the communion table some Sundays ago, that getting people to talk was his superpower. "But also, I'm just easier to talk to than you. No offense. You're intimidating. I'm a nobody. People don't want to embarrass themselves in front of you. They don't give a shit about what they say to me. They don't think I expect anything of them."

"I don't either," the reverend said in response.

"I know this. But it takes time for people to learn that. They have to be ready to talk to you. And when they do, they probably tell you things more truly than they'd ever tell me."

"Except you."

"Except me?"

"I know nothing of your past."

Aside from that first day—*I need a tether*—Michael has been reserved about his personal life. He revealed himself only once, seemingly by mistake, as a brief aside during a Bible lesson on selfhood in Corinthians, when he mentioned a woman named Esme who had no sense of self, a lack so present it broke their relationship; then he immediately backtracked and said she was perfectly fine and deserved happiness, and he changed the subject to a tirade against Paul, who he believed distorted the word of Jesus Christ. When the reverend later met that woman, the one who said she was a former fiancée but still wore a metal wedding band, there was no question it was her. The reverend gathers Michael has built an image of himself that doesn't fit with being a man of the church. But why? It's clear he had a strong up-bringing in the faith. Yet outside this church, he seems ashamed of it. When he goes out, he covers up with a scarf, sunglasses, and hood, as if he doesn't want to be seen. Like he's running away.

But we all have secrets.

"You don't need to know my past," Michael said. "That was a different life. You know my present. Born again."

"I suppose that's more than I can say about them," he said quietly, referring to the others who stayed. In all honesty the reverend doesn't want his church to become a shelter and is grateful that people have been finding their homes. But now all that are left are the homeless. He'll need to figure out what to do.

Michael peers out into the courtyard. "Maybe it's time to turn off the computer and get started."

"Let's wait a little longer. Nobody listens to stay-at-home or-ders. More will show. The QR codes. The traffic." The reverend clenches his fists. "Have a little faith."

"There's faith, and there's facts. I thought you liked both, Reverend."

"There's also patience. We'll wait just a little longer." Tired of sitting, he gets up and paces around the pews, as if each revo-lution will make it that much more likely for people to suddenly appear on the benches with Bibles in their hands. The reverend's ankles are sore at first but settle into the movement, his soft leather shoes brushing against the floor.

On the fifth revolution, he gives up. "Let's go, then."

Michael shepherds the five other residents from the sanctuary to the courtyard. He walks ahead excitedly and opens the door with a flourish. The courtyard is set up with long tables lined with party trays filled with mashed potatoes, roasted salmon, fast-food french fries, bagels, baklava, and kale salad. None of the food seems to match. "Something for everyone," Michael says. "No matter what food you believe in, it's here." The reverend expected all this. What he didn't expect are all the decorations. There are streamers and balloons and a big poster board with a photo collage, showcasing the reverend's father and grandfather and even one old sepia print of his great-grandfather, setting down the church's first brick. In front of this is a round three-layer cake that says *Happy Anniversary!* in scraggly liquid letters.

"Who did this?"

"I did," says Michael.

"Where did you find that photo?"

"You showed me."

"And you know how to bake?"

"I learned."

The others dig into the food right away, filling up their paper plates to the brim. The reverend doesn't get any food for himself, just takes a seat at the end of the table. Michael joins him there, similarly plateless.

"Aren't you hungry?" asks the reverend.

"Not really."

"Yes you are."

"I'll eat when you eat."

"You're just trying to make me eat."

"But aren't you hungry?"

No. He's getting old and hunger means less these days. Food has become a homework assignment in health. An equation of fiber and vitamins. "I'll eat, but nothing healthy. Bring me a slice of cake."

"Joke's on you; that cake is made of zucchini."

"I wish you hadn't told me that."

Michael is a good man. But is it enough? Will he want to inherit this place? The reverend is getting old and won't be around forever. Even before thinking about things like that, there are the economics to consider. The property taxes, even with partial exemptions, are astronomical. And the utilities aren't subsidized. He would need more government grants. The one he received to form a temporary shelter helped. But is it sustainable? Will it last?

And who are these new people?

"Excuse me," says the man who just walked into the courtyard with a woman who appears to be his wife, by the way they are gripping one another for dear life. "All right if we join?"

After a beat, the reverend recognizes him. He came here once, a month or so ago. The man's shiny blonde hair has become greasy and he now has a shabby short beard, but his eyes are the same, and the reverend has a gift with names.

"Please do come in," says the reverend, standing up. "There's plenty of food. Joey, is it?"

"Yes. And this is my wife, Rosemary."

The reverend examines this woman, whose disheveled hair is pulled back into a nest of braids that have come half undone. She's wearing loose, dusty jeans, a black button-down shirt, and white socks underneath black leather ballet flats. The socks are soaked in blood.

"Do you have a first-aid kit?"

"Of course."

"It's embarrassing," says Joey, "obviously we have our own, but she insisted on leaving before I had time to get it . . ."

The reverend waves off his concerns and says he'll be right back. He's surprised to find the woman, Rosemary, following him down the hall. She doesn't say a word. He respects her implicit wish for silence as he leads her to the house next door, his living quarters, and points her to the bathroom, where there are bandages and ointments in the closet and a tub for washing the wounds. "Would you like any help?" he asks. She shakes her head no.

When he returns to the courtyard, Michael and Joey are deep in conversation.

"Duct tape! I can't believe it." Michael's shaking his head.

"Believe what?" asks the reverend.

"This man's a genius," says Michael. "He says he was able to keep his house attached to the Empire State Building this whole time just by using duct tape."

"It's stupid," says Joey. "But it's the first thing you learn at prepper camp. Duct tape solves everything."

"And it's still connected?"

"Only until tomorrow. My wife asked me to cut the tape. She wants to be far away from that building now. Long story."

"I think we have our newest congregant," says Michael. "We need more smart guys like this."

"Are you a follower of Jesus Christ and his teachings?" asks the reverend.

"Kind of," Joey says. "I went to church as a kid. Lutheran. I hadn't been for a long time, until the Unmapping. Then, for the first few days, I went again. I told my wife I was looking for our car. Instead I found a church and I sat there all day reading the Bible, feeling like a failure. I did the same the next day, and the day after. Whatever church I'd happen to find. It was your church one day. You remember, Reverend. And I remember those green glass windows." He swallows and takes a breath. "And then my wife . . . disappeared. That's when I knew true and total failure. So I stayed home on my porch and waited for her. But—and here's the even more awful part—I lifted a Bible from a nearby church. I read it on our porch all day, every day. While I waited for Rosemary, it was the only thing that gave me respite, if only for the briefest moment. I'd be reading about something totally bonkers, pages and pages on how to sacrifice a calf, and then on other pages it's just like, bam, a simple 'Love thy enemies.' I don't know which is harder to understand, like on the one hand it seems very complicated to learn and memorize all these elaborate instructions on killing a calf for sacrifice, and on the other, how is one actually supposed to love thy enemies? It seems impossible. And then it hits me. There's something in the impossibility that's worth looking at and sitting with. And for a moment I'm like, I found it. Why I am the way I am, why the world is the way it is. We need the impossible. When we don't have it, we go mad. So. There." He leans back in his chair. "To answer your earlier question, I don't know if I'm faithful. At the very least, I'm curious."

Michael, who has been listening intently this whole time, nods. "There are a thousand contradictions in the Bible," he agrees. "It's impossible to understand. Yet we try to understand it. That's all we're asked to do."

"I guess so. But I also lied to my wife and stole a Bible. I've shorted stocks and ruined lives. And when Rosemary showed up this morning, I didn't care about anything in the Bible. I'd have sold my soul to the devil if it had brought her back to me sooner."

"But you didn't."

"I don't think I'd make a good congregant."

"You're here," says the reverend.

"Yeah," says Michael. "And it sounds like you've already reached, like, advanced levels of Bible study. You'd fit right in." He looks around at the nearly empty courtyard and bursts out laughing.

"Can I ask you guys something, though?" asks Joey.

The reverend braces himself for the inevitable question about why they don't celebrate Christmas.

"Yes, and I have an answer." Michael jumps in, once again reading the reverend's mind, and launches into an explanation of why celebrating Christmas is a distraction from the words of Jesus himself, whose life should be celebrated, yes, but in different ways at different times of the year . . . and as he speaks, the reverend thinks, Yes, Michael is a good man. His voice takes up the space. People love him when they listen. And although the reverend knows nothing of his past, he can help guide his future . . .

"That's interesting," says Joey. "But I wanted to ask something else. Is there more coffee? The pot's empty—"

◆　◆　◆

He's making coffee again. He's the coffee man. It took six weeks of arm-in-cast and in that time he perfected the art of doing everything with one hand. It was painful. Everything. The explosion itself—yes. And the weeks of recovery. Pain like he'd never known. He refused all sedatives and painkillers, though. Terrified of going down the path of his pillhead brother. So he experienced it. He wanted to know what his body was doing. What it was going through. He was alive. He was lucky, he knew that. Thanks to some woman he barely remembers, he is alive and that meant pain and he lived every moment of that pain. He lived more in the past six weeks than he'd ever lived in his life. Despite hardly moving. Despite sitting in a hospital bed, in and out of sleep, watching the news with the captioning on, unsure if he was dreaming all the strange things on TV. Until he was kicked out of the hospital bed and forced onto the streets with a map of shelters, and the first one was two blocks down, this church. Pilgrim Highway or whatever. He hasn't seen the sign since he walked inside, and he hasn't been back out yet. He could ask someone where he is but he can't hear anything since the explosion and he hates saying, "What?" Except the noises in his head. He can hear them loud as ever, no matter how much he pulls down his hat. It's a funny fedora, nice brown leather, and he found it on the street just outside the church. It makes him look good. Even if it doesn't keep out the noises. Those noises only ever say: *Pow!* There are explosions in his brain, reliving what happened, as if that would fix anything. *Pow pow pow.* It wakes him up at night and then he falls back asleep and it wakes him up again. Sometimes he's so sure something's happening he jumps out of bed to find the fire. But there's nothing.

It's crazy, these explosions in his head. And makes him feel crazy but also very sane, like, how much is always happening beneath the surface? How little can we hear? He goes inside himself and he can hear. He can *hear.*

Still. Phone calls are useless. He tried calling home but couldn't even hear the phone ring. So he asked that guy Michael, who seemed way too cool to be in a church, to make the phone calls for him, and if someone picked up, he'd tell him what to say. He wanted to call his parents. He called their landline every day. But they never picked up. He assumed they ended up living at Rockefeller Center. That's where they work, and they get there every day by three in the morning to make everything spick and span by six, when the "real" workers arrive. So they'd have shown up there that first day, and then unmapped with the building, and then stayed there forever. He'd read about how people like his parents made their jobs their new homes. That could be easier than dealing with everything there was to deal with these days. Probably not much easier for his parents, who now get to clean all day long in a building that hates them, yet can't find their second jobs or their third. So no. No one ever picked up his landline phone. Not even his brother, who never used to leave the couch. Probably he's out on the streets somewhere. Maybe he overdosed. It's better not to wonder. He hopes his parents are relieved of their burden. From two annoying sons to none.

Now this son has a place to stay and food to eat and something to do with his time: coffee. Anyone else tries to make coffee? He tells them to stop. He's the coffee man. "I make the coffee here," he says, hoping the words come out okay. They do. People listen. Even Michael's not allowed. Especially since he cut off his cast, at the six-week mark like the nurse said—although she probably didn't mean for him to do it himself, but why do you need to pay a doctor a thousand dollars to cut through a piece of paper?—so now that he has both arms back, he feels like a coffee wizard; he can make two pots at once, he knows the best proportion, uses the best water—unfiltered—and boom. The magic stuff that makes your brain wake up. Why would anyone want a downer when they could have coffee instead? The world is crackling and you can feel it, hear it, after your third cup. Your own body crackling in time to the rhythm of the pulse that keeps pulsing. He can hear his own pulse. It feels like the ocean. Like he is an ocean. The truest blue. They say there's no true blue in nature. Only the deepest purples, or a trick of the light. Let him be blue in the light. Let him soak it in and let it out. He's the coffee man. He's invincible. He survived an explosion without doing anything at all. Now he gets to live in a place where no one looks down on him. Even if he's nothing yet. Yet. He turns on the coffee maker. The "on" light shines the brightest blue. He could do anything. He could change his name and be anyone. He could be anyone. He can be anyone.

20

It's hard to say when things started turning around for the better. Is it possible to pinpoint a particular moment when everyone stopped running around trying to live in a broken world and started instead trying to fix it? No—not everyone. There are still those who've thrown up their hands in surrender to whatever may or may not happen, without the will, interest, or time to care. But it certainly feels as if everyone is thinking about this—the Great Fix, the Remapping, any of the many names used for it—and people are not only thinking about it, but doing something about it, so many people it feels as if we've reached a tipping point. How did we get here? When exactly did we cross this tipping point after which everyone seemed to agree that something had to be done about this? Was it exactly fifty-one percent of the global population? Or at least of the New York City population? Twenty-five percent? Three and a half percent? There are studies on social movement tipping points that say each of those things, and other studies saying this is an impossible thing to study. Yet so is a beginning. Let's say everyone agrees there's exactly one person who made the difference between then and now. But that person is a product of their education, so perhaps it was their teacher we should thank, or their teacher's mother for forgetting to take her birth control pill, or the inventor of the pill, who gave the teacher's mother the confidence to go without a condom, or the genes that give us the urge to procreate.

Impossible though it may be, Arjun, social media associate at New York City's Remapping Department, has been tasked with finding the beginning of our story's end.

So if you ask Arjun, he'll say it began in the Bronx. That's where Julian Reed, known colloquially as JR, was camping out in Hunts Point Riverside Park alongside over a hundred cousins and friends and neighbors when, in early January, he woke up to find his apartment building across the street.

It had been two months since he'd seen it. He'd abandoned it on the first day of the Unmapping to search for his little brother, Antony.

At first, JR thought he dreamed it. "I'd been having fuzzy dreams since Christmas," he admits to Arjun, who's recording the video interview on his phone. "Those dreams where you're not sure if you're awake or not." But when he stepped closer, he realized it had to be the real thing. His home. "I'd forgotten how ugly it was. In my dreams, our house was a lot more visually appealing, I'll say that. Don't kill me, Mom." It was a skinny row house with four floors chopped into four different apartments, all moldering brick and shutterless windows and a garish front door, the door JR's mom had painted in a fit one night, sick of the row houses on her block all looking the same. She wanted theirs to stand out. So now it's the brightest acid green. "It looks like someone puked up Mountain Dew. Also it wasn't the right paint for weatherproof doors, so it started chipping off right away. I couldn't have been happier to see it, though."

Before that, JR had gotten used to the idea that he'd never go home again. "I had a new home. Riverside Park." He was willing

to pretend that was where he wanted to be. But then, right before his eyes, his family's apartment building showed up, with his
name scrawled on the wall-mounted mailbox.

"I woke up my mom and my girl and my uncle and my favorite
cousins—wait, edit out that part, can't have my cousins knowing I
have favorites. So I woke them all up and told them about it. I said
we had to go in all together. See, it wasn't just my apartment, but
our whole family's—we rented in the same building. But my mom
was scared to go inside. She said she worried she'd never leave. So
I went in first. I tried my key and it worked. It worked, motherfucker! You can bleep that, right? As soon as I stepped in, my mom
changed her mind and barreled in after me. She was like a dog
who'd just come home from the dog park, picking up all the blankets and putting them down again, sniffing the empty refrigerator.
We'd cleared everything out when we moved our things into the
park, but I guess she thought some food would regenerate. She was
half right, because I found a couple bottles of liquor stashed deep
in the back of the pantry. I don't know how we missed them. We
had a big party even though it was only nine in the morning."

But JR didn't want to leave Riverside Park. There was the fact
that his brother Antony had run away again. "Not like before.
He'd gotten in the habit of taking off for a night or two at a time.
No idea where or why." Every time he returned, their mom yelled
at him until her throat got hoarse and she promised that if he
slipped away again, she wouldn't let him come back, but she always did, and always will. So they wanted to make sure he knew
where to return, which they couldn't exactly do in a house that
didn't stay in one place.

There was also the fact that JR and his friends had built something special in the park, which had become a sort of community
distribution hub. It started as an informal texting network: When

you needed something, toilet paper or bottled water or a good bottle of tequila, you texted JR, who knew which of his contacts had extras on hand and could facilitate a cheap sale. Then people with extra stock—often mistakes after panic-buying things like breadmakers and lifetime supplies of deodorant—ended up dumping it off at the park for easier facilitation, where he'd hang on to anything for at least a week until it sold. As it became clear how efficient JR's system was, it grew and grew, receiving donations and wholesales, until he hired an assistant—his girlfriend, Jackie—to manage the requests while JR spread the word and informally vetted applicants to become runners.

So he wanted his house back, and he wanted the park, too. He wanted both to stay together. On top of that, JR wanted to figure out a way to save the city. "Everyone was talking about big picture 'how do we stop the Unmapping,'" he says to Arjun, who is still dutifully recording, "but why not the little picture? One building at a time. When I saw our house, I wanted to do whatever we could to keep it here." So JR had an idea. As the party continued and the hour grew late, he convinced everyone to stay awake until four. Then his family stayed inside the building, huddled by the first-floor window, while JR stood outside it, and they all grabbed his left arm, while his right extended outward to hold the hand of his girlfriend, who was standing on the lawn, and who held hands with someone else from the Riverside camp, who held hands with another, and another, until their chain of hands crossed the street and reached the row of trees that marked the park's entrance. And when the time drew closer to four, JR grew nervous that either his arm or his mom's arm or somebody's arm would get ripped clean out of its socket, or that perhaps it'd be a clean cut down the property line, so he insisted on his arm being the only one sticking through this window; the others could hold on to him from inside the building, yes, to hold a finger or his elbow as he pressed up to the side of the building. He told everyone to keep talking as if nothing was happening, no countdown or anything like that, nothing that would cause him to flinch and pull his arm free at the last second, no, he didn't want to know what time it was, he just wanted to exist, staring at the acid-green door, with one hand holding his girlfriend's and the other being squeezed on every digit by his family, and he felt himself get a little gassy and woozy and thought he might close his eyes for one second when someone said, "It's over." And it was. It was 4:01 and, even though every building around him was different, he was still in one piece. His house was still there, and the park was, too. And the chain remained unbroken.

It was not JR's first attempt at something like this. Back in November he'd tried lassoing together the nearby buildings, hoping for a little more consistency and stability to their operations. He tried all sorts of rope in all sorts of positions and all sorts of knots, connecting laundromats and hardware stores and office buildings and gas stations around their signs or pipes, then loosely across the street to loop around the trees in the park. But each time, his ropes would be empty the next day, lying languidly on the ground. When an abandoned fruit market showed up, he tried tying the rope to each stall, creating a maze of crisscrossing lines in and through and out of the market, but the next day, it had fully disappeared, along with all the rope.

He'd long ago given up on his tethering idea when his home showed up.

That was months ago, JR tells Arjun now on a warm and windy April day. He's standing at the edge of the dock at Riverside Park while Arjun, crouched on a nearby rock, films him. Of course they couldn't form a human chain around the whole city, JR said, but the night's success gave him renewed energy to find a solution. JR told everyone he knew he'd give them five dollars if they came up with a good idea and five hundred dollars if it worked. His girlfriend's second cousin suggested duct tape. He had read in Bluzz how one man used duct tape to attach his home to the Empire State Building—supposedly. There was no proof of this, because by the time of publication, the man had taken the tape down. Still. Worth a shot. And it worked. For the most part. Most of the buildings they connected with duct tape stayed together, but some disappeared. It was either bad luck or poor placement or some troublemaker cutting through the tape. But for the most part, they were able to put their neighborhood back together, building by building. Or at least *a* neighborhood. Sometimes this new neighborhood broke apart, with entire blocks moving to Manhattan, but when that happened, they'd just keep building, making the city whole again. "My girlfriend keeps talking to me about ants, so I've been watching them," JR told Arjun. "Their anthills get kicked down every day and they just keep building. Each one doesn't know what they're building, exactly, they just know where the next grain should go. We don't know what we're building, exactly, or what it will look like when we're done, but we believe in the next grain of sand. All we're—"

"Wait," Arjun interrupts. "Before I forget. Any anthills around here? That'd make excellent B-roll." He looks around. The dock is surrounded by a combination of grass and gravel, which is taken over by tents, scattered with the occasional boulder, and rimmed by rusty sheet metal. But beyond the lot there's a grassy lawn lined by trees, some of which are blooming, the tight purple redbuds, white cherries, and a single luxurious magnolia. The park's greenery in this decay feels like a gulp of water on a hot summer day.

"I don't know, man. Ask Jackie."

"Okay, okay. Continue."

"As I was saying, all we're trying to do is make the world a little better. If anyone wants to join, we have a spot for you. That includes you, Brother. You're welcome back at any time. We'll always have a home for you. That good?" He says this to Arjun.

"Wait, wait—don't forget the boilerplate."

"The what?"

"The script."

"Oh, right." JR uncrumples a piece of paper from his pocket. "When we rebuild," he reads, "we need to make sure to do it right. Duct tape is step one. Step two, thanks to the city, are the concrete stabilizers. In the meantime, we're installing solar, microwind, and storage batteries wherever we can to make the grid more resilient. We're researching ways to remap the city every day. New York is becoming a model for the rest of the world, from Rio to Cairo. From Rio to Cairo? No, sorry, I can't do this. Can't you put that in a caption or voiceover or something?"

"Sure, that's fine."

Arjun takes his phone off the handheld tripod. "I once had the same thought about ants."

"Damn, and here I felt so original."

"Great interview, though. I'll edit and post this to the city account ASAP."

"Thanks. You sure? I feel all rigid when I'm talking on camera. Like, canned. 'All we're trying to do is make the world a little better.' I feel like a PR salesman." He moves his arms robotically. "Greetings, earthlings!"

"Are you a PR man or a salesman or an alien?" says Arjun.

"All three!"

"I wonder, though. What you said about the new neighborhood. What will people call it? Hunts Point? Or New Hunts Point?"

"Maybe, yeah, and we'll all be in New New York."

"Or Double-New York."

"Newer York. Newest York."

"But who will call it that? Tourists or locals? Like, tourists always call my home city New Delhi, when all of us who live there just think of it as 'Delhi.'"

A cloud briefly passes over the sun. Arjun knows there is a hurricane in the forecast, record-breakingly early in the year for this region, but that's still days away. "Let me edit this now. While I do, can you get someone to take a new photo of you? A candid shot holding duct tape. Hopefully somewhere with a 'Free Antony' wheatpaste in the background."

JR's girlfriend comes up to him. "JR, there's an issue in block three. We need you now."

"Hang on. I need to take a photo for Arjun."

Arjun shakes his head and shoos him away. "To be honest, I was just trying to get rid of you. I need to edit this video."

Arjun doesn't care to know why JR is needed in block three. The Unity Collective may or may not be the gang formerly known as UNCUT, but the city isn't asking this question, and neither is Arjun. What does "gang" mean anyway? JR knows a lot of people and has a lot of friends and it seems that everyone likes doing him favors and giving him free meals, which Arjun benefits from sometimes. Maybe some of these friends drop off mysterious boxes labeled mysterious things like *office papers* and *the good stuff*. But if JR does run a gang, what does that mean in a world with no concept of territory? Even with the remapping efforts, the city continues exchanging neighborhoods with neighborhoods. But certainly there seem to be fewer shootings in this new world. Arjun wonders what it would be like to grow up thinking you had no option other than to join your local gang.

And then you move somewhere far away. Suddenly anything seems possible.

When JR leaves, Arjun sits down cross-legged on the dock at the edge of the park. He stares at the sky over the Bronx River as he considers the best ways to cut this video. *We want people to be encouraged by our progress* was his new boss's only directive. He likes his new boss, Emily. She lets Arjun have creative control over his assigned social media posts for the Remapping Department, mostly because she's too busy to review his drafts. This is a welcome shift. Everyone is always busy, but in the past, that translated to "stop and wait for your superior's okay—oh wait, now it's too late," whereas now, it means "do everything now and figure out the logistics later." Everyone is still busy, but the attitude has shifted from "don't do anything" to "please do everything."

Arjun replays the interview and realizes he forgot to stop the recording when he and JR were talking about New New York. He wonders what his family would have to say about that—maybe Delhi will truly become New Delhi now. It was the first city to unmap in India. Before it happened, Arjun's father agreed with him that it was a terrifying prospect, and they bonded over the effort to get his mother and grandfather to leave the country. They sat on the same hard brown couch and crouched over the phone as they spoke to Arjun's mother on video chat, exhorting her to meet them in New York, or in Toronto, or in Montreal, or in Trenton, where Arjun's father owns apartment buildings. Anywhere but India, where, Arjun and his father feared, things would quickly devolve into chaos. But Arjun's grandfather continued to refuse to leave the city he had known his whole life, and his mother refused to leave her father. Nothing had changed in that respect. So Arjun and his father instead decided to help them prepare. They shipped hundreds of portable phone chargers and GPS trackers and told them to pass these trackers out to everyone they possibly could. Arjun's father flew to Delhi to install a small solar panel on their roof and a microwind system on their windows. The wind slowed to a trickle in the heat of day, when the sun was strong, and picked up at night, and with this combination, there was always enough for the air conditioner and a quick phone charge. When his neighbors learned about it, they wanted one for themselves, too, which was exactly what he'd hoped for. He'd invested a lot in this microwind company, purchasing thousands of systems for himself to help them get off the ground, and was now eager to resell them at a markup to those who could afford it and at a discount to those who could not. Arjun was glad that all these boxes were finally disappearing from his bedroom and from their storage unit. It was so successful his father hired a dozen people to help him install them, and he decided to stay to oversee this new venture. Arjun was supposed to join his father on that first flight to Delhi, before it unmapped, but then he got the job transfer to the mayor's PR department—the one he wanted—so he kept putting it off, just as his father kept putting off the return to New York City, and Arjun found he enjoyed being in the city without the overbearing presence of his father, and his father seemed happy to be doing something useful in Delhi, so it seemed this postponement would become permanent. His family quelled Arjun's continuing concerns—what if you run out of water; what if there are riots?— with a weekly video call, telling him of new life in "New" Delhi, making it sound just fine. To a city of chaos, what's one more drop of chaos? It doesn't hurt that so much of the city is made up of interwoven parts. There are the massive compounds of the wealthy that have everything they need inside, and the labyrinthine alleys and slums with walls bleeding into each other, so that entire neighborhoods move together and stay together. His grandfather has never been happier: His doctor and the doctor's extended family have moved into the apartment building and there are still Vishnu temples on every corner, and cashew candies everywhere you look, and cigarettes offered left and right, with thousands of carts pushed around the streets selling water and food and more.

Arjun technically still lives in his father's condo but sleeps most nights on site in Hunts Point—where he liaises with the Unity Collective—in a trailer that the city provided to field workers like him. He shares it with a program coordinator named Vaughn Dobson. Vaughn likes to sleep while playing bass-heavy electronic music and smokes marijuana five times a day, but otherwise, he's friendly enough. He keeps offering edibles and blunts to Arjun, each time forgetting and remembering that Arjun doesn't smoke due to the panic attacks, but Arjun doesn't mind the secondhand feeling of it, and he makes Vaughn watch *Miami Vice*, and the two of them laugh through it, so he's pleased with the living situation, with the easy commute and built-in best friend, even if the divider between their sleeping quarters is too thin to keep out Vaughn's snores.

Theirs is not the only trailer on these streets. Every research institution in the New York metropolitan area is here, studying the city and the solutions for keeping it together. Some companies have been working with concrete, others with a strong epoxy-based glue. Others study the question of what moves and why. They have no unifying theory as to how this all works, no simple answer, so they test as many things as possible. The big "why" is still up for debate, although many have agreed upon global warming as the answer, so while the city responds and adjusts to its unmapped reality, the world needs to do more to draw down greenhouse gas emissions, and Arjun is generally aware that world leaders are trying to come to an agreement on just this, but haven't they been trying this for decades? Will they really do it now? Then there are the more granular whys: Why do buildings move and not trees? What makes a sidewalk decide where to go? Why is the Empire State Building so impossible to contain? Even with the concrete stabilizers, the Empire State Building keeps stomping through the boroughs like King Kong on the loose. It has been successfully affixed to several neighboring buildings, but never to any locational anchors, like a river dock or a tree. The result is that entire blocks fly together through the city. It's become its own moving neighborhood and global tourist attraction. Ever since the women in red jumped off the observatory on Christmas Day from the eighty-sixth floor, presumably jumping to their deaths, only to be blown back by a strong wind onto a two-foot ledge on floor eighty-five, the public's fixation on the Empire State Building has only increased. The women were cleared out and arrested, but no one could say exactly for what—they seemed unaware of the explosion at Rockefeller Center, and mentally disturbed; apparently, they believed they could fly. So they were let go and assigned mandatory psychiatric assistance, and there hasn't been anything in the news about them since.

The only reminders of that day come from Franz Gleason, the strange, old former head of Gleamwood City. Franz's face keeps appearing on Arjun's social media timeline, in selfie videos backgrounded by a fuzzy panorama of sometimes mountains, sometimes beaches, and occasionally the side of a highway. He's on the run, after having taken full credit for the Christmas bombings. Apparently he'd believed that the only way to stop the Unmapping was—for reasons that are hard to gather—to destroy as many TruTrees as possible at one time. When that didn't work, he realized his great mistake. His first video missive was an apology. Franz still believes he was responsible for the Unmapping: In the past, it was because of his failure to shut down Gleamwood City's TruTree business. But now he believes that his belief in the Unmapping's existence was what caused it to happen. He criticizes Bluzz for spreading the story and creating the social tipping point in New York City, and every other media outlet for continuing to report on it. He also says that global warming is fake, that the moon was built by aliens, and that GPS satellites emit carcinogenic radiation. Arjun figures he's just trying to stay relevant after Gleamwood City shut down and liquidated its assets. Maybe he'll start selling sponsorships for snow globes.

For the most part, Arjun tries not to think about Franz, even as he keeps appearing on his timeline. Arjun tries to focus on the here and now. And right now the city needs to be fixed, and that takes work, and he's working hard—which, yes, involves social media, including the frequent use of his increasingly popular John Bobson account, which always promotes Arjun's city account posts with some sort of snarky commentary, but he doesn't worry anymore about whether or not he'll lose followers or receive fewer likes. He posts without emotion or anxiety. It helps that he runs now. It turns out the nerves in his body needed somewhere to go. With the guidance of his therapist and after much trial and error, he's switched to a half dose of clonazepam per day, which makes him feel more alert and surprisingly less anxious. Whenever he senses the familiar crinkles of anxiety, he goes running, and if he's not able to run, he squeezes his hands in a rhythmic pattern, and if that doesn't work, he jumps up and down in the bathroom until he's calm. There is no feeling like the feeling after a hard run, laid flat out on your bed, waiting until your body regains composure. For several minutes you feel the cells in your body move back and forth and everywhere. You can feel your shoulder connect to your stomach. Your head pulses with blood from the toes. The city is alive in the same way. It is coming back together.

As Arjun hits Upload on his video, a text comes in.

ESME: You good with sushi?

She'll be here at noon for a date in the park. Yes, they go on dates. Esme's living and working up in the Palisades, an hour's drive north, but she comes down whenever she can for lunch, which feels almost like their old lunches, only now they switch off buying each other food, and instead of talking about their old jobs with vivacity and passion, they talk about their new jobs with vivacity and passion. Arjun feels for the first time like he has a voice that matters; he's gone from dreaming to doing. And Esme, meanwhile, has gone from doing to dreaming. Whatever she's studying seems very complicated but she talks about how happy she is to help scientists with their creative work. "We can study things without understanding them," she says. "It's like gravity. You can't see it, but you can study the things surrounding it. Dr. Sokolov gives me assignments and I'm not always sure how they fit in—like global and local PFC pollution percentages—but somehow it's all part of her vision."

On the one hand, everything has changed. On the other, it feels just the same, like they've come back to the best parts of themselves and one another.

The other thing that makes it different is the kissing.

Arjun doesn't count that strange night in Gleamwood Gardens as their first kiss. No, that was a blip in time. A drunken anomaly. If you ask him about their first real kiss, he'll tell you about the second time they had a lunch date at Riverside Park, in mid-January, when he brought homemade parathas stuffed with curried potatoes and cashew candies shipped from Delhi, and when she said goodbye, she looked at him, as if asking what would happen next. And he knew it was time. But who would lean their head in first? And how long would the kiss last? His fingers were cold and stiff but his face was hot. The kiss itself was suddenly happening and then suddenly over. It was quick. Who went in first? Him or her? He wondered if it would happen again, and if so, if he would be similarly confused at who was doing what. He liked the feeling that he was making no decisions, but responding instinctually to something else between them; it was going to happen, and then it was happening, and then it had happened, and it all felt inevitable. The kissing felt more familiar the next time and even better the time after that. But that's all. Esme wants to take things slow. And Arjun is left wondering what these incredible feelings are—he thought that he was in love for two years, but now there is something different, maybe not love, but something somehow more intense and less intense at the same time. It makes him both unbearably nervous and unbearably happy, and he's trying to live with these feelings and somehow enjoy them. His worries still live in his head like tiny little friends who urge him on: *Look at me! Look at me!* But there are many other things he'd prefer to look at. Like the redbud trees in the park behind him. Like the nice breeze that cools the sweat on his neck. A wet, misty breeze that tastes like salt.

"How is it?" asks JR as he crouches down beside Arjun on the pier. "How's the video?"

Arjun gives him a thumbs-up. "So far so good. Twenty likes and one repost."

"Only one repost? Who's the one?"

Arjun shows JR his phone. "Some guy named John Bobson." John Bobson reposted the video with the words These idiots. But Arjun knows the power of anger to spread an idea. "I think he's a troll. Don't worry about him."

"Well, it's a good start," says JR. "Maybe I should do what that guy Franz says. I believe this video will go viral!" he shouts to the sky. "If I believe it, it'll happen! Isn't that what he's saying now? He caused the Unmapping by getting people to believe in it. And now people can stop it by not believing it anymore."

"I don't believe you can replace a belief with the lack thereof. It can only be replaced by a different belief," says Arjun.

"Like what?"

Arjun shrugs. "Don't know. That's the problem."

JR repositions his crouch to face Arjun. "How about, oh, I don't know. The fact that pollution caused the Unmapping and humans are the scourge of the earth?" JR leans close and says quietly, "Isn't that right, John Bobson?"

Arjun's throat catches. "What do you . . . Oh, I get it. Good joke. I'm John Bobson. Very funny."

"Yes. A joke, from me to you, Ar-John. Here's another joke. Isn't it funny that John Bobson opened his account the same day you found us?"

Arjun blinks three times.

"Don't worry," JR laughs. "Your secret's safe with me. We have each other's backs. Right?"

Arjun nods warily.

JR claps his hand on Arjun's shoulder and pushes himself up, leaving Arjun alone on the dock once more.

Unlike the rest of the city, where the skyline changes daily, the view from this park is always the same. A river, and, on the other side, another park. Many of the trees have bloomed pink. The sky is hazy and colorful from smoke from some wildfire somewhere—Arjun doesn't know where, but he knows how the fires make the air a lovely orange. A warm front is coming from the ocean soon, followed by a nasty storm to wash it away. He looks at the Bronx River below him, a tributary to the East River. The East River is the strangest river. Esme once told him that it's not actually a river at all, but a tidal strait between two bigger bodies of water. He's since looked it up to learn that a real river is supposed to flow in one direction only. But the tidal strait, some days it flows one way, some days the other, and sometimes it just sits there, stuck between the two. The Bronx River similarly sometimes flows up, when the East River tells it to. Today it appears confused, like the water can't decide which way it should run. Arjun watches a sail of aluminum foil blow past him. The topper of a dish from the potluck in the park behind him, he guesses, detached from its jalapeño poppers and taken by the wind. The aluminum foil lands on the water, floating on the surface beneath his feet, first going north, then south, then pushed eastward, until it gets sucked down into a small whirlpool. Arjun watches to see where the foil ends up. But it doesn't end up anywhere. He looks on the surface of the water in both directions, but there's no glint of silver, no hint of foil. The river took it and it's not giving it back.

"Is that snow?" he hears someone say from behind him. And indeed, miraculously, in sixty-degree weather, white fluff is falling from the sky. It starts with a few flakes and then it's everywhere, drifting slowly through the air, then pushed hard by a westward wind to the dock. More white flakes appear, dotting the sky and raining down sideways. One lands on Arjun's leg.

This is not snow.

"It's cotton!" someone else calls out. Arjun does not look back to see the people who are talking, just lets their voices drift into and through him.

"Cotton?"

"Must be a seed from a cottonwood tree."

"No cottonwood trees in New York."

"Sure there are, at Soundview, just across the river. And that wind today."

"Yep, the wind is something."

Arjun leans back and closes his eyes. The voices behind him fade and come back.

"Maybe a cotton factory exploded."

"Where's there a cotton factory?"

"Don't ask me."

"Then why would you say that?"

"Wherever it is, it exploded."

A strong wind picks up. Eyes still closed, he holds out his hands, feeling the wind, imagining the softness of the delicate flecks of cotton. He continues listening to the people around him, as if they're talking to him, through him, as if he's dreaming them into reality.

"You caught one, baby! Make a wish! Then I'll blow it free."

"What do I wish for?"

"Anything you want, but keep it secret."

"Mama, you blew before I could make my wish!"

"That's okay, muffin. Catch another one."

"I . . . can't . . . !"

"Stop crying, I'll catch one for you."

"I . . . didn't . . . make . . . my wish!"

"Baby, it's okay. Look, your brother caught two."

Arjun opens his eyes. The cotton is falling more thickly from the sky. It's like living in a snow globe. He tries to catch one, but the simple act of trying to catch a bit of the fluff creates enough force in the air to push it away. He tries to catch another and similarly fails. Then he holds out his hand and waits for a piece of cotton to blow into it. When he feels the whisper of a touch, he clenches his fist, then opens it to examine his prize. There's a slightly damp feeling to the piece of cotton. The tiny center is hard and white and surrounded by soft, translucent tendrils. The wind picks up, blowing the seed from his hand, as more cotton falls around him. Yes, it's like living in a snow globe. If he were to make a snow globe, it would be his grandfather's favorite temple in Delhi, so everyone there could experience snow for the first time. What if he made one of these snow globes, and then it really did snow in Delhi? It would be a miracle. But this has been a year of miracles. Miracles as big as flying buildings and as small as the pinky finger that has learned how to stay still. As big and invisible as love. The miracle of existing. The miracle of moving. He wants to tell the world about what it means to run. To feel your nerves cycling in and out of one another. The entire body, circulating. And how, in the moments after the run ends, this flurry of bodily activity briefly increases. Or it seems to, when contrasted to your static body, when you finally stop to listen. You lie on the couch and feel your pinky talk to your eyeball as your chest flickers with static. And then things settle. Maybe the world just needs to let off some steam. He has the feeling that if he ever truly understood his own body, like how a heart can pump blood and a lung can squish out oxygen, he'd understand the Unmapping. He'd understand the world. If you understand one thing completely, you understand everything. He knows this is impossible. But he is Arjun. His father's son. He can do the impossible.

A blaring noise comes from the phones all around. It wakes him from his snow globe daydream. An emergency alert.

He knows what it will say.

A hurricane is coming to New York City.

ACKNOWLEDGMENTS

Writing this novel would not have been possible without the support and help of many other people. Thank you to all the talented writers who read sections or entire drafts of this over the years, including Jeremie Amoroso, Aviad Eilam, Leslie Ekstrom, Cynthia Folcarelli, Brian Grittner, Kent Haeger, Len Kruger, Zack Latino, Michael Macagnone, Ian Nytes, Marly Owens, C. S. Simpson, Leslie Spitz-Edson, Chris Stevenson and the Petworth Library writing workshop, Amy Tercek, Alexia Underwood, Chuckry Vengadam, and Christine Welman. To Mike Tidwell, who told me it wasn't good enough when it truly wasn't, motivating me to improve. Thank you to the lady from the Petworth workshop who showed up once, heard the first chapter of this book, and found me again years later to tell me she hadn't stopped thinking about the story. Thank you to the wonderful teachers who've been mentors over the years: Bud Smith, Johannes Lichtman, and David Yoo. Thank you to the authors who don't know me but have inspired me nonetheless, particularly China Miéville with *The City & the City*, Mohsin Hamid with *Exit West*, Karl Ove Knausgaard, Kim Stanley Robinson, and countless others. Big thank you to the lovely Illika Sahu for showing me India, and again to Chuckry Vengadam for help-ing me with cultural research. (Any errors or inaccuracies about anything in this novel are entirely my own.)

Thank you to everyone at Bindery, Girl Friday Productions, Audiobrary, and Lavender PR for bringing this book from vi-sion to publication. Meghan Harvey and Matt Kaye, you created a beautiful endeavor. CJ Alberts, Kristin Duran, Brittani Hilles, Shira Schindel, Reshma Kooner, and Julia Whelan: Thank you for all you've done to champion this book. Charlotte Rose and Ibrahim Rayintakath: Your artistic vision blew me away. Tegan Tegani: Your edits were difficult and necessary and made it one hundred times better. Marines Alvarez: You picked this book out of a pile and gave it a chance; our visions fit together so beau-tifully, and I admire the community you created. Thank you to Marines's Bindery, for being early fans of the book even while I was still revising it. And thank you to Annie Romano, my amaz-ing agent at Olswanger Literary, who believed in this book when I'd lost faith.

To Andrew Quinn, who lives on in my dreams. To my father, who lives in the red sky. You both instilled in me early on the de-sire to create a book and make a small mark on the world.

To my family: Brian, Charlie, Colin, Coraline, David, Elena, Jeff, Kelly, Molly, Sean, and Vicky, for being a stable source of joy. And especially to my mother, Pamela Robbins, with a love words can't describe.

Most of all to Seth, who, for years, supported and inspired me without fail; who was a fount of strange ideas about this strange novel, ninety-nine percent of which I ignored, but all of which simmered in my head over the years and made the world feel full; who read multiple iterations; who stayed up late to read and edit while I was in the thick of revisions; who did the laundry and the cooking whenever I had deadlines (and whenever I didn't); who always makes me laugh, even or especially on the worst days. You are my love and my muse; you are everything to me.

THANK YOU

This book would not have been possible without the support from the Mareas Books community, with a special thank-you to the Producer members:

Amy Church
Audrey Quinn
Brittney Cornelius
Cadence Rochlen
Caitlin Vanasse
Cristina B
Dawn May-Christ
Eric Calamari
Heather Hulscher
Jennifer Down
Jenny McEldoon
Kayla Chapman
Kia Borner
Margaret R Camp
Megan K
Meredith Hackerson

Reads with Rachel
Ruaridh K
Sara Conrad
Sarah Sharfi
Sarah Tucker
Suzanne Wdowik
pawsitivevibes
Fortunesdear
Ramona
melodygrant
alana
Calliyanna
GenoTheCat
watalienaite
velosigraptor

ABOUT THE AUTHOR

DENISE S. ROBBINS is from Madison, Wisconsin, the city where she grew up and to which she returned after sixteen years of living and working in climate activism on the East Coast. She lives with her husband in a yellow house circled by oaks and pines and two owls. She is a Pushcart Prize–nominated author whose stories have been published in literary journals including the *Barcelona Review* and *Gulf Coast*. Read her work and get in touch at www.denisesrobbins.com.

Mareas Books is an imprint of Bindery, a book publisher powered by community.

We're inspired by the way book tastemakers have reinvigorated the publishing industry. With strong taste and direct connections with readers, book tastemakers have illuminated self-published, backlisted, and overlooked authors, rocketing many to bestseller lists and the big screen.

This book was chosen by Marines Alvarez in close collaboration with the Mareas Books community on Bindery. By inviting tastemakers and their reading communities to participate in publishing, Bindery creates opportunities for deserving authors to reach readers who will love them.

Visit Mareas Books for a thriving bookish community and bonus content:

mareas.binderybooks.com

MARINES ALVAREZ has been creating content across a variety of platforms since 2011, building a vibrant and engaged community of story lovers. Profiled by *Rolling Stone* and *Vulture*, Marines is a community builder on- and offline, crafting reviews that invite readers to think critically about media and representation. She is also the cofounder of BookNet Fest, a yearly bookish event that brings together readers, authors, and reviewers around a shared love of books.

YOUTUBE.COM/MYNAMEISMARINES

TIKTOK.COM/@MYNAMEISMARINES

INSTAGRAM.COM/MYNAMEISMARINES

BSKY.APP/PROFILE/MYNAMEISMARINES.BSKY.SOCIAL